THE RECRUITS

Answering the Call

J.M. CRANFORD

WESTBOW
PRESS®
A DIVISION OF THOMAS NELSON
& ZONDERVAN

Copyright © 2016 J.M. Cranford.

All rights reserved. No part of this book may be used or reproduced by any means, graphic, electronic, or mechanical, including photocopying, recording, taping or by any information storage retrieval system without the written permission of the author except in the case of brief quotations embodied in critical articles and reviews.

Scripture quotations marked NIV are taken from the Holy Bible, New International Version. NIV. Copyright 1973, 1978, 1984 by International Bible Society. Used by permission of Zondervan. All rights reserved.
Unless otherwise indicated, all scripture quotations are from The Holy Bible, English Standard Version (ESV). Copyright 2001 by Crossway Bibles, a division of Good News Publishers. Used by permission. All rights reserved.

This is a work of fiction. All of the characters, names, incidents, organizations, and dialogue in this novel are either the products of the author's imagination or are used fictitiously.

Author Credits: Master of Arts in Bible and Theology, veteran Captain in U.S. Army

WestBow Press books may be ordered through booksellers or by contacting:

WestBow Press
A Division of Thomas Nelson & Zondervan
1663 Liberty Drive
Bloomington, IN 47403
www.westbowpress.com
1 (866) 928-1240

Because of the dynamic nature of the Internet, any web addresses or links contained in this book may have changed since publication and may no longer be valid. The views expressed in this work are solely those of the author and do not necessarily reflect the views of the publisher, and the publisher hereby disclaims any responsibility for them.

Any people depicted in stock imagery provided by Thinkstock are models, and such images are being used for illustrative purposes only.
Certain stock imagery © Thinkstock.

ISBN: 978-1-5127-7970-7 (sc)
ISBN: 978-1-5127-7971-4 (hc)
ISBN: 978-1-5127-7969-1 (e)

Library of Congress Control Number: 2017904045

Print information available on the last page.

WestBow Press rev. date: 03/28/2017

*"'Not by might, nor by power, but by my Spirit,'
says the Lord." (Zechariah 4:6, NIV)*

Dedicated to my beloved children: Jessica, Olivia, Sadie, and Lucas

ACKNOWLEDGEMENTS

I would first like to thank my parents, Bob and Betty Hoyt, for your support of all of my adventures, including this one. Dad, you read, re-read, and read again my material, offering constructive criticism and praise even when it hurt. I will never think of flashbacks in the same way. Mom, you bolstered me with your praise and excitement throughout the lengthy process, making me feel that I could do this. Thank you both for believing in me.

Secondly, my sister, Amy Cook, provided me the most detailed criticisms that inspired me to add a bit more of this character, clarify a bit more of that character, and develop more emotions and relationships in the scenes. Sis, your encouraging words and vote of confidence kept me moving forward.

Thirdly, my children and grandchildren bring me the greatest joy, not to mention a lot of useable material. I am blessed beyond measure with you all.

Finally, my husband, Scott, supplied me with encouragement, affirmation, resources, advice, and patience to achieve my dreams. My love, I am so thankful to journey this life with you.

Thank you, Jesus!

CONTENTS

Prologue .... *xiii*

Recruitment *1*

Assessment *103*

Basic Training: Phase I- Indoctrination *159*

Basic Training: Phase II- Qualification *205*

Basic Training: Phase III- Maneuvers *257*

Commencement *295*

Epilogue *311*

PROLOGUE

Sergeant Riley lay naked, battered, and bruised, yet the odd floating light that emerged from the wee farthest corner brought him warmth and peace as it expanded and filled the alcoves of the container. Soft pillows of air crept through the spaces beneath his deadened limbs as a cool breeze brushed across his lacerated face, filling his nostrils with new life as he inhaled and expanded his lungs in relief. In desperation, the déjà vu of joy clung to the most remote recesses of his mind while the blasting sound of the music that had bombarded him from the outside with its random chants of quick rises and falls, off-beaten chimes, and snake-like rattles against the relentless pounding of the Doumbek faded into the distance.

His captors had been diligent about breaking him, housing him like a rabid dog in a box-like contraption that confined his shoulders and constricted his knees in a bent position. Although even his mind fogged in the depravity, he calculated that he had been their prisoner for about seven months now, the raising and lowering of that aggravating music aiding his count.

The captive had long given up on deciphering the noises; instead he cradled up next to one of the two air holes to avoid the onset of claustrophobia. When the fighter first had the strength, he used the foreign melodies to cover the sounds of his own music, but the caged one had been trained to keep it down. "Quiet down in there!" a low, raspy, accented voice shouted from outside the door as a dull thud further emphasized his point. "Or you'll get no food!"

The small amount of gruel or hardboiled egg seemed worth it at first, but the gaunt skeleton became too emaciated to gamble that away. As the prisoner lost the ability to muster much of a voice, he resorted to worship in his head even though that effort became a challenge as his days were filled with slipping in and out of consciousness.

As memories of his childhood, his initial tours in the service, or even his most impactful relationships swirled through his mind, the prisoner lost awareness of whether they were dreams or just thoughts that occupied his time.

★ ★ ★

"Hamilton, did you get those weeds pulled around the tomatoes?" Mrs. Riley hollered from the front porch as her boy walked down to the park with his bat and glove in hand.

"Yes, ma'am," the ten-year-old bellowed back over his right shoulder, determined to reach his destination.

"Hamilton Clyde Riley, you hightail it back here right this moment!" his mother insisted in her most serious voice.

Although the middle name intended to honor his father, the use of it made the hair rise on the back of the child's neck every time. With all due respect to his hard-working patriarch, that name sounded so old-fashioned and downright embarrassed young Ham.

However, he knew when Mrs. Clyde Riley resorted to her baby's full name, she meant business. A lack of immediate obedience would either mean a good whoopin' from dear old dad right after supper, or worse yet, no dessert. Now given that Irene long held the coveted title of the best baker, according to every Sunday social he had ever had the privilege of attending, missing out on that night's specialty served as torment. Flaky, doughy peach cobbler, light and moist German chocolate cake with homemade coconut praline frosting, or even sweet and tart apple crisp from their very own tree in the yard motivated even the orneriest of boys into compliance, and smelling the delicious desserts cooling in the breeze of the fresh summer day stopped him dead in his tracks as he contemplated his next move.

"Blasted woman!" the stubborn child grunted under his breath while still gazing with fleeting desire at the edge of the ball field. "Why do you tempt me?"

★ ★ ★

Sergeant Riley's cramping stomach and lower intestinal growl alerted him back to his present state.

"Food!" the husky, foreign voice yelled from the other side of the manmade cage as a narrow chuck hole fashioned from a mail slot opened and a tin plate of slop hit the base and splattered over the edges.

Even though it pained the soldier to bend his body farther to retrieve his nourishment, no matter how minuscule or how undesirable it tasted, his thin, frail, claw-like fingers reached for the dog dish as his mangy foot tapped and swooped it closer to the other end of the box. How the withering fighter would have withstood additional scrapes or a few more bruises to get his head down there to lick up the spilled scraps, but he just could not manage the contortions anymore. With the air holes fixed at the opposite side of the entrance and his body long since depleted of strength, the weary and rigid captive remained in a steady position for the optimal amount of oxygen intake.

★ ★ ★

"Flutter kicks! Now push-ups! Now flutter kicks! Now push-ups! Now hold!" his drill sergeant barked at the platoon full of eighteen- to twenty-year-olds that had volunteered to be shipped into shape. "Don't let your chest touch the ground, Private Riley! Don't you do it!"

* * *

The soldier's breathing raced and the tightness of the muscles around his ribs ached as his eyes opened to face the discouragement of the darkness that had surrounded him for eons. Not even the faintest of shadows slithered through the end of the long pipe protruding out of the side of the contraption. Defeat crept in as the distant memory of his old drill sergeant threatening him to persevere, build fortitude, become battle ready seemed like kid's play in comparison to his present circumstance. Would the military man have enlisted if he had known what his service to his country would ask of him? How many of his fellow combatants would have run back out that door instead of signing on the dotted line if they were forewarned of possibilities like this? Would the servant still have come to know Jesus as Lord if he hadn't?

* * *

"Oh, Riley, you have just got to get back here for Christmas! Why, we have a snow dance coming up at school, and I just can't be the laughingstock of the town and not show up. You just got to get home!" Penny insisted after accepting his collect call.

"I'll do what I can, hun, you know I will," the long distance lover tried to reassure her. "I just can't control these things. I've put in for leave, but my first sergeant says I just might not have enough rank yet to get it."

The smack of the receiver and the subsequent dull alarm of the dial tone overwhelmed the distant beau with helplessness. How could he keep his girl happy when he lived on the other side of the country? Didn't she know her beloved prepared for war? Ranger school had been no small feat, and it required every last ounce of his inner strength and mental focus to succeed.

* * *

Frustration must have been mounting outside of his cage as the biting tones of enemy voices ebbed and flowed between the alternating pitches of that repetitive, eerie music. Unable to maintain his concentration, the captive exhaled and considered defeat. Just as his desperate attempts to cling to his years of training cracked and crumbled, the hopeless one squinted his sandy dry eyes and labored every last drop of his thinking ability on the quiet when that tiny sparkle of light wafted its way in and around and somehow even through him.

"**Hamilton**," this radiant voice reverberated wherever the light had made way.

The low and peaceful tone calmed him as it seemed to fill him yet remained outside of him all at the same time. "Yes, Lord," the weakened soldier pried apart his dried lips to reply.

"**You must remember all that I show you and then go and do**," the Lord directed, His words pushing light to every dark corner.

"I am weak, Lord, and I am bound," the disciple pleaded.

"I love you," the Lord renewed. "**Trust me. There is work yet to be done**."

In a magnificent flash of cool blue tones, pictures of people and places and happenings flooded the follower's thoughts as though he were at a private showing of the next box office hit. The reel of images resembled his own memories but of times not yet past, and the warrior awakened, alert and aware that he no longer stumbled around lost in his weakened subconscious or dreaming in his faint slumber. The visions overwhelmed his sleep-deprived mind, and the soldier knew that he wanted to remember, hoping that his brain was not too frail to do so, yet an inner confidence offered assurance. As it lured the scenes along a path that traveled through his eyes to his mind and then imprinted on his heart, strength pooled in his aching joints and stretched along each muscle. His spine zinged and popped as it shot to attention at the command.

"Thank you, Jesus," he cried, tears streaming down his face and salting his tongue.

Demanding his attention, a tinkering at the lock of the cage and then the flat backs of the metal bolts jostled as the door creaked and hissed and then gave way. His heart pounded through his inner ear, beating from the shallow marrow of his frail bones, yet he felt no fear. The intrusion called his tattered frame to attention, alerting his bodily systems to respond.

The stillness and silence permeated for a long length of time of which he could not quite discern, and then the peculiar sound of humming penetrated the barrier. The inviting tune rang deep and rich as higher pitches arose in the background while footsteps rustled about as if several people rushed in methodical sequence, accepting in earnest their assigned duties leaving no need for idle chatter. A large, dark hand grabbed the bottom of the door frame while its partner reached for the side. The plump, groomed digits looked soft and gentle, not war-torn and ragged, and the melody in the foreground expanded, unhindered as it heaved its way up and over the threshold.

Behind the enticing tone, a stout black lady in a white polyester uniform that zipped down the middle crawled in on all fours to reach him. Her massive afro constrained by the confines of the space showcased a metallic red clip that held back her bangs, and her chocolaty morsel eyes exuded gentle sweetness. "Come on now, honey," the woman spoke with angelic compassion as she squeezed into that small space. "We gonna get you outta here now."

"You are?" he muttered, his voice cracked in its efforts.

"Oh, sure thing, now," she assured him. "No worries."

The careful attendant reached for his broken ankles and cradled them in her warm padded hands to set them straight without causing even a tinge of pain. Her tender touch enveloped his bruised and scraped shins that had taken the brunt of his movements and guided his fragile body towards the entrance. The awakening eyes of the captive could then make out two other silhouettes waiting just outside his box. Dressed like orderlies, they rushed to assist their leader in placing his feeble body on a canvas stretcher while the large woman eased her way out of the doorway much like she had made her way in. As her feet touched the ground and the other figures stepped into motion, she changed their tune.

"Hallelujah, hallelujah," her voice echoed everywhere in its deep baritone pitch.

The other two chimed in harmony, praising the Lord as they worked to tend to his every wound and warmed him with a white, heated sheet. Certain that he smelled that fresh nostalgic fragrance of the fabric softener his grandma used to launder, the war-torn prisoner glanced to his left, surprised that his captors still remained. They appeared unaware of his extant rescue because they sat at their card table playing a game almost as if in slow motion. The notes of the angelic singing waved across their faces like a television screen losing its broadcast signal.

The delicate woman refocused his attention on his rescue as she knelt down to eye level and brushed the back of her hand against his sunken cheek. Her grin and nod invited him to participate in their praise.

"Hallelujah, hallelujah," the believer eked out, tears pouring from his eyes, strength welling up from some unknown place.

Six months had passed since the mysterious yet miraculous rescue, and the freed soldier grew anxious to finalize the poking, prodding, and interrogating and focus on the next mission. He had wearied of the debriefings and mandated physical therapy that consumed his days, leaving him little time to put his thoughts to paper and prepare his records. In utter desperation, the questions droned on in cyclic repetition in an effort to comprehend just how the prisoner had arrived at the checkpoint out of nowhere.

"So, the reports from the soldiers guarding the border station indicate that you just walked up to them and rapped on the window," Major Mercado, the third army psychologist to interview him, questioned with that familiar tone of disbelief.

"Yes, that's right, sir," Sergeant Riley replied, sitting upright in his metal chair and resting his cupped hands on the brown table that divided them.

The interrogation room reminded the soldier of those cop shows on television where the voices echoed off of the cold, block walls and the lights blinded their detainee into submission. The elongated window in the door exposed the occasional passerby while the looming mirror on the wall behind the interviewer kept the target wondering who was listening and why it needed to be so covert. In full disclosure, the debriefing team recorded every meeting, so the rescued one knew that his sessions were not private. So much for creating a calm, inviting, resting place for him to recover and share as much intelligence as he could remember.

"But you don't seem to fully recall how you got there?" Major Mercado continued.

This line of questioning always left the witness in such a conundrum. A part of him wanted nothing more than to let loose and give them every single fantastical description that he could articulate, yet the staunch, almost defensive reception that he faced limited his enthusiasm.

"I've tried to tell you all, but no one seems to want to take me seriously," the sergeant replied.

"Well, why don't you give me a try?" the medical specialist suggested.

"I have said it so many times, but I will tell you again. There were three people that rescued me. One of them removed the door by the hinges, and then the other two helped to lift me out. They tended to my wounds, warmed me with some blankets, and then carried me through some woods and down a hill to that road. They set the stretcher down there and then pointed me towards the guard station. They said the folks there would take care of me," the rescued one maintained.

"But you don't know who these people were? Where they came from? Or even how you were able to walk?" the questioning continued.

"Well, no, not really. I mean, they did not identify themselves, and I certainly was not going to refuse their help. I don't know exactly how I was able to walk, but once I stepped off of that stretcher, I had some strength back. I didn't race down there or anything. I mean, I took my time, but I just moved one foot in front of the other," the frustrated soldier claimed.

The major shuffled through the paperwork in between his own random note taking, and Sergeant Riley could tell that this guy lacked the foundational ability to put all of the pieces together either.

"The medical reports indicate that you sustained significant injuries during your captivity. Broken bones, dehydration, weight loss, multiple scars from severe lacerations," Mercado read aloud.

"It was a miracle, sir! I am not joking! I don't know how else I can possibly explain it to you. I'm not crazy! God intervened!" the warrior pleaded for understanding as he examined the eyes of the man across from him.

His insistence and gape caused the psychologist to pause and soak in the words. The sergeant could see the contemplation waging war in his interviewer's mind, but a quick blink, a shake of the head, and the seed was tossed aside.

"I understand your religious convictions, Sergeant Riley," Major Mercado attempted to resume control as he cleared his throat. "The previous notes make that quite clear. Although I don't discount your devotion to your beliefs, you have to understand that we cannot simply report that this entire ordeal can be set aside and chalked up to the big man upstairs. We need something a bit more concrete than that."

Four manila folders, two mechanical pencils, and one yellow

tablet were all that the recovering patient had requested for his own private stash. Along with his Bible, he kept them in his brown leather satchel wherever he went. The veteran disciple knew that most of his superiors would not understand the contents of his scribbles, so he did his best to keep them as his own personal journals.

"Sergeant Riley," his commanding officer approached him in the day room. "Good news. I have received your next duty assignment from higher up. You ready to get out of here?"

"You know I am, sir," the sergeant affirmed.

"Let's go meet in my office," Captain Schaller proposed.

"Yes, sir," the sergeant approved.

Valuing each page, the fervent follower returned them to their respective folders and stacked his records with care, securing them with his black, leather-bound Bible before slinging the satchel over his head and across his chest. Once in the office, Captain Schaller recited the orders with encouraging motivation while the sergeant chuckled under his breath, recognizing the humor the Lord used sometimes.

"So, it looks like you are going to the Midwest," Captain Schaller summarized. "A recruiting station will be a nice break for you and give you a chance to ease back into the swing of things."

"Yes, sir," the sergeant grinned.

Here the US Army was sending him to a recruiting station in the middle of hometown USA, assuming they were gracious in giving him active duty pay for a cushy job. The disciple could not help but smirk at the irony. Sure, the US Army signed his paychecks, but the warrior knew in his heart that he served a different commander in chief. The military was merely his cover. His true purpose in life was to lead others to Christ. His next mission for God's army: four lost souls in Central Illinois.

RECRUITMENT

CHAPTER 1

Sergeant Riley

The speeding train came to an abrupt halt at the isolated depot just on the south edge of downtown. One of five passengers in the railcar on the trek from St. Louis, Sergeant Riley could see on the concrete platform out of his window that a horde of corporate types chomped at the bit to get on board. The private soldier felt relieved to be getting off at this stop instead of enduring the demanding masses the rest of the way to Chicago.

A consummate professional, the noncommissioned officer (NCO) stood to collect himself, zipped his black, short-waisted coat, and secured his uniform cap on his head to ensure no gusts of wind or pushy mobs would knock off his head cover. As he walked to the front of the cabin and retrieved his long green duffle bag and black rolling chest from the large carpeted storage bins, the doors slid open, and the briskness of the winter cold air livened his face.

Many of the civilians straightened up and stepped aside as the uniformed soldier departed the train. Some of the waiting passengers fumbled to put their hand over their heart or tip their brow in a salute, unsure of the proper etiquette for such an encounter, but the humble service man passed by before they came to a decisive conclusion. Most of his assignments operated behind enemy lines or on military bases, so this stint in the heart of common folk made him uncomfortable and would require some getting used to.

The visitor no sooner passed the cement benches than the crowd resumed their frantic push to get out of the cold and onto their commuter transportation. They had spent enough of their precious time ogling the military man. A rare sighting for sure, time was money after all.

Preferring to move and operate in the background, the former sniper was more than relieved to have his audience proceed with their normal activities. He found he could do his best people watching from that point of view. As the newcomer strolled towards the courtesy terminal, he spotted the taxi driver motioning him in that direction. The guest figured his uniform exposed his approaching position; however, he appreciated the driver's punctuality.

The husky cabbie greeted his client and opened the trunk for his passenger's luggage. "No doubt you are the sergeant I'm picking up?"

"Yes, sir," the soldier replied.

"Oh, don't call me sir," the gentle giant corrected. "I work for a living."

Recognizing the line of military talk that signaled the separation of the officer ranks from the enlisted, the sergeant appreciated the welcoming banter. During the exchange, the camouflaged disciple fought to maintain eye contact while placing his own gear into the back of the bright-yellow Nissan Cube that served as his hired ride because he aimed to show love to people by being present with them, ensuring that they knew that he was paying attention.

It was a small act of service and one that had morphed into a covert tactic in this stage of the global spiritual warfare. All the while the faithful follower would pray that the Holy Spirit would move in him or help him to discern the needs of whomever he encountered. The waging warrior had trained enough at his gift to ascertain in a short amount of time whether someone served the enemy, served the King, ran from the conflict, or remained stuck somewhere in the middle. As per his training, he referred to the last set of folks as collateral damage.

Much like the battlefield in traditional warfare, civilians milled about their everyday lives, oblivious to the staunching effect of the fight until the looming discomfort forced a response in one of four ways. One faction joined the enemy, fearing its punishing blow more than anything else or buying the lie that the evil side would, in due time, win out anyway. Some surrendered their lives to the King of Kings, gripping to the truth of victory. Others fled with their backs to the conflict, convinced that they could avoid the scene altogether and pursue a life of nothing but happiness on their own strength. Or still another group remained stuck in the middle, clinging to a false reality that they were neutral and neither working for the darkness nor for the light. This section existed in the chaos of the world, surviving each day by its own accord.

Sergeant Riley understood his posting as a fighter in the spiritual corps of combat arms, so he served on the front lines. That meant that he fought to gain ground and defend those that battled this sort of placement whether they even realized it or not. That was his calling.

As the visitor stared into this driver's eyes, he discerned without hesitation that this prompt fellow was collateral damage. Sometimes these folks resisted, settling to ignore the chaos in, around, and through their lives. The blinded patrons reasoned it away with the greatest of ease, and the clever enemy surrounded them with enough propaganda to keep it that way. The darkness used all genres of media: television, radio, print, the Internet. They were crafty, he had to give them that, but the strength of their ploys paled in comparison to that of the Holy Spirit.

The sergeant understood full well that words alone did not draw attention to the belt of truth, but communication was required to yield the sword. His gifts of discernment and evangelism helped him gauge with astute accuracy how aggressive the warrior needed to be and when. As this particular gentleman seemed distracted by his breastplate, the military man deciphered that his chauffeur was far from making a decision. Sergeant Riley figured that this former enlisted vet was unaware that a decision even needed to be made. "Prior service, I see. Where at?" the sergeant asked with his unconcealed southern twang as he closed the hatch.

"Second Armored Cavalry Regiment out of Fort Polk, Louisiana," the driver touted as he dug for his keys and scrunched into the driver's door. "Lanes training at the JRTC. You know, the Joint Readiness Training Center?"

"Fort Polk. The good ole bayou. Really?" The sergeant offered his praise while taking his place on the opposite side.

"Hooah!" the driver grunted in reply. "I was no paper pusher, Sarge. No offense."

"Oh, none taken," the sergeant engaged in the friendly exchange.

Sergeant Riley accepted that his contact had assumed that he was a desk pusher since he was assigned to the recruiting station in town. Most soldiers in this type of position for the armed forces were young, attractive, and well-polished, although often not well-seasoned. The new recruiter realized that he was not a spring chicken, and maybe he had been considered attractive once, but the notion of the assignment itself set the tone.

"You sound like you might be from somewhere down in those parts," the cabbie retorted.

"Can't say that I've ever been to Fort Polk, but I spent a lot of time in Georgia," the sergeant confessed. "That's likely the sound you hear."

The driver grinned and then hopped off of memory lane. "So where we headed?"

As Sergeant Riley reached into the outer compartment of his satchel to retrieve his pocket-sized day planner, he knew this guy must have thought him archaic, using an ancient tool like a paper planner instead of an electronic one, and perhaps he was right.

Technology was by no means his strong suit, so the passenger flipped to his contacts and recited the address. "116 Cypress St."

"Shoot, that's not far at all, Sarge," the driver barked as he punched the meter and sped away.

The serious military man thought how silly the two of them must have looked in this submarine-like vessel that they were passing off for a car these days. The lean and fit soldier always committed to maintaining his physical ability to answer the call of the Lord as well as oblige the requirements of his cover, but he still had to cram his active frame into the tiny motorized contraption. If he had not witnessed the feat firsthand, he would have questioned the probability of his hired ride, nearly three times his size, to accomplish the challenge.

Although his escort must have been fit once upon a time to have served at the JRTC, his stature suggested he had long since retaliated against the strict regimen of daily exercise that the military required. The sidekick wore no coat, his own body's insulation keeping him warm enough for the tiny heated space. His knit, short-sleeved shirt hung to his knees in hopes of covering his sagging belly, and his baggy jeans bloomed so as not to constrict him during his long hours on the road. His shaved hair looked like a one-guard Caesar cut, but the sergeant surmised that this style choice had a lot more to do with his lack of hair and unwillingness to work with it than his previous years in the army. While his nails appeared to be manicured with his mouth, although his two thumbnails looked long for a man, his smoker's growl combined with the overwhelming scent of Old Spice attempted to mask the cigarette vapors trapped within the confines of the car.

Reminiscent of his months in captivity, a bit of claustrophobia crept its way in with them that morning, so the freed soldier leaned on the Lord. *Jesus, help me,* the sergeant prayed from within. *I rebuke these caged feelings and demand that they flee. Lord, soften my heart instead to serve this here man you've sent to me for however long I have with him.*

Right away the driver cracked his window, allowing the gust of crisp February air to make a once through the vehicle. "Not too cold for you, Sarge, if I get a bit of circulation in here?" the cabbie presented his best hospitality.

The sergeant replied, "Not a bit. Uh, ya know, I just realized that I don't even know your name."

"Randall, Randall Hornsby at your service," the man touted, being sure to keep his eyes on the road as he made a right turn.

"Well, Hornsby, it's a pleasure to meet ya, and no, I appreciate the bit of air in here," the sergeant added.

"Ditto," the driver replied as he slowed the car, made a u-turn, and zipped into a graveled shoulder in front of a corner house. "Told you it was close."

"Wow, we're already here?"

"I'll help you with your bags," the oversized man offered as he struggled to reach his seatbelt release.

"Not at all," Sergeant Riley interrupted as he raised his hand to stay the movement. "That won't be necessary, but I appreciate it. Is a $20 okay?"

"Sure thing. I'm pretty sure I can make that change."

Hornsby jostled his lean to his other side in an attempt to find his wallet in his back left pocket.

"No change necessary," the passenger insisted. "Please."

"Why, thank you, Sarge," the driver accepted. "And, welcome to Normal."

"Thanks again, Hornsby. Say, do ya have a card or somethin' in case I need your services again?" The visitor aimed to keep the contact possibility open.

"We are kind of a small operation around here, Sarge," the cabbie chuckled, "so no cards or anything of that sort. Just give us a ring. I own the place."

"Roger that!"

The obliging sergeant reached out to shake Hornsby's hand, which seemed to surprise his new acquaintance a bit. Good old-fashioned handshaking proved to be another lost art and thus a present day covert action of seed planting. The simple act of touch in this obscure way allowed another means for the Holy Spirit to connect with a lost one. Sometimes the unassuming person realized that something happened during the exchange, that something was a bit different about a touch from Him, while others just focused too much on the propaganda to even notice. The oblivious ones had become desensitized, but the sergeant always got a bit of a thrill deciphering the results. He often restrained himself from blurting out, "Did you feel that? Did you feel Him?"

Although the trained soldier had learned to control his tongue in this way, he suspected that his facial expressions still exuded his anticipation, and he smiled in relief at Hornsby's response. His new friend displayed that fine mixture of reassurance and yet confusion. The cabbie conveyed that he appreciated their encounter and would be pleased to have another one day. With that confirmation, the sergeant closed the door behind him and waved as he watched Hornsby zoom off.

Sergeant Riley then draped his precious satchel over his head, hoisted the green duffle onto his shoulder, and pulled the black trunk with his other hand, pausing at the gate to absorb the landscape. As he eyed the two-story farmhouse with dull white metal siding, the narrow height fell into the background and rested on an unlevel front porch that had been converted from an overhang. By enclosing the original opening with cedar planks painted to match the siding and inserting some windows to allow in the natural light, the cock-eyed room added depth and character. Although the cement block foundation stood sturdy and upright, the abstract pattern of the chipping gray paint revealed it had weathered the storms of time, and the ice-brittled lawn with random spots indicated it pastured a dog on occasion.

As the keen observer took a couple of steps to his left and peered along the side of the house, he saw a single-lane driveway off of the main road and a mismatched garage addition. The brown cedar planking on that part of the structure seemed out of place since the owner maintained the color consistency at the front, but as the intuitive mind gazed to his right down the rest of Cypress Street, he observed how this hodgepodge approach fit in with the rest of the neighborhood.

Interspersed amidst overgrown trees with lawns seeded for functionality, not for adornment, ranch-style homes exhibited varied combinations of wood and metal, and a couple of the larger homes presented divergent garage add-ons as well even though most of the neighbors just lined their cars in the gravel drives. In the next block just past the railroad tracks that trailed its path to meet the hustle and bustle of the big city, stood a dark brick building with a corporate office attachment and some playground equipment fenced in off of the back side.

Although the sergeant's particular mission field involved adults, he always enjoyed watching others work with the young ones. Because the shimmer of the morning sun reflected that foggy haze where darkness and light met, the aging combatant could not quite read the earthy brown sign with black lettering, so he burned a mental note to scout out the facility another time.

Comfortable with the lay of the land, the newcomer unlatched the chain-link gate, positioned his belongings inside the yard, and secured it behind while maintaining his scan for further signs of a four-legged visitor rushing to greet him. Satisfied that he could relax, the soldier paced with ease up to the porch, pried open the storm door with his patent leather shoe, re-gathered his luggage on the fake grass carpet, and rang the bell. The courteous visitor hoped his arrival would not startle his new landlord, but the soldier had sent prior notice that he would be arriving in the wee hours.

As the high-pitched yelps of a small pooch broke through the silent stillness and sounded the alarm—a confirmation to his cursory intelligence survey—the overhead light flickered and a stern voice resounded from within. "Lulu, stop your incessant barking!" the adamant woman ordered. "I have it! I told you someone was coming this morning."

Permitting himself a faint grin, the sergeant raised the back of his hand to cover his mouth and clear his throat so as not to offend the two having the rather odd conversation.

"Now scoot back so that I can open the blessed door," she scolded back at her little pal.

The barking never did die down, but the front door creaked opened and the old woman peeked sideways around the edge, her squinted eyes and unadorned fingernails the only body parts exposed. Sergeant Riley hoped that she had not had trouble with intruders or scammers in the past, but her mannerisms thus far left him quite unsure.

Without further delay, he removed his cover, secured it under his left armpit, and extended his right hand. "Morning, ma'am," he offered. "I'm Sergeant Hamilton Riley."

The aged woman held her ground while the two adults ignored the relentless barking of little Lulu.

"I am the one that hopes to rent your upper room?" he tried to maintain a smooth demeanor to keep her calm.

Still no response, so Sergeant Riley attempted to make friends with the canine. The small yet mighty lap dog bounced around his ankles with her black curls and beige goatee minimizing the fierce effect that she fought to convey.

"Well, you must be Lulu," he knelt down to offer his palm.

As the ferocious-minded dog increased her howl and her growl and retreated to the prone position to be at the ready, the sergeant accepted defeat. "I'm sorry," the polite figure apologized as he stood back up. "Maybe I'm not even at the right place. Are you Ms. Hoback?"

Still the awkward silence remained, and the stunned Sergeant Riley held his position until he caved to the unspoken tension, secured his cap back on his head, grabbed his luggage, and headed back out to the road.

"Yes," the woman interrupted his movement as she broke free from her barricade, "I'm Ms. Hoback. Come on in. Just ignore the dog." That was it. With no further explanation, the strange woman ordered him into the house, expecting his compliance without further discussion.

Having been forewarned that his landlord was difficult, the renter conceded so as not to make matters worse. Yes, difficult was the word used by a pastor friend with reluctance. Jarrod had tried to be polite and not gossipy as he provided his aunt's contact information. The endearing nephew loved his aunt, she was family after all, but she could be hard to get along with, especially at first.

Jarrod had divulged that Gladys Hoback was a retired English teacher from one of the more diverse high schools in the area and had never been married. Old Aunt Gladys had never been married and no children, but she loved the Lord and considered it her responsibility to help others—just in her own special way.

Jarrod revealed that his aunt managed the leasing of the family farmland as well as one of the farmhouses. On occasion, for a few worthy applicants, she rented a small studio apartment on the second floor of her home, and the pastor was hopeful that he could at least put in enough of a good word for his faithful friend to warrant a telephone interview, a prerequisite for his aunt's standard operating procedures. It must have worked because one day the sergeant got a call from his pal giving him the green light to give her a ring.

"Good luck, man," Jarrod offered with caution.

The sergeant could not help but minimize the concerns of his dear friend. With all that he had endured during his many years in the service, the dedicated soldier was not fazed by the likes of an old woman that had grown rigid around the edges due to a life of being alone. Shoot, he figured much the same could be said of him.

The phone interview had been short and to the point. The sergeant preferred that type of direct communication, so it did not deter his efforts. Ms. Hoback asked very reasonable questions, or perhaps it was more along the lines of expressing her more obvious concerns.

"How long do you plan on staying?" Gladys asked as soon as he greeted her on the line.

"Well, ma'am," the soldier responded, "the assignment is for three years, and it is my hope that I can make your studio my home for the duration."

"Three years, you say. Did my nephew tell you I charge $250 a month?"

"Yes, ma'am, he mentioned that," the sergeant answered.

"I expect cash on the first of every month. I don't want any checks bouncing, and I don't want to hunt you down," Ms. Hoback directed.

"Oh, yes, ma'am. That will not be a problem," he provided.

"I also won't have any loud noises and no girls up there," she scolded.

"Ma'am, yes, I totally understand. You need not worry," he obliged.

"Oh, I won't worry. It just won't be allowed!" the retired school teacher corrected his phrasing.

"Yes, ma'am," he shortened his response to avoid any further miscommunication.

"Well, when are you going to be here?" The aged bachelorette must have concluded that he was worth the risk, at least for a trial run.

"Well, ma'am," he explained, "my train arrives on 12 February, but it is scheduled to get in early, around 0600 hours."

"0600 hours? I don't talk like that, Mr. Riley," Ms. Hoback interjected.

"Oh, yes, forgive me, ma'am," the sergeant apologized. "Old habits die hard. That would be six in the mornin'. I hope that is not too early for you?"

"No, that will be fine," the former farmer directed. "I will see you then."

A probable precursor to his uncomfortable arrival, she hung up the phone with no unnecessary pleasantries. Sure, she was abrupt and brash, but in his line of work, he had dealt with far, far worse.

Now that he passed her physical inspection, the staunch landlady led him into the dining room just inside the front door and placed her coffee mug down on a doily as she retrieved a small silver key from her robe pocket to unlock a gray metal door on the wall that resembled a circuit breaker box. The pencil notations on the inside of the panel matched the corresponding labels on the keys that hung from thin wire loops attached to color-coated push pins. The ingenious system that embraced the advantages of proper key control declared that Ms. Hoback would have made a fine supply sergeant in her heyday.

Gladys retrieved a brass piece that dangled from a neon-orange, spiral elastic bracelet, jotted a note on the panel roster, and locked the case behind her. Before issuing the tarnished key, she scolded little Lulu who had not yet halted the intruder alert, grabbed her coffee, and steered toward her new guest who still waited near the door.

Trying to gather and analyze intelligence while maintaining a level of respect for the older woman, the sergeant was surprised to find Ms. Hoback in such good shape for her age. She looked slender and fit, and she walked with perfect agility, although he doubted that she participated in any formal exercise. It was not as if it were not possible that she could be a member of the local gym, but the older woman struck him more as one of those old-fashioned types that believed hard work was all the exercise needed to maintain a healthy lifestyle.

The precise woman wasted little time on other superficial traits, leaving her hair shoulder length and permed to minimize the maintenance and no make-up. The bachelor did suppose that her bare face could be a result of his early morning arrival, but he suspected it was more routine than that. Her hazel eyes revealed no traces of mascara balled on the eyelashes or hints of color on the lids, and the thin lips had a normal pink hue. Women that wore lipstick often drained them of their natural brightness. No, the trained scout gathered that she embraced her God-given appearance—less the perm, of course.

Ms. Hoback kept her cheaters hung about her neck with a purple flowered chain and nothing showed beneath her turquoise terry cloth robe, so the observer figured she was a nightgown sort of gal. The house slippers were more like tan leather moccasins, more practical than the fluffy sort.

"This is your key," she offered it over to him. "Don't lose it, or I will have to charge you to have another made."

"Yes, ma'am." He accepted the neon ring, certain he would not lose the reflective accessory.

"It will let you into the garage service door out back and then into the back entrance. Head up the stairs, and it will then let you into your apartment. Breakfast will be served promptly at 7:00 a.m. each morning, so don't be late," the landlady explained.

"Oh, Ms. Hoback, I was not expecting you to provide breakfast," he chimed. "Jarrod explained to me quite fully that I would be on my own."

"Well, that is my policy, of course, but I am just letting you know that I will have breakfast down here. Eat it or don't. It's your choice, but if you are late, you won't get any. I have to have the dishes done on time and get to my day," the ole gal snipped, as she turned back around and off to the kitchen to his right. Lulu pranced right behind her owner, no longer concerned with the stranger.

Still confused by the entire exchange, the sergeant glanced to his left into the living room where dull orange carpet laid since the early 70s. The solemn room had no television, but a set of brown metal TV trays wedged in between an orange and brown flowered loveseat and a beautiful hand-crafted rocker with a floral-patterned cushion provided some vibrant accents. Next to the chair, he spotted the Bible and a notebook on an end table that doubled as a magazine rack full of almanacs, and on display under the front picture window, a mahogany hope chest rested with a delicate doily runner laid across its top. Opposite the main entrance to the home from where he made his detailed observations, the inquirer previewed the short hallway that connected a bathroom towards the right and a bedroom to the left where a multi-colored, handmade afghan draped over the end of a brass-finish bed frame.

With the enticing aroma of bacon fat wafting through the air and the mouth-watering sizzle popping in the pan, the combatant decided he better skedaddle to his studio and finish surveying the place later. After he marched around to the garage, through the service door, and up the stairs, the guest balanced his trunk on the landing while he fiddled with the lock until the door gave way and opened into the cozy gabled room. With years of disciplined simplicity under his belt, Sergeant Riley's initial assessment heralded the pine scent traces of cleanliness and the basic comforts of home.

Under an octagon window to the right that looked out onto Fell Avenue sat a two-top square oak table with matching chairs while the opposite side boasted an efficiency kitchen with a sink the size of a saucepan, two lower cabinets, a microwave atop a dorm-sized fridge, and a hot pot. The problem solver figured there was enough room there for a small coffeemaker as well, providing ready access to his daily staple. Neatly placed beneath the two normal-sized windows that peered back over Cypress, he located the sofa component of that brown and orange combination from downstairs. The pullout mechanics hidden underneath the cushions caused the center to sag just a touch, welcoming him to his new space with a frumpy grin. The rounded nightstand and stained-glass floor lamp completed the ensemble.

Realizing that his inventory lacked a water closet, the renter hoped that sharing the facilities in the main house was not the grand plan. Willing to work through the uncomfortable details with Ms. Hoback after breakfast, the recruiter rolled his trunk over to the couch and laid it on its side to second as a coffee table, leaned his duffle against the arm of the sofa, unlooped his satchel from his neck, and placed it atop the dining table. The soldier then returned to the pullout, draped his jacket across his bag, and secured it with his hat.

Not wanting to miss his gracious invitation to a fine spread with his new roommate, the early morning traveler scurried over to the kitchenette and refreshed his face with some cool water and skipped back down the stairs. When Sergeant Riley rapped on the front door, Lulu once again sounded her required alert.

"Come on in and take a seat," Ms. Hoback yelled from within. The protective woman appeared to have let her guard down in record time, and even Lulu took one look at him as he entered, perked her tail back up, and took her leave back to the kitchen.

"Is there something I can help you with, ma'am?" he hollered in her direction.

"No, no. I have it all covered. Just take a seat and help yourself to the coffee. Your place is the first one on the west side," she ordered back.

The combatant appreciated her use of the cardinal directions. He was hard pressed to find anyone these days that used them so readily, but they steered him to his exact setting just to the left of hers at the head. It was apropos that Ms. Hoback be placed at the helm; it was her house, after all, but if he had to guess, he would have thought her old school enough to insist that he sit at the end since he was a man.

As the caffeine enthusiast sat and poured himself some coffee into the rose-accented china cup placed on its dainty saucer, Ms. Hoback carried in a serving tray of piping hot vittles with Lulu nipping at her heels. The determined woman gave a heaving sigh as she leaned to set the fixings in between their two place settings, and as the gentleman rose from his seat and reached out to offer some aid, she ordered him back down again. The stubborn landlady did not want him throwing her off balance with good intentions.

The hot juicy bacon that had been tempting him all morning lay in crisp curls just as he liked it, while the eggs fried over easy, pile of toast, mason jar full of jelly, potato hash, fried apples, and fried cornmeal mush with real maple syrup widened his eyes and made his stomach growl. To his recollection, the southern gentleman had not enjoyed fried cornmeal mush since childhood.

"Wow, Ms. Hoback," he doted, "you are treatin' me like royalty. You did not have to go to all of this trouble, but I sure do appreciate it."

"Oh, it was no trouble," the stern one struggled to accept the praise. "Breakfast is the most important meal of the day. I normally cook like this, but of course, I had to increase the portions now that you are here."

"Well, I am truly honored, ma'am," he replied as he gave her a slight bow of the head and placed his hand to his chest, signifying his comments were from the heart.

"I can my own jellies and apples, so those items are always at the ready in my cellar. I usually make up a large batch of mush every other week and keep the pan in my refrigerator. I don't make the syrup, although I could, but I do use the real thing. Is there really any other kind? The potatoes were leftovers, so I only had to put on a few more eggs and strips of bacon because of you," she reasoned away.

"Well, still," he refused to ignore her hospitality no matter how much she tried to thwart him. "I am obliged to be at your table."

"Don't make a fuss about it," the former educator corrected. "What are your plans for the day?"

"Well, ma'am, after this fine fill," he offered as he patted his gut, "I need to head down to the office. It is just downtown on Broadway."

"Really?" the local resident questioned. "I don't recall ever seeing an army station down there, and I've lived in these parts my entire life."

"Yes, ma'am. It is not a station really," he explained further. "It is just an office where we recruit folks for the army. It is not a big operation at all, so I am sure it can be easily missed."

"Are you sure?" she pried. "I've walked to town a million

times, and I am a very observant person. I am always aware of my surroundings."

"Yes, ma'am, I'm sure," the polite sergeant answered. "I don't recall how long that particular office has been in that location, but I know it has been nearly twenty years."

"Well," the head of the table scoffed, "I will just have to walk down there myself one of these days and check in on you. What are you going to do if it isn't there and they sent you to the wrong place?"

"Well, ma'am, I am pretty sure my assignment is accurate," the interrogated one kept his calm at her insistence. "But I tell you what. Why don't you join me down there one day, and I could take you to lunch or something?"

"Oh, no need to do something like that. I always make better lunches here than you could ever get at a restaurant, and they charge so much," the frugal farmer contended. "No, I will just check in on you and then get back to my day."

"I would be honored," he resounded as the topic came to an abrupt end.

The grateful sergeant offered to help with the clean up, but Ms. Hoback declined. She preferred to wash her dishes herself because she knew how to get them clean, and it would take her longer to explain to him where everything went back into its place than if she were to just do it herself.

While the diligent woman cleared the table, her guest excused himself, hustled up to the studio, retrieved his coat, cover, and satchel, and hurried down towards the office to be sure that his landlord's concerns of a possible misplaced assignment were without merit.

CHAPTER 2

The Replacement

As the sergeant trekked down the sidewalk, he noticed the student housing that had saturated the area. The robust bungalows and grand Victorians that perhaps once entertained affluent adults or maybe even games of kick-the-can or hide-and-seek lay in impending decay for the sake of progress as the remnants of the previous night's drunken entertainment left its mark on the landscape. Porches full of tattered furniture that provided more comfortable seating for the masses, gutters clinging to the edges of the roofs by the last rusted screws, and windows encased by frames desperate for fresh paint proclaimed the rescinding dominance of the family unit.

To continue its need to impact and expand, the university converted homes into apartments, apartments into parking decks, and even parking decks into some newfangled combination of both. Although the modern approach to the ever-growing problem looked impressive with the ingenious architecture and stone accents, the relic preferred the down home feel of family and neighbors.

Still early in the morning for the average college student, the bright-eyed recruiter hiked unabated along the cement walk as the corporate traffic raced down College Avenue on their way to the east end. When the green stick figure lit up, Sergeant Riley continued his steady pace across and then east one block, past the town's library and then south on Broadway. Relieved to find the recruiting office wedged back behind the rear of a drum shop and the employee parking lot of the post office, the former sniper understood why the ordinary building went unnoticed to the untrained eye. Because the tiny station faced an entire block of stone with no store fronts, it thwarted any temptation for window shopping or a need to meander. It existed as more of one of those places for "he who had eyes to see."

When the middle-aged replacement reached the door, he was surprised to find it still locked and the lights off. A bit unnerved to find a military operation not running with the efficiency it should, even for a covert spiritual operation, the newcomer decided to reserve judgment until he could further assess the current duty sergeant, although his experience suggested that his predecessor took advantage of a lack of accountability.

"Sergeant!" a high-pitched voice called from down the hill to his left.

As the footloose and fancy free fellow in uniform skipped towards him with a youthful spring in his step, the sergeant blinked and squinted to clear the cold fog that clouded his vision, convinced that his eyes deceived him. Although the war-torn soldier lacked experience with the college-aged crowd, certainly this fledgling could not be the administrator of this fine facility.

"Sergeant! You must be Sergeant Riley," the giddy steward blurted as he reached out his hand to welcome the new recruiter.

"And you must be Sergeant Fowler," the combatant resolved as he grabbed the kid's hand with a firm grasp.

Just as his demeanor insinuated, the lad reacted with a weak attempt at a brute exchange, conveying in an instant that this guy's journey had been far different from his successor's. With red hair tapered beneath his cap that accented the faint freckles on his tender complexion, the ginger looked about eighteen. However, having just completed his own three-year stint as a recruiter, his appearance had to be part of his gift of disguise.

As Sergeant Fowler reached to unlock the door, the keen observer caught sight of the edges of some tattoo ink on his forearms. Far too trendy for his taste, the consummate professional again fought against his disposition to judge, but Sergeant Riley wondered how in the world the Lord planned to use him in this place. With his predecessor's physical ability to blend into the college town surroundings better, and all but one of his targets so young, the new recruiter felt inadequate.

"Sorry I kept you waiting," Fowler provided as he tossed his coat across the back of his chair and placed his cap on the stack of papers in the corner. "The little one kept me and the wife up last night, and then they are just so sweet and cute! It is hard to leave them in the morning, especially when you have to face the cold."

Unable to relate, the bachelor kept silent rather than force a disingenuous reply. Sergeant Riley had never married, no children he was aware of, and duty always took precedence for him. With this relaxed assignment aimed to ease him back into the routines of normal society, the staunch NCO wrestled with the reasons that this soldier gave for being tardy.

While the young man continued to spout on about his beautiful life, the sergeant opted to take a quick visual inventory of the place to help calm his nerves. The bleak office stocked with the necessary amounts of office furniture and advertising materials showcased a standard issue gray desk with a matching swivel chair and some black plastic seating for guests. Behind the desk stood three, dull gray, metal filing cabinets and a coat stand, and the compliant military man would have preferred its use as opposed to tossing the uniform coat across the chair.

Even though the front lobby supplied two brown bookshelves filled with black manual binders and some military magazines, the opaque plastic protectors and thin layer of dust hinted that they had not been cracked in ages. The yellowing on the desk computer revealed its age as well, and the technologically-challenged newcomer tensed at the thought of conquering the electronic beast.

In his cerebral schematic, Sergeant Riley rearranged the desk but granted the advantageous positioning of the other components. With only a view of a solid brick wall across the street, the freed captive felt the importance to bask in as much natural light as possible because darkness had taken on a whole new meaning for him since his rescue. The preference was not driven so much by fear as much as it was by appreciation of access to the sun.

"Excuse me, sergeant?" Fowler broke through the mental plans and scrunched his eyebrows in concern at his replacement.

"Yes, Sergeant Fowler, pardon me," Sergeant Riley rebounded. "I was just orienting myself to the place."

"Absolutely," Fowler spouted as he proceeded with his rant. "No problem. I was just asking if you wanted to go over any paperwork that you may have brought with you?" Fowler took his seat behind the desk, crossed his arms and laid them to rest atop a large table calendar in front of him, leaned in and cocked his head as his mouth grinned from ear to ear.

The jolly nature of this guy rubbed the sergeant wrong somehow. Although the experienced disciple embraced exuberant joy, Fowler struck him more along the lines of someone that either did not know of the darkness in this world or refused to acknowledge it. With his forerunner expressing that pie-in-the-sky kind of demeanor with the wide eyes and constant twinkle, the cautious skepticism that the sergeant had developed over the years triggered the gears to engage his emotional wall. The defensive posture confused him a bit given the mission they both shared.

Because Sergeant Riley had grown accustomed to the authoritative role of giving orders, mentoring the novices, setting the pace, the idea of this young fellow facilitating the hand-off, counseling him on the history of the station seemed almost backwards. Already this assignment in Normal felt all kinds of different, but the obedient soldier moved forward with the mission which required an interview with this Opie Taylor.

"I am not aware of any paperwork," the reliever confessed.

"Really?" Fowler sounded bewildered. "Are you sure there is nothing? Personal notes? Perhaps some miraculous vision that needed documenting?"

Sergeant Riley fidgeted in the guest chair and strained to maintain his stoic, professional posture with this line of questioning. Sure, he understood that he and this young whippersnapper fought for the same team, but his journal was personal, and the experienced fighter had no previous indication that he would be expected to share it. He had labored with mindful discretion to decode key components without divulging too much detail in case his notes fell into unbelieving hands. As the interrogations during his recovery had dragged on and he accepted the reality that no one aided his spiritual mission, the loner had succumbed to the idea of tackling this one solo. However, the doe-eyed ginger staring at him, smiling, waiting, forced him to reconsider his position.

"Listen, Sergeant Fowler," the older comrade began his explanation, "my journal is very personal, and I had no intentions of really sharing it."

"Oh, believe me, I understand," Fowler responded. "I felt the same way."

He felt the same way? The only scars this lad seemed to display were the self-imposed ones hidden beneath his shirt sleeves, and those appeared to be more of a fashion statement than battle wounds. The tried and true warrior hated to be presumptuous, but his gifted intuition was rarely off the mark about these things.

"I'm sorry," the sergeant chimed in. "I mean no disrespect, uh, Sergeant Fowler, but I am not sure if we are truly talking about the same thing here."

"Oh, sure we are," Fowler rattled. "That is exactly how I got assigned here too."

"Do you mind elaborating?" the sergeant begged.

"Absolutely!" Fowler complied. "To make a long story short, I joined the army because I was not sure what else I wanted to do with my life. School was never really my thing, and I had my girl—that's my wife now—and I needed to provide for her somehow. Well, fast forward, and I was stationed at Fort Eustis, Virginia, learning how to drive a truck. I had no special affection for vehicles really, but that is where they put me. Anyway, I was playing guitar for a band on my nights off, and well, I eventually got saved. The actual event took place in my barracks room at the time. I had one other bunk mate, but he was not in that night. I had been partying a bit too much, but a couple other guys in my unit had been witnessing to me. The Lord spoke so clearly to me that night, like the games and riding the fence had to stop. Well, I'm sure you know exactly what I'm talking about. Fast forward a bit, and I married my girl. We have a baby girl now, did I tell you that part? Well, anyway, fast forward a bit more and the Lord spoke to me so clearly one night after some fervent prayer with my mentor. He showed me in my uniform reaching a bunch of young adults like myself at some frat party. There was so much more, it all came so fast and furious. I tried to write down as much as I could when I got the chance. Next thing I know, I got reassigned here to recruit. The sergeant I replaced really spent a lot of time with me to get me started."

Sergeant Riley struggled to put the pieces of the puzzle together and keep up with the frantic pace in which his predecessor recited his story. So, he gathered that they both were given a vision to reach the lost in this area, and lacking sovereign intuition, the army reassigned them to this spiritually strategic locale. During his own particular encounter with Jesus, the captive observed four different civilians, glimpses of them hurdling obstacles in their daily lives, and the sergeant's heart grieving in desperation for them to heed his message as he shared the Gospel.

Although some of the intricate details lacked clarity, Sergeant Riley was able to discern some specifics about his primary targets. While a Spanish-looking guy played soccer and smelled like taco meat, the athlete looked almost paranoid as he continued to scan the surrounding terrain. The teenage girl cried over a crib, and a grade-school boy trotted alone on his way to school with his hair and clothes disheveled, his innocent gaze fixated on the ground as if he was unaware or indifferent to his surroundings. The one older guy looked muscular and strong, but his beating heart exuded a soft compassion. Although the speed of the scenes blurred the finite circumstances, all four were bound with heavy chains that hindered every movement as they muddled through their unattached existences. As two weights forced the necks down, two others pounded on the hearts.

During the divine preview that came during his captivity, the older recruiter visualized his engagements with the marks in the course of their regular lives, and the Holy Spirit allowed a glimpse of his disguise under the cover of the US Army but in a secluded place that the Lord had set aside for this soulful purpose. With a segment of accountability reporting, the Comforter indicated that the sergeant would not be pioneering this post but instead would replace a position that had been well established. Sergeant Riley had just begun to link some of the components together in a reasonable sequence when the captain in Germany ordered him into the office to present him with transfer orders and a reassignment.

The surrendered servant always marveled in amazement at how the Lord guided his faithful followers with just enough light to guide one step or two at a time. To get one's feet to marching, He placed a strong sense of direction and purpose on the heart, a comforting cornerstone, so to speak, but when it came to the movement itself, He never let the soldier get too far ahead. It would not be following then, would it? Nope, it would look a bit more like leading, which always got the soldier in trouble. Always concerned with maturing growth, Jesus allowed the puffy-chested will or aggressive logical mind to stumble along for alittle while until He restored them, making them strong, firm, and steadfast.

Even during his out-processing in Germany, the sergeant had

been briefed that this recruiting station was a small, one-man operation, so the transfer knew he would be filling someone else's shoes. Given the nudgings of the Holy Spirit, the disciple concluded with confidence that the duty sergeant that he was replacing had been a double agent as well.

The new recruiter could accept all of that, but he had assumed that the outgoing administrator would be older, wiser, more of a mentor for him instead. The spry tenderness of Fowler affected his military pride as well as his Christian walk, or so he thought.

Jolted with the call to surrender and submission, the bewildered disciple shook his head as he lowered his rightful position. Having figured that his last assignment tackled his temptation for unrighteous pride, the sergeant recognized that he was relegating self-glory ahead of glory to God. The early wake-up call corrected his inward disposition. "I apologize, Sergeant Fowler," Sergeant Riley confessed. "I've been prideful and frankly a bit too possessive with my reassignment. It is a challenge not to cling to how I think it should go."

Without hesitation, Fowler forgave the humble replacement, and the two delved into a thorough, productive debriefing session. Fowler shared in great detail his call to reach some students in Theta Chi as well as some successes and failures he had along the way. He surrendered his contact list of helpful, faithful saints and important support locations in the area and had even been so kind as to put them in a pocket-sized address book for his successor. The predecessor did not know then that the older sergeant had been technologically-challenged but had only been prompted to do so during a power outage one day. Making his own assumptions, the hipster expected the newly appointed duty sergeant would be, well, much younger, and with youth came a common affinity to all things digital.

The two perused a detailed map of a camp about thirty miles south in a farming community named Clinton, and Fowler shared his thankfulness for the facilities, the staff, and the valuable training he and his recruits had received there. "I mean, you may have another plan of attack, but I am telling you, this Bible boot camp was absolutely amazing for my mission!" the enthusiastic guide recalled.

Sergeant Fowler detailed how this camp, Fort Gideon, was founded as a summer church camp some years back, and a former soldier had joined forces with the staff to implement a challenging but effective discipleship training course for adults. This fellow, by the name of Akpore, merged his intricate knowledge and experience of molding immature privates into the fundamentals of basic soldiering skills and his deep-seated passion for spiritual formation into a full-fledged basic training program for the willing Christ warrior.

"It is amazing!" the zealous ginger continued. "I mean, he took all of those same things we learned at boot camp, you know, marching, weapons, land nav, all of it, and he used those skills to teach about the spiritual disciplines. This dude recognized that a lot of Christians were never taught the basic combat skills, but for the spiritual battle, ya know?"

There it was again, that unexpected encounter with the workings of the good Lord that could make even the toughest of skeptics smile in gentle reminder that He was sovereign. The outgoing administrator seemed none the wiser that his replacement hailed from that little, sleepy town of Clinton. Shoot, although it was just a half-hour south of Normal, it was reasonable to ascertain that the rural community was where the sergeant first mastered his southern twang. It seemed odd to folks that such an accent could start so close to the boundaries of Highway 74, but the morphed dialect was undeniable.

Once they had gone over the nuts and bolts of the operation and its amazing ability to serve its dual purpose, Fowler again asked for the sergeant's journal. "I understand the vulnerable nature of the contents, but believe me, it was so helpful to have my previous duty sergeant review mine and offer me some insight," Fowler treaded.

"Absolutely, Sergeant Fowler," the new recruiter conceded. "I would appreciate your input."

It did prove helpful. Sergeant Fowler recognized the older target from television, although he was not sure where the local celebrity resided now. "I can't remember exactly which little town he's from, but it is over by Peoria."

Fowler could not offer any information on the girl nor the Spanish target, but he showed his substitute some Mexican communities on the map. Although there was no definitive indication that the guy was Mexican, that seemed to be the largest Latin population in those parts. The schoolboy, however, was a different story, and the predecessor remembered that the kid had been a previous target as outlined in the cold case files.

With the unexpected breakthrough, Sergeant Riley's eyes sparkled and his grin relaxed at that tidbit of intel, even more thankful that he submitted to Fowler's request. Service to the King could never be done alone; that was not His ultimate desire, and the disciple was remembering that truth all too well. Marching with the Master was always stronger where two or more were united in His name.

Pausing their discussion to rifle through one of the filing cabinets, Fowler searched for the frayed folder that had been left in storage and bounced back to the desk in triumphant delight, file in hand. Together the two soldiers perused the sparse documentation about an eight-year-old child that grew up less than a mile from that very office. The cursive notes indicated that the mark had three older sisters, his mom and dad were still married, he was a regular church attender, and he was a good boy for all intents and purposes, but the assigned recruiter at the time had annotated only a few comings and goings of the child in the area. None of the intelligence provided clear evidence that he, or she, had ever approached the lad.

The sergeant's chest tightened as envy rose from beneath his collar, jealous that this kid had been sought out at such an early age. Expecting the same pursuit would have saved him a lot of heartache and given him more time to serve the King, he wished that the same could be said of him. Concern also forged its way into the mix at the realization that the first mission had been unsuccessful, and the unformatted notes lacked proper dating techniques, concealing the age of the case.

According to Fowler's recollection, it had neither been assigned to his predecessor nor the one before her. With a cursory calculation, the new recruiter surmised that this target who had been about seven or eight years old in his initial vision was now about eighteen or nineteen. Here Sergeant Riley would have been expecting a child but instead would be encountering a young adult.

CHAPTER 3

The Tenant

As the darkness of the short winter month settled in, Sergeant Riley finished the intense review of the recruiting operations with Sergeant Fowler. Because the two diligent combatants had delved with such vigor into the exchange, they resolved to undertake the physical recon of the surrounding community another day. For now, the tired traveler would unwind in his new home and the exuberant husband would return to his precious baby girl.

After Fowler locked the door and shook hands with his new-found friend, he skipped back down the hill while Sergeant Riley tucked his hands into the pockets of his jacket and lowered his head into the southern-blowing winter wind.

Although the Sergeant's first day was winding down, he could tell the college proper had come alive as students rushed here and there, huddled together as they discussed their options for that evening's festivities. Surprised that the busybodies scrambled about unaware of his military presence, the newcomer enjoyed the evening walk less the fumbling stares that he had already experienced earlier that same morning. With a hurried step to warm his body that was still acclimating itself and the day's accomplishments calming his drive, the disciple seized the mountaintop moment to devote himself to some meditation. "More of you, Lord, and less of me," the follower spoke aloud in hushed tones.

The moist heat in his breath joined with the coolness of the brisk air as they danced their way out into openness of the atmosphere, and the astute observer watched their union twirl and spin as if in its own special waltz. The private dance warmed his heart as a reminder that the warrior was never alone because he served a great and mighty King, the God of the universe who put all things into motion. Even the air from within him and the air just outside bowed to His majesty and revealed His magnificent glory.

As the rejuvenated renter fumbled through his pant pocket for the orange spiral bracelet that served as his keychain, the silhouette rocking forward and back against the sheer drapes in a methodical cadence distracted the former sniper's progress. While the housemate peered through the slight separation of the two panels, he hoped the neighbors would not consider his methods sketchy or creepy, but he wanted to gather a bit more information about his landlord.

Sitting in her rocker, reading her Bible with the aid of her glasses, the long chain still draped about her neck, Ms. Hoback basked in her solace with her furry companion curled about her feet, offering comfort and warmth. Although the slight turn of her smile conveyed an abiding peace in her solitude, the stillness of the scene seemed empty without the remnants of a husband or children to frame the walls or fill a corner.

With the realization of the familiarity that resembled his own impending existence, the bachelor envisioned himself in her place, sitting alone in retirement in a home that creaked and hissed to the echoes of quiet. The sojourner had always justified his circumstances as par for the course with a demanding career that involved constant travel; however, Ms. Hoback's settled life seemed different.

As the single tenant strode through the service door and up the back stairs, his flooding thoughts continued the silent debate.

With his service to the King and the country, the sergeant survived in the preoccupation to his call. Day in and day out, he gleaned from the Word, prayed without ceasing, seized quiet moments to meditate, or worshipped even in the mundane. With all the ways that his missions consumed him, the idea that others operated with as much vigor without the continuous stimulation of adventure was difficult to imagine, and even more incomprehensible was the divided service that spouses and children required. Sure, he dabbled in a parental capacity when directing troops, ensuring they ate their greens, adhered to the lights-out procedures, and succumbed to the ritual expectation of proper personal hygiene, but he knew he was a temporary substitute, a stopgap in the maturation process. Like many folks that practiced the discipline in short spurts, he often thought he could have done a better job with some of the hoodlums assigned to his ranks, but even two months in the trenches of combative training paled in comparison to decades of childrearing.

But what about his housemate? Ms. Hoback displayed emotional stability, and she operated with more than enough organization to multitask with the best of them, a requirement for motherhood for sure.

As the door opened to the basic flat, forcing his mind back from contemplation, the distracted sergeant remembered that he never resolved that logistical issue with the bathroom, so he marched back down the steps, hoping that Ms. Hoback would not be too displeased with the necessary interruption. Before he touched the doorbell, the male renter could hear Lulu scampering to greet him.

"Lulu, stop the blasted barking!" Ms. Hoback conveyed her impatience with her four-legged companion.

"Sorry to disturb you, Ms. Hoback," he began, "but I needed to ask you a quick question about the latrine."

"Latrine?" the old gal questioned.

"Oh, yes, excuse me, ma'am," the house guest apologized. "I mean the bathroom."

"Mr. Riley, I know full well what a latrine is," she chided back.

"I was an English teacher after all. I embraced all facets of our beautiful and intrinsic language."

"Oh, I see, pardon me, ma'am."

The firm educator interjected, "I simply want to remind you once again that we do not use military lingo in this house. I have nothing against the service, and I am thankful for our fine men and women that have defended this country of ours, but we are not on a military base, and as such, I would prefer that you show enough respect to use proper American speak."

After accepting his pardon with a quick nod, she explained with no apparent disdain that there was a three-quarter bath in the garage built into the spandrel. It was not extravagant, but it would serve his purposes, offering him a toilet, sink, and modest-sized shower. Ms. Hoback further detailed that she would appreciate his conscientious conservation of water by limiting his showering to once a day and no more than fifteen minutes to boot. With his dedication to the stringent protocol of the military, she was confident that he could adhere to her expectations. Like the strict supply sergeant that she could have been, Ms. Hoback added that all renters were on their own for any consumable amenities such as toilet paper, soap, and the like since she did provide the water after all.

Even though the growing cold crawled against the back of his neck, the grateful tenant concentrated on her instructions and even asked about her day. His genuine inquiry softened her edge, although the quick retort that she had worked on farm issues indicated the visitor could take his leave. After a pleasant "good night," Sergeant Riley hurried back to the warmth of the garage.

Once back into the protection of shelter, the scout discovered the door in the spandrel, although he was unfamiliar with the meaning of the word. Upon his initial assessment, he assumed the small space was a closet, but he was pleased to discover a sink similar in size to the one in his room above resting upon a narrow cabinet that had just enough space below and around the piping to house some toiletries. The oval mirror plastered near the slant of the ceiling looked rather feminine with its ordained curves and gold accents, but it too would be appreciated for its ability to help him shave. The round toilet with black seat and rusted posts looked accessible near the narrowest corner, and the wood frame centered on a floor drain formed the homemade shower. Rubbing his hands across the inside walls covered with some sort of aqua-colored marine paint that aided its ability to repel water, the sergeant smirked at the cleverness of the makeshift unit and commitment to utilize dead space in the most advantageous way.

With the refreshing mechanics of his private latrine assisting his first night's slumber, the following morning the prompt recruiter awakened to establish his new Normal routine. He wanted to get out into the morning air, fill his lungs, prepare his mind, and exercise his body. Although the physical habit had been a job requirement, the disciple cherished the bouts of solitude that his jogs provided because the silence and separation aided his focus on his relationship with the Holy Spirit. So much of his energy was exhausted on the front lines, attuned to the Lord directing his actions towards one person or the next, aware of the ever-present danger at each turn that the focused soldier grew desperate for these moments of renewing submission, restoring his entire being: mind, body, and soul. The fighter embraced them as opportunities to meditate on a Word that he was trying to hide in his heart, listen with precision to the leading of God as He flooded his thoughts, lift up his concerns to the Master as he pondered on loved ones while preparing his body to continue his mission. Even though his fitness readied him to respond to the needs of the US Army, Sergeant Riley desired to keep it strong and agile for the call of Christ because of the eternal nature of his alter mission.

After a few cursory jumping jacks and push-ups to get the joints mobile and the blood flowing, the jogger set out east along Cypress towards the facility that assisted children. With the obscurity of the morning's darkness still about him, the sergeant remained focused on his footing, avoiding patches of ice here and there along the side of the road until he negotiated the tracks and eased his step. As the security lighting near the brick building illumined the path across the parking lot and past the monkey bars, he raced towards the front office door and then ran in place while reading the signage: "Baby Fold: Established 1902, Foster Care, Hammitt School, Adoption Services, Pregnancy Counseling, Residential Treatment Center."

For a facility that appeared to serve more than just infants, the name seemed rather odd and exclusive, and with the close proximity to his home station, the recruiter disregarded the allure of coincidence. Instead he wondered if the Holy Spirit was prompting him towards a clue to his saintly pursuit. As he resumed a slow and steady pace along the shoveled walk, the observer noticed the bus stop and posted pick-up schedule at the corner of Linden Avenue and felt another nudge, urging him to pay special attention. The experienced disciple recognized the alerts that suggested components of the mission's puzzle, but he knew he had to cling to his struggling patience to piece them together.

Sergeant Riley zipped across the wide street and weaved his way around some of the neighborhood on the other side until he stumbled upon an outdoor shopping area that had a familiar appeal. To the trained eye the entire encampment had a strong military presence with the dark brown brick buildings positioned with purpose into a housing section, some central logistical facilities, and perhaps even a small school. Although the unsuspecting shoppers may have reveled at the secluded, self-sustaining qualities of the transformed complex, the historical details still maintained its initial significance amidst the progressive makeover.

Again the Holy Spirit moved the heart of His servant at the sight, and Sergeant Riley wished he understood why. Almost like a dream, the recruiter felt the cries of small children smothered around the giggles of others well up from somewhere deep inside, and he knew the Lord hurt for that place. The unusual insight startled him because it was so different than how Jesus prompted his emotions in the past.

During times of consciousness, the Holy Spirit directed his steps, urging the sergeant to veer this way or that, or perhaps even engage with that person or another. Over time, the experienced veteran developed a keen sense of his target's stage along the faith journey, or lack thereof, and wielded the spiritual armor proportionate to the task. Sometimes the warrior fought on the offensive or sometimes the defensive, but most often the heart of Jesus, the emotional component, occurred to him during dreams.

A deep sleeper by nature, the hard-working soldier relished his bouts of unconsciousness as a necessary form of rejuvenation, but on occasion, the Spirit would guide him through a vision of moments past or in the future and affix so deeply to his soul that he could remember them when he awoke. The images portrayed a high view of the spiritual battle and aimed to either provide insight into how the Lord once felt, giving the sergeant some historical perspective, or it previewed a future event. The episodes were not always chronological or methodical in their unfolding, but they did capture the essence of God's will.

Because the encounters were difficult to verbalize, the recipient avoided doing so except to a few select mentors in whom he could confide. Two of the sergeant's close friends were in tune with the workings of the holy spiritual realm, and then a mentor that spoke the boldness of the promises of the Word focused on truth. This group of battle-ready friends was imperative to the success of his faith journey.

Since his captivity, however, the Lord had awakened the soldier to more heart issues during his active periods. It was as if the two methods had melded as a result of that last conflict. The change sent him on a brief cerebral journey through his faith walk, and the long-time disciple was able to affirm that through each major trial in his life, he had grown more suited for the battle at hand. As if he gained another combat patch on his uniform sleeve or a service ribbon on his chest with every step, the warrior had transformed from a lowly private at the beginning, having no idea what he was doing, relying on the investment of others to disciple him, to a sage leader.

As the scout fumbled across some hardened snow drifts and ice patches in the low visibility of the present darkness, he knocked the sheet of ice covering the sign with the back heel of his shoe to expose the words. "Formerly the Illinois Soldiers' and Sailors' Children's School," it read. The veteran had never heard of such a facility, a typical confirmation that he could expect an emotional ride on this assignment. "Lord," he whispered into the stillness of the morning, "could ya please spare me any physical pain on this one? I still feel the aches of the last one at times, and my bones could use a breather."

CHAPTER 4

The Scout

After spending countless hours with Sergeant Fowler reviewing intelligence, threat levels, topographical layouts, logistical routes and points, and contingency plans, Sergeant Riley was relieved that the weekend had arrived. Drudging over SOPs (Standard Operating Procedures), reporting requirements, and accountability standards in a week's time had his brain clamoring for a break.

The next two days alone gave him ample opportunity to recon the area a bit more and test a local church body for his own spiritual support. The sojourner had been on plenty of assignments where a biblical community operated in the concealment of night or in a secluded place with just a few faithful followers. His last assignment had been that, and he was looking forward to participate in freedom. The disciple did not *have* to go to church, but he *got* to go to church, and he was going to bask in it.

Ms. Hoback had notified her tenant that breakfast was not going to be served on the weekends. Even she needed a time of rest, and the devout woman fasted every Sunday as an act of worship, so she did not want to put herself around a lot of food.

As a matter of personal principle, the disciplined combatant did not fast as a routine, although he accepted the practice as one of the classics and respected her commitment to the restraint. For him, it became too mundane and ritualistic that way, although he knew that was not the experience for every believer. Like any virtue, there needed to be a balance between surrendering to the Spirit and a carnal effort to "be good." Fasting was this sort of tightrope for him. If the staunch rule follower made it too commonplace in his life, he started to control it himself. His mind would wander into the realm of keeping fit or prideful obedience. No, he had to allow the Holy Spirit to remain at the helm, so the sergeant fasted when the Lord urged him.

Jesus knew just how to direct him too. His typical challenge would be, "**Is he or she worth it?**"

That was the sergeant's call sign. Those were his marching orders to fast and pray for a specific purpose for a designated time, and he witnessed the Lord's mighty movement indeed. Sergeant Riley had often wished that he could reach those mountaintops on a regular basis like Ms. Hoback seemed to be able to do with that particular discipline, but he had to accept his limits. He never again wanted to tip the scales and embrace a vice, masking it as a virtue.

For this first Saturday in Normal, the scout headed to the mall. He loathed shopping and tried to avoid it at all costs, but the bus route on Linden made a round trip there every hour. In quick step, the soldier marched down Cypress, past The Baby Fold, and waited at the corner until the punctual bus halted and released its doors.

The accommodations were clean, and the hard plastic seats served their purpose, while the rows of windows provided ample view of the city. The robust, middle-aged, female driver guided the mighty machine back to the downtown area and then east along College Avenue. Within just a few blocks, the confines of the university fell behind and the corporate influence arose as the view displayed shops and restaurants and shops and restaurants.

The never-ending slew of eating establishments that thrived so close to each other baffled the economic principles of competition. Fast food chains, upscale venues, and mom-and- pop shops advertised pizza, ice cream, steaks, or specialty imports. One could buy fresh-baked bread, Indian samosas, and a sugary donut while getting a watch repaired and a day's worth of groceries before the travel cup of coffee got cold on its way back to the car. The landscape looked like a rich man's flea market on steroids, shouting convenience from every turn, crying materialism, consumerism, individualism, give me, give me, I want more.

Oh, the over-stimulated observer sighed with frustration at the scheming ploys of the enemy. Just because witch doctors, artillery rounds, or waterborne illnesses did not prevail in this culture, the masses sauntered through life as if the spiritual battle existed in some other remote corner of the world. Even when the battle seemed daunting, the warrior resolved to remember the real victor.

Gripping to the curve into the complex, the public transporter eased to a halt as the brakes blew their excess air and delivered the sergeant to the beckoning warmth of Eastland Mall.

Lord, more of you and less of me, he prayed as he made his way through the turnabout.

The mall was packed. If the temptations of treasure did not lure them in, the avoidance of the cold outside gave them a nudge, and it served as a congregating place for the young and old alike. There were herds of teens playing their silly games with rival schools, vying for social standings. Older couples or groups of women donned their sneakers to get in some cardio as well as current gossip. Lovebirds promenaded, displaying their affection as a public promise. Families corralled their tots as they attempted to gather some necessities while giving the kids a chance to get out of the house. Even local hoodlums tried to stake their territory at the corner of the food court or the water fountain. It was the quintessential melting pot of madness.

Without his military uniform to draw any unnecessary attention, the sergeant could people watch and engage when prompted. Although he preferred more intimate settings for the workings of the Great Commandment, the soldier accepted that the good Lord had beckoned him into another transformational stage that somehow involved the allures of the average American.

As the disguised scout canvassed the layout, he warded off some aggressive sales people a couple of times. The bachelor did not need his nails manicured with the miraculous workings of the compact-sized wonder buffer, nor did he care for the numerous applications of the looped scarf. He did not need one himself, and he had no lady friend to please with the fashionable and versatile accessory. He did, however, stop for a cup of joe, but resisted his favorite oatmeal butterscotch cookies. It was there, just outside of the coffee shop, that the watchful one paused to soak in the artistry of the next display while blowing the steam away from his face.

The simple exhibit was just a beige wall between the food vendor and the next large clothing retailer, but a local photographer had been astute enough to utilize the hardened canvas as a backdrop to his work. High school senior portraits seemed to be his primary specialty, but the artist had a few family pieces as well. The large one at the top row in the center with brown overtones seemed to attract the most attention as passersby pointed and whispered.

The portrait showcased a family, very typical in most ways, with a proud father, tender mother, the token boy bearing the youthful image of his pops, and a beautiful daughter with endearing wide eyes. Posed in a library or den, something about the eyes lured the sergeant in. It was the mom, her green eyes sparkling, exuding joy from her inmost being, her gaze enticing him with a strange combination of nostalgic familiarity and present significance. She was a fellow combatant for certain. Even the matted gloss finish could not mask the glow that accompanied the presence of the Holy Spirit.

"Uh, excuse me, sir," the sergeant interrupted the vendor who was taking advantage of a lull to complete some paperwork. "Could you tell me where you got that photo?"

Assuming the trajectory of the point, the attendant answered without breaking his concentration, "Oh, that one has been a real attention getter. I can't tell you how many appointments we have booked with it, too many to count for sure."

"Are you the photographer?" Sergeant Riley insisted.

"I am a photographer, yes, but I can't lay claim to that particular one," the artist admitted. "That would be our owner, Daryl Lee. We have his cards here, if you would care to book a session with us."

The assistant scrambled to open a small rollaway cabinet that served as a temporary office for the studio's booth.

"Oh, no, that won't be necessary," the sergeant interrupted. "I was just wondering if you knew the family in the photo."

"I don't personally, no, but I know they are a real family, not models. Hard to believe, isn't it? Daryl likes to capture the raw innocence of Americana, especially before they become a sensation."

"Sensation?" the inquirer responded, unaware of the reference.

"Sure, the kid hit it big, years later of course, but it still draws the crowds," the helper disclosed.

The kid. The sergeant scanned right past him at first, but now he could see it. The dark hair, strong chin, and that look that puppies have that reveal that they are going to be big when they grow up. The boy was his older target before the wonder years.

The eager soldier probed further, "So you are telling me that the woman in that picture is his real mom?"

"Sure thing. Ha, that's funny," the employee chuckled. "We never get any questions about her. Rather ordinary looking, if you ask me. I think this may be a first. Everyone else always wants to know about Brock. They want a detailed account of how Daryl knows him, how old he was at the sitting, what he was like back then since they are from the same hometown. That's one of the reasons that Daryl stopped manning this site himself. He loves the business it draws, but hates to relive the story over and over. That's why I volunteered. I'm not originally from around here, so I have no direct connection really. It hasn't hurt my own prospects, though, if you know what I mean."

No, the sergeant did not know what he meant, and according

to the perverted wink and sly smirk, he did not care to. Instead, the pursuer focused on his next step and decided he would take one of those business cards after all. Gloating in delight, the assistant assumed that he had converted yet another reluctant patron, and for now, the sergeant was content to keep it that way.

With his mind filling with plans of action, the soldier opted to make his way back to the bus terminal just outside the food court. When the mega transporter rolled in, the doors exhaled, and Sergeant Riley greeted his driver with an accomplished smile.

"Had enough already?" the plump gal nodded, figuring he was not the shopper type.

"You could tell? It is not really my thing, but I found it productive," he chuckled back to her.

"How did you get out of there with no packages?" She extended the conversation, giving the young teenagers just a few more seconds to sprint for her doors.

"It wasn't easy, believe you me!"

As the swarm of youngsters stormed the gates, the bystander stepped past the local chauffeur and escaped into the first row. After the gaggle flashed their passes and took off towards the back, Sergeant Riley turned to preview the other passengers. As per his protocol, he attempted to make eye contact with each and every person and offered them a gentle smile of acknowledgement. Although that practice had become second nature to him, the humbled disciple recalled how uncomfortable and downright unnatural that small gesture was at first.

They are going to think I am some kind of creeper, he used to tell himself. *Guys are going to think I am soft, women are going to think that I am coming onto them, and parents are going to think I am a pervert. This cannot possibly work.*

The enemy implored doubt and the culture advocated the masses to keep to themselves, but step by step the Holy Spirit revealed to him that these small acts of obedience produced much fruit and prepared him for greater challenges. That was how a lot of the transformational process worked. With each baby step, with each little success, the task got easier and the soul developed genuine care for others. It started as a simple act of external obedience, but over time it became an internal instinct.

"Thanks again for the ride!" the soldier bid the driver farewell and walked the rest of the way back to the Hoback house.

As he passed by the bay window and raised up on his tip-toes just enough to see the landlord rocking in her chair again with her eyes closed, Sergeant Riley paused and debated whether to disturb her. If she were having some time of prayer or even trying to take a late afternoon nap, he did not want to interrupt, but the urging pressed harder, making the thought too strong to ignore. About face and back to the front, through the storm door, and with a gentle knock, the Lulu alarm sounded in full force.

To his surprise, no forceful command for the pooch to pipe down sprang from the west side of the house, and the belabored silence concerned the watchful tenant. Soon enough he heard some footsteps approach the door, the thud of the latch release, the creak of the door, and the steps fade away as little Lulu attacked his shins with her typical over excitement.

He did rather enjoy the little dog, but her nails could do a number on the skin. For now, however, he was far more distracted by Ms. Hoback's demeanor. "It's just me, Ms. Hoback!" the respectful soldier replied towards the living room as he knelt down to pet the hyper little fur ball. "Lulu, relax girl. I see you!"

When the visitor received no response and had the canine satisfied with enough belly rubs on her full, widespread, back pose, Sergeant Riley stepped towards the front room and peeked around the corner. "Ms. Hoback? Are you okay?" he inquired.

The ole gal just sat swinging in her rocker, staring out the bay window, deep in thought.

"Am I interrupting?" he continued. "I can come back another time?"

"Oh, no, Mr. Riley. Please come in. Take a seat," she managed to answer without shifting her glance.

"Are you feeling okay today? Can I get you something?" the gentle friend probed.

"Oh, I'm feeling just fine, just reminiscing in my mind," the old woman replied. "I like to do that sometimes, you know? I don't want to ever forget."

"Well, what are you thinkin' on, if you don't mind me asking?"

"Oh, just a little of this or a little of that. I like to think about Mama and Daddy, old farm days, and the sort." The joy glittered from her face as she spoke.

"Mmmm, oh yeah," he relaxed, confident that she was good. "Speaking of former times, I was meaning to ask you about a place I ran past the other morning during my PT, uh, I mean, physical training, you know?" The quick learner corrected his speak before he rattled her pleasant state. To his relief, she just turned her gaze towards him and waited for his question with no further critique of his misstep. "It was just east of here a bit," he pointed, orienting her to the location. "Something about a soldier's and sailor's home?"

Sergeant Riley was quite pleased at the radiance that exuded even more from her face at his inquiry.

"Oh, yes, the children's school," she answered.

"Yes, that's right. What is that place?" he urged her on.

"You mean, what was that place?" the educator corrected.

"Yes, ma'am. What was that place? Did you know of it?" Sergeant Riley continued.

"Oh, I knew it quite well, Mr. Riley," Ms. Hoback smiled as she looked back to the picture window.

Without the rigidity that he had grown accustomed to, the tender spirit caught in a bout of nostalgia recited a small tale about her stay at the home. Her daddy was neither a soldier nor a sailor, but during the time of the Great Depression that hit just after she was born and when her mama came down with a terrible bout of influenza, the home opened their doors to other families in need.

The Recruits

Not knowing how else to manage with Mama sick and all, Daddy put Gladys and her older brother Roy in the home until Mama could tend to them again. She must have been just about three at the time, so Roy must have been about six or seven. Her baby brother had not been born yet.

Gladys did not have a lot of memories of the place, but to her recollection, they had lived there about a year. What she could recall were warm and joyful thoughts about a heavy-set, old woman that hugged them a lot and read them stories at night. The retired English teacher figured she got her love for books from her. If anyone asked Roy, now, he would tell another story altogether. He hated that home even to this day and just downright forbade any talking of it. Since the boys and girls were kept separate, Gladys could not say for certain what happened to her brother there; besides, she would have been too young to understand anyway. From what little Roy had said over the years, they expected the boys, even the young ones, to do regular chores to keep the place in good order. Gladys always reasoned that he just missed Mama something terrible, and Daddy was too busy eking out a living to visit much.

However, Mama did recover, unlike a lot of folks taken down with the sickness back then. Gladys and her brother returned back home just in time for Mama and Daddy to announce the impending arrival of their little brother. It was a wonderful homecoming gift.

"So, what happened to that place after that?" Sergeant Riley probed further.

"Oh, it stayed on for awhile. At some point they started taking in troubled kids, and then the foster care system started," she explained. "Eventually, its purpose and funding ran out as the facilities started declining. Some of the buildings were demolished and some turned into the stores that you probably saw out there."

"Hmm, interesting stuff," he added. "I never heard of such a place. And The Baby Fold just up the road?"

"Oh, it had a similar calling," Ms. Hoback replied. "It tended more to orphaned children that needed adopting. They eventually joined with the foster care system too."

"Wow, two places and so close together?"

"Oh, yes, it was a different time back then. Folks tended to pull together back then, help one another out. Some of it was good and sometimes not so good." Her thoughts still focused on the past.

"Well, I won't keep you, Ms. Hoback," the attentive visitor apologized. "I'll see you Monday morning for breakfast."

With no response, he just let himself out, giving little Lulu one more good head rub before he secured the front door behind him. Unsettled by the encounter with his landlord, the concerned tenant worried about her, yet the another part knew that everyone needed a little time of quiet and deep reflection. He just wished that she had more friends, people to socialize with, or ladies to encourage her at times like these. The familiarity made him ponder what his life might be like at her age.

"Hey, Mary, it's me, Ham. I just thought I would call and check in on you. I'm in Normal."

CHAPTER 5

The Support

With Sergeant Fowler taking his last week in town to prepare for his permanent duty relocation, Sergeant Riley assumed sole custody of the office keys. In keeping with his adherence to protocol, the prompt professional arrived at the recruiting station well before official opening hours, hung his coat on the army-issue stand, and just sat and stared at the computer, contemplating whether to turn it on or not. He realized that this newfangled contraption could aid his efforts, but for now, he just did not have the heart to accept the challenge. No, the old soul would attack his mission with some old-school tactics.

"Hornsby?" the recruiter asked the man on the other side of the phone.

"Well, Sarge, how are you doing?" the husky voice replied. "You settling into Normal okay?"

"Absolutely, thank ya kindly," the sergeant echoed.

"What can I do you for, Sarge? Need a ride?" asked the kindhearted driver.

"Well, not exactly," the sergeant answered in hesitation. "I do need some transportation, but something a bit more permanent than a cab. I was wondering if you could direct me to a reputable dealer for a car. My work requires me to travel out into the region a bit farther than I originally anticipated, so I am going to need my own set of wheels after all. I am not looking for anything fancy, but I would hope that it could at least last me the next three years."

"I see," the driver resounded with an understanding tone. "Well, Sarge, I can't say that I know of anyone in particular, but I tell you what. I got an old Mazda that was my boy's. It has no bells and whistles, but it is reliable."

"Really? Your boy doesn't need it?" Sergeant Riley prompted.

"Ah, no. He dumped that thing with me as soon as he made enough money to buy himself something sweeter. I just keep it around here for a rainy day," Hornsby confessed.

"Well, how much do you want for it?" the recruiter inquired.

"Shoot, I will just let you use it, Sarge, as long as you keep the regular maintenance up on it," the cabbie offered.

"Oh, Hornsby, I could not let you do that. Let me give you somethin' for it."

"Shoot no," his friend insisted. "We don't want to have to go through the hassle of all that. I trust you to do right by me, Sarge. You just take care of it while you're here, and then you can leave it back with me when you head out of these parts."

"Well, Hornsby, I don't know what to say. If you are sure, I would be mighty obliged. I promise to take care of her and treat her right," the grateful one committed.

The two made some final arrangements, and it was agreed. Hornsby would pick up his friend from the recruiting station at noon, the sergeant would treat him to some lunch at the Old Country Buffet, and then the pair would drive to the maintenance shed out west of town where he housed the loaner.

The disciple was baffled at how his day had started. Not only had the Lord prompted him to call his new buddy, Hornsby, but He provided above and beyond his expectations as per usual. The close follower was just so thankful and felt so unworthy to be led with such care. It also struck him funny how the Lord used this non-believer to offer such graciousness. Moments like these served as a reminder to the soldier that every single soul mattered to the Master as it was His desire that none should perish, and each person bore the glories of God whether they realized it or not. All good virtues found in the heart of another were planted there by the Wondrous Creator, calling it back to where it belonged. Sure, a lot of folks claimed those righteous attributes for themselves, boasting about their own desirable traits, but surrender put it all in the proper perspective.

In an instant, the Mazda started up, although a high-pitched squeal bellowed from the front end. During the transition, Hornsby had explained that the alternator belt always loosened on this thing, but the noise would die down once she warmed up a bit. With his concerns satisfied, the sergeant headed west on Route 9 to meet up with a very important support contact.

Through a wintry wooded countryside interspersed amongst the bedded farm fields, the disciple lost himself in the silence. Mary had sounded relieved yet surprised to hear from him, and he accepted the expected adoration from his widowed sister-in-law who had never forced him to maintain a relationship. With Edward long since passed and her remarried and all, it was awkward at best, not to mention she always managed to blurt out some critical opinion about his mother. Oh, she did not mean any harm, and Hamilton knew that full well, but his mother was such a dear treasure to him, and he struggled to hear anyone speak ill of her.

Irene was a tough nut, to say the least. With Clyde gone for weeks at a time on the railroad, it was just the two of them most days. Edward was sixteen years his senior, so the older brother seemed more like an uncle, leaving Hamilton somewhat of an only child.

Mary—well, Mary was always in the picture. She and Edward had grown up in school together and were sweet on each other since they could talk. No one thought twice when they went down to the courthouse in the center of town and got hitched one afternoon. That just made it all official, and to the young Ham, Mary was a doting sister. She never seemed too bothered with Mrs. Riley until she and Edward had kids, and according to Mary's version, Irene had proclaimed on more than one occasion that those kids were not her blood relation. Oh, Mrs. Clyde Riley loved on them and spoiled them with her delectable treats, but those comments never did sit right with Mary, and his sister-in-law let it be known.

Perhaps his male instinct, or perhaps his age, kept Hamilton from paying too much attention to the rising angst between the two women over the years, but from his point of view of the opposite sex, friction and hurt feelings were almost expected. The difference from one set of problems to another rested on the subject matter, and he had learned to keep his nose out of those issues.

As he expected, Mary begged him to make a trip to town for supper and a catch up. The sojourner in turn committed to try to fit it into his busy schedule, and the pair left it at that. She never did push him, and he always felt relieved because it unsettled his emotions to go back there. Sometimes the pain lingered longer than his war wounds.

Akpore had picked the location, a Mexican restaurant, the best in the area, he claimed. They would not be rushed at the table, they would receive great service, and the food was both filling and delicious. Along with an impressive culinary review, the place in Pekin proved easy to find.

His new mission contact greeted him just inside the front door with a huge bear hug, which triggered his instinctive stiff reaction. The stoic professional was unaccustomed to such displays of public affection in his line of work, but he had been briefed that soldiers in the civilian world were more demonstrative with their thankfulness for the support of fellow believers. Although his etiquette training incited his mind to lower its guard and accept Akpore's gracious act, his counterpart's size alone left him no other choice.

The taller and stronger-looking Akpore reached one arm around the sergeant's neck while patting the back of his head with the other, and the maneuver brought back memories of childhood.

The exchange felt like that wrestling hold that his older brother locked on his buzzed head right before skinning the top with his knuckles. The painful and embarrassing memory prompted a cringe in anticipation of a full-fledged noogie, but the present pats proved to be signs of genuine affection.

At the request of a place for both privacy and longevity, the restaurant host, who spoke impeccable English, sat them in a corner booth close to the kitchen. With a heavy African accent, Akpore introduced the protocol for the basic training camp's initial assessment and routine training schedule, requiring the sergeant to follow the conversation with attentive determination. While the listener found the dialect an interesting mix of Spanish and Italian sounds with a hint of French, the well-traveled military man had little to no exposure to the language in particular, and he suspected his new friend could say the same about his very own southern drawl.

According to the brief history, his new teammate originated from Angola and the accent stemmed from his native tongue of Portuguese. Akpore had immigrated to the United States with a student visa, became a citizen, joined the marines, married, and then settled in central Illinois as a civilian. Due to their combined armed services experiences which heightened their passion for this assignment in particular, each of them resounded that there was nothing more unique than serving in God's army while defending the country as well.

Akpore elaborated, "When I first approached the camp staff about incorporating this intense discipleship training, I was a nervous wreck. The Lord had put this passion inside of me, and I was bursting at the seams to follow through with His plan, but I doubted that others would understand my vision, my calling."

"Had you seen something like this done somewhere else? I mean, how did you know this idea was going to work?"

"Oh, I didn't, brother," the dreamer confessed. "The Lord brought it to me, and it took a lot of work to get the plans organized, develop a presentation, so that I could communicate the concept. They did not bite at first. The leadership there had a lot of questions for me, but they were encouraging as well. I kept going back to the drawing board, and they continued to give me audience."

"So, obviously, they rallied behind you at some point," Sergeant Riley affirmed.

"Praise the Lord, brother," Akpore put the credit in its rightful place. "We collectively made this process a reality, and my cadre followed shortly after."

"So, is the cadre all former military?"

"My basic training instructors are all prior service in some capacity. I thought it imperative that these leaders understand the foundational elements of the military, so that we could capture the essence of the value of its transforming and team-building qualities. Yet, as disciples in the grace and mercy of our Lord and Savior, Jesus Christ, my core cadre must exhibit that unique ability to differentiate between training a recruit for the spiritual warfare that we face and the conventional warfare of man."

Mesmerized by the efforts of this group to embrace discipleship and be intentional about their efforts, the sergeant beamed at the ingenious attempt to mimic the US Army's processes at the entry level. The conversation brought the Lord's placement of him to an actual recruiting station full circle.

The description of the process did the comparison justice. The recruiting personnel spread the Gospel at every opportunity wherever the Lord placed them. The assessment phase replicated the ASVAB (Armed Services Vocational Aptitude Battery) but focused on spiritual giftings, and Fort Gideon, well, it imitated basic training at its best as it provided a secluded place for each new believer to be indoctrinated into the world of true discipleship, using the spiritual disciplines as the vehicle. The camp was a living and breathing testament to the reality of the spiritual warfare that they all faced, and it strove to prepare each member of the messianic army to serve in their real-world placement with the confidence, security, and drive that the Holy Spirit alone could invoke.

"I am not sure how familiar you are with the area," Akpore interjected, "but the facility is near a small little farming community called Clinton."

Sergeant Riley chuckled. "Believe it or not, my friend, I was born and raised in Clinton."

"You don't say," Akpore smirked. "Well, I'll be. The good Lord is doing something mighty with you, my friend."

"Yep, no denying that!" the soldier conceded.

"So, are you familiar with Fort Gideon then?" Akpore continued. "I believe it was started back in the fifties as a summer church camp."

"Strangely enough, I don't know a bit about it," the sergeant replied. "I never did church camp as a kid, and most of my wilderness excursions were done out at Weldon Springs over there."

Located just east of the Mexican restaurant in a small town called Mackinaw, the initial testing was administered by a wonderful couple named Carl and Trish who owned the place which doubled as a Christian daycare by day and a community learning center by night. According to Akpore's assessment, these two seemed like the odd couple, but together they exemplified how opposites could unite to create a formidable team. The duo combined their individual callings to utilize that building to its fullest potential while serving the King with every aspect.

Although the couple was a mighty force, Akpore was certain the sergeant would have strong feelings about them one way or another when the newcomer met them face to face. "It is a real hot or cold type of thing," he attempted to describe the pair. "It is hard to put into words. They evoke a strong reaction from people. When you meet them yourself, you will know what I mean."

The sergeant was intrigued, to say the least, and his discerning spirit accepted the challenge.

Akpore continued his praise of his camp staff, describing another power couple, but for very different reasons, who served in two different capacities at the basic training center. The studious Captain Peters loved the Word but struggled to relate it to real life in others that did not share his same passion for that discipline. He upheld the backbone of the academic portion of their program. His wife Thorpe, a small yet mighty powerhouse, exuded a gift of softening hearts with her unassuming exterior while challenging the will with her ability to communicate her expectations. She led one of the platoons, and her groups were always a reckoning force. Her knack for training compelled the most diverse personalities to work as a team.

A consummate renegade, Burroughs embraced the camp's purpose and vision but preferred the path less traveled. While leading his platoon, he always managed to put his own spin on the processes, keeping it interesting and taunting the imagination. He proclaimed to represent that type A/B personality that tended to always think outside of the box.

Akpore himself wore dual hats as he led the third platoon and directed the entire program. Fort Gideon employed other full-time support staff that belonged to the facility itself, and those folks served the effort by preparing meals, maintaining the grounds and facilities, and safeguarding supplies. Their commitment was imperative to the success of the place year round, but they did not participate in the actual training schedule.

External recruiters like Sergeant Riley played a key role because each one was expected to provide input into the assessment process as well as the strategic planning of the camp. Through a series of preparation sessions, all cadre and recruiters would meet to discuss platoon placement, leadership positions, and even insights into effective role-playing during combat scenarios. They would aid the formation of ability groups for physical training as well as growth opportunities for known weaknesses. In essence, these players were the hinge between the civilian world and the success of the basic training cycle to prepare the recruits to answer the call and march with the Master.

"Wow!" the sergeant exclaimed. "It sounds like such a huge responsibility."

"Well, of course, my friend," Akpore responded with delight. "But no worries, it is not by our might nor by our power that we face this battle. Remember, it is by the power of the Holy Spirit in which we bear His armor."

"So, how do I exactly fit into all of this?" Sergeant Riley wondered. "I mean, I'm actually in the US Army. If I participate, what is my deadline for finding my recruits?"

"Well, it is a lengthier process than you might imagine given the logistical constraints," Akpore explained. "We have to administer the assessments in groups of eight or about the size of two squads. So, to get three full platoons, it can take almost six weeks just to run everyone through the testing. We then have to meet to go over the results, make recommendations, assignments, and so forth. A full basic schedule then takes eight weeks, so we need sixteen weeks at a minimum for one full cycle. Now, that is assuming all of the recruiters have enough soldiers to fill the spots."

"So, do you run it year round?"

"No, the camp still operates its youth cycles in the summer, so we have the property for one cycle in the late spring and one in the early fall. We do have some specialty courses out there through the winter months, but those are more for veterans," Akpore answered.

"So, where do my folks fall in the mix?" Sergeant Riley felt the pressure to meet some sort of deadline. "What do I need to do to prepare?"

"We are finishing up some assessments now for our cycle starting at the end of April, so you won't go this round," his contact replied. "I think it is too soon for you to be considered for this year's training at all. You just hit the ground. We will have regular meetings with the recruiters to see how well they are coming along, and then we fit you in based on the readiness of your recruits."

"So, Sergeant Fowler briefly explained to me that this regional operation involves folks from all sorts of specialties," the soldier delved further. "He said you have recruiters from all walks of life."

"Oh, absolutely! Right now I have a gal that cleans houses, a financial planner, a school counselor, a plumber, and even a web designer. All kinds."

With the nuts and bolts of the program situated and their bellies filled to the brim with fried tortilla chips, Akpore invited the sergeant to join him the following week at the Eastside Educational Center to meet some more of his counterparts and get a feel for the assessment phase. The team had a lot of work ahead of them, and they needed to be warriors together to see it through.

Thankful for the support troops the Lord had placed in and around him, the humble sergeant accepted. This assignment teeter-tottered between his military career and the next chapter of his own life and faith journey, and he knew the mighty Lord must be moving for such a time as this.

"Just try not to worry," his advisor gave him some assurance. "Some respond quickly and some take a lot more time. The pace is not really yours to set, and the sooner you accept that, the better."

CHAPTER 6

The Recruiter

With the week coming to an end, Sergeant Riley was determined to make a trip out to the town of Washington where the main studio of that photographer started. Knowing full well that the Holy Spirit directed him for a reason, he needed to follow up on as many leads as he could to find his targets. Gracious enough to lend him her road atlas, Ms. Hoback insisted that he take the entire book with him because she took great pride in taking care of her things, and she did not want permanent creases on Illinois. The abiding tenant reconned the map before heading out on his planned route.

Opting for the more scenic version of Old 150 rather than the freeway system, the recruiter preferred to scout out the little towns in between. The purpose of this first trip was not about rushing as much as it was about absorbing his surroundings, gleaning from his whereabouts. Although nothing extraordinary jumped out at him along the way, Washington itself proved quite interesting even at first glance. As he traveled west on Business 24 to enter into the farming community, the sergeant arrived at a tried-and-true roundabout right in the center of town. It was not like the current design in Normal that was an obvious attempt at being retro, but it was a genuine circle encased by a town square that had survived the decades.

The well-kept facades of the two-story buildings conveyed that the historical society took great pride in the traditions of their small city, and the life-sized nativity scene that still covered the fountain fixture in the center park projected to all that passed through that Washington preferred Christianity. Since that winter holiday had long since passed, that Christmas adornment spouted a bold statement in this day and age, and the sergeant intended to discover if all that he witnessed thus far was just for show, was more of a statement for morality than steeped belief, or was a genuine base for the Messianic movement. The people themselves would be the true litmus for that particular test.

Because it did not appear as congested as the other legs, the focused driver opted to park on the south end of the traffic pattern and took a closer look at the allure to this bedroom nook. That particular side paled in comparison to the other three because its clean, white exterior was not quite as updated.

At one corner a closed game room with dark windows showcased board games, canisters of dice, and shelves full of fantastical figurines. Several long tables placed about indicated that this store catered to those customers that hoped to spend hours upon hours challenging one another in imaginary duels between dwarfs and elves or magical journeys through strange lands. Rather impressed, the sergeant had never seen this type of business succeed in such a remote place, so the owner must have been doing something right to maintain his niche.

Next to the game room was a hair salon that was also closed for business and appeared to operate by appointment only, and the clerk at the office for the Chamber of Commerce was on a break according to the paper sign on the door that resembled a clock whose hands marked her expected return. No wonder this segment of the square sat empty; the vendors were not even present and did not survive on regular foot traffic.

As he cased the perimeter by foot, the observer admired a beautiful flower boutique that served the teen corsage crowd as well as higher-end floral designs. Signs of the upcoming prom theme already adorned one of the arched windows while large stands of bouquets prompted lovebirds to finalize their summer wedding arrangements without delay. The realty company shared space with a prominent lawyer's office, both promoting their longevity in those parts and the ability to take care of the entire slew of home buying requirements in one locale.

The north strip was perhaps the most beautiful of all because the power-washed, brick fronts had been restored to their former glory, and the revamped signage portrayed a subtle hint of elegance with a taste of nostalgia as the letters curled and the beige colors blended with the background. At the east corner the caramel corn shop filled the cold air with wonderful smells of melted butter and warm sugar, and the workers inside hurried to prepare the various batches of flavors before the coating hardened. While two gals baled the white fluffy kernels, the third one with a strong grip poured the sticky brown goo, and still another drizzled melted chocolate on pieces spread across a large metal sheet pan. The adjoining space attracted the antiquers as well as those patrons looking for modern pieces that replicated times long past, and their glass case displayed a weathered Red Flyer wagon surrounded by planters fashioned from repurposed wood pallets.

The mercantile, however, grabbed his attention. First, the bronzed footprints on the sidewalk laid claim that President Abraham Lincoln had tread this track, and secondly, the sweetheart tables in the lofted window begged passersby to come on in and experience a romantic piece of Americana. From the street view, it looked like a good old-fashioned soda fountain shop like those appearing in a Norman Rockwell painting, and when he pushed open the wooden door and heard the overhead bell ring, he could see that they stayed true to their initial advertisement.

This place was amazing. Rows and rows of glass self-serve canisters ran the length of the wood-planked store and enticed customers with every type of pieced candy made to man. Scads of jelly beans, soured assortments mimicking everything from worms to baby pacifiers, and even those waxed bottles filled with flavored juices begged for consumption. One could opt for various flavors of jellied rings or SweeTARTS that looked like building blocks. There were chocolate treats filled, coated, or left bare, and hard candies that were meant to be savored and not chomped that ran the gamut from the minty tones to the more exotic spicy sorts. Why, the sergeant even found his all-time favorite, the French Burnt Peanut. Although he was not sure that France could lay claim to this confectionary masterpiece, the combination that tempted the palate with the perfect blend of sweet and salty was out of this world.

Displaying nearly every candy bar, patty, or nugget that had hit the market over a fifty- year span, one of the outer walls lined from top to bottom with the wrapped options promoted tantalizing pleasures for both the young and old alike. That package of shredded gum that looked like a pouch of chewing tobacco, cartons of sweet sticks that released puffs of sugar dust that imitated cigarettes, and a small burlap of crunchy pebbles that resembled gold bombarded the guests with sweet memories. One could tantalize the tongue with crystals that popped or savor the long-lasting chew of the Charleston. Oh, how this place must have struck a chord within the inner child of every patron.

As if that inventory were not enough to tempt the taste buds, behind the cash register waited freezers full of hand-dipped ice cream that could be blended into a milkshake or drowned in syrupy seltzer water. Three different kinds of slushies churned in a self-contained machine, and processed meat sticks of all sizes and flavors stood guard at the scale that weighed each small paper sack that was filled with the chosen individual pieces. The mastermind behind this quaint little place was a genius, and it was evident to all how it maintained its place on the square.

As the novice visitor placed his own selection of a few red, candy-coated peanuts interspersed amongst a sampling of the popcorn-flavored jellied beans upon the scale, he glanced back at the wall of fame directly behind the entry door. According to the poster-sized pictures, several nationally known celebrities either frequented the store or knew the owner because the autograph on each was addressed to this same "Elaine." Lo and behold, an action shot of Brock Bradford found a place in the top right corner.

"Excuse me," the sergeant interrupted the middle-aged gal that waited on him. "That guy in the top right looks familiar. Does he live around here?"

"Oh, he is homegrown. Well, sort of. He was not born here, but he was raised here, so we claim him as our own," the woman conveyed with such pride.

"Really? Wonderful," he added. "Is he still around the area?"

"Oh no. He took off after high school, but he visits now and again. He makes a point to always come see Ms. Elaine when he does. Make his rounds, you know," she added.

"I see," the sergeant participated.

"His folks still live in town, though, well, kind of," the clerk continued.

"Kind of?" he questioned.

"Well, the Chief, his dad, is at the nursing home. Dementia, ya know. Poor guy. He was always such a force. Ya know what I mean? Hard to imagine him so—what's the word—fragile," the gal carried on.

"Ah, yes, terrible thing," the sergeant responded with true sympathy.

"Yep, Mrs. Bradford still lives in their same house, but I guess she is at The Village nearly day and night," the woman offered.

"The Village?" the sergeant inquired, unfamiliar with that local term.

"The nursing home, ya know, The Christian Village," she replied as if he should be aware of all Washington slang. "Rumor has it that she hardly leaves his side. He doesn't deserve it if you ask me. He did not make a lot of fans when he was in charge of the town, but it never seemed to sway her love or loyalty. That's a mighty fine woman if you ask me. I know I couldn't do it."

The sergeant felt a bit uncomfortable with such personal details about a couple he knew nothing about, and the clerk's willingness to divulge the town's gossip was a bit alarming. He could imagine the stories that passed across that counter over the years. However, the information did prove helpful, so he scooped up his purchase, strolled back to his car, and headed for The Village.

In the solitude of his car, the recruiter considered how he was going to approach Mrs. Bradford, and he tried to bury any hesitant thoughts that popped into his head. What if she thought him a creeper? What if the staff insisted that only family was allowed into the room? What if he could not convince her that he had righteous intentions? The doubts could be powerful.

As he parked his compact ride and gnawed on a few of his delectable treats with the main entrance to the home behind him, Sergeant Riley rehearsed how he might strike up conversation with his target's mother.

"Hello, Mrs. Bradford? I'm looking for your son."

No, that sounded like her baby was in trouble.

"Mrs. Bradford, hello, I'm wondering if you could help me locate your son?"

No, that sounded suspicious.

"Well, hello? Are you Mrs. Bradford?"

No, that definitely imitated a stalker's line.

Oh forget it! Disappointed in his options, the disciple trusted that the Lord would provide the right words and the best way to deliver them so that she would receive them. With that settled for the moment, he rolled up his little paper sack of goodies and thrust them into his coat pocket.

After mashing the sequence of numbers posted above the keypad which in turn released the lock on the right, Sergeant Riley stepped through the automatic doors and surveyed the entrance. Down the hall, straight ahead, the trained scout spotted a few cafeteria workers hauling a cart and a nurse eyeing a clipboard as she passed. As he glanced down the left wing and found it bare and quiet, the strong odor of industrialized cleaner drifted over which drew him farther in the opposite direction.

Pacing down the right wing corridor, the undetected guest passed by a small sitting room full of residents perched in wheelchairs. Some were watching television, some were playing cards, and others just sat and stared into the abyss. It broke his heart a bit, so the disciple raised a quiet prayer for their peace and comfort as he continued through the double doors and stumbled past a nurse's station where two gals reviewed a log sheet about meds. Either the ladies were unaware of his presence or unconcerned with his motivations because neither hesitated in their conversation.

Concerned that the relaxed safety of this building put its staff and residents in jeopardy, the guarded military man resisted the temptation to get side-tracked. Instead he begged for the Holy Spirit's guidance as he peered into each room while maintaining his respectful position in the center of the corridor until he recognized her.

She was much older than that portrait at the mall, but to his delight, the unassuming woman wore the same hairstyle that had grayed at the edges, and her face displayed the same muted tones of make-up. The serene lady exuded the compassionate peace of Christ just as she had in that family picture from years past.

Oh, Lord, give me strength and take control of my tongue, the sergeant pleaded as he raised his eyes towards the ceiling.

"May I help you, young man?" Mrs. Bradford asked as she looked up from her book.

"Yes, ma'am, I'm hoping that you can," Sergeant Riley proceeded, tip-toeing past the threshold. "The King sent me." The surrendered disciple knew how corny that sounded as soon as those words left his mouth, but the power in that phrase was undeniable.

As the recipient inhaled a deep breath and released it with such surrendered relief, dropping the book to her lap, it was obvious that she knew what he meant. Mrs. Bradford had been waiting decades for reinforcements, and Sergeant Riley had been an answer to her prayers.

Sitting next to the sleeping giant that once safeguarded the entire community, the two carried on with ease as they nibbled on some candies. Mrs. Bradford was like that grandma everyone always hoped to have because her kindness, gentleness, and loveliness encouraged the sergeant as he shared about his journey to her and ultimately to her son. The doting mother reciprocated, making herself vulnerable, retelling bits and pieces of her own Christ walk that included falling in love with the big lump of a man next to them who had never surrendered his own life to Christ. The burden deepened her struggle yet built her faith all the same.

"Can I ask your opinion about something, Sergeant Riley?" the gentle woman proposed.

"Of course, Miss Ginny, anything," he responded, hoping that he could offer her comfort somehow.

"I know his mind is long gone, and when he does sound coherent, it's as if he were stuck in his early twenties or something, but since he is physically still here, do you think he can still accept the gracious gift of Jesus and know Him as Lord and Savior?" her tone searched for some answers.

"Well, Miss Ginny, I can't say that I rightly know," the helper confessed. "I mean, I want to believe that it is never too late as long as there is breath."

"Yeah, me too," she uttered as they both sat in silence and stared at the body resting under the covers, the rise and falls signaling its survival.

Neither of them grasped the boundaries and wonders of the Master and how He penetrated hearts. They each knew how they had experienced Him in their own life, and, of course, they both held firm to those shared within the binding of the Word, but some circumstances just did not seem so cut and dry. The Chief was one of those, and this disease seemed to baffle even the keenest of scientific minds.

"Sergeant Riley," she broke the silence, "would you come see me time and again, so that we can pray together here for Chief and the others in this home?"

"I would be honored," the soldier admitted.

"I know you won't be able to stop by all of the time, but we both know you have to come this way to find Brock," the mother grinned, her thankfulness for the Lord's dealings with her son beaming from her face.

"That we do, Miss Ginny," the sergeant obliged. "So, you are not aware of any plans for him to be here until next fall? That seems so far away, but the Lord works in decades, centuries, and generations, doesn't He?"

"Isn't that the truth," Mrs. Bradford agreed. "To Him next fall is coming quick."

With a promise to let him know if her son was going to be around sooner, they parted ways for the time being after laying hands on the Chief and uniting in prayer. Before heading all of the way back to Normal, the sergeant hoped to first swing by the local coffee shop that Mrs. Bradford had recommended. The express hut had unpredictable hours and may not be open, but the trip inside the store itself would be well worth it, in her view. The regulars always boasted about the inviting décor of the place as well as the high-quality product, and the coffee lover just could not pass it up.

Even if the drive thru station was open, the sergeant was determined to scope out the gathering space. It did proclaim to be "The Place Where Coffee and Community Come Together," so he wanted to see how true that was for himself. Mrs. Bradford had also divulged that this particular coffeehouse was owned by a Christian family, and the experienced traveler always enjoyed establishments that served the Lord and the world together. It could be a tricky challenge, but doable, and it did not hurt that they served his favorite beverage to boot.

The parking out front was slim pickings, but the driver managed to maneuver his little ride to the side until another car could guide itself out of the space without running into the pillars in front of the building. Good thing this place was not a tavern. Those colonial-looking beams could be an easy target for those hindered by the wiles of alcohol.

The sergeant high-stepped his way into the main hallway and then into the shop itself. The dark, earthy aroma of freshly brewed coffee welcomed him at the door, and the cool blue tones of the walls against the deep brown hues of the tables bade him to relax. Whoever designed this space had a hospitable gift. The short line at the counter gave him ample opportunity to ogle the bakery case and peruse the colorful chalkboard menus at the back. The coffee hound was soaking in every scrumptious bit of the place, thrilled that he had taken Mrs. Bradford up on her suggestion, so even he was taken aback when his true purpose smacked him right upside the noggin.

There she was. The female, target number two, tried to go unnoticed behind the counter as she filled cups with syrup or threw beans into the grinders, but the scout was well-trained and could have spotted her a mile away. His years as a sniper proved so valuable in more ways than he could have imagined, and today it got close enough to bite him.

The objective avoided his gaze for now, ducking back into the small kitchen as soon as she was able. She looked younger in person than what he had imagined, and she was a pretty girl, but her obscure movements and mannerisms conveyed that she did not want to draw unnecessary attention to herself.

The staff did not wear nametags, and the wooden placard only revealed the barista and the back of the bar representative. While the one worked the monster of an espresso machine, the other manned the cash register. The sergeant supposed that the dish washer or designated cup filler-upper was not worthy of the welcome wall, and he did not want to just ask her name given it was his first time in the place. With the staff being aware of the locals, he settled in his mind that he would have to visit with Mrs. Bradford a bit more than they first suspected.

★ ★ ★

"Mrs. Bradford?"
"Please, Sergeant Riley, call me Ginny," she insisted.
"Yes, ma'am. Well, Miss Ginny," he replied.,"you know how I was telling you that I have a mission to locate some other folks? Well, I found one, and I think I might need your help. Would you be willing to meet me up at The Blend next week? My treat."

CHAPTER 7

The Contact

As she entered through the glass-paned door, Sergeant Riley rose from the seat without scooting all of the way out of the booth and gave her an enthusiastic wave. Mrs. Bradford unzipped her coat and made her way over to her new friend, avoiding the gaggle of teenage girls scurrying to the booth next to theirs.

"I hope you don't mind the adolescent vibe going on in here right now," he apologized, remaining on his feet until his guest took her seat. "I think the high school just let out, or maybe one of the junior highs. My age gauge may be a bit off."

"Oh, I don't mind at all," she offered with a gentle smile. "It reminds me of when my kids were that age."

"It's just that it was about this time when I saw her here last week, so I figured we had a good shot of observing her again today," the soldier explained. "What can I get you to drink? Coffee? Tea? Hot cocoa?"

"Oh, that is not necessary, Sergeant Riley. I am happy to purchase my own drink," her calm way continued.

"Please, Mrs. Bradford, it would be my pleasure to treat you today," he insisted.

"Well, okay, but only if you remember to call me Ginny."

"Well, ma'am, I can meet you halfway and call you Ms. Ginny," the southern gentleman suggested with a wide grin.

His gracious guest accepted his plea bargain with a slight nod and opted for the daily flavored brew. With his orders in hand, the sergeant negotiated past the young swarm of girls at the booth next to them which had multiplied after pulling up one of the four tops and at least six other chairs. According to the slew of whispers and expletives, something important was going on there, and to his relief, he was not being prompted to pursue it. Instead the nimble man skirted around the bedazzled purses dangling from the backs of the chairs, hopped over a couple of overstuffed backpacks with similar adornment, and arrived at the end of the order line.

The stout, youthful fellow behind the cash register with enormous button-like black discs stuck in his earlobes causing them to droop seemed relieved that the soldier was not ordering anything blended or doctored up with a quarter of a squirt of the sugar-free flavored syrup or some soy adaptation of one of their special lattes. Just two regular cups of joe appeared to give the crew a much-needed break from the late afternoon rush. When the sergeant spotted his girl working at the back counter in quiet diligence, the patron pointed back over the wall of the whole bean display behind him towards the booth and asked if someone could bring them over when their drinks were ready.

"Absolutely, dude, no problem," the cashier replied, keeping his seat on the small, metal stool. "We have all of these other drinks in front of yours, so it may be a minute."

The diehard military man clenched his teeth and pursed his lips to calm himself, remembering that he had not been out in the civilian world that long and that he could not, and likely should not, get all authoritative on folks. His natural instinct wanted to highly suggest in his most stern command voice that this young man raise himself from his conveniently placed cushy seat to assist the older lady behind the espresso machine who was fumbling through the endless line of cups and rushing to level the grind pulls to churn out the barrage of specialty requests that the line of tweeners had ordered. Perhaps the back of the bar designee could even offer assistance to his gal on the back wall. She was laser focused on keeping her back to the slew of clientele while keeping her diligent hands productive by grinding beans, changing filters on the coffee machines, filling up the airpots, and squirting the exact amount of syrup in the line of to-go cups. Unlike the fellow taking the money who rested with satisfaction with his performance of the clerical duties, his gal seemed to have the heart of a hard worker. He liked that.

For now, the proper professional just smiled at the guy, continued to observe the ladies striving to please their customers, and eased around the horde of zealous adolescents waiting for their creative concoctions and flirting with each other with that very loud, awkward pitch. Besides, the setup was perfect to get his recruit over to his table. The cashier did not look anxious to jump at the chance. That kid had been distracted yet again by his cell phone.

While Mrs. Bradford and the sergeant waited for their drinks, the pair engaged in meaningful conversation. With her cheeks flushed and eyes lowered, Ms. Ginny admitted that she felt just a bit guilty for feeling relieved to have a reason to get out of the confines of the Chief's room if even for just a little while. His slow decline left her in a strange state as if she had two lives that were both on temporary hold. She loved her husband dearly and would love nothing more than for him to recover, but the reality was clear. He was not going to be getting out of the home. Her friends, those from her ladies' Sunday school class at church especially, did their utmost to check in on her and continue to invite the suffering soul to outings. Mrs. Bradford accepted on occasion, but the devotion she had to Chief kept her at his side most days. Without knowing how much time they had left together, she opted to cherish them, regardless as to whether he could understand or appreciate it. Hers was a strange combination of being a widow, without her beloved husband, and still bound to the vow she had made nearly fifty years ago. Mrs. Bradford had long since relinquished her fight to understand it all or explain it to others because she knew what the Lord had placed on her heart concerning the Chief, and she rested in that.

"I think it is the short days of winter that get to me sometimes," Ginny thought out loud as she watched the traces of the sun's rays through the large picture window across the room fade into the blue mist of the winter's afternoon.

The slight lift of her head and the broad smile that overtook her face alarmed her fellow warrior. The sergeant straightened his back as the figure reached past him and placed a steaming, glass mug of coffee on the table.

"This is the Sumatra," the soft voice interrupted. "And this one is our crème brûlée flavor."

"Thank you, dear." Mrs. Bradford patted the young girl's hand after she had laid some napkins next to the mugs.

The youthful server retracted her hand from the touch and squinted her eyes at the older woman, trying to recall how they might know each other. "Do you need anything else?"

"No." The sergeant cleared his throat. "That will be all for now. Thank you, uh…?"

With no response, the girl just looked at him, eyebrows narrowing even further, then turned and walked back towards the kitchen area. The deep laughing sighs from across the table broke his concentration.

"What?" he attempted to understand his comrade's response. "I was hoping that she would tell me her name."

"I can see why you asked for my help. You haven't worked with women much, have you?" The kindhearted smirk softened his guard.

"Well, what made you touch her hand?" the scout asked, hoping for some guidance on how to proceed.

"Oh, I guess I just learned that by being a mom," she answered, the love for her own children pouring from her eyes.

"But I could tell that her response was a bit concerned. I mean, she pulled her hand back quickly," he probed his advisor further.

"Well, Sergeant Riley," Ms. Ginny consoled, "first, you will have to understand that as a woman and a mother, I can approach people in a much more intimate way than a gentleman such as yourself will be able to. No, with you it is going to take time and consistency to break through that girl's walls. She has been hurt and deeply."

"I know, right?" the recruiter concurred. "The intelligence that I received gave me some of the history there, but I have no idea how I am going to approach her. I mean, she has no idea who I am, what I am about, or what I even want. I feel so out of my league right now, it is not even funny."

Her chuckle managed to confuse him further.

"What? What am I missing?" he pled.

"Oh, dear Sergeant Riley," Ms. Ginny just shook her head and smiled at him with that endearing affection reserved for mothers. "You remind me a lot of myself when it came to the Chief and even Brock. Early on I used to talk the ears off of the Chief, thinking I might be able to reason him into believing, and when Brock was little, well, I just prayed daily that I wouldn't mess up the Lord's plans for that boy. Shelby was a little different. As girls, we had our way of connecting, but those boys. Lord knows how I struggled understanding how to deal with them."

"So, how did you end up doing it?"

"Well, I like to think I settled into a means of sowing seeds with all of them," she replied. "Mine might have been a more quiet version of service, but I stayed committed to my faith and love for them, focusing on the gifts that I could see within them, resting in the hope that the King would bring help."

"Well, you can clearly see that I'm in need of help myself," he winked, understanding her sincere gratitude for his presence.

"Well, I'll tell you what," she offered. "If you commit to meeting me over at The Village once a week or maybe even every other for some time of fervent prayer, I will meet you over here for coffee on alternating visits. We can just chat, you know, catch up while you observe the young lady and gather more information. You likely won't stand out so obviously if we are together."

"Oh, would you, Ms. Ginny?" he answered with utter relief. "I would be so obliged. Are you sure it won't be too much on you?"

"Oh, no," the humble woman lowered her head in embarrassment. "It would do me good to get back out among the town folks a bit. But I am not going to let you buy! We will have to go Dutch!"

"Agreed," the pleased partner held his hand across the table to shake on it, catching the cool stare of his second target near the garbage cans.

Encounter

He did not want to go on this trip. Sure, it was nice to get a little rest and relaxation in the sun after the grueling cold weather training exercises, but after the recent breakup, Sergeant Riley was not in the mood for vacationing in a lover's paradise.

"Oh, come on!" a teammate prodded. "Sun, rum, and now you are free for the ladies! At least just come and chill for a bit, get your mind off of things. You can't just sit around here and mope."

To get the guys off of his case, he caved, realizing a change of scenery may be good for him. The all-inclusive resort was that for certain. A far cry from the pothole- ridden, narrow road that wound around the foothills, the lush green entrance to the gated compound foretold that this secluded treasure had everything that the heart desired: five- star restaurants, a picture-perfect, white sandy beach, a never-ending supply of drinks adorned with spears of fresh fruits, three different crystal clear pools, impeccable accommodating service, and plenty of organized activities. Snorkeling, parasailing, horseback riding, fitness classes, and even a night club kept the clientele engaged within its walls.

The soldier, however, opted to catch up on some much needed sleep and soak in the warmth of some sun while reading a good book. For this week, he had snagged a small paperback at the airport about the history of the white witch. He had an ingrained passion for learning the background story on all of the places that he visited even if they were steeped in mystical legend. Being more of the serious, cut-and-dry type, he did not get too wrapped up in the allure of it all, but instead found himself refuting the holes in the fables. Some of that was just part of his years of military training, but part of it was planted there in a divine capacity.

"Come on, Sarge," a teammate begged from the other side of the suite door. "It's our last night, and you have not done a thing. It's a big festival they are putting on. Just come out for a little bit."

"All right! All right!" the more reserved comrade hollered back. "Go ahead without me. I'll get changed and then find you guys out there."

With his fists dug into the pockets of his tan cargo shorts, his loose-fit, white button-up offering some breeze to seep through, and those blasted flip-flops letting the granules of sand pass across his pink toes, the sergeant perused the festivity's offerings strewn about the torch-lit walkways. Limbo was out of the question, although the middle-aged woman dressed in a primitive grass skirt and bikini top demonstrating the technique made it look easy. The full bottles of liquor offered as the prizes were not a temptation for him either. The dance lessons were good for the newlyweds, but the interlocked bodies twirling about with giddy expressions of love spewing from their eyes reminded the bachelor that he was alone. The lazy river was still full of man-filled inner tubes, keeping the curbside bartenders busy, and the booths of local artisan vendors were selling everything from caricatures to beaded jewelry. The flickering flames against the backdrop of the clear dark night provided that magical, intimate aura that drew the tourists in droves to this type of escape.

After a once around, the skeptic had his fill, but as soon as he lowered his head and stepped on the stone pavers back towards his room, the ruckus at the main colonnade caught his full attention. The sergeant raised and tilted his head to catch darted glimpses of a tall, black, priestly figure with gold-rimmed glasses, a neatly pressed black suit peeking out from underneath a bright white robe with black trim that fell just past his knees. A thick, heavy gold adornment hung about the stately figure's neck, and he carried a wooden tool of some sort in his hand. The white hat with black trim sat on his head almost like a crown, and it reminded the soldier of the cardinals he saw rushing past the turnabouts manned by the Swiss Guard at the Vatican when he was in Rome, but this VIP was no Catholic priest.

The looming height and proud chest of the man demanded attention, and his four assistants did not need to work to rally the patrons. Instead they were forced to guard the icon almost, organizing the guests to form a line. A concerned spirit welled up from within the sergeant like a three-alarm blaze as his sniper-trained eyes captured the scene in its crosshairs. The soldier was frozen in his tracks as the lapping waves ebbed and flowed their enticing song from the beachfront behind him and the frenzied crowd blocked his route back to his suite. The panoramic view slowed to a creeping crawl as his mind absorbed the intel; even the elongated shadows of the visitors cast in the dancing glow of the fire sticks rubbing their hands in slithering delight communicated a battle- ready message.

Ladies tugged and prodded their unassuming spouses over to the religious figure for a chance at a memorable experience while on the island. Most of the nudged fellows did not hesitate for any other reason than the line was beginning to snake around the waterslide with the tail end rattling in excited chatter. As each couple stepped up to the threshold in front of the infamous celebrity with their lovesick hands intertwined in eager anticipation, one of the cleric's enormous claws reached to cover and swallow up the united grasp as the other one rose high into the sky and swiveled the drum-like wooden instrument in concert with the low-pitched chants.

I rebuke you in the name of Jesus! Jesus! Jesus! Jesus! the sergeant's heart bellowed in utter distress, knowing that his silent prayer may disclose his camouflaged position. *Oh, Lord, these people have no idea what they are doing. Oh, Holy Spirit, move, interrupt, have your way here!*

As the sappy couple stepped aside after receiving their native blessing and just before the next victims took their position, the coal burning eyes paused from the ceremony, realigned towards the sandy shore, pierced through the clueless bystanders, and locked with the pale blue ones honing in. The sergeant had been exposed, but he did not care. The soldier wanted his combatant to know that he was there, calling upon one far greater than anything his foe might be able to conjure. The laser-focused gaze lasted mere seconds but seemed like hours as the rest of the chaotic noise fell off into the distance. The slight raise of the enemy's upper lip just on the right side of his mouth tried to convey victory, but the calming peace and assurance of the Word rode atop the waves of light and wiped the grin away, leaving a disdainful pucker in its place.

"*You, dear children, are from God and have overcome them because the one who is in you is greater than the one who is in the world.*" (1 John 4:4, NIV)

Marching with the Master Minutes

June 2003

Cadre: Akpore, Thorpe, Burroughs, Peters, Beyers

Recruiters: Dinkheller, Lockenour, DeSutter, Irions, Stroud, Martin, Conger, Kohler, Navas, Linthicum, Northrop, and Riley

The group opened with prayer for each recruit as well as the planning of the camp.

1. Each recruiter reported on their progress to date. Dinkheller, Lockenour, DeSutter, and Northrop have each located all four of their recruits and have begun processes for engagement. The remaining eight recruiters have at least located two of their targets. Locating the remainder will be the primary focus while creating engagement opportunities where needed and responding as necessary. Continual surrender to the Holy Spirit is of the utmost importance for these maneuvers. Time is of the essence. Support systems will be activated on an as-needed basis.

2. After a thorough presentation by Captain Peters, the list of Spiritual Disciplines for the basic training have been finalized. They are: Meditation, Study, Confession, Fasting, Mentoring/Accountability, Prayer, Service, Simplicity, Submission, Worship, and Solitude. During each proceeding meeting, Captain Peters will delve further into each discipline and how it might be incorporated into the field training exercises. Each member should consider these disciplines in his/her own life and be prepared to discuss personal strengths and weaknesses.

3. The Beyers will review their assessment-testing worksheets for any necessary revision and/or updates and will report back to the group at the next planned session. This information will assist recruiters in detecting potential gifts which will aid the assessment process as well as placements during basic.

4. Logistical Support: Funding sources have been identified. Although each source is an individual financial supplier, they have been identified as possessing the spiritual gift of giving. Akpore will be responsible for finalizing the funds needed for the camp and providing necessary reports to those donors. Trish Beyer will be responsible for thanking the donors on behalf of our organization as well as feeding ongoing prayer needs to our prayer partners.

The group closed in silent prayer as we listened for any further promptings of the Holy Spirit.

Godspeed,

Akpore

CHAPTER 8

The First Targets

Four months had passed, and the sergeant had gotten no further with the female target other than to resolve that her name was Darby West and she grew up in Washington. She still avoided him just as much as she did everyone else that passed through the place, and each time the disciple prayed about engaging her, the Holy Spirit prompted him to wait.

"**Patience, Hamilton**," the Lord reminded him. "**She will come to you.**"

So that was his directive, and the anxious recruiter struggled adhering to it. The soldier had learned patience over the years, of course, but he wanted to get something moving. He felt that he was lacking diligence at this assignment. Target one, Bradford, had not made any attempts to visit his folks or anyone else in the area, according to his contact information. The former caged one contemplated a drive up to Pontiac to force a potential run-in, but the idea of prisons was still too fresh of a combat wound for him, and again, the Holy Spirit urged him not to go that route.

The female target was steps away from him almost every week, but he could not do anything about that quite yet other than to smile and be gracious whenever he had even the remotest of chances. The Spanish target was nowhere on the radar yet, nor the young man that was supposed to live within a mile of his home base. Shouldn't he be doing more? Shouldn't he be doing something to get this ball rolling? Weren't their souls at risk? With all the information that the scout did have, why was the King taking his sweet time about allowing him to share the Good News? Sometimes it felt like the former sniper was stalking the enemy camp, identifying multiple ways of penetrating the perimeter, yet the theater general was more concerned about luring them out, capturing them one by one instead of dominating the whole lot of them at once.

The ever-learning disciple had to be mindful that the Master's ways were not his ways, no matter how much he transformed into His likeness. The sergeant had no way of knowing the intricacies of these people's lives nor their spiritual ripeness for the harvest other than by the workings of the Holy Spirit, and when his impatience welled up, he knew he was focused too much on his own efforts rather than the Lord's. The never-ending balancing act of living in this world and not being of it sometimes sailed along smooth waters while at other times it nipped at the heel.

However, his time at the coffee shop was not without some success as the recruiter gathered intelligence about the young girl through the idle chatter of gossipers at nearby tables. Some older gals whispered about her mother who struggled to raise Darby on her own, while older teens tossed about rumors of promiscuity and unsavory guys allowed to spend the night in the house. Even young men would throw their two cents in as if they were in the locker room, claiming they had managed a base or two with her. The protective sergeant had to hold his tongue most times, but he was able to square away a few of the boys with just a stern, threatening glare, his rough exterior and serious stare doing the trick. With the ladies he had to be a bit more genteel. He kind of gave them more of that "Really, girls?" look, which resulted in an immediate change of topic. The professional did not always react, but sometimes he just had to when his carnal nature screamed *defend, defend, defend*.

Along with Mrs. Bradford, the meetings with Akpore and the

crew helped dilute his inner rage to take matters into his own hands. The team had become a support group of sorts, spending ample time discussing challenges they were facing, so that their prayers could be specific and intimate. Prayer had been the cornerstone of their gatherings. Many times the sergeant had experienced groups of believers that threw up prayer as if it was some mindless chant that they were obligated to spew out as if to put a Christian stamp on their meeting, but these comrades were different. They grasped the concept that prayer was key. Prayer was powerful. No situation was too menial, and everyone was given all the time needed to explain the entire scenario being presented.

"Well, I shared with you all about my first recruit, Bradford," he updated his fellow fighters. "He does not live too far away, but he hardly ever comes around. His mom, Ms. Ginny, she's been helping me, and she believes that his shame keeps him away most likely because he calls her whenever anything good comes up. Otherwise, she doesn't hear a word, unless he has to. Anyway, she saw in the local paper that his class reunion is coming up this fall, and she is sure he will come for that."

"Was she able to provide you any other intelligence?" Akpore probed further.

"Well, I shared with her some of the vision that I had on him," Sergeant Riley continued. "She was not familiar with the contents other than to admit that her husband's family had some deep ties into the occult, and she was confident they stemmed from that."

Although Akpore and Burroughs nodded with that look of familiar understanding, a few of the others could not help but let out a concerned gasp. The sergeant understood. He was a bit frightened of that part of evil himself during his first face-to-face encounter.

As soon as the new recruiter had met Trish and Carl, he understood Akpore's description of them. Giving that instant shock value, the looming height of the wife over the husband accentuated the clash of her overt personality to his reserved one that ushered in the second phase of awe. Because of their unique blend of external contrast and mission-focused commitment, they had the sergeant in stitches. He loved their lively display, and he loved them too. The front-row follower admired the Lord's ingenuity to grab the attention of folks, but he relished even more His choice to move mountains with the least likely of pairings.

Trish always cut to the chase and got to the heart of the matter while Carl took time to reflect on the present obstacle. The two of them together helped the sergeant to migrate through his own confessions of his personal hang-ups and habits of taking control to the encouragement of staying the course. They had become invaluable to his own walk as well as his current mission.

"If the Lord told you to wait for her, sergeant, well then, I think that is what you ought to do," Carl advised.

"You should ask those young men, talking trash about her, if they know Jesus!" Trish insisted.

"No, Trish," Carl chided. "He doesn't want to cause a ruckus."

"He doesn't need to cause a scene," she continued her defense. "But if they claim to know Jesus, then he can pull them aside and set them straight, but if they don't, well, then he might as well start praying for them and figuring out how he is going to share the Gospel with them while he is waiting around for her."

The sergeant always got a kick out of watching these two go off into their own little world as they debated one thing or another. The two always veered off on some tangent, but somehow they sooner or later made their way full circle back to him, and when the lot of them joined in prayer together, the mighty Holy Spirit moved. Without fail, the third wheel left encouraged and ready to fight for the Lord another day, and the two of them walked away all sappy, holding hands and making goo-goo eyes at each other. It was a sight, but it made the bachelor a bit jealous for a love like that, a partner for life battling anything that set its target on attacking the unity of marriage. For the moment he was content enough to have the privilege of seeing it front and center.

Captain Peters proved to be an amazing study partner. He and Sergeant Riley challenged one another in dissecting the Word, investigating the world behind, in, and in front of the text as a full-blown exercise in iron sharpening iron. Peters' wife, Thorpe, helped the recruiter consider the social intricacies of non-verbal cues, especially as they related to young women. Because the combat veteran served with males his entire military career, he needed that added insight into the ways of women. Burroughs and Akpore focused more on the basic training element and proved to be viable strategists in the art of spiritual warfare. Burroughs' expertise hailed from more of the enemy's point of view, while Akpore was a logistical guru. Altogether, this motley crew was tried, true, and at the ready, and the sergeant felt honored to be found fit to be amongst them.

These ties in particular led him to his third target when Akpore pulled him aside before one of their scheduled meetings in the upstairs of the educational center. "Don't be discouraged, my friend," the leader offered encouragement. "I think I am able to help you directly."

"Oh, yeah? How so?" the soldier responded, unsure if he was missing something in the translation.

"I think that Hispanic recruit that you have been looking for is working at that restaurant that we met at last year. He is a new waiter there named Salinas. Friendly gentleman, very friendly!"

The exuberance jumped from the sergeant's face. "Are you serious, Akpore? Are you sure?"

"Yes, I'm pretty sure that is your guy," Akpore replied. "Want to start having dinner there with me before our meetings? Give you a chance to make a connection?"

"Oh, I would be mighty obliged," Sergeant Riley accepted the help. "You're sure the wife won't mind?"

And so, a full year had passed since arriving in Normal. West was growing more and more accustomed to the regular's patronage to the coffeehouse, and he could tell that she began to eavesdrop on his serious conversations with Brock Bradford. Although Ms. Ginny had given him the logistical details to ensure an encounter with her boy and even some family history to better understand his visions and get her son's attention, the acceptance of the Good News was turning out to be a long process because this guy thought he had life all figured out already. Now that the recruiter just got a good lead on Salinas but still no direct contact with his fourth target, the sergeant accepted that it was unlikely that he was going to be able to participate in the basic training cycles this year either.

"Remember what Akpore always says," Carl tried to keep him from feeling too defeated. "You have to wait for the Holy Spirit's timing. It will happen! You know that to be true!"

"Well, that doesn't mean he just has to sit around like a bump on a log," Trish added.

"Trish, dear," Carl tried to correct her, "Sergeant Riley has been working diligently ever since he joined us."

"Well," she continued anyway, "have you asked everyone you know? You said he lives right by you, right?"

"Well, I know his childhood home is right by where I am staying, but I don't know if he still lives there."

"Have you been canvassing the area?" she interrogated.

"Trish," Carl tried to intervene again, "of course he has."

"Yes, ma'am," the sergeant replied. "I run every morning and try to take a different route. I've eaten at most of the popular joints that the kids go to. I've tried to ask around. I even went as far as showing his picture to my cabbie friend, but no success."

"What about your landlord? You said she has lived there her entire life?"

Ms. Hoback! The sergeant was dumbfounded. Because the grateful tenant never did seem to catch the ole gal in another nostalgic mood, he never thought to pry much further into the guarded woman's recollections. She insisted upon her privacy, and he had been out on the road so much it slipped his mind.

"Well, there you go!" Trish rested her case.

The landlord layered in knee-high beige boots and a mid-calf-length, pale blue, pillowy coat shoveled her front walk with her mammoth-sized suede mittens and rabbit-fur-lined trapper's hat after the afternoon's glistening fall. What a sight! As Sergeant Riley put the Mazda into park, he rushed over to her and tried to offer his services. "Let me finish that for you, Ms. Hoback," the southern gentleman insisted, reaching out for the shovel.

"Oh, now, I am fully capable of tending to my property," the stubborn woman replied, raising her head in an attempt to communicate through her brown, hand-knitted scarf that had been wrapped three full times to keep the chill away from her face.

"Oh, I know you are, ma'am," he continued. "But there is a real chill out here tonight, and it feels just a tad slick. Why don't you let me finish this here, and I will even throw a bit of salt down for you, and you could wrestle us up some hot cocoa."

"Well, you do know that I make the best!" she contemplated his offer while still holding firm to the handle.

"Don't I know it!" he agreed. "And I was thinking on a cup of it on my drive back tonight."

Little Lulu gave consent from the chair on the front porch, hopping and barking at the return of their housemate. Even the excitable pooch knew better than to be out on a night like this and opted instead to guard her keeper from the confines of the shelter.

"Well, make sure that you get all of the way down to the cement. I don't want thick ice patches growing over the night," the educator instructed. "And make sure you clear out around the gate, so that it doesn't get stuck open when you come and go."

"Yes, ma'am! Will do!"

"And don't dilly-dally," she hollered back at her helper before closing the porch door behind her. "You know my chocolate is best when piping hot. I don't want to waste good milk if you're going to let it grow cold."

"Oh, no, ma'am!" he affirmed. "I'll be along pronto!"

Having finished the walk, the mindful renter leaned the shovel against the corner between the porch wall and the inside door and tapped his heels against the threshold to shake off any remaining loose snow. Lulu hopped, yelped, and danced in circles, waiting for him to greet her properly. The smell of delicious, sweet chocolate wafted from the kitchen as Ms. Hoback steadied a tray full past the dining table and in through to the living room.

"I thought we could sit in the front room tonight and watch for snowflakes next to the street light," the ole gal offered, pushing the curious little mutt away from her feet.

"Oh, yes, ma'am," he obliged, placing his gloves, satchel, and hat on the table. "Would you like me to get that for you?"

"No, thank you," she insisted. "But you could grab Lulu before she causes me to lose balance and spill."

Get Lulu? Now that was a challenge. That feisty dog had some sixth sense about people picking her up. She would lie on her back and wiggle from left to right when her belly was being rubbed, but the moment those hands formed around her, she bolted like a flash. It was impossible to catch her, so his best bet was to shoo her in the opposite direction until Ms. Hoback could secure the tray on a stand that she already had positioned at the ready. He felt like a farmer trying to corral the evening's chicken dinner.

"Now, if you are going to have to put your mug down on the end table, make sure you grab one of those coasters out of the drawer first," the stern woman ordered.

The soldier knew the drill and placed one of the felt-lined squares closest to him so that she would not continue to worry about it. The sergeant needed her full attention tonight.

"Ms. Hoback, I was wondering if you might be able to help me with something," the interviewer began his interrogation.

To his delight, the ole gal seemed interested in his story about being called to locate a few lost souls in the area as she sat in silence and hung on his every word. He rather thought her a bit too rigid for such open dealings with the movements of the Holy Spirit, but the warrior seized the moment with his attentive audience and continued his tale with encouraged vigor.

Although his landlady preferred the more liturgical practices of the church body universal, her own mama recited claims of receiving miraculous workings of the Lord. Although Gladys had not experienced much of Him by way of pomp and circumstance, she believed in the ways of the Holy Ghost since she was a small child.

Although the prisoner of war never thought of his rescue as either pomp or circumstance, the forgiving fellow understood the dramatic reference that his elderly friend used to try and relate. Either way, he had to remember to make a point to thank Trish for her insistence because Ms. Hoback did have some valuable information for him in regards to his fourth recruit.

While the matriarch still sipped on her mug of winter delight, allowing the tiny marshmallows to melt themselves into the mixture, the sergeant hurried over to his satchel to pull out his file which now included the cold case documents that he had received from Sergeant Fowler. To his utter amazement, Ms. Hoback recognized the young boy immediately. Brian Hoyt had been a pupil in her wee worship class at church. According to her assessment, the picture of him at eight looked like the spitting image of him back at age three when she served him.

"Oh, he was a bit of an odd child, if you know what I mean," the Sunday school teacher recalled, rocking her chair back and forth in slow succession as she gazed at the snapshot with a fond grin. "Oh, he was quiet, kept to himself, not rowdy like those other boys. He minded and all, but he rarely said a word even if you asked him outright, and he never bothered to try and play with the other kids."

The ole gal remembered some elder sisters that used to fetch him after the main service, and the folks seemed polite and attentive, but once the tot graduated from her class, she did not keep up with him. To her recollection, the family sat together in the service, and the faithful attender strained to recall the details of the tragedy that struck them years after. By that time, the university had purchased the church building that was situated just down Fell Avenue next to the library. They tore that beautiful, brown brick building down and made it a parking lot, and it crushed her heart something terrible. She was a fifth-generation Hoback that called that place home, and now it was nothing but a yellow-lined blacktop that hosted empty cars.

"Nope, once they rebuilt way out east of town where all of the new housing was going up, I just couldn't bring myself to go," Ms. Hoback recalled with a painful grimace. "It was so far to drive, so much traffic to weave through to get there, and they did not even keep the organ. Nope, I just started walking over to the campus church after that. Mama and Daddy would be right disappointed in the whole lot of them."

"But as far as you know, the Hoyt family continued over there?" the sergeant probed.

As far as the Normalite knew, they had, but she was certain that they still lived at the same house just a few blocks over on Normal Avenue.

"How do you know that?"

"Well, the campus church is right next to it," Ms. Hoback stated. "The university has pert near bought up everything around it, but it is still there, and I see the missus tending to it on occasion. I can't say that I've seen Brian, but I am sure that I have seen the girls now and again. They are stunningly beautiful even still."

Oh, what relief that the recruiter felt to get such a hopeful report. With his mind racing, his cup of hot cocoa empty, and Ms. Hoback showing signs that it was getting close to her bedtime, the thoughtful tenant strong-armed her into allowing him to carry the tray back to the kitchen, wash out the dishes, and set them to dry in the rack overnight.

CHAPTER 9

The Final Targets

Akpore waved him over to a table just opposite the entrance. March may have come in like a lamb, but it went out like a lion and had not seemed to let up yet. As soon as he reached the table, Sergeant Riley used his napkin to wipe the excess water from his cover.

"So, which one is he?" the soldier asked with anxious anticipation.

"Oh, you aren't going to miss him, my friend," Akpore assured him. "He is serving us tonight."

"Wonderful! Great job!" the enthusiastic sergeant praised.

"I come here often enough, so they try to let me choose my seat," the leader explained. "I did not ask for him specifically, but I did see him serving the table next to us, so I knew this was his section. He already came to take my drink order, so he should be back out promptly."

And so it was, and when the recruiter observed his third target gliding in from behind the swinging doors, skirting around a busboy heaving a full load, past a leaning waitress where he gave an endearing tap on the behind and a pause and a wink at a beautiful patron heading towards the bathroom, even the lonely sniper knew just how friendly this guy was. It stirred a surprising defensiveness within the recruiter, but then he pushed that aside to focus on his mission. Undoubtedly there was still hope.

Twice a month for the next year the sergeant and Akpore met up at the Mexican restaurant to build a rapport with Salinas, building their own rules of engagement while continuing to strategize on making contact with Hoyt. For such an ordinary fellow, the fourth target was turning out to be quite elusive.

"I just can't seem to find him," the sergeant confessed.

"But you have seen the mom?" the camp leader inquired.

"Yes, I have seen her a few times pulling out of the driveway, but that is about it," he replied in frustration. "I have even gone up to the front door twice, but no one answered. I just don't understand why this is proving to be so difficult, and I am getting pretty irritated about it. I mean, I've attended their church. I have scouted out the girls' homes, their spouses, and even the grandkids. I know his grade school, junior high, high school, and his major. I tried going into one of his classes at the university not too far from the station and made as if I was lost, but I still did not spot him. I have even researched the tragedy and reconnoitered the cemetery on the anniversary, and let me tell you, that visit was far more painful than I had imagined."

Seeing how troubled the recruiter had become during this final quest, Akpore delved further into the details like any good mentor would. With no constraints for time, the sergeant put all of his stoic military presence aside and retraced his emotional journey with his friend. It boiled over during that trip to the grave site.

* * *

It started with research of old newspapers at the Normal Public Library which led him to the obituary, and with dread he discovered the graveside service was held at the Clinton Cemetery. With so much personal loss in that little town, Sergeant Riley was hoping not to go back, but his mission left him no other choice.

"Mary, I am going to be heading down your way later this morning for some work stuff, so I thought I would see if you might be available for lunch?" the brother-in-law resigned.

"Oh, Ham, that would be wonderful!" she replied with genuine enthusiasm. "Do you want to just have lunch over at the house? I could make that tuna salad with the bean sprouts that you love."

"Oh, no, Mary, that won't be necessary," said the soldier, not ready to get that comfortable with the past. "Why don't we just meet up at a restaurant or something?"

"How about The Shack?" she suggested. "You always loved that place."

"Are they still open?" he sounded astonished. "Well, I'll be."

"They sure are. They have updated the inside a bit, but the menu is still the same," Mary replied. "The prices are higher, though. You can't get a burger for a quarter anymore."

"Well, inflation and all!"

They settled on noon which gave the sergeant ample time to scout out the cemetery and see if anyone from the Hoyt family showed up and appeared approachable. As he drove his little lender down Highway 51, the prodigal was pleased to see that they had widened and repaved the road. The south of Bloomington was growing closer and closer to Heyworth, and even that little blip of a town had plenty of new housing. Wapella did not look too far different than what he had remembered, still sporting the notorious purple house, and by the time Clinton arose on the horizon, the former maroon was shocked to see that the highway had been redirected around the town. He reckoned that Center Street was a much quieter thoroughfare these days without all of the semis bustling past.

As he veered to the left to take the old business route through town, the stately grounds of the old Homestead property, home of the annual Apple 'n Pork Festival, stood tall, proud, and well manicured. Just the sight of that grand Victorian mansion filled the air with those delicious smells of ham cooking in the wooden smokehouse that he always thought looked more like an outhouse. He loved traipsing around that place every fall as a kid, filling his gut until it nearly burst with caramel apples, funnel cakes, corn on the cob, and black, kettle-cooked ham and beans. The skilled Riley always waited in line to twine his own string of homemade rope and rested on the curbside as the local square dancers did their jig before heading home on his bike. It was the one time a year that Mrs. Clyde Riley let him go hog wild with his sweet tooth and birthday money.

At the four-way stop, the soldier turned right and then down the long hill along the edge of the cemetery. Oh, that deep valley was one of his wintertime favorites. He did not know how they managed it, but the powers that be never sold any plots along that edge, leaving it for all the town's folk to sled down every time enough snow fell. Now, Mrs. Clyde Riley was too formal to get herself down onto a toboggan or old aluminum trash can lid that seconded as a saucer-style sled, but she would drive Ham over regularly. In typical Irene style, she would sport a flower-patterned dress, tan-toned hose, clip-on earrings that matched either her brooch or her pendant necklace, a head scarf to keep her curls in place, bright red lipstick, and a blanket to run across her lap as she waited in the car like a hired chauffeur, watching her baby boy slide down that hill until he tuckered himself out. Then it was straight home for a piping hot bath in their soaking tub that was too short to sprawl out in, so the thawing adventurer scrunched and exposed his knees to the cool air until he could slide his entire head under the bubbles while Mother whipped together some homemade hot cocoa on her prized gas stove.

Before the sergeant stopped by the maintenance office to see about some directions to the Hoyt headstone, he decided to swing towards the west side to his own family's plots. He turned into the cemetery at the second to last entrance on the south side, up along the narrow drive that curved first to the right and then to the left. Directly off from that first bend rested the small Civil War plot that leaned just a smidge and marked his great-grandfather, Otis Riley. Since just the one relative was laid there and he could see it from the car, the generational military man decided not to stop. Instead, he drove farther up the path, maneuvered the sharp turn and big loop to the right, and just sat with the car idling for a few moments. He had not been to his mom and dad's burial places for ages. Just to sit there and gaze out over towards them mustered that battle of tears and emotions that he had trained for decades to master, and the surviving son smacked the steering wheel. He should have brought flowers, a wreath, something! Mrs. Clyde Riley had trained him to care for the memories of others, yet after all of this time, it had slipped his mind to come prepared.

That failure drew him out of the car. With as light a foot as possible, he stepped across several rows and guided himself over to it. Oh, Mary, she had been so good to pick up where Mom had left off. In the two vases cemented in the flanks of the pink-hued granite stone, a small bouquet of fake flowers matched the spring's décor.

"Mom, I miss you so much!" the visitor spoke out into the damp morning mist. "No, I haven't brought you any grandkids, but I love the Lord just like you always wanted."

The soldier knelt down close enough to run his fingers across her engraved name without resting his knee on the dew-soaked ground. His left hand rested on the top of the stone as he lowered his head and allowed one small tear to break free of its rightful place. In an attempt to gather himself before any others followed, Sergeant Riley stood upright, rotated his stance a quarter of a turn to the left while keeping his left heel planted, composed his absolute best position of attention, and saluted the patriarch, Clyde O. Riley, a World War II veteran.

As he lowered his salute and eased his stance he reported with the utmost respect, "Sir, I think you would be proud, sir."

While the respectful descendant paced the rows to pay homage to his grandfather who fought in the Battle of Little Big Horn, his uncle who had served during World War I, and, of course, his dear brother who survived Vietnam, the soldier stopped dead in his tracks as a marker just one row behind Ed's took him by surprise. Situated right next to Aunt Hazel's but still in the row purchased for his kin, the trained sniper kept his rising composure while he surveyed the roads around this section of the cemetery to ensure that no cars were en route. With no onlookers, he marched over to the gray speckled headstone labeled "Hoyt" and stepped closer to better see the name below to the left. It read, "Robert A., 1960-1998," and the right side identified Betty, born in 1958, with a lone dash after her name.

It just could not be the same folks, but the names were right, the age was about right, the fact that the husband had passed but the wife had not. No, there had to be some sort of mistake. Besides, Aunt Hazel, the beloved town librarian, was a notorious spinster that spoiled Hamilton to the dickens because she never had any children of her own. Perhaps her family plots had been sold since that was the case. Surely Mary would be able to offer him some reasonable explanation at lunch.

After returning to his car, Sergeant Riley pulled up next to the maintenance shed and tapped his fingers along the steering wheel like a pacesetter at a military parade, waiting for someone from the Hoyt family to come pay tribute to their fallen father on the anniversary of his unexpected death. Even though the skies began to drizzle, forming droplets on the windshield, the trained scout could still see through the song and dance that performed its gentle pitter patter as he waited in disciplined silence. When no one showed up, he headed for The Shack.

As he debated whether his nerves could take much more on this roller coaster ride, Sergeant Riley resolved to take the route down West White Street. Although the road would end smack dab at the restaurant just beyond the small rural hospital, it also meant that he would pass straight in front of his old home at 808. Long gone were the blooming flower gardens, bursting blueberry bushes, overgrown apple tree, and Irene's favorite resting spot, the porch swing that swung from two posts out in the middle of the yard. The inviting landscape had long been overtaken by the ever-expanding car dealership that had purchased the house upon the passing of his dear mother.

The grown boy told himself over and over that he would not look, not do this to himself today, but his trained eye, his softening heart, this strange phase that he was experiencing during this mission forced him to lift his foot off of the accelerator and absorb every nook and cranny of the place without having to full out use the brake. Although his childhood home, now a rental, had been kept clean and tidy on the outside and a new two-car garage had been erected just in front of the tiny one stall where he practiced easing out the enormous black Chevy Impala with white top, the imposing concrete walls of the surrounding business consuming the place bit by bit hit him like a dagger. This was why he never visited this town.

"Ham!" Mary darted right over, demanding a full-fledged embrace as soon as the brother-in-law stepped through the door. "I've missed you!"

"Hello, Mary," the skillful sergeant patted her on the back while observing his surroundings. "Let's take a seat." The gentleman guided her over to a booth in the corner and allowed her to gush over him until after they had placed their order.

"I just can't believe you are here," she stared, smiling from ear to ear. "How long has it been?"

"Oh, geez," he readjusted himself in his seat, knowing full well it had been far too long. "A long time!"

Before she had an opportunity to rehearse the progression of years until they could agree on the actual date, time, and place, the recruiter seized the small window to address his present situation.

"Mary, I could really use your help on an assignment that I'm working on," the sergeant initiated the debriefing.

"Me? Help you with work? It frightens me a little bit to see how that is even possible," Mary played along.

"Well, you see, I have this recruit, and well—" Sergeant Riley struggled to find the best way to phrase the situation. "Well, I was doing some background checking on him, and to my surprise, the boy's father is buried in our family's section here at the cemetery in town. Do you happen to know any history on a fella by the name of Robert A. Hoyt?"

Mary's enthusiastic smile melted into a serious look of concern and her head lowered in defeat.

"You do know something!" the interrogator demanded.

With care and trepidation, Mary disclosed the entire situation, admitting that she knew nothing until Ed's last days. She figured that the copious amounts of painkillers aimed to ease his discomfort loosened his grip on family secrets, but even Irene did not attempt to deny the allegations when confronted later. As the sister-in-law recalled, dear Aunt Hazel found herself pregnant and unmarried during a time period and in a community that was quite harsh on such conditions. Supposedly she had relocated to Normal for about a year for some advanced classes on library stuff at the university, but in reality, she took refuge there to deliver. Seeing as the baby boy's father was long gone somewhere, the infant was put up for adoption.

"Oh, what was the name of that place?" Mary tried to remember. "I thought it kind of funny when Ed told me. The Baby Home? No, shoot, I can't remember, but it is there in Normal somewhere."

"The Baby Fold?" the nearby tenant surmised.

"Yes, that's it. The Baby Fold."

Sergeant Riley folded his hands and rested them against his mouth in an attempt to keep himself calm as the turn of events unraveled over a greasy cheeseburger and a side of hand-battered onion rings.

According to Mary's rendition, Aunt Hazel never got to have a relationship with her son, but the adoptive parents did allow for regular updates through the facility. From Ed's disclosure, what the beloved aunt could not outright do for her own child, she expressed by coddling little Hamilton who was just a year younger than her precious Bobby. As Hazel's executor, Ed himself made the final arrangements to secure a final resting place for the Hoyt boy along the row that had been established for his birth mother's line. No one had any idea that it would be filled at such a young age, but thankfully, Ed had not lived to see that day. He would have felt responsible somehow.

Ed had, however, tracked the young man as best he could, using The Baby Fold as a mediator to help pay for the boy's college. Bob had attended Blackburn in Carlinville, Illinois for his bachelor's, but then pursued his Master's in Social Work at Tulane University in New Orleans.

"According to Ed, he had a real passion for jazz, and given his history, it is no surprise really that he went into the social services," Mary divulged. "Apparently he was really smart, a great guy, and he settled in Normal with a bunch of kids. I think he had some big job over at one of the hospitals in Peoria, though. I can't remember all of the other details."

"Yeah, he had three girls and a boy," the sergeant added. "His boy, Brian, is one of my recruits."

"You don't say? What a small world!"

* * *

"Indeed," Akpore chimed into the story, having sat listening to his beloved friend release his pent-up anxiety. "I can see how taxing this has all been on you, my friend."

"Akpore, Hoyt is my relation!" the sergeant blurted. "And I'm beginning to think that this wild goose chase was no accident."

"Remember, I told you He was moving," the leader recalled in abiding amazement. "I knew He was doing powerful things in you and through these recruits."

"But I've already missed the last two summer cycles, and this one may be my last chance. Next February is the end of my tour, and I have no idea what I am doing next," Sergeant Riley explained the urgency. "This kid has already been wandering around out there, and I don't want to be the second recruiter to miss him."

"Now, now, sergeant," Akpore calmed him. "You cannot rush these things, and you are forcing this too much. Some of them take so much time. You cannot grow weary. Brother, you are only to be obedient to the leading of the Holy Spirit. I can attest that you are doing that. The Lord is working mightily on your behalf and on the behalf of the targets. You have to rest in that. You are so close with the others. You have been so diligent. Focus on them for right now, and I am sure you will have recruits ready for a cycle this summer. I have been praying hard for you, my friend, and I know this to be true."

Throughout the years that the sergeant worked with his team of supporters, they always managed to provide wise and sound counsel at just the right moments. Every time the sergeant felt frustrated with his progress or hopeless about his opportunities, that fine group of warriors bolstered his efforts, focused his intentions, and bathed him in prayer. Time had nearly run out when he made the call.

"Trish?" the sergeant blurted out on the phone.

"Hey, sergeant, so good to hear from you! Are you ready for tomorrow night? I just can't wait for this final testing session. I just get so excited every time a class comes through and the last five have been so powerful. I have…"

"Trish, sorry to cut you off, but I got him!" he interrupted.

"You got him? What do you mean?" she replied in confusion.

"The kid. I got the kid. I got to run, but expect him to be there tomorrow night, and don't forget to tell Carl. Oh, and remember, Salinas' English is still a bit rough. Go easy on him," he rushed.

"Thank you, Jesus!" was all that she could get out before he disconnected.

Sergeant Riley was running late for his appointment with Mrs. Bradford, and he did not want to disappoint her. He had so much to share but so little time. His encounters with her had grown to be so deep and emotional, and he was bursting to share with her a detailed and moving dream he had had about the Chief. The disciple was a bit hesitant to outright proclaim clear answers based on his visions, but then again, she had come to understand how the Lord spoke to him during these times, and the gentle woman appreciated his willingness to be so vulnerable with her.

The dream had not occurred just once, which was a sure indicator that there was a message in the mix. Some parts were vague and confusing, the specific meaning reserved for the Chief himself, but others seemed quite vivid and understandable.

As the pair walked about the outdoor botanical garden situated between the cafeteria and the east wing at the village, he recreated the scene for her.

> *The Chief was a young man, talking to another guy about some fraternity-like organization. It was not a college frat, but it was a brotherhood of some sort. He was the one trying to talk this other guy into joining, sharing about the trips they make to Vegas, the importance of Washington DC, and the advantages of calling upon the ring.*

Again, some of these details were a bit sketchy to the sergeant, but he did not let it deter him from the possibility of bringing Mrs. Bradford peace in the end.

> *Anyway, this guy began to share the Gospel with Chief. He scoffed it off and tried to dismiss the comments as sheer rumor, but the man was direct and bold. Soon the Chief found himself stuck in a corner of sorts. On one wall, he kept seeing pictures of his relatives long passed, admiring their successes and lofty positions within this private group, but when he looked at the other wall, he kept seeing your face like when you were younger, maybe like when you first met, and you had tears. He saw the kids too, behind you in a*

closet. They had these big dark cloaks being piled on top of them, suffocating them almost.

Then the Chief was laying in a bed much like his bed here at the home. He was still young, but it was that bed. He had two big chains wrapped around each arm, and he was pulling them. One was life when he was young, like a boy, and the other was him as an old man, decrepit and alone. He was just laying there struggling to maintain his grasp, then, finally, he breaks free from the one that was pulling him toward that generational wall that aged him and isolated him, and he turned and grabbed the other one with both hands. He kept yelling to the witness that he chose Jesus, and then he scooped you up into one arm and freed the kids from drowning in the closet with the other.

"Now, I don't know what each part of that means, Miss Ginny, but I do know this," the sergeant elaborated. "When your husband goes back to years past in his mind, he is reliving this. I can only hope that it means that there, in the caverns of his mind, he is brought to the choice for Christ again that once upon a time he had ignored."

Forcing her eyes to flutter in adoration, tears streamed down Mrs. Bradford's face and her chin quivered as she fought to control her silent sob throughout the telling of the vision. She knew the Lord had brought her hope by way of this courageous veteran, and the abiding spouse released the decades of tension in her neck and shoulders.

"I know your words are truth, sergeant," the endearing wife and loving mother confirmed as she squeezed the arm that escorted her steps. "I have seen that struggle in him when his mind is elsewhere. Sometimes as I reach for his hand and he pulls away, he calls out my name. I know now to hope for him to grab mine with both of his. Then I will know, and I will have my peace."

ASSESSMENT

CHAPTER 10

Hoyt

A Midwestern day in late August in the city of Normal, the sun could not decide whether to tuck behind the low-lying, gray clouds, offering hints of the fall to come or remain at high noon, enticing any patrons to retreat into the coolness of one of the shops. The masses of college students had not yet returned to flood these city blocks that boasted a serene taste of Americana.

While the socialite moms with their trendy clad crew scurried along to the children's museum situated just off of the roundabout, the slow-paced retirees with their rigid exteriors that had long lost patience for all things hurried embraced their run of the place for just a few more days. The townsfolk milled about the stores or chatted for hours at a curbside table, enjoying the calm before the clamor of compact cars, mountain bikes, and skateboards overwhelmed the scene.

Hidden away just a half a block north on Broadway behind the post office stood an unassuming store front. Its dull cement block exterior revealed that it was built to last but had still not been scathed by the modern influences of bold colors. The short metal overhang that cast a thin shadow covered just the top of the door, offering no relief for any passersby and dated the place even further as if it were still stuck in the 1970s. The uninviting glass door with a generic paper "Open" sign was sandwiched between two equally dreary display windows, one of which read "Recruiter" in arched black lettering while the other advertised "All are Welcome". Both notices lacked the art of provocation, aiding the facility's obscure existence.

However, the bleak announcements did snag the attention of one young man that day. Much like the place that projected a mild allure, this demure fellow hunched at the shoulders as if he had been trying to hide from the popular crowd for years. He stood at about six two, early twenties, with a rail-thin, weak build, and the greasy tinges of his dark hair reflected the sun as it prepared another peek. Although his mop was not fashioned in any particular style, the tousle had been cut just enough to swoop some bang away from his eyes and keep the edges off of his ears and shirt collar. While his khaki cargo pants treaded on the flood-zone stage, his striped indoor black soccer shoes creased at the toe as if he had found them in his size at the local thrift store where he discovered a non-NFL brand Green Bay Packers jersey, a steal since he was deep in Bears territory.

He did not rush towards the door as if he were running behind for an appointment, but instead, he blinked to clear his vision and cocked his head in contemplation as if noticing the station for the first time. Coming to an affirmative conclusion, the man-child pulled his hands out of his pockets and guided them toward the grip of the door like an irresistible magnetic pull. After tugging twice, he realized that he needed to push, and when he lowered his head to hide his eyes under his dark tufts, the tiny bell attached to the hinge of the inside of the door rang its high-pitched tone to announce his arrival.

Springing up on cue at the sound of the alert, the well-trained professional seated at the dull gray desk placed near the front of the barren shop rushed to greet him. Unlike the visitor, this man stood lean and strong and proud. While the crisp, light-green shirt boasted several commendation ribbons on his left chest, the thin black tie maintained its rightful place just above his belt and dark green suit pants. The recruiter looked about late forties as his flat top was darkening in that stage that sandy blonds began their salt-and-pepper phase. His skin bore a bit of weathering as if he had earned this more subdued assignment after many years in rougher terrain, and when he opened his mouth to cock his southern drawl, his metal-capped molars confirmed he had seen harder days.

"Hallelujah, you're here! Come on! Get on in here. Been waitin' for ya!" the sergeant demanded as he waved the young man in and bustled around to the front of the desk.

After thrusting a black plastic chair with metallic legs directly across from his own work station, the elated attendant wiped the chair with his rugged hand to remove any lingering but invisible dust and scurried back to the other side. The sergeant pulled a brown leather satchel from a hook on the coat rack and returned to his gray, roll-away chair. As he rummaged through its contents, he muttered to himself under his breath, "Let's see here."

The young man's eyes bugged and brows rose up beneath his bangs. "Waiting for me?"

"Yes, wonderin' when you were gonna get in over here, but been waitin' for ya," the sergeant reassured him. "Come on. Right here. Have a seat. I'll get your file."

The visitor looked frightened and bewildered as he kept glancing over his right shoulder towards the entrance, contemplating whether he should back out slowly or rush the front door before the military man even noticed. "I, I, I think you must have me confused with somebody. I, I just decided a few seconds ago to step in here. There is no way that you could have been expecting me."

As the driven recruiter ignored the grumbles and gathered his supplies, the young man held his ground and peeked around the room, noticing a few brochures, a few more empty chairs, some bookcases in the back, and then caught a glimpse of one of those old Uncle Sam posters where the stern-looking, bearded man's finger seemed to be always pointing at you no matter what angle you looked at it. Nothing struck him as out of the ordinary. No one else seemed to be there. As he strained his body to his left to peer down the hall, he spotted a door marked "latrine" and wondered if it was at all possible that someone else was in there and this confident recruiter was confusing him with that person. While he tried to remain still to listen for further movements, the nervous guest heard no noise other than a no-frills, metal fan in the back right corner, oscillating on low. Every time its air passed across the sergeant's desk, it raised the edge of the paper stacked in the top right corner.

Satisfying his search, the meticulous sergeant eased out a smudged manila folder held by a few paper clips with intermittent frayed edges and placed it on the desktop. Making numerous glances between the contents and the young man, the recruiter reported aloud to an unknown audience for reassurance. "Yep, looks a little thinner in person. Shoot, even got the same shirt on here. Yep, it's you all right."

Alarmed and confused, the college kid strained to catch a glimpse of the documents and responded with a slight raised tone in his voice, "What? What do you mean? It can't be me. I mean…"

"Ah, I, see," the brash sergeant interrupted, "you seem a li'l confused. Thought you decided just to come in here by chance, did ya?"

"Well, yeah. I, I was just walking by, and I, I saw the sign. You are a recruiter, right?"

"Yep, you got that right, son."

The sergeant turned back towards the computer and pecked like an injured chicken with the right index finger and then the left.

"Well, I just, I just … maybe this is a mistake."

"No, no. There's no mistake," the sergeant replied as if the young man's conversation was inconsequential to the task at hand.

"But, I just, was just thinking, about coming in. I almost turned away at the door."

The sergeant chuckled in response. "It's noted that you struggle with obscurities."

"Well, who noted? What was noted?"

The young man's voice quivered, stuck somewhere between demanding an answer and scared that he might draw the sergeant's undivided attention as he wilted into the seat provided for him. The latter prevailed as the recruiter stopped his attempt at typing, swiveled his chair to face the target, and rested his folded hands on the desktop between them. "Ahhh, I see. We need to kind of start at the beginning with you, give you the whole picture."

Shocked at the rumbles of bravery swelling up from somewhere within, almost as if his life depended on this final plea, the student proceeded to question, "Well, yeah, I mean, I almost didn't walk in, and then I decided I would kind of, maybe, come see what you are about."

The recruiter found the comments almost comical. "See what I'm about? Ah, it is not what I'm about. It's what you're about."

"What I'm about?"

"Yes, this is what you are about, recruit."

The echo of the sergeant's drawn out use of that title made the timid adolescent straighten up in his seat and roll his shoulders back as if accepting some rite of passage. The gleam in the boy's eyes as they perked up to this apparent call of duty soon faded back to the haze, perhaps even more confused now than when he first walked in that door.

"I was briefed by, uh," the sergeant paused, unsure of how to explain the situation, "um, the previous duty sergeant that you had passed by these doors since you were about eight years old but never so much as glanced at the window to see your own reflection."

"Eight years old? You've been expecting me since I was eight?" The recruit could not decide whether to be flattered or even more frightened.

"You betcha. Said you grew up in these here parts, wanderin' around down here on your bike for ages. Always lookin' down when you walked, though, even back then," the sergeant continued. "Said most times you were just lookin' for loose change and would head over yonder to old Randall's store for candy."

As the target squirmed in his chair and stared up at the ceiling in desperation, trying to recall the handful of times that he had ridden his bike from his house about a half mile away to Randall's store for candy, the vulnerable recruit winced at the disclosure of such intimate details. Randall's had been gone for eons and most of his candy runs were to the little shack of a store, Hendren's, that was just on the other side of the alley behind his home. Although he now had this eerie concern that he had been followed all along, he never remembered this place or felt that he was being watched at the time. His mind strained through childhood memories like an online newsfeed, frantic to make some kind of connection with this odd but alluring conversation.

The youngster remembered speeding around the college quad on his yellow bike with the image of a horse's head blowing in the wind on the chain guard while dodging Frisbees or weaving around lovestruck couples lounging on blankets. With fond recollection, he envisioned the family walks to and from the church that used to stand just a few blocks north. Although the house of worship was positioned in the midst of college central across from the towering dorms and next to the public library, few young adults attended; however, his family filed into the fifth pew to the left of the podium every Sunday like clockwork.

With disdain the recruit recalled the expectation to dress up, him in slacks and a button- up shirt while his three older sisters flaunted their floral dresses. Although the baby brother hated that part of the service more than anything, the obedient one complied every week while the girls fussed and bickered about whose tights belonged to whom and something about how someone spilled something on someone else's favorite sweater when that someone borrowed it earlier in the week without permission. The verbal barrage never ended with those girls and their drama surrounding clothes, and it made him thankful to be a boy. However, that did not mean that the girls left him alone. Oh no, the trio critiqued his clothes with equal vigor. "Are you wearing that? Those don't even match. You can't wear brown shoes with black pants. Mom, please don't let him go out like that."

As the distracted visitor did a once over on his outfit for the day, he wondered if the girls would have approved of his khaki pants with green shirt.

"Ah, none of that was in vain, recruit," the sergeant drew him back to his present circumstance with a tone as if he were tracking his review of the past. "All along there has been a glorious plan for your life. You were magnificently and wonderfully made, and you have a very unique purpose in furthering God's army that only you can fulfill. We want you….yes, you."

"God's army?" the recruit asked as he stared, puzzled, with wide eyes down that pointed finger, so reminiscent of the one from the poster hanging on the wall just to his left.

"You see, even when you were in your mama's womb, the God of the universe knew you. He had great plans for you, plans to prosper you, even then. Everything about you, your looks, your personality, your intellect, your strengths, your hang-ups, your experiences, everything is part of what brought you here today!" The sergeant settled into his role as the ultimate salesman.

Hoyt absorbed the comments. The God of the universe knew him? Now he was certain that the sergeant had him confused with someone else.

The recruiter interrupted his target's thoughts once again to continue his pitch. "He has been quietly whispering to you, hoping you would want to be a part of his family unit, and now here you are. He has been preparing me as well, just for this time, this place, this here, this now! Today is your lucky day! You are just what we have been looking for, and now we have found you. Let me tell you about God's family unit, God's army, and why you want to be a part of it. I do not want you leaving here today without having all the information that you need. You want peace? We got it. You want joy? We got it all. You want truth? I will tell you the truth. Can you handle the truth? You want love? God is love. Shoot, God is all things good. That is why they call it good. It is just an extension of the word GOD. Get it?"

The overwhelmed recruit cringed at some of these comments. He first tried to recall any voices whispering to him but could only think of a few times he was frightened as a child, riding his bike in the dark, hoping with bated breath that no one would jump out from behind a bush to nab him. His mother had often warned them about local crime that infiltrated college towns, but most of those seemed to involve a loud frat party or tailgating at a football game. Other warnings were more for the girls, not being swayed by prowling men, or the general "don't talk to strangers" speech. Hoyt could not remember anyone approaching him with a whisper or even face to face, for that matter.

The seeker longed to hear more about this peace. Raised with three, strong, independent sisters, he had wanted peace from them until he had more peace and quiet than he knew what to do with once he moved out of the house and into the dorms. Perhaps the goal was to answer that unsettled nagging question about what he was supposed to do with his life. The successful student had just graduated last spring and still had no idea what he was going to do long term, so the wayward one went ahead and enrolled in a few summer classes just to keep his spot in student housing.

The runt of the family desired joy, more moments like the ones he shared with his dad, and the logical thinker pursued truth, concluding it was the best way to go. He felt he could handle it unless it was going to be overly critical, of course, then he would rather not.

Love, now that was something the young man had no experience in and made him blush to even think about. As a child he often thought a brother would help fill that need to belong, but with no more additions to the immediate family, the sole male searched for that best buddy that so many others seemed to have. Much later he crushed on the occasional girl but never ever had the courage to act on it

Following the Holy Spirit's unique leading, the sergeant brought his target back in focus. "Let me give you a bit of your glorious history. When God created the universe, He breathed life into man, Adam, in the Garden of Eden. He loved Adam, loved living life with him, talking with him, caring for him. He gave Adam dominion over the land and the animals, and then the Creator saw fit to give Adam a human partner for relationship as well. He gave Adam a woman named Eve, and He intended intimate relations for them, blessing them with offspring of more humans to fill the earth, have more relationships, and have more help taking care of the land and the animals. It was all great until Adam and Eve disobeyed God and ate from the forbidden tree. They caved to that carnal issue of man thinking he knows best. You know it. You know what I am talking about. You have caved to it yourself. Thankfully, God was not done with mankind then, and He is not done with it now. He gave them consequences, but He also kept loving them and making a way for them to have relationship with Him."

The obliging church attender knew that he had heard all of this rhetoric before. Was this sergeant really going to start with the whole Adam and Eve thing? Hoyt remembered hearing this in Sunday school many times but thought it boring, sappy, and unrelated to his life whatsoever.

The recruiter carried on, "Eventually, an entire people group was formed to be His army here on earth. They were the nation of Israel. God prepared an unlikely leader for this group of misfits. His name was Moses, and like you, he did not expect to be a highly sought after recruit. He felt ill-equipped to lead. He was disliked, he was distant for a time, he doubted himself and God, and he just felt downright unworthy to wear the uniform. But also like you, he eventually was willing. He led that group like a champion, and God gave him the Ten Commandments that would serve as the written law of how God wanted His army to have relationship with Him and with each other. Ten instructions that engulf all that relationships and life are supposed to be about. Ten doesn't seem that hard, now does it? Shoot, it seems like doing ten push-ups. Can you do ten push-ups, recruit?"

"Push-ups?"

The wimpy target glanced down at his right bicep, trying to flex in a way that would make it look like his normal arm position, but he knew that he would be hard pressed to do any push-ups, let alone ten. Then, Hoyt tried to imagine Moses doing push-ups. And what in the world was that sergeant talking about, Moses with a uniform? The student did not recall any pictures of Moses in some uniform other than a robe tied by a string and a big staff. The skeptical one thought the sergeant must be confused with his Biblical history. Sure, the boy had not been a stellar Sunday school student himself and had not even finished confirmation like the girls had, but he knew enough about his religion to know that back then they did not wear uniforms like that. And according to that "Moses" movie that his grandma always made them watch on TV when it aired, the one where Charlton Heston played the lead, Moses was always strong and in charge, not anything like what this soldier-preacher seemed to imply.

The same was true about the Ten Commandments. What in the world did they have to do with relationships? He had never heard that before. They were some set of magical rules that parents reminded you of when you did not obey them or gave you a lecture about while reading the newspaper about some criminal getting caught and put in jail. "The Ten Commandments say do not commit murder. That is what he gets. You hear me, kids? Obey your mother and father and do not commit murder and go to prison."

"Well, I tell you what. It is harder than you think, and it was harder than they thought too," the sergeant continued reciting his epic. "This army called Israel was getting swallowed up. They wanted this and that from the other side, and they lost their way.

But have no fear. God did not give up on them, and He has not given up on you. He took care of this situation, well in advance."

The riled sergeant paused, relaxed his eyebrows that had grown stern as the story went on, and cracked a smile on the right side of his mouth.

"Oh, young recruit, I could go on and on. I could tell you of great battles won by the smallest, youngest, and least likely of men like David. I could tell of losing ground sometimes, like the exile into Babylon. You will learn all that and more in good time, soldier, but now I want to get to the secret weapon that is available to you right here, right now. You see, fast forward in this saga, and we get to what we call the Holy Spirit that can reside in you as it resides in me and all others that have joined the army of God. You see, the Holy Spirit is the actual Spirit of the God of the universe. There is none greater, and He will empower you, recruit. How? How is this possible? How is this so? Ahh, recruit, that is the greatest triumph of all human history," his nostalgic tone heaved as if the storyteller had survived each episode himself.

"You see, recruit, a long time ago, God put his New Covenant into motion. He sent His son to the earth to be born as man. He was the God-man as He was fully God but fully man. His name was Jesus, and He came as ransom for us. The enemy thought he was winning. He thought his control of the armies could not be defeated. The lawless one laughed at the sting of death, but what God had in store for him, he could not even see comin'. He was not expecting a child to be the Savior of all mankind," the sergeant created the battle scene like a famous movie critic.

"Sure, when he got suspicious here or there, he tried to outmaneuver us, but that snake was always one step short. Tried killing children about Jesus' age when he was about two or three, but no go. He later tried to tempt him into sin in the desert when He was all alone when He was about thirty. Again, Jesus survived unscathed. He tried to confuse Jesus' men with deeply religious questions and trickery, but Jesus stayed the course. Even the night before His final earthly sacrifice, He tried to diminish His fortitude, but Jesus surrendered to the mission. Ah, yeah, and then they crucified Him, thought they had killed Him, put an end to His reign, but they were walking right into our hands. You see, Jesus died, but then rose again, having defeated the enemy's hold once and for all. The Savior appeared to His troops, told them all about the ultimate plan, and He sent the Holy Spirit to reside in each of His followers, so that they could continue the fight for all those that would simply follow Him."

Hoyt was downright mystified at this description of Jesus and the battle that seemed to ensue during his ministry. This graphic depiction was a far cry from the long-haired Jesus in white flowing robes with a kiss of sunlight radiating from his face and children laughing and sitting on his lap while little lambs grazed in the hills in the backdrop. As this sergeant portrayed an epic war that had played out in the battlefield of real life, he spoke of this Holy Spirit as Jesus' final secret weapon, a tried-and-true expert in this cosmic spiritual warfare that still waged. The curious visitor perched on the edge of his seat in anticipation of the rest of the story.

"Now we are here at you, recruit," the sergeant's words left their distant place and floated straight back down to his target as they faced each other once again, eye to eye, the presence of the fan still offering an occasional breeze to ward off the heat of the day. "Simple, yeah, seems simple enough, but that's where you come in. Right here, right now, recruit, you have to choose whose army you are in."

The mesmerized recruit eased back into his chair once again, stunned by the sergeant's directness.

"Don't wanna be in any army, you think? Hate to break it to you, recruit, but ain't no such thing. Sure, you may have walked in here thinking that, but you can't walk out thinking that. Sure, you can walk out, you can play pretend for a while, but the enemy ain't gonna leave you alone now that you know the truth."

The truth? Although Hoyt could not deny the feeling of despair infringing on him on one side and some place of strength and safety that seemed to warm him on the other, the timid student was unsure what he knew. As he sat in the middle of the invisible tug of war, his heart pounded louder and louder inside his chest.

"You don't wanna believe the truth? Shoot, ain't no such thing. Once you walked through my door, recruit, you were faced with the truth. You're not here by accident. So now, what's it gonna be? Let me break it down for ya. You got one choice to make right here, right now. There's a battle goin' on out there, and you pretendin' that it isn't, ain't gonna work no more. You're either fightin' for the enemy or you are fightin' for the God of the universe, the King of Kings, the Alpha and the Omega, the Lord of Lords!" The sergeant's words reverberated through the office like an echo caught in the valley of a deep cavern.

Hoyt heard the claims penetrate his mind and a still voice expected a response.

"You have to choose me or not choose me."

The timbre rang strong and confident, yet gentle and peaceful at the same time. Because the pronouncement resounded in his head like a dominating force, the recruit suspected others could have heard it as well, yet he knew it was meant for only him. The office, the sergeant, everything else faded into the background as he buried his face in his hands, his elbows resting on his lap. The invitation felt so real, and he had waited his whole life to hear that voice.

"I love you, Brian, but you need to choose right now. You either choose me, or you do not choose me."

The soft tone sounded so familiar somehow, a place of rest and security, yet its power wielded some protective shield from terror and darkness that licked their lips for just the slightest hesitation, chomping at the bit to have their turn with him. Overwhelmed with this sense of someone searching in earnest for him, wanting to be his constant companion and friend, someone loving him so dearly while the realization of his failings silently confessed that he was so undeserving, the isolated target released his pooling tears that had sprung from his soul.

"I choose you, Jesus," the humble words spewed from his mouth out into the open as they brought an invisible embrace unlike he had ever felt in his life. All darkness seemed to flee as if it never existed as he re-uttered those words out loud over and over again in adoration and thankfulness.

The sergeant's confident voice comforted him. "You made the right choice, son. Of course, you don't deserve all of this at your disposal. You think I did? Shoot, I was worse off than you, recruit. Don't you worry about them tears neither. That always happens when someone joins. Now, come on, sit up tall, be proud in whom you serve. You leave all that other stuff to the Lord. He'll get that all worked outta ya in due time. He always does. We gotta get you ready."

Wiping his face with his shirt sleeve, the timid recruit gaped at the sergeant with admiration, attentive to the forthcoming direction for his next steps.

"Let me make sure we get your name in here right." The sergeant reviewed his file again as if the contract was now complete. "Brian Robert Hoyt. Good, looks good. Now, we gotta find out what your special gifts are and get you started on your basic training. Report back to me at 0800 hours tomorrow."

Still rattled from the emotional upheaval that had just resulted during a last-ditch effort to inquire about military service and set a course of direction for his life, Recruit Hoyt remained dumbfounded in his seat not ready to leave. Part of him still wanted to cry, part wanted to ask more questions, and part of him wanted to race home and talk to his mom. He was not quite sure what to think or feel or do, but the sergeant's order seemed emphatic.

"Yes, go on. Yes, you can walk out that door. Remember, Recruit Hoyt, you will never be alone again. You are one of us now. You just enjoy this day and how thankful you are, and I will see you bright and early tomorrow morning. Remember, today is the first day of the rest of your life, recruit."

CHAPTER 11

Salinas

Salinas turned onto Leopold Street, a hard right into the parking lot, and into a spot opposite the building. After placing the compact beater into park, he reviewed the address that the sergeant had written on the back of the business card. As he strained to read the sign through his rearview mirror, just enough of the moon's light hit the letters to decipher "Educational Center". Even though the title seemed accurate, the playground equipment and toddler trikes secured in rows within the fenced yard to his left threw him. This school for kids did not seem at all like a place to hold assessment testing for God's army, but this was where the sergeant had directed him.

As his motor sputtered to a halt, the apprehensive recruit pried open the rusted door and strolled toward the entrance. When he cupped his hands around his eyes and peered through the window on the left door that advertised the operating hours, the immigrant noticed the alarm system blinking its operating lights. Amidst the casting shadows he recognized a check-in counter and three classrooms. Remembering the instructions to enter through the solid white door on the right and his curiosity with the left satisfied, Salinas scanned over his shoulder as he reached for the other handle.

Without resistance the door opened, and the tentative Latino ascended the looming staircase with keen awareness of the echo he produced with each step as he leaned his weight towards his toes. After pulling the door at the top of his climb, he studied the carpeted path of the hallway and proceeded towards the room at the end. While the carpet absorbed the noise of his arrival, muffled tones of other people grew louder. Two doors on the left, one on the right, and the one straight ahead marked "The Scott Wenzel Library". As the tester reached out for the handle, someone from within had beat him to it.

A tall, thin lady with an inviting smile greeted him and then swooped in for the hug as she drew him into her bosom. "Hi. Welcome. I'm Trish."

Startled by the uncommon display of affection from this culture, the observer noticed the large, raised scar peeking out of the top of her shirt when she leaned into him. As the blood rushed to his cheeks, his inner child longed for the familiar embrace that he had experienced often from his mother, aunts, cousins, even neighbors. Parts of him longed for the comforts of home, battling against the American he strived to become.

"Come on in." She released him from her grasp as she looped her arm around his, ushering him into the room and over to the desks assembled for the class. "You sit right here," she ordered as she guided him down into a seat. "Now, can I get you something to drink? Coffee? Tea? Bottle of water?"

"Give him some breathing room, Trish," a man spoke with impatience as he headed toward them, marker still in hand from writing on the white board on the other side of the room.

"I'm only making him feel welcome, Carl," the woman defended.

Apparently, this tit-for-tat had not been their first rodeo because they spoke to one another as if no one else was listening. "I know, honey, but you got to let people get in the door first," the man switched his tone, showing his affections for the intent, although her methods seemed to embarrass him. "Let them pick their own

The Recruits

seats, sit where they feel comfortable." The man's attention now directed on Recruit Salinas, "Sorry, dude. If you want something to drink, it is right over there. Get what you want. We will be starting in just a few minutes."

Salinas noticed that this Carl seemed about his own height, about five nine, while his "honey," whoever she was to him, had to be at least six two. Most couples in his country were the same height, but never was the woman so much taller than her mate. When he shifted his view down to her left hand, he saw she was wearing a wedding band. *So, the observant one concluded to himself, what an odd pairing.*

Although Carl exhibited an olive skin tone, the foreigner did not detect an accent in his voice, so if the teacher was a fellow Latino, he had long lost the allure of his verbal charm. The slight slant to the husband's hazel eyes also set him apart from the Spanish norm and pushed the leader towards the racial category of the integrated sorts.

When Trish followed Carl back to the white board to finish their preparations for the class, Salinas opted against any refreshments and remained in his seat to survey the rest of the room. A tall, athletic-looking, dark-haired, middle-aged guy made small talk with a cute, fit, light-brown-haired gal at the drinks table. Their conversation looked innocent enough. Just a few feet from them sat a beautiful, young, thin redhead in one of the chairs in the far right of the front row. As she leaned toward the front of the seat with her hands locked in her lap, she seemed to anticipate the excitement for the night's event. Over his right shoulder in the last row, a nerdy-looking kid with dark, greasy hair stared at a pencil, drumming out of tune with his free hand. With a strong sense of style, Salinas resisted the urge to judge the dude's mismatched apparel of khaki cargo pants and yellow t-shirt. As a transformed expert in fashion, the Hispanic recruit surmised that this guy lacked the influence of a good woman.

As he turned to assess the other people in the room, Carl

chimed in. "Recruits, if you could all take your seats, we will begin. We have a lot to cover tonight and not a lot of time to do it."

Like obedient soldiers, the entire room complied and maneuvered into the metal chairs attached to the faux wooden desktops. Witnessing the embarrassing struggle to squeeze into the tight opening, Salinas relished his decision to stay put.

"I would like to welcome you all here to our little classroom," Trish's eyes gleamed with the high pitch of her fairy-like voice. "As you may know, my name is Trish, and this gorgeous man here is my husband, Carl."

"Okay, Trish." Carl grabbed her arm as if to get her attention back on the task at hand as well as the class's. "They don't want to hear that."

"Well, Carl, I can't help it. You are gorgeous, don't you think so, guys?"

As she searched the room for what seemed to be a rhetorical question, Carl interrupted before anyone had the chance to form a reply. "Trish, stop. Okay, recruits, we have a packet for everyone. Trish, here, hand them out," he ordered her in a tone that wavered between affection and frustration.

The demonstrative wife complied and passed out the packets one at a time as she paused and gazed right into the eyes of each recruit as if her analyzing stare calculated some data from each soul in just a few seconds. Every "here you go" varied, hinting at her brief determination. Some of the phrases rounded into soothing confirmations and others descended like an apology. Some pepped with excitement, and some burrowed like a question. Salinas's nerves twisted in anticipation of the line she would serve him, but with her head tilted and eyes blinking like a doe, she imparted a simple, "I love your glasses, by the way. So GQ."

Not knowing how to read Trish, Salinas battled all kinds of conflicting emotions. Considering himself an experienced lady's man, the recruit swarmed in his confusion, unable to categorize the comment as flirtatious or motherly. Their proximity in age veered him toward the forward box, but the presence of her husband countered that line of thinking.

After the female instructor finished her rounds, she rejoined her husband at the front and continued her suspicious ogling of the class.

"Again, sorry, but we don't have a lot of time, guys," Carl reiterated.

"Carl, we have to give some kind of introduction," Trish insisted.

"We just don't have time, Trish," Carl replied, and the tit-for-tat began again, leaving the rest of the room somewhere in the near distance.

"Well, Carl, if we don't give some kind of introduction, they are not even going to know who we are."

"You already told them you are my wife!" Carl tried to satisfy her and move on with his duties.

"Sweetie?"

"Okay," Carl conceded, trying to put the brakes on this runaway train. "As we said, I am Carl and this is my wife, Trish. We own this daycare center, and at night we give different classes up here. We do stuff like financial stewardship classes, marriage enrichment classes, and, of course, assessment testing, which is why you all are here. Right?"

Giving that reassuring nod to the left and to the right, the room confirmed they were all in the right place at the right time, although none of them looked confident in what they were doing there.

"Good!" Carl confirmed. "Then that should just about do it. Oh, before I forget, this is our daughter, Chloe. She is in the final stage of her instructor training course, so she will be observing us tonight and may be helping during the exit interviews."

As he pointed towards the beautiful ginger in the front row, the shy young lady shrugged her shoulders, glanced back towards the class, and waved, covering her sheepish grin.

Salinas had assumed she was one of them, a recruit. With a

youthful look and a timid demeanor, how could she already be so far in God's army to be in training as an instructor?

"Can I continue?" Carl had hoped Trish was satisfied with his introduction and would allow him to resume.

"Yes, thank you, dear," Trish permitted with a genuine approval. Her knight in shining armor had won her heart once again.

Salinas wished that his own wife would one day look at him with that abiding admiration, that passionate endearment. He knew he did not deserve it, but he longed for it all the same. He loved Anna and their two kids, and he tried to be a faithful husband and reliable provider, but no matter what he did to "be good," he always, eventually, somehow failed.

The skillful performer must have misread Trish, though. Based on her obvious commitment to resolve conflict with words of kindness and her sincere public affections towards her spouse, he reasoned that Trish loved Carl.

Oh, these circular emotions inflamed uncomfortable fright, and the assessment had not even started. The testing process was supposed to identify his true spiritual gifts, those unique aspects of him that God wanted to use for His own purposes, God's army. Salinas doubted the sergeant's promises that he even had any. Women—manipulating them, swaying them with is suave charms, and tossing a few Spanish compliments in their direction was his typical MO, but this night already challenged him to re-evaluate his perceptive abilities.

The sergeant had reassured his third target that surrender to Jesus Christ and enlistment in God's army forged a new man. Although the recruiter even affirmed that accepting the gracious gift of redeeming salvation would ignite a rebirth, the recruit felt that old self pulling within him. The muck did not disappear like a magic spell as he had hoped, and Trish was a tell-tale sign as her overt mannerisms rattled the purging within his spirit. While Salinas had once claimed the ability to read females as his own gift to the world, now the loosening grip on the power triggered a fierce internal war.

The tantalizing snare had been there, residing in him, consuming him for longer than he could even remember anymore. As part of his Hispanic culture, the sly offering controlled part of his identity, part of his manhood. Even his own father had often bragged about the scores of sexual escapades that accompanied the maturation of young men, and like a rite of passage, the patriarch had even arranged for a local prostitute to take his thirteen-year-old son's virginity. With a round of beers for all of the boys, the celebration on the front stoop of their adobe home washed away any lingering uncertainties.

Like the opening of that mythological Pandora's Box, the young Salinas became aware of his body, his mannerisms, his smells, his words, his tone, and even what he owned or lacked. Every thought focused on one task, getting another notch in his belt. Like training for a prizefight, he was determined to be the champion.

As the never-ending thirst for more begged him to widen his territory, the agitated mama's boy grew weary of his meager, rural offerings. When word had gotten back to the hillside village that his eldest brother had made his way across the border to El Norte, Salinas set that as his next target. If he could just get there, he could have more. He could have more money, more things, more women, opportunity for white women, and a more satisfying purpose. The driven one was convinced that he could be someone truly special if he could just get there.

As the recruit sat in the library in the middle of Illinois, he recognized that former man was still in there. All of those desires now battled against shame, enticing him to hide them if at all possible. Although Salinas felt desperate to start over, he had no idea how. How could he erase his whole life? How could he make his wife forget all of his misdeeds and trust him again? How would his white, American in-laws ever see beyond their illegal, Mexican, cheating son-in-law? How could God recruit him for His army? He was a failure, a fraud, but he still…believed.

The faint hope resonated in there, urging him to hang on. Within his very core the sinner knew he could never be good on his own, but that comforting warmth, echoing within his heart, reminded him that he had been forgiven and that Jesus would transform him.

"I am with you always, Artemio. You do not fight alone."

CHAPTER 12

Hoyt

Never breaking his focus from the paper, Recruit Hoyt finished his test and laid his pencil down so as not to disturb any of the others seated in front of him. As a seasoned college student, he felt comfortable with taking tests, having long since gotten over the anxiety of them. With the detailed instructions provided by Carl and Trish, the obedient participant answered the questions as honestly as possible without trying to force a particular outcome.

"Just take one question at a time and really select the first answer that comes to your mind," Carl advised. "It may not all make sense to you now, but when we compile all of your answers, we will go over them with you individually during the exit interview. Believe me, you will not leave here without knowing your gifts."

"This assessment is more for you than for us. It is likely that we can already detect many of your gifts." Trish tried to be comforting, although her invasion of personal space triggered guarded skepticism. From her intrusive hug to the salutations with each packet, the mystery behind her expressions and comments suggested a secret waited just behind her garbled clues. "But you need to know your own gifts," Trish's eyes scanned the entire room as her sing-songy voice imparted an edge of condemnation.

Carl, on the other hand, issued methodical instructions. "Well, that is not altogether accurate, Trish." As he turned his attention away from his wife and back to the class, he continued his directive. "Higher up does take these results seriously in finalizing your active duty placement. You are going to be answering all kinds of questions. There will be some about what you like, some about what you don't like. There will be some about experiences you may or may not have had, personality traits, what you are good at, what you are horrible at, just all kinds of stuff. Then there is your heart, where it is tugging at you. That is where we really come in."

"That's my favorite part," Trish chimed in as she looped her arm around Carl's and leaned into him with a public caress.

An unemotional person by nature, Hoyt tensed and scowled at such displays. Sure, he did not begrudge anyone true love, but he was raised to believe that affections were reserved for behind closed doors. As the queasy one strained to remember his own parents' acts of engagement, he wondered what Chloe must have thought. Because his seat faced the back of hers, he could not see her facial expressions unless she turned to look back at the class, but the recruit had not detected any nonverbal cues of displeasure.

"During the exit interview, we will go over your results and dig a bit deeper into your heart condition," Carl smirked and tossed a wink at Trish, hoping that she picked up on his clever pun.

"Carl," Trish scolded with an affirming love pat, "you are going to scare them."

Shaking his head at her ironic remarks, Recruit Hoyt thought Trish's dramatic ways usurped even his sisters'.

"I want you all to feel totally safe in our care," she tried to be comforting again. "This is not a medical matter of any sorts."

"Well, now, that could be debatable," Carl caught his chuckle before it escaped his mouth.

"Carl, stop, you're terrible," Trish encouraged him again with another tender pat on the shoulder, signaling that she appreciated his dry humor.

"Okay, enough of that. The desires of your heart will help make that final determination of your placement, as I stated before. In a nutshell, the composite outcome will result in a ranking of sorts. The first area on your list will be to review your packet, thoroughly pray over it, and determine if you will meet their present needs. If so, they will take your packet and begin to process it for your final assignment—place, particular tasks, stuff like that. If they pass up on you, it goes to the next in line and so on. No need to worry about that stuff now. Get going on your tests, and we will tie this all up at the end." Carl turned to the recruits to give them the green light and then escorted his bride over to the drink table.

Still bewildered by the animated couple, Hoyt waited for someone in the crowd to howl, "Get a room," but no one took the bait. Instead, in unison the class eyed Carl and Trish to the table and turned to their tests. As an ardent rule follower, he did the same.

Finding the questions rather straightforward, the studious one selected scenarios worthy of engagement and identified activities that leaned towards the unpleasant. Most of the questions were phrased as "would you rather" type of situations. While a few forced him to weigh how he felt against the "right" thing to do, Hoyt needed to know his gifts, get some answers for his real purpose in life, and he did not want to interfere with the assignment process, so he adhered to the instructions to answer honestly.

Some of the personality questions were similar to ones he had encountered during a high school class and sometime even in college, so the novice recruit was not too surprised by those, but the experiences posed a challenge. As a relegated loner, Hoyt lacked many interesting life experiences, although he maintained a pretty normal life.

Air puffed out of his nose at the amusement of that thought. Coming from the town of Normal, he always got a kick out of referring to himself as normal. He was normal from Normal, and to boot, he lived on Normal Avenue, and he never understood why no one else seemed to get the humor in that clever quip. As the sounds of closing booklets and rustling paper distracted his witty tangent, the student saw that most of the others were finishing up their tests and Carl and Trish promenaded back to the front to explain the next steps.

"Okay. Is everyone finished?" Carl surveyed the room. "Great. Okay. Trish will go around and collect your test. Go ahead and do that, honey."

"Absolutely," she confirmed with delight and made her way to one desk at a time much like she had passed them out. "Thank you very much." The domineering woman congratulated each recruit with such genuine pleasure in their efforts although she had not even evaluated the results yet. As she retrieved each packet, she paused for another brief gaze to ease their soul.

When she had just about collected that last one, Carl resumed with his instructions. "Thanks, honey. Recruits, we need the room to be quiet for these exit interviews, so we will have to ask you all to remain in your seats and remain silent. Trish, Chloe, and I are going to one of the other classrooms that you passed in the hallway on your way to the library here. One of us will come back here and call you one at a time to follow us for your interview. Upon completion of your interview, you will exit the premises immediately and await further instruction from your prospective recruiter. Any questions?"

Assuming the rhetorical nature of his remarks, the entire room just glanced at each other, wondering if anyone would conjure up the guts, but none did. All the recruits sat in surrendered silence as Carl headed out with Trish directly behind as she stumbled over herself trying to look back with that endearing farewell look on her face. Chloe rose from her seat like a gentle flower, making her way behind her parents like a soft petal swept up in a cool spring breeze.

During her voyage, Hoyt could see that she was nearly as tall as her mother with a similar long, thin build. She looked nothing at all like Carl as her skin was fair and her hair had an angelic-like shine to it. The young man's nerves tightened and his gut wrenched as he watched her gallop out of the room. Something intrigued him about the beautiful young woman.

Although she had remained silent during the testing, her mannerisms exuded a quiet strength. Like a perfect blend of the emotion that favored Trish and that edge of sensibility that aligned more with Carl, Chloe conveyed a bridled version of them both.

Hoyt's eyes popped with the realization that he might draw Chloe as his interviewer. The angst battled between desire and fear. If the doe-eyed, redhead called his name, he would finally hear her speak and have a chance to get to know her more, but his fear warned him that he would have to speak back.

CHAPTER 13

Salinas

As the door handle turned and the bottom sweep brushed against the low pile of the carpet, the recruits held their breath in anticipation of the next instructor and the next interviewee. When Carl popped his head past the threshold, the united sigh released their sails.

"Salinas?"

Unwilling to delve any deeper into his emotions surrounding Trish, the conflicted recruit relaxed in utter relief that Carl had called his name. "Sí, I mean, yes, that's me," he answered, wiggling out of his confining desk unit.

Motioning for the recruit to lead the way down the hall, Carl secured the door behind and then brushed past the wandering participant, keeping his eyes fixated on the pages within the manila folder. Other than the swish of their own footsteps or the muffled sounds of female voices echoing against the barren walls, the two walked in uncomfortable silence for what seemed like an eternity until Carl opened the last door on the left and darted into the examination room.

Salinas hesitated and eyed the two opposite entrances, listening for a clue to the interrogative process. He could hear that Trish was in the one to the left, her theatrics continuing in there, and he strained to make out a woman's voice behind the other door. By process of elimination, he figured the more subdued interaction was facilitated by Chloe. As he struggled to interpret the high-pitched words, Carl beckoned, "Salinas? Let's go, man."

Expecting a traditional classroom or some space similar to the staging area in the library, the recruit was surprised to walk into a crowded living room with a bright seaside mural on the wall and a tiny blue-jean lounge chair with matching ottoman situated in the corner tattooed by one too many spills of red juice. The white canvas couch looked like a dwarf between a full- length one and a love seat, and a six-cubicle green shelving unit overflowed with children's books, a bald baby doll with traces of a black-penned scar across her head, and odds and end pieces of toy school buses and monster trucks. As he peered down the narrow hallway to his left, the observer spotted Carl sitting at a square, tall table in the kitchen.

As Salinas pulled out the mocha-colored wooden bar chair, he noticed the shiny appliances and smooth oak cabinets in the galley kitchen. The paned door squeezed between the refrigerator and oven must have led to a deck since they were on the second floor of the building, but the opening allowed for some natural light into the compact space.

"When we built this place, we lived up here for awhile, so we made it into an actual apartment. Sometimes we rent it out, but whoever lives here has to deal with the sounds of all the kids downstairs during the week," Carl sensed Salinas's curiosity.

"Oh," Salinas's voice cracked and quivered, showing his trepidation.

"Give me just another minute here to tally your responses," Carl directed.

"Oh, yeah, sure thing," Salinas answered in his best American slang.

As the minute dragged, the nervous recruit felt the sweat trickling near his brow, so he lifted his black-rimmed glasses just enough to catch it with the back of his sweater sleeve before it made its way to his cheek. Because his wife rode the cusp of relevant fashion and took great pride in making him look stylish and important, his eyewear served to convey a particular trend more than aid his vision. She had advised that the marbled finish matched his graying curls and made him look sophisticated. Although the modest statement was not intended to be a disguise, it helped him look like he belonged in their well-to-do town.

Carl tapped the stack of papers back into shape to indicate that he was ready to begin. "Looks good, Salinas. I can see that you answered as openly and honestly as you could. I know it took guts to answer truthfully about your legal status. Good stuff, man. Good stuff."

"Thank you very much, sir," Salinas's multiple-word sentences unveiled more of his lingering accent.

"You can't be so formal with me, man," Carl insisted. "We are brothers now."

"Yes, okay, I will try."

"Good," Carl replied, appreciating short and sweet responses, "because we gotta get to know each other a bit here tonight."

"Yes, that heart thing." Salinas aimed to prove that he had been listening to every word.

"Ha," Carl laughed as he pointed back at Salinas. "Yeah, man, that heart thing. Good, good, you like to pay attention to detail. Love it."

Hurrying past the pleasantries, Carl pressed on with the interview, asking the recruit how he immigrated to the United States, what attracted him first to his wife, and other questions that were not listed on the test. As if the session was a time of abiding confession, Salinas felt relieved to respond and break some of the lying chains that had kept him in bondage. Fighting back tears, the immigrant did his best to summarize his tale, cognizant of the time constraint and his instructor's strict adherence to the consideration of the others still waiting in the library.

The Recruits

Salinas had first traveled to the US when he was nearly seventeen by way of an elaborate underground human smuggling system. Athletic enough to pass for a member of an elite soccer club that crossed the border twice a year to play colleges in Texas, the middle son had taken over his oldest brother's job as a carrier to earn money to pay the outlandish rate. Desperate and determined to make it to the land of opportunity, the disguised teenager maintained his composure and recited his assigned script during the grueling lines and interviews for his student/athlete visa. With that token pass in hand, the hopeful traveler saw the light at the end of this proverbial tunnel.

As instructed, the imposter gathered his supplies and packed his name-brand duffle bag with his name-brand shoes, three pairs of underwear, two navy blue t-shirts, one pair of casual jeans, three baggies of snacks, the basic hygiene items, and his identification. After growing out his curly locks for three months, he paid to have his hair shaved into the required faux-hawk style that dominated the athletic scene and suited up in the polyester black sweats with the appropriate team insignia on the back and the left chest. With the rest of the team, Salinas boarded a charter bus, knowing that he was not the only decoy but unaware of which ones were or even how many. As commanded, the escapee worried about himself.

At the border crossing one customs officer strolled down the aisle of the bus looking for suspicious characters, while the other guided the coach to the gatehouse to review the documentation. In an attempt to appear undaunted by the brief inspection, the phony closed his eyes and pretended to sleep until the vehicle proceeded past the station. Like the emotional rollercoaster of a surprise party, the encounter generated immense tension followed by exalted relief as the guarded boundary faded into the distance.

Once the freedom train released its parking brakes and switched off the ignition, the players trekked in obedient silence behind the token student guide and filed into the visitor's locker room. After selecting his own cubbyhole, Salinas adhered to the specific instructions, shoved his gear into the designated space, and waited in the line for the team trainer to tape his ankles while the rest of the athletes suited up. To ensure that he filled the last place in the queue, the wanderer ambled to the bathroom two times, patting his stomach as if to indicate a mild case of indigestion had been the culprit.

Finally after sitting in awkward silence as the meticulous trainer bound both feet with layers upon layers of green-hued wrap and beige tape like a fragile package traveling long distance, the amateur actor stretched his socks over the protective padding and re-laced his shoes, giving the medical staff ample time to exit the room. When the catch of the door sounded the all-clear, he rifled through the first-aid bag, snatched the electric clippers used to remove hair from head lacerations sustained during the course of a game, and shaved his faux-hawk flat.

As the clicking gallop of cleats echoed across the cement floor and past the door sill of the field entrance, Salinas rushed back to his locker, changed out of his sweat suit, and shimmied into his jeans. After shoving his costume into the duffle, the fugitive fled through the disarmed emergency exit and searched for the silver minivan with the "Soccer Mom Aboard" window sticker. Escorted by a Latina assigned to shuttle him to the north, the runaway tossed his bag into the back row and positioned himself in the passenger's seat until he reunited with his older brother in an ordinary town in the middle of Illinois just a few miles from the educational center that prepared him for a different life journey.

Under the watchful eye of a friend of a friend, the fresh apprentice worked the Mexican restaurant circuit in the area to earn some cash, practice some English, and assimilate to the culture. At the cantinas the newcomer started in the back, washing dishes and cleaning the restaurant after hours. Once he communicated well enough to retrieve napkins or straws, simple requests from the English-speaking patrons, he promoted to the position of bussing tables, but soon enough his dynamic personality and zealous drive to congregate with the gringas elevated him to the coveted role of waiter. With hours of listening to American pop music and watching daytime soap operas to enhance his game, Salinas worked the crowds, climbed the ranks, and earned the highest tip count night after night. Even though the servers did not get to keep all of the gratuities, the spanking new immigrant relished in his convincing knack to woo the ladies, his charm working better here in the States than he could have imagined. He enticed the young American, rebellious girls like the forbidden fruit, and so it was with Anna.

"Sorry to interrupt you, man, because that is compelling stuff, and I definitely feel you, but I got to get you out of here on time," Carl interrupted, struggling to be compassionate to this recruit while adhering to his deadline: mission first, people always. "I need to give you your list of gifts, and then I have one final question for you."

"Sì, yes, of course." Salinas knew too well how intricate operations could be. He cupped his hands against his mouth and blew the compressed air from his pent-up lungs as he waited for the big reveal.

"Your number one gift is... evangelism."

The recruit's hands dropped to the table as he straightened his back and crinkled his face in shock. Evangelism? Him? The only evangelists he knew were the ones that he watched on television, and the recreational performer shook his head at the notion of engaging the masses at that level. Sure, his old self would have clutched the hunt for fame with its grandiose persona and all its lavish perks, but with a changing heart and sordid past, was he supposed to announce to the world on live TV that he was an illegal, a liar, a cheat? As he sank back into his seat he questioned, *Lord, do you know what you are doing here?*

With no time for debate, Carl continued, "Serving and hospitality were neck and neck for second."

Now those traits made more sense given his litany of successes at the restaurants. Perhaps the buried traces of these unsanctioned characteristics enticed the oblivious waiter to strike up conversation with the sergeant when they first met.

"That is all you need to know for now," Carl concluded. "You will learn more later during the transformational process, but that is a great start. Now, my final question, and then you have to get going."

With no idea what in the world he was supposed to do with this information, Salinas pushed his mind-boggling concerns aside and focused on his instructor's last question.

"If you had no obstacles—not money, people, places, nothing—what would you choose to do for the Kingdom?"

Salinas expected a simple question, one that he had to just answer yes or no to and go on his way, but this challenge was loaded. Sure, he had plenty of pie-in-the-sky dreams, many of which dictated his life's course, but now all that was different. Now his thoughts staggered in the context of the Kingdom, and the untrained disciple felt unworthy to receive the invitation into the righteous association. *Who am I, Lord?* he cried from within. *Who am I?*

Catching him by surprise, his mind flooded with visions of his ardent trek from his motherland to the heartland of Illinois and all of the people he encountered along the way. The memories of shady places and the biting whispers of the pervasive darkness gnashed at him even now.

"You don't need to answer me, Salinas," Carl's commanding tone snapped those taunts back into submission. "Whatever the Lord brought to your attention He will use. Just takes steps in that direction."

With the puzzling clues still overwhelming his sense of reason yet enforcing a strange sense of peace, the interviewee accepted his final marching orders. "Is that it?"

"Yes," Carl responded as he closed Salinas's folder. "Your recruiter will be in touch."

CHAPTER 14

Hoyt

Hoyt busied himself, trying to avoid any unnecessary attention from the remaining recruits in the room as they waited in requested silence for the final phase of the assessment. As he studied the engraved picture that hung on the wall to his right, the recent graduate contemplated the photograph of the big-bellied, bald guy with wisps of curly hair flipping out like firecrackers atop both of his ears. The jovial gentleman wore wire-rimmed glasses with clear frames that lit his bright, twinkling eyes and accented his jolly grin, narrow lips, and sizable front teeth. Standing with his hands glued to his sides, the man posed in front of a mid-sized freight van that had been renovated into a traveling library for kids. The gold inscription read, "In loving Memory of Scott Wenzel... beloved husband to Julie, father to Victoria, and educator to all."

Hearing the swelling approach of footsteps, Hoyt whipped his head towards the closed door and held his breath in an attempt to decipher the heaviness of the gate. With the stylish Spanish guy assigned to Carl at the last intrusion and just a handful of participants still waiting to be called, he knew his turn was coming and that either Trish or Chloe would wield the next two folders. The threatened young man still could not decide if he was more afraid of Trish for her personal space issues and intimidating glances or Chloe for her beauty and sweetheart demeanor.

The nervous Nellie gasped for air and sealed it into his protruding chest as the door creaked and Chloe peeked around the edge. "Sorry, but, let me see." As she paused to review her notes, running her finger across the name on the label, his eyes bulged, his cheeks reddened, and his throat tightened during the fight to sustain his pulmonary hold. "Mr. Bradford? I mean, Recruit Bradford?"

In relief Hoyt controlled his exhale through his nose and nodded his head at the proven answer to his question. He was more afraid of Chloe.

When the muscular old guy removed his reading glasses, tucked them into his front pant pocket, and edged his way out of his desk, the innocent admirer smiled as he overheard Chloe greet her interviewee. "Hello, Mr. Bradford. Shoot, I mean, Recruit Bradford. Please forgive me, that takes some getting used to."

"No problem, I understand. I'm getting used to it myself," the gentleman excused her as he stepped in front and out the door, so that she could institute the protocol of securing it behind them.

Although Hoyt had majored in mathematics, it did not take much deductive reasoning to conclude that he was going to get assigned to Trish on her next run or Carl after that. Now that he knew Carl could be a possibility, the hopeful participant threw up a little prayer request and turned back to analyze the humble tribute to this Mr. Wenzel. As he pondered the story behind the man, the pitter-patter of stretched steps broke his concentration as he felt the tension return and the heat crawl up his neck from under his shirt. Too soon after Chloe's entrance to be Carl, the kid knew the odds were stacked against him as the door flung open in typical Trish style.

"Recruit Hoyt, you are with me!" the animated instructor zoomed in on him without hesitation.

The sheepish student eased out of his desk when a sudden tug stopped him in his tracks. When he looked down to find his anchor, the tip of the pencil he had placed in his right pocket snapped off, releasing him from his seat. With his head hung and eyes peering through his tousled bangs, Hoyt turned towards the door, trying to ignore the others in the room that watched his every step, doing all they could to contain their laughs. The notorious oddball knew this trek all too well, and the trail conjured up some of his worst childhood memories that dated as far back as grade school when he existed in the shadows of his infamous three older sisters.

The beautiful girls ruled the unspoken social classes and led the ranks in unbridled school spirit. Leading the masses in rhyming cheers of valor, the three basked in the adoration of the student body and even the faculty. When classmates, teachers, and administrators discovered the lowly little brother lacked the familial thread of empowering magnetism, the instantaneous shock expressed itself in mild disdain, leaving them to refer to him in the third person.

While the Hoyt girls mulled over their copious options of friend groups and club invitations, he struggled to find someone to sit with at lunch. The youngest member of the notorious family dreaded that part of every school day. In the confines of the classroom, the lackluster pupil hid amongst the crowd and could even do so in the hallways, but as the loner stepped past the threshold of the cafeteria with his paper lunch sack in hand, all eyes seemed to gravitate like a swooping feather clinging to his every move. With a calculated scan to the left, the whispering voices echoed away in a distant fog.

"No, really, he's their brother."

"What? Really? But..."

With a hopeful scan to the right, the initial remarks were cut off as young Hoyt searched in desperation for a pair of inviting eyes to catch his. In moments the stifled echoes upsurged until the chaos blurred with the mass of screaming kids. Accepting the inevitable results, the brother drooped his head and proceeded with a methodical pace to the far left corner table that hosted a couple of other lonely lunchers. In between bites, he inspected his food like an undercover food critic making mental notes of every tantalizing morsel.

While the ingrained memories kept the recruit's thoughts preoccupied all the way down the hallway, Trish halted at the last door on the right to allow him to pass. Distorting her face as though the walk in forced silence had been a cruel form of punishment, she waved him through with her exaggerated expressions. With industrial shelves stacked with paper towels, toilet paper, baby diapers, and various soaps lining the walls, the large storage closet transformed into a comparable interrogation room. Two wooden rocking chairs with floral cushions squared off in the middle of the room while a tall brass floor lamp shined on center stage. "Finally, we made it," Trish released her gasp as if she had been holding her breath since she shut the door on the library.

Analyzing the exaggerated reaction, Hoyt could not determine if she was just dramatizing the situation to convey that she hated not being able to interact until now or if she had some real medical condition that precluded her from long bouts of holding her breath. He never was very good at picking up on those types of social innuendos, especially from girls.

Trish solved the mystery for him. "I just hate that Carl insists we be quiet, especially when I just can't wait to get to know someone."

Hoyt dreaded the limelight and found little satisfaction in his audience of one. As he squirmed in his seat to settle on the most advantageous position, the interviewee rocked back and forth in short, quick succession with his hands folded in his lap and squeezed between his knees. To avoid the lingering stares of Trish who just sat there smiling at him as if she wanted to pinch his cheeks, the recruit cleared his throat, forcing down the lump with a swallow. Thankfully, that strategic move seemed to make her snap to.

"You are just so adorable," she was talking out loud again as if he was not there.

"Uh, thanks."

"A different hairdo could really make all the difference," Trish assessed further.

As the target ran his fingers through his hair and wiped them on his pant leg, he absorbed the uncomfortable bluntness of this lady.

"Have you seen my Chloe?" her tone expected a response.

Dumbfounded at the unrelated nature of this line of questioning, Hoyt wondered what in the world was going on. Was his exit interview really going to be a style consultation or an interrogation on his perception of her daughter? If the direct heat from the lamp was not causing him to sweat, this interaction certainly was.

"Sorry, but we don't have time for that," Trish answered herself before he found the courage. "I am already going to be in trouble with Carl for running behind on my other folks. Though my husband is just so adorable when he is angry, I promised to try my very best to stick to the schedule."

"Okay," was the only word Hoyt could formulate.

"I always like to start with a favorite family memory," Trish said, breaking her focal point as if remembering one of her own. "I just adore my precious family, and I like to hear where others come from."

"Um, what kind of family memory?"

"Oh, something joyful, and perhaps, funny," her focus re-engaged on him in full force.

"Uh," he shuffled through his mental catalogue for the slightest hint of a funny story. Humor was just not his strong suit, and although the detainee entertained her inquiry, he was not convinced that she was going to be satisfied with his normal from Normal routine. "Well, I do have one little story from my early childhood that always makes me laugh."

"Oh, wonderful. Let's hear it," the interrogator leaned forward in anticipation, causing her target to recoil.

"Well, the church that we went to growing up..." he began to set the stage, hoping she would be as amused as he had been.

Although the staunch routine of the place felt redundant as the regally clad reverend preached about God as if he was so far up in heaven that he did not even bother with the tragedies of life on earth anymore, his family committed to the drudgery week after week. The themed message conveyed that God made the world as part of His dutiful obligation, and, in turn, grateful Christians reciprocated by attending church. As a congregation bound to the biblical narrative, the pastoral leader talked about God's son, Jesus, and how He died for all sins. The premise of the contemporary significance aimed to assure the congregants that a moral life could be obtained if they so desired. As one of the most stressed aspects of the service, the money basket passed without fail, and on occasion a small snack in the form of juice and bread was dispersed so that together they could bow their heads in solemn thankfulness for their good life.

As diligent members of the institution, his family followed the liturgy like dominoes as they took their seats, stood for a couple of familiar hymns, sat back down for an eloquent interlude, and then up once again at the prodding of the organ. However, every now and again the lead pianist would select some old hymn in a challenging key, stretching everyone to either pick a super high octave or a very low one.

The recruit remembered hearing his dad's voice strain at the attempt to follow the ladies. In the beginning Mr. Hoyt would go the high route until his falsetto skipped and weakened, forcing him to plunge to the low register mid-sentence until the male part descended so deep that he had to climb back to the high one again. As the two of them caught each other's eye from the peripheral of the hymnal, encouraging each other to hold it together, they felt the impending rage of his mom about to pounce as she glared at the two of them with righteous condemnation while carrying the tune with ease. Back and forth they glanced for support until the laughter could not be contained and the pair burst forth in unison, relieved to let it go and acknowledge in camaraderie the failed attempt to stay on key.

"Oh, I love it. So precious." Trish gazed at him with those glossy eyes like it took all of her strength not to pinch his cheeks or embrace him in another hug. "You have a wonderful relationship with your dad. I can tell. I can feel your love in that story."

Okay, now the weirdness escalated. The storyteller considered his tale amusing, making him giggle even after all of this time, but now she had gone and sapped it all up. The crux of the conflict involved a guy being forced to sing along like a girl and failing. It had nothing to do with how he felt about his dad or love or anything like that. Why did girls always have to read into everything so much?

"You are just a gem," her oozing continued.

With the heat rising in his cheeks and sweat beading under his bangs, the timid recruit looked up at the clock in a desperate attempt to distract her again and get this show on the road.

"Oh, my, here I go again. Carl is going to have my head," Trish declared after checking the time. In haste the interviewer opened the manila folder that had been resting on her lap. "Well, I must say that your results look fantastic. Good job!"

"Uh, thanks," the student shrugged, not knowing what he had done to deserve her adoration.

"Your primary spiritual gift is…giving." She stared at him, hoping to decipher any nonverbal cues to his reaction.

"Giving. Okay. Got it. Not sure what that means, or what I am supposed to do with that, but got it," Hoyt tried to stay her enthusiasm with his typical monotone reply.

"Oh, giving is just wonderful, and when done well, it is more subtle than you might think," Trish explained as if she were narrating a scene to a mystery novel. "Giving provides the bulk of the financial needs of the Kingdom, but it is covert as well. Oh, how exciting!"

Feeling the pressure of the responsibility of financing God's work, funding God's army, Hoyt labored to conjure up any particular excitement. Would it require building a large church? Employing a network of pastors? As a minimalist, money just never served a purpose for him beyond the basic essentials, so the results sparked the curiosity of the immature disciple.

Having learned good old-fashioned hard work from his parents and fiscal responsibility as well, all four of the Hoyt kids detasseled corn for the junior high social studies teacher, Mr. Sharp, every summer since they were about twelve to have the money they wanted for extras. Of course, the girls always bought designer clothes with theirs, but he put all of his earnings towards a new, royal-blue Raleigh ten speed, and he still had that same bike.

"The other runners up are… administration and mercy," Trish now sounded like she was a game show host, announcing the grand prize. "Now those are two that you don't find together very often. Good for you."

"Uh, thanks," he mustered once again, not knowing what he had done to make her so enthusiastic. These were gifts, after all. He had done nothing to create them or deserve them.

"Oh, I so hope I get to see how this turns out," Trish spoke as if this was a four-act play and they were in intermission.

"Ah, yeah. Me too," he blurted out the first thing that came to his mind.

When the interviewer closed the folder, stood back up, and strolled towards the door, the tall woman turned to him with her head cocked and eyes still gleaming, "It has been a pleasure to spend this time with you."

What? That was it? They were done? Hoyt sat stunned underneath the ever-growing heat of the floor lamp. Although the strange process resulted in the revealing of his top three spiritual gifts, the perplexed recruit did not know what he was supposed to do with them or what he was supposed to do next even. The rule follower wanted answers, a logical outline of his next steps because he was confident that God's army did not want him making it up as he went along. Considering further probing would enable Trish more time to study his inmost being, the compliant nature won out as he reached into his right pocket to make sure his pencil was tucked away.

"Your recruiter will be in touch," Trish confirmed as she squeezed his left arm, dying to comfort him with affection one last time.

Encounter

Like most sixteen-year-old boys, Brock thought he knew how the real world worked better than most adults, so when he snagged a deck of tarot cards from his grandma's house, hoping to practice on one of his best buddies, his allure to the family's long history of secretive power seemed innocent enough. He thought at most Glen would be impressed and at worst he might be a little scared. Either way, they were sure to have some fun.

Home alone for the evening, the boys headed down to the basement to see what they could conjure up. As the anxious teens huddled in the musty-smelling dampness of the back storage room behind the gray card table that his folks used for bridge, Bradford demanded total silence from his audience of one. With the faint flicker of a lavender-scented candle that his mother used in the kitchen after she fried food, the apprentice concentrated, trying to replicate his grandma's slow, deep chant that started with a soft, gentle invitation and ended with a bellowing command as he flipped and paused and flipped and paused. The imitator surveyed the room, hoping for a sign. Perhaps the flame would fade out and then reappear or the dog would bark or something that would signify some strange atmospheric build up, but he did not expect it to really...work.

Just as the trainee turned that last card, he felt a thin layer of oil on the skin of his arms, triggering an immediate, bone-chilling sensation in his gut. The confident, cocky youth had never felt so petrified in his entire life as the intrusive presence's dark and eerie arrival oozed its slithery hands around them. The piercing look in Glen's eyes indicated that his friend could feel it too. Although their sharpest night vision could not detect a visible figure, they knew they were no longer alone.

As Brock's neck muscles tensed and his heart pounded through his chest, he battled the urge to scream or run or do something, but the novice was frozen in disbelief. The unexpected ringing of the phone upstairs in the kitchen broke through the silent attack, and without hesitation the two sprinted up the wooden staircase, hands grabbing several steps above to help shorten the distance.

Bradford reached for that handle like a lifeline. "Hello? Hello?"

"What are you doing over there?"

"Grandma, thank goodness! Uh, we got a real situation over here," he managed to utter in between deep gasps.

"I told you not to mess with this stuff! Well, you better listen to me now, son!" Assertive old Grandma Bradford directed him to dispose of the cards in the fireplace while she tidied up the rest of his mess from her front parlor back up in the big city.

That episode was the first and the last time that Bradford intervened with that other world. He knew from that frightful experience that all of that hocus-pocus with his grandma's psychic business was true, and the unsuspecting teenager accepted her assessment that he carried the family gift, one that she advised him not to exercise.

"For our struggle is not against flesh and blood, but against the rulers, against the authorities, against the powers of this dark world and against the spiritual forces of evil in the heavenly realms." (Ephesians 6:12, NIV)

CHAPTER 15

Bradford

"Wow, I can't say that I'm surprised about discernment," the sergeant commented from across the line. "I figured that just from my vision of you back in my box, and I can see leadership as well. You certainly have had plenty of experience with that with your athletics and even at the prisons, but now you are going to learn how to use those for the Kingdom."

"It is so hard to wrap my mind around this whole thing, Sergeant Riley," the recruit replied. "It makes sense on paper and with some of my experiences, as you say, but I am having real trouble imagining myself as a Christ warrior. My grandmother is probably flipping in her grave about now, and I cannot even begin to picture how my coworkers are going to take this! I have this reputation of sorts, you know."

"I know, Bradford. Believe me, I know, and you don't need to get overwhelmed with all of that right now. Once you get through this basic training and get some discipleship under your belt, you will be better equipped for the battle at hand," the wise recruiter advised. "You can trust in what I am saying."

"I know I can, Sergeant Riley," Bradford lowered his level of anxiety. "You haven't let me down yet even with all of the arguments and debates I threw at you."

"You had me on my toes there sometimes," the sergeant teased. "I had to do a lot of study to answer some of your questions, especially when you misquoted a lot of scripture. You know, stuff like the palms of the hands revealing someone's life."

"Yeah, well, a kid is taught to obey their elders, and when my grandma shared her version of the secrets to life with me, I assumed she was right."

"Sure, sure, but palm reading is just a bit off base from the truth of the Bible." His instructor kept the conversation light. "And then there was that talk about knights descended from Solomon's temple and the real truth of history without religion. You really gave me a run for my money."

"I am glad that your pursuit was not without reward," Bradford teased back.

As the two confirmed the logistical requirements for basic, ensuring that the senior correctional officer had solidified the necessary leave from work, the recruit sighed in nostalgic relief that those years of discussions broke down his argumentative walls. The war-torn fortress had been rebuilt, filling the holes with a miraculous salve that saturated him with more concern for his father's condition and patience for his mother's meekness.

Sergeant Riley assured the new soldier that he would maintain his prayerful relationship with Ms. Ginny in his absence and contact Bradford immediately if there was a change in the Chief's condition.

"Is there anything else I should know before I catch the bus tomorrow?" the recruit probed.

"Bradford, some of this stuff may come easy for you, and you may find some of the folks challenging, but I want you to particularly concentrate on discerning the Holy Spirit," the sergeant advised.

"What do you mean? How exactly do I do that?"

"Well, based on your family history and the dabbling with the other side of the spiritual world, so to speak, you have grown a bit comfortable with its power, in my view," Sergeant Riley expounded. "You have to learn that the power of our side is truly stronger."

"I know you have hinted at that before," Bradford admitted.

"Yes, and you may have to concentrate on resisting the habit of going to that side," the recruiter attempted to provide caution with unavoidable concern. "It is going to have to be a renewing of your mind."

"What's that noise? Are you outside?" Bradford chimed in, happy to get off such a serious topic.

"Oh, yes, I'm walking my landlady's dog," the sergeant huffed, accepting the change in direction.

"You, walking that little ball of fur that you were telling me about? Ha! I'd love to see that about now," Bradford started the teasing again.

"Yeah, well, Ms. Hoback had a doctor's appointment with some tests and little Lulu here has been acting a bit confused, so she was hesitant about leaving her alone for that long," the recruiter explained. "I got my buddy, Hornsby, to give Ms. Hoback a ride in his cab, and I offered to keep the pooch company. Lulu is a good girl, really."

"Oh, I'm sure she is, you old softy!"

With that, the conversation ended on a light note, and Bradford concentrated on gathering all of the supplies atop his king-sized bed, so that he could check off his list as he packed them in his bags. *Toiletries, two towels, two washcloths, ten pairs of underwear, one pair of running shoes,* he perused the list.

In his absence he had made arrangements for Mrs. Piña to have her own key to keep the place clean and tidy. That gentle woman had mothered him for the last twenty years, doing laundry, dishes, dusting, the floors, and she spoiled him with homemade tamales twice a year.

The bachelor had first heard about Mrs. Piña from the check-in gal over at the gym. One morning after a tough workout on arms, Bradford forewent his usual crunchy granola bar breakfast and took some time at the counter to enjoy one of those fancy protein shakes with peanut butter and chocolate. As he boasted about his single status, the freedom to come and go as he pleased, the reigning king of his own domain, the unaffected attendant girl asked him how he kept his place clean and acceptable for visitors with such a demanding career and lively social life. Of course, his mother sanitized that place from head to toe when he allowed her to come up for a visit, but the proud and strong stud could not admit that to someone of the female persuasion.

"Well, I'm in the market for a new housekeeper," Bradford announced in hopes of saving face.

As fate would have it, the gal's mother, Mrs. Piña, was an immaculate housewife and looking to pick up a few extra bucks on the side. With just a simple jotting of the phone number, the domestically-challenged bachelor sealed the deal, and the faithful servant tended to him every other week ever since.

Now, as the recruit contemplated about life differently since becoming a believer, he wondered if his arrangement with Mrs. Piña hindered his willingness to commit to marriage. He soared in his corrections career which served to keep his ego inflated even after the fall of his football dreams. He maintained an active sex life, boasting about it with the guys on a regular basis, and he employed a devoted elderly lady to ensure his other needs were met. Why did he need the hassle of a wife?

As he sat on the edge of his bed, Bradford shook his head and cringed in shame because he used to think that way and not that long ago. How could he have gone so long in his life not knowing that he was missing out? How could he have convinced himself time and time again that he deserved to be adored and revered by so many? Why in the world would some of his friends send their boys to get advice about life from him?

As the former elitist's thoughts raced in an effort to make sense of his present circumstance, he envisioned what it must have felt like to be small, thought of as insignificant, and desire that quality. How could he even begin to make up for so many of the terrible wrongs? In his mind Bradford understood the sergeant's insistence that the recruit did not have to, that there was really no way that he could, that Jesus's ransom more than made amends for all of that, but the new follower grappled with disbelief.

"By all means," Sergeant Riley expounded, "if you are feeling led by the Holy Spirit to give someone a call, apologize, reach out and ask for forgiveness, then do so, but believe me, brother, you are not going to be able to go back and right every wrong. There's not enough lifetimes left for that."

"Thanks a lot," Bradford responded, knowing that his recruiter was exaggerating his situation.

"You know what I mean," the sergeant replied.

Bradford desired complete understanding, but his mind raced sometimes in the still of night or even during lulls in the day, replaying missteps in his past, imagining how he would have done things differently. All of those little tidbits that his mother would share with him about patience, kindness, and even omniscience conveyed new meaning, and the remorseful son had to admit that she was right. Mrs. Bradford, of course, would never boast or brag about it, but he wanted her to know. If only he had been more considerate of others. If only he had been more respectful of women. If only he had embraced abstinence and not brushed it off as sissy and petty. If only he had managed his money better. If only he had embraced family more. If only he had gone to church with his mom, or summer camp, or VBS, or any of the umpteen Godly opportunities that she had arranged for him.

Sometimes the barrage made the new believer writhe in guilt and kept him awake, and sometimes the joyful replaying of the past in his mind with different choices eased his thoughts and directed him into a full night of peaceful rest. Nothing like this had kept his mind so occupied in the past. Sure, work riled him up, and even some of the more dramatic and rocky relationships that he had endured, but not his own actions.

How could he be a productive warrior for the King when he was so dark and stained? What was God thinking when He sought after him? Didn't Jesus know that there were far more pure hearts than his out there? How could He use him?

CHAPTER 16

West

When Sergeant Riley saw West seated behind the cash register that late morning, he found her bright eyes and exuberant smile rather contagious.

"Sergeant Riley!" she greeted him with a quick salute and a wink. "Great to see you. Let me guess? Our single-origin bean in a to-go cup?"

"You know me too well, don't you, West?"

"Remember, they call me Darby in these here parts," she ribbed.

"Well, I'm an old dog, West," the recruiter played along. "Don't go tryin' to teach me new tricks now."

Because the morning rush had wound down and that late afternoon crowd had not been released from school yet, the young recruit took his order, processed his payment, and filled his cup. Her helper had assumed the dish washing and supply restocking duties.

"Decided to let someone else do that job finally?" Sergeant Riley asked as he nodded towards the kitchen.

"Well, as you know, I'm not so inclined to hide out as much as I used to."

"Thank the Lord for that," he added, content to just stay at the counter to catch up with his female recruit. "So are you ready for tomorrow? Got your hours covered and your affairs in order?"

"You make it sound like I'm headed off to war or something, Sarge," West teased.

"Well, not war exactly yet, but you're definitely going to be doing some soldiering," he remarked.

"Uh, I know. I can hardly wait!" she responded. "My mind is just running a mile a minute. I mean, I've always wanted to go out and experience something, have adventure. I knew there was something in me that wanted to, to, oh, I don't know, to take on the world somehow."

"Oh, He'll give you adventure, all right," the sergeant embraced her enthusiasm. "He's going to use you, West. With your gifts of leadership and wisdom, He has some mighty plans in store for ya."

"I know. Can you believe it?" she conveyed her shock. "Me? Wise? I thought that innocent, young girl that interviewed me after my testing must have made a huge mistake. I mean, one look at her and you can see that she is so good, but yet I get wisdom? You know that I have made absolutely horrible choices, so I cannot understand how that is even possible."

"You were fighting Him before, though, West," the recruiter explained. "Now you will be working with Him. It's a whole different ballgame."

"Oh, I hope so," she sighed in relief as the novice soldier closed her eyes and allowed herself to just imagine for a moment. "I have to confess that I am a bit concerned about dealing with all of the other women at basic. I mean, I've never really gotten along too well with other girls. Guys, now, I probably got along too well with them in the past, but I just hope there is not all of that gossiping and clique forming and stuff."

"You don't need to be worrying about that now," the sergeant attempted to ease her mind. "Drill Sergeant Thorpe has plenty of experience, and she will not stand for any nonsense. It is going to be a good experience, West. You won't regret it a minute. Now, you got your time away all cleared with Carrie and Yvonne?"

"Oh, they have been wonderful. Between the two of them, they have made sure that my shifts were covered, and Carrie even surprised me with all of the supplies that I needed from my packing list," West replied. "She even bought me my very first Bible."

"Well, what about the one I gave you?" he teased.

"Well, that was a used one that you already had." She did not want to offend him, although she knew he was not that sort. "Carrie thought it imperative that I break one in from scratch."

"Well, good," the proud recruiter winked back at her. "Sounds like you are ready to ship off and get this thing going."

West's face got serious as she glanced back over her shoulder to make sure that her words were private, "Sergeant Riley, I just can't thank you enough."

"It's been my pleasure, Darby, really," he answered, reaching for her hand to give it a big squeeze, knowing full well that any more words out of that girl might bring them both to tears right there in the open.

BASIC TRAINING

Phase I: Indoctrination

Marching with the Master Minutes

September 2005

Cadre: Akpore, Thorpe, Burroughs, Peters

Recruiters: Northrop, Dinkheller, Martin, and Riley

The group opened with prayer for each recruit in 1st Platoon.

1. The indoctrination will set the tone for etiquette by explaining salutations, responses, general commands for stances, and some interspersed exercises to keep them a bit off balance. The engagement will be direct and forceful but not demeaning. Similar to how Jesus called His disciples, the goal of this approach is to encourage them to submit to cadre authority. In the Gospels Jesus gave His men no explanation at the time, leaving them often wondering what was happening and why, but the first step of the training to be His disciple was to follow by faith.

2. The discipline of Simplicity will be emphasized during the occupation of the barracks and securing of issued and personal items. Thorpe will teach all female recruits since they will be housed in one billet regardless of their platoon assignment. Burroughs will instruct his platoon who will occupy the third set of barracks, and Akpore will handle his male soldiers in the second set of barracks.

3. PT will commence upon completion of billeting setup. Thorpe will lead the first ability group which will set a faster pace. Because these soldiers are already physically capable of maintaining the pace, she will initiate the discipline of Meditation with them. They will consider the majesty of

God's creation first, then memory verses, and finally the discipline of Prayer by listening to the voice of the Holy Spirit. Akpore will lead the second group. Although a bit slower-paced than the first group, they will start with basic cadence calls, then memory verses through cadence calls, and working themselves up to running in silence whereby they can consider God's creation and then listening to His voice. Burroughs will lead the third group. This group faces the most physical challenges for one reason or another, so they will spend more time on cadence calls to get them to stop focusing on the physical struggle of running and moving as a unit. They will then follow suit through memory verses and eventually to the discipline of Prayer. It is the aim of PT that all soldiers will be able to maintain a routine of exercise to keep them prepared for battle but also to utilize that time as a means for Meditation, Prayer, and perhaps even Solitude and Worship. The soldiers in 1st Platoon will be assigned to the following ability groups for PT:

   a. 1st Group w/ Thorpe – Jensen, French, Clannin, Hinthorne, Salinas

   b. 2nd Group w/ Akpore – Morris, Meredith, Miller, Esper, West

   c. 3rd Group w/ Burroughs – Schume, Shaw, Desche, Insetta, Bradford, Hoyt

4. Peters will be leading the discipline of Study through the classroom setting. One key component of each lesson will be to search for Jesus's teaching or practicing the disciplines in the Gospels. Memory verses will be assigned during these times.

5. Drill and Ceremony will be taught and practiced throughout to encourage uniformity and general group movements.

The group closed in silent prayer as we listened for any further promptings of the Holy Spirit.

Godspeed,

Akpore

CHAPTER 17

Bradford

The humid air trapped in the bus by the scant openings in the passenger windows stamped out the coolness of the fading morning air while the radiating September sun tried to make its way up, warning that today would be hotter than the last. Bopping to his own private tunes, the stocky, black bus driver seemed uninhibited by the stifling heat as the small mounted fan blowing across his face offered some refreshment. As he glanced into the oversized rear view mirror on occasion to check on his precious cargo, the trained transporter maintained his jovial facial expressions, showing no real concern. He just carried on with his uplifting songs, never missing a beat as the jiggling seats seemed to almost join in unison.

Bradford was seated too far in the back to be able to distinguish any of the words or even the melody, but his annoyance fought off its own form of superlatives because this ride was taking longer than he had anticipated. Although the shine of the dark gray vinyl and the lack of tears in the fabric indicated that the seats had been reupholstered, the knotted lumps and metal prods from underneath the cushions proclaimed that the innards had not. With the lack of shade from his window, the over-the-hill recruit scrutinized the other passengers, contemplating the obvious gap in age.

In an effort to fight the nagging heat and disheartening youthfulness of his fellow travelers, the recruit forced his mind into bouts of historical contemplation. No matter how the campaign began, the unsettling bewilderment always wandered back to the same question. Why did it take him so long to get to this point in his life?

By and large he considered himself a good person. He never set out to intentionally harm anyone and only gave others what they had coming. The athlete, friend, brother, co-worker, and son was well-liked as far back as he could remember.

When the Bradford family had moved from Chicago to the small town of Washington, the youngest child had to admit that he was a bit skeptical at first, but now he thought of that place as home. When his dad had been appointed police chief, Brock and his sister gained instant notoriety.

Not only did Bradford have the right name, but he resembled his dad with a sturdy, tall build, and dark black hair. With a natural giftedness for sports, popularity followed, and then there was the girl. From the sixth grade, he snagged the most sought after one, and although they experienced a rocky relationship, the connection enhanced the allure that all the other students envied.

By the standards of a typical spoiled child, he had life in the bag. Bradford worked hard for the things he wanted and ignored his deficiencies. Although his dad's position forced him to stay out of too much trouble, it cleaned up any that he may have gotten into. As the baby of the family, his mom catered to his every need as long as he showered her with a token amount of hugs each day. Her precious Brock could do no wrong in her eyes. So from an early age, the self-proclaimed stud ruled his world. What could he be lacking?

Following his father's wishes, Bradford left the comforts of home to play football in college and major in criminal justice. Even though he and his teenage girlfriend fizzled out after the move, he had developed alternative plans to address his more pressing needs while impressing his peers at the same time. No longer under the scrutiny of his little tight-knit community, the predator believed that sort of prey ran rampant in the boundary-free zone of the college setting. Even though a new territory would require him to re-establish his dominant identity, his stature, rugged good looks, athletic prowess, and confidence soon resolved that minor setback.

Throughout the years, the popular Washingtonian had maintained lifelong friendships with other athletes from high school, and together they committed to attend the scheduled reunions and reminisce about their glory days. With each passing year as their hair thinned and beards grayed, those events came around faster and faster. His twenty-fifth shook him to the core, causing him to re-evaluate some of the choices that he had made over that quarter of a century.

Twice divorced for years now, Bradford knew no one would be too surprised when he showed up stag, but he usually had a nice piece of eye candy to accompany him. With the last gal swarming him, being so needy, desperate for marriage, the devout independent dared not entice her to be his date. The former athlete had contemplated reaching out to a few others but decided instead to use this time to play the field a bit. Because his confidence never failed him, he had no inkling this time would be any different.

As he recalled that night, he climbed out of his red Ford Raptor and strutted toward the hall in anticipation of his animated reception. With each step his chest swelled, knowing his mere presence would bring all the accolades he needed to recharge. As per usual, the local favorite drew the attention of the guys as well as the gals. While the fellows wanted to vicariously relive his path along his small stint in the NFL which had been cut short due to a rare leg break before his rookie season barely got under way, the ladies swooned to his near-celebrity status. The night had progressed just as the former prom king had imagined, so it seemed by chance that he struck up a conversation with some random guy at the bar while he waited for his drink.

The stranger claimed his friends called him sergeant, which matched his cool flattop and rugged stare. Although the guest did not mention much else about himself, he seemed to know an awful lot about the local superstar. "Say, aren't you that ball player?"

"In the flesh," was Bradford's typical response.

The challenge when interacting with an unknown fan started with the need to decipher the core of the connection without coming right out and asking. During the course of natural conversation, Bradford honed in on key words that referenced the location where the infatuated admirer first saw him play. With intermittent eye contact and the occasional nod of the head accompanied by an amused smile, Bradford appeared to appreciate their praise, a trait he had learned best from his dad. All the while, he contemplated a clever way to either end the conversations that he did not want to pursue or lengthen them, depending on his audience. However, on the night of the reunion, the expert had failed to figure out which way to categorize this guy, so he entertained him a bit longer than usual.

"How's your mom doing?" the sergeant had asked.

"Oh, good, you know, hanging in there."

Was this sergeant someone he had gone to school with? Because the gentleman was not wearing one of those cheesy badges with a name and high school yearbook picture, Bradford could not recognize him. However, the way that the inquisitor spoke with such familiarity about his mom, he presumed this guy came from Washington.

"Good to hear. I'm sure she misses your dad," the sergeant's southern twang ended each comment.

"Well, he's not dead or anything. Sure, he has Alzheimer's, but she visits him at The Village every day," Bradford responded with some offense. After all the polite consideration the star offered this stranger, proving his gracious intent and willingness to engage in conversation, the presumptuous tone miffed him enough to grab his drink and consider his escape.

"Yeah, sweet lady. Prays for him every day, and for you too," the sergeant leaned in to be heard above the crowd.

Bradford's head jerked back at those comments. "I'm sorry, do I know you? Are you a friend of my mom's or something? Did she send you here?"

"Ah, shoot, no. I am not really an old friend, but we served together," the sergeant laughed off the target's growing frustration.

"Served? Uh, my mom never served. I'm not sure what you are talking about, sir." The well-polished hero's tensions rose as he reasoned that this dude was not all the way with it, and he was certain he would begin his exit. As he raised his glass to squirm out of the tight space, a splash of rum dripped down onto the visitor's lap.

"Ah, that's right. I forgot, that you only believe in the powers of darkness like that stunt you pulled in the basement," the sergeant played his trump card.

Halted in his tracks, the target accepted the challenge to engage further with this mysterious know-it-all. Who was this stranger? How would he know about one of his biggest fears? Grandma had said she would never tell his folks about that night, and to his knowledge, she never had. The favorite grandchild knew he could trust her, so how in the world did this sergeant know about it? As his mind searched for a reasonable explanation to the absurd encounter, Bradford surmised that the antagonist must have known his grandma or perhaps even shared in her hidden abilities and sensed its presence. "What are you getting at?" the enraged competitor mustered in response.

"Just that there is one far more powerful, one that you don't need to be fearful of," the sergeant answered with a straight face, knowing that it would strike his opponent's curiosity.

"Okay, listen. This whole conversation is getting a little out of hand, and I don't really think this is the time or place for this kind of thing." Bradford knew he was no saint by any means, but he also knew he did not want to dabble deeper into any darkness. More powerful? Shoot, whatever caught up with them that night in the basement produced more power than he wanted to mess with. He preferred the strength he now mastered in the carnal world.

With an absence of any expression, the sergeant handed the recruit one of his business cards, patted him on the shoulder, and left him with one final word. "When you are ready to join the light, give me a jingle."

Before Bradford could decipher the slew of words amongst the overwhelming background noise and request a further explanation of the light this fellow spoke of, the sergeant was gone, lost in the sea of old schoolmates.

As the brakes of the vehicle screeched to a halt and hissed their air behind the tires, the buoyant driver pulled on the long metal arm to open the bi-fold door and let the midday heat swarm in. "Welcome to Fort Gideon! Godspeed!" Before the final farewell settled on the passengers, a tall, lean black man with a green camouflage uniform and wide-brimmed hat charged up and into the bus shouting, "Let's go, recruits! Let's go, let's go, let's go!"

CHAPTER 18

West

West raced to the head of the line at the foot of the steps that led to the cabin, her home for the next eight weeks. Although the daring adventurer never had a problem leading the way, she thought she might keep that part of herself at bay for this experience, although taming it would take practice. When the lady drill sergeant beckoned all females over to the last building with a loud and commanding voice, West's natural bent towards risk taking kicked in.

"Listen carefully, recruits," the pint-sized drill sergeant extended her syllables as if they were all hard of hearing, "You will enter the doors behind me, one by one, in an orderly fashion. The first person, you, recruit?" The uniformed soldier paused and looked down from atop the front stoop, demanding an answer.

"Uh, West?" the recruit replied.

"That sounds like a question. Is it West or not?" the drill sergeant grew impatient.

"Yes, drill sergeant!" the recruit answered as instructed during the gaggle at the bus stop.

The cadre leader, satisfied then with her response, turned to eye the rest of the group. "West here will enter first and take the bunk at the end of the bay on the far right. The next person in line will take the bunk opposite her on the far left, the next will take the right, then the left, and so on. Do you understand?"

"Yes, drill sergeant!" they all chimed in unison, trying to stifle the fear laden in their voices.

"You will place your duffle bag on the trunk at the foot of your bunk. You will then stand at ease until all recruits have secured their spot. Do you understand, recruits?" the accent in her voice strengthened the longer she spoke.

East Coast? Chicago, maybe?

Wasting too much time thinking about the root of the dialect, West almost forgot her. "Yes, drill sergeant."

"At that time," the commanding female's instructions continued, "I will give you the introduction to your first discipline. Now move!"

The lot of them screeched and quivered their token, "Yes, drill sergeant," out as they scurried into that cabin like frightened little mice. Since arriving at the camp, the recruits were hurried off the bus, forced in a line, given quick and sharp instructions on how to address their instructors and negotiate a couple of different stances, a few push-ups because they said it helped to shake out the nerves, and then beckoned to the cabin at the end of the row.

The only intelligence provided to West prior to her arrival was that the core instruction revolved around learning and practicing spiritual disciplines. Although the novice to all things biblical had no idea what spiritual disciplines even were, let alone how to put them into practice, based on the looks of the other gals, she figured that they felt much the same way.

Rooted in the school of thought that information yielded power, the strong-willed young woman conceded to the insinuated notion that the cadre at this facility did not embrace her same enthusiasm for divulging all details and answering all questions when she attempted to articulate her concerns at their initial training bombardment. Instead, she accepted the predominant notion that they would tell her what she needed to know and when.

After following the orders without issue, the compliant group of girls stood at the end of their bunks, waiting for further direction as the drill sergeant moseyed down the bay like a Wild West gunslinger, glancing at each of them as she passed, appearing to make some mental notes. The small yet mighty leader sauntered all of the way down and back before she stopped on a dime and turned to face her crew. "At my command, you will all gather around me at this empty bunk to my left. You will do so in an orderly fashion. Once everyone is situated and quiet, I will begin to explain how you will arrange your items. Do you understand, recruits?" the drill sergeant bellowed once again.

West figured this mantra was going to be the routine at this place as she found she was already growing tired of the, "Yes, drill sergeant." The recruit struggled to tolerate guys that touted such demanding authority, let alone women, and second thoughts about her decision crept into her mind like nails on a chalkboard.

"Recruits, fall on me!" the drill sergeant gave the green light.

The entire bay rustled over to the bunk closest to the door without so much as a snide bicker, a disgusted glare, or even a not-so-accidental push. Contrary to her previous experiences with women, West approved of the abiding cooperation.

"The first discipline you will learn here is... Simplicity," the drill sergeant sounded out the word as if English was not the common language.

Drill Sergeant Thorpe opened the narrow wardrobe locker that housed a small wooden chest and slid out each drawer to display its contents. At the end of the bed, she lifted the lid of the trunk, pulled out the two-sided insert, and placed it on the floor. The organized instructor then proceeded to teach the group how to fold their issued t-shirts, socks, and underwear, and identified which drawers they were to be placed in and how.

After the methodical leader hung the drab green uniforms that looked like they were a half- century old and made for men, she positioned the polished boots next to the chest, a travel bag of hygiene items on the top, and all other bulky personal gear in the bottom of the trunk. The insert allowed for smaller items like pens and paper or pictures from home.

Proceeding to the beds, the precision of the hospital corners looked doable, but the scratchy wool blanket lacked the inviting appeal of comfort. When the drill sergeant had finished her mock display, the efficient space screamed neat and tidy. "Simplicity is about simplifying your life, so that you can begin to stop focusing on yourself so much. This is your first step. You have all that you need right here. Now, you will have thirty minutes to duplicate my example here with your own things and change into your PT gear. That means Physical Training." The skilled drill sergeant articulated her orders and vacated the premises.

The chant of "Yes, drill sergeant" followed right behind.

The fear of the unknown still permeated enough to keep everyone focused on their task at hand without as much as a peep. Having never witnessed such adherence to the rules, West wondered how long this level of cooperation was going to last. The fighter within wanted to break the silence, ease the tension, but even she had not conjured up the guts for that quite yet. For now, the curious trainee would comply.

Right on time, the slew of girls filed out onto the concrete slab just outside the dining hall, awaiting further instructions in abiding silence. At this point, the women were still separated from the men, all eyes forward.

"Your physical training will be your introduction to the disciplines of Meditation and Prayer," the fit black male instructor paced in the front of the formation, his voice deep and commanding, his accent thick. "You will be divided into ability groups. To my left is Drill Sergeant Thorpe. She will be leading the first group. The middle group will be next, led by me. The last group will be led by Drill Sergeant Burroughs, on my right."

Not recognizing that name from their initial instructional phase, West strained to peek out the farthest corners of her eyes to catch a glimpse of Drill Sergeant Burroughs without moving her head and breaking her stance. From what she could gather he looked short, stocky, probably about mid-forties, and his rough edges accented some lingering glimmers of a baby face. Although his athletic build had softened since his glory days, he still exuded that "Don't mess with me" exterior.

The primary drill sergeant continued his directions, "I will call out names on my list in order of first group, then second, and so on. When your name is called, you will sound off with a 'Yes, drill sergeant,' step behind your line, exit your formation to your right, and fall back in with your new group. You will move at double time. Do you understand, recruits?"

"Yes, drill sergeant!" the panicky bunch shouted as one chorus.

The powerful refrain grew the unit by an inch, but as West maintained her statuesque stance, she hoped that her name was not first. A leader by default, this time she did not want to be the guinea pig that stepped up instead of back or turned left instead of right. She preferred the comfort of watching a few others stumble through those mistakes, so that by the time he called her name, her anxious nerves would be calmed.

Relieved to spot a few familiar faces during the process, West recognized the Spanish guy from her assessment testing and now knew that his name was Salinas. A spry-looking guy, he got called to be with the first group. She also noticed Hoyt from that night at the testing, although he got placed behind her in the last group. When she eyed Bradford trotting towards the third group with Hoyt, her eyes brightened and her face broke a rule—she smiled, remembering their first introduction at the coffee shop.

Serving as the barista that day, West still projected her conservative front, so she did not make much small talk with him other than to tell him to enjoy the pumpkin latte. When the large man picked up the dainty cup and licked the whipped cream, she recalled the irony of a big, strong guy ordering such a feminine drink.

With a strong, rugged edginess, good dark hair with just enough body to hold the swoop on top, a clean taper around his ears and neck, and even those deep blue eyes tempted onlookers to take a prolonged glance. Although West considered herself a conservative on the emotional scale, his mature demeanor intrigued the young woman, but when she saw other patrons turning their heads to catch a glimpse of him as he walked to the far corner booth, the rebel scoffed and refocused on coffee.

To her surprise, Bradford ambled over to the same booth where the sergeant spent his afternoons once or twice a week. Although the barkeep did not know the recruiter at the time, his gentle way and endearing eyes that conveyed a fatherly concern left a deep impression on her. With every serving, his polite accent proclaimed his genuine thankfulness for the care she put into each cup. Even that first time when the sergeant sat with that older gal, he gazed into West's eyes as if he knew her—the good in her, at least. She thought it had been buried too deep, but he seemed to think it was just below the surface somehow.

The hardworking employee grew familiar with the pair little by little as they met there time and again over the next several years. Bradford's drink choice changed from the cavity-forming sweet kind to the more adult versions like the bold flavor of the Americano, but the sergeant stuck with his usual, the featured bean of single origin. Bradford's demeanor transformed over that time too. When he first arrived kind of cocky, the stud prepared to battle the sergeant, but as time went on, she noticed him soften, eager to listen, even fighting back some emotion now and again. On the day that she witnessed the two men grasping hands across the table as Bradford bowed his head, tears dripping down his cheeks, her curiosity prevailed, and the quiet observer was determined to find out why they had been meeting.

Feeling a twinge of guilt for spying on them all of this time, West debated her approach. With little experience in social engagement, she tended to occupy herself at work with her own stopgap mind games as she formed imaginative opinions about the variety of folks who frequented the establishment. The hometown café drew all kinds: teens, moms, kids, elderly. She served hipsters and an occasional emo, but most folks ran in the middle of the pack. As per the request of Yvonne, her trainer, West invoked enough cordial pleasantries but kept even the regulars at arm's length. Always avoiding genuine closeness, the private young woman realized that she would have to lower her guard and make the first move towards Bradford or the sergeant to accomplish her goal. Since the military man attempted conversation with her on a regular basis, she opted for the path of least resistance.

As the tentative barista finalized her tactical strategy, she had no idea that her next move would catapult her life into a frenzy of change and growth. The renowned transgressor never imagined that the trail would lead her to a place like Fort Gideon for basic training as a soldier for Christ.

Jumping jacks, more push-ups, flutter kicks, and then some basic stretches to warm up, the first group took the lead and strode off in silence. It caught her by surprise then when her group ran, forced to sound back the cadence calls. West had no idea what any of this had to do with meditation or prayer, but like most aspects surrounding this God's army thing, she had to hurry up and wait.

As the runners repeated every line of the cadence and watched their feet so as not to step on the person in front of them, the intelligent young lady rolled her eyes at some of the lyrics.

"When my Granny was ninety-one," Drill Sergeant Akpore's powerful accent coming through with each line.

"When my Granny was ninety-one," the group had learned to mimic every fluctuation.

"She did PT just for fun," his melody landed on point.

Although the thought of someone's granny doing PT in her ripe old age challenged the recruit's willingness to repeat the silly songs, she admired the tenacity of the main character and the cleverness of the rhymes.

Two laps around the fading green parade field and safely back at the second space on the concrete slab, the cluster followed their drill sergeant's direction through some post-run stretches.

"Place your right leg over your left leg and s-t-r-e-t-c-h!"

Bent over, grabbing their toes until the blood began to pound in their heads, they could hear that third group approaching in the distance as they sang the same simple tune over and over.

"Left," Drill Sergeant Burroughs called out.

"Left," the group resounded, struggling with their rather slow-paced run.

"Left, right," Drill Sergeant Burroughs chimed as if giving orders.

When that final section echoed their leader's call, West saw the lot of them stumble about, trying to step with their left foot as they shouted left, and the right foot when they got to that word. Even though Bradford trailed, he moved with little difficulty, but Hoyt still tripped over himself, so she lowered her head against her leg to mimic the stretch and hide her grin.

After Drill Sergeant Akpore excused the entire company, West scanned the first ability group, searching for an approachable female. Because that sector ran in silence and curiosity had gotten the best of her, she fixated on finding the reason.

CHAPTER 19

Salinas

Salinas hurried into the cabin with the other men because the recruits had been given twenty minutes to shower, change into their drab green uniforms, and form back into their original platoons on the court outside. Frazzled with the quick turnaround, the aesthetically aware student deliberated the deadline. As an acclimated immigrant, he had grown accustomed to long, hot showers, making sure every part of his body smelled like cologned soap, and primping his hair just right. The modern conveniences so prevalent in the States integrated into his daily life like threads of fine linen, but the strict demands of the camp asked that he depart from the distracting comforts.

The stringent schedule allowed no room for idle chatter either, yet the agile runner wanted to talk with someone in his ability group to see if they had any idea why they seemed to be the only formation that operated in silence that morning. Drill Sergeant Thorpe set the faster pace even though she was a woman, and a small one at that, and her one directive: maintain the tempo and take in the view.

With his scampering instincts on full alert, the physical challenge sounded acceptable, and since he always paid careful attention to his surroundings anyway, aware that the police could be tracking him at any moment, the absconder bolstered even more confidence in the task. As a matter of survival, the settler watched people too, leery of unwarranted glances, always wondering what their reaction to his illegal status would be.

As normal tricks of the trade, Salinas had developed elusive techniques, making the chances of getting arrested and deported slim. Avoiding bar fights and never committing any hard crime formed the basis of the steady climb to normalcy, but when he acquired a car and started driving, knowing that the slightest fender bender could draw unwanted attention, the gambler elevated his game and tight fisted the steering wheel. Although the stakes seemed high, the freedom was worth it.

Marriage and children created another threat level as school functions, block parties, and even birthday parties increased his social footprint. As a bachelor playing the field, he could pretty much love them and leave them, and even if an infatuated follower came around the restaurant later, asking questions or miffed that he did not call, the experienced player could finagle his way out of the situation because in most cases the white women wanted to downplay their pursuit of a Mexican waiter. However, if one of the enthusiasts developed a fanatical obsession, Salinas just switched to one of the other restaurants in the circuit. As a matter of routine, the affectionate husband kept a honey or two on the side even after he and Anna made it official because his wife did not run in his circles and he did not run in hers. With her feelings in mind, he pursued targets that fell outside on the fringes.

Anna was beautiful and sophisticated and brushed off his flirtatious advances at first. About once a month she frequented the restaurant with a group of five or six girlfriends. Standing out in the crowd, her fit and trim figure, gleaming, long dark hair, sparkling green eyes, and picture-perfect smooth skin enticed the full staff. While Salinas imposed his innate knack, getting the gals to giggle and flirt back with ease, Anna repelled his efforts, shooting him that look that indicated that she was flattered but not interested.

Her polite refusal stirred his desires even more, and the chase intensified.

The doting server dug deep into his arsenal. He insisted on waiting her table. He showered her with poetic accolades of beauty in Spanish. He diverted his attentions to one of her friends to spark some jealousy. He even ignored her a little bit, but none of his manipulative tactics penetrated her hardened exterior. Never having to resort to such depths before, the overachiever's frustrations mounted as the months droned on without any hints of success. Just when the agitated pursuer considered defeat, resigning to the friend corner like a scolded pup, the troop marched into the restaurant with heads hung low.

On her way to the bathroom, one of the gals elbowed their regular waiter and confessed that Anna's nana had just passed, and the close-knit friends gathered with the intentions of fostering some good cheer in celebration of the old woman's life. Balancing in a field of unchartered emotional territory, Salinas kept a respectable distance that night until Anna leaned down to retrieve her purse in preparation for her leave. By impulse, the consummate romantic knelt beside her, picked up her bag as a peace offering, stared right into her eyes as the mesmerizing twinkle flushed his face, and told her he would light a candle for her nana.

Salinas cringed at the utterance of the endearing oath. He had no idea where the sappy salutation came from. He was not a religious person, really. As an act of obedience to his faithful mother, the son endured his token Easter and Christmas Sundays in the gilded sanctuary of the local cathedral, but apart from those obligatory experiences, the skeptic failed to see God very active in his world. Church seemed more of a tradition for pining mothers and praying grandmothers.

His ma and abuela harped on him to pay homage to the saints for revelations of paths unknown, protection from lurking danger, or safe passage for a dead relative, but his compulsory participation aspired only to appease his two favorite women. Perhaps that habitual practice in his childhood, albeit infrequent, prompted him to speak to Anna that way. During his pious attempt to offer his condolences, the skilled thief had no inkling his combination of words would unlock Anna's heart and affections.

Gazing back with remnants of tears re-forming their sullen pool, his primary target thanked him for his kind words and told him how much they meant to her. The prowler was in. Although he had no intentions of stooping to such a morbid tactic, the success of the maneuver rejuvenated his ego, and the skillful con artist continued his charade by sustaining the somber façade until her car left the lot. After a cool wave, he darted back to the kitchen and strutted his happy dance.

With a solidified cornerstone, Salinas courted Anna, biding his time, moving with gentle intentions to further crumble her fortified boundaries, his true love growing for her yet not transforming enough to make him give up his extracurriculars. Convinced that his other primal needs were irrelevant to what he had going on with Anna, the schemer busied her with his deceptive focus on religious matters, knowing full well that the subject matter interested her. The performer sympathized with her spiritual search, dramatizing a fictitious instinct about a sense of God's presence during the circumstances that led them to each other. Living for the moment, Salinas advanced one step ahead of her with no qualms about the seductive dance he twirled.

In an effort to minimize her own distractions, Anna never brought her alien boyfriend around her folks because they would not embrace the multi-cultural relationship. However, when the proper girlfriend discovered that she was pregnant, clinging to some hope that God was still in it all, she begged for her man to remedy the situation.

Trying his best to continue his wholesome charade, Salinas gave in to the idea of marriage. Deep inside he knew that was what his girl wanted, and he did long to be this wonderful guy that she thought he was. Just at the slight mention of a proposal, Anna sobbed and hugged him like a school girl on a pink teddy bear won at the county fair, when all the while he wondered how he was going to pull this one off. In desperation the bachelor resolved that the sanctity of marriage would be enough accountability to change him. He would re-train his mind and just choose to be that guy, be faithful, be a provider, submerge himself into her world, but his overzealous attempts could only be sustained for stints at a time.

As skepticism grew in the eyes of his in-laws, the phony questioned the depth of their reluctant approval. In a frail attempt to honor their daughter's adulthood, the couple never summoned the courage to confront him about his late nights or frequent schedule changes. As he mastered just the right amount of spin to impose on a tale to keep them at bay, knowing that his lies could be possible and hoping for their daughter's sake that they were, the chameleon steered the rocking boat, and once the baby arrived, the captain steadied the rolling tide. When the second baby came, the thick layer of binding tar sealed the hull of trickling doubt even more.

Salinas intended to keep his secret life away from his loved ones. If a side gig approached danger close, he switched to a different restaurant and reported to the family with animated enthusiasm that he had received a promotion with more opportunity for management. While his odd hours masqueraded his movements, the braggart touted to his co-workers about the ease by which he fooled even the closest of relationships. In his estimation, loved ones wanted to believe, so they did.

Finding the thrill of the game increasing in direct proportion to the close encounters of his two worlds, the offender pushed the envelope of chance a bit farther each time. After a while, Salinas spent so much time and energy maintaining the irons in the fire that he forgot about the moral limits of acceptable behavior. It was what it was.

However, that day in the restaurant, the persistent sergeant brought him smack dab back in touch with reality. The serviceman first appeared like any other customer, asking for the specials, trying his hand at a Spanish word here or there. "Hola, amigo. I like you, Salinas," the sergeant was always so complimentary. "You are a real people person. I can tell."

Although Salinas got a kick out of white people's meager attempts to speak his language, the flourishing waiter always congratulated them with such pomp and circumstance. The consistent ploy made for good tips and guaranteed a return visit. "Gracias, sergeant," was his typical response. "I do my best."

As the pleasantries migrated into more personal conversation over the years, the cocky waiter laughed inside, thinking it funny that this sergeant thought he knew something about his server. If the probing customer only knew how good he really was. Because the sergeant tipped well and interacted with genuine interest, the infamous character appeased the light attempts at ongoing engagement.

"Oh, before I take off, I got a message for you, Salinas," the sergeant blurted out one day.

"Oh, yeah?" Salinas, willing to play his part, "What's that, señor?"

"The games have got to stop. Lives are at stake," the sergeant's eyes bored into an intense focus, expressing his serious concern.

Taken aback at the abrupt change of pace, Salinas deliberated the source of the attack. Did the patron know he was an illegal? Was it something to do with the underground circuit? Was this staunch professional a cop, and all of this time Salinas's radar suffered a malfunction? He decided to play dumb, "No entiendo. I mean, I am not sure what you mean."

"Your wife has truly become a believer and the Lord will not continue to be mocked," the sergeant's voice laid down the gauntlet.

"Oh, my wife. I see," the sly waiter relaxed now that he knew this was nothing to do with immigration.

"No, Salinas, I don't think ya do, but you're goin' to and soon!" the sergeant pounced.

"Again, señor, I don't understand what you are getting at,"

Salinas countered, confident that the sergeant had no way of knowing about his dual life.

"Salinas, you've been workin' for evil far too long. You have a real chance to work for good now, be the man that I know that you really wanna be. No more pretendin'. No more lies, false promises, other women," the sergeant struck a deep blow.

The ardent performer swallowed hard and cleared his throat as the stage fright froze him in his tracks. How could this guy know any of this? They shared small talk over enchiladas and tacos, and most times the military man was busy talking with that African friend of his. Salinas never saw the regular customer outside of this place, so there was no way this stiff collar could know anything so personal.

"You can be a new man, Salinas. The old can be gone, or you can keep riding this thing out the way you have been. Your choice!" the sergeant softened his approach.

For perhaps the first time in his life, Salinas felt exposed, and not just caught, but revealed, as if the mask fell off during a packed-house performance. Although he did not know why, the unexpected barrage triggered a welcoming assurance that had lain dormant for decades, and as the pleading patron converged, the guilty one felt bare, vulnerable, pierced. By instinct Salinas wanted to trump him, dig some prop out of his treasure troves, but he kept coming up empty-handed. The evader just could not think under the scrutiny.

"You don't have to carry this anymore. Jesus wants to clean you white as snow," the sergeant spoke as if he was able to see the inner turmoil.

When the sergeant grasped his hand, gently pinning it to the top of the table, Salinas could no longer deny his struggle. With that single touch, he knew at that very moment that he could either tap out or fight on forevermore.

"He is real, Salinas, and He loves you."

Normally Salinas would have been aware of every movement in the entire facility, but during the exchange, he lost all sense of what was happening around him. The fighter focused on the glass blue eyes that drew him into the drama of a great clash until love swelled and consumed the adversary within as if it had been there all along. The truth cut deeper than the love he reserved for Anna, wider than his concerns for himself. Finally, the surrendered target confessed in a whisper, "I don't know how."

"I am here to help," the sergeant affirmed, calming the quivers pulsing through the recruit's hand.

CHAPTER 20

Hoyt

With the swarm of activity imposing utter exhaustion, Hoyt appreciated the fast pace at which the nights progressed and ushered in a cavernous slumber. With his repetitive former existence of going to class, working at the take-out pizza shop where his sole responsibility was to cut the pies when they came out of the oven and box them up, then back to his single dorm room for homework, the mundane faded into a distant memory. Although his obsessive-compulsive tendencies favored the reliable routine, the excitement that the camp evoked brought living to a whole other level.

Lost in the recesses of REM, the startled soldier toppled off of his bunk when the drill sergeant flipped on the lights and bellowed his "rise and shine". As the visually challenged one fumbled around the floor for his dark-rimmed glasses, he missed the convenience of his contacts. Even though the realist boycotted the introduction of the tiny pieces of manufactured eyeball skin at the onset, his sisters had talked his mom into getting him a trial pair. With his fear of foreign objects bypassing his protective lids, his middle sister pinned him down on the ground and pried his lashes apart to force him into compliance. The violated little brother was not sure which part of the incident made him feel worse—the idea of fabricated matter clinging to his pupil or the pathetic reality that his sister could still hold his arms down with her knees and overpower him enough to accomplish the mission.

With prevalent signs of sleep deprivation, the tired soldiers managed to don their PT outfits again and muddle through another run, chanting their "left, rights." Straining to ignore the stomach cramps and sore thigh muscles, Hoyt banked on Drill Sergeant Burroughs's promise that this part of the training would get easier.

After a quick shower, change of uniform, and a few tidying chores within the billets, the trainees filed back out onto the cement slab where this time, instead of separating them into ability groups, Drill Sergeant Akpore assigned them to platoons. Finding Drill Sergeant Thorpe's leadership style less intimidating than the other two, the consummate loner marched over to the first section and waited while the female cadre positioned them into four rows of four people like a preschool teacher.

Although statistics was the least desirable subject of the math disciplines, Hoyt relished the lean in his favor when the few faces that he recognized popped into his line. Salinas had sat near him at the assessment testing, and he remembered Bradford and West from that night too. Unsure that his comrades would reciprocate the recognition because his glasses hid a large portion of his face, Hoyt accepted his miscalculation and adjusted himself to allow West to slide into the first position. In silent acknowledgement, the quartet nodded to one another like a melodious chorus as they held their stance and listened for further direction.

Drill Sergeant Thorpe paced back and forth in front of their platoon as she enlightened them on the significance of the camaraderie and teamwork required by the squad unit. They were battle buddies for the duration of this training and would learn to operate as one while also maintaining the integrity and functionality of the platoon as a whole.

Each member would take turns acting as squad leader, but the group would be assigned one permanent platoon leader.

Hoyt appreciated the commutative and associative nature of this dynamic and could only hope that he was not the chosen constant. Thankfully, she named some tall, thin kid from the first squad. Jensen, the token recruit in charge, strutted to his position front and center.

Thorpe then instructed the unit how to conduct the accountability reporting, each token squad leader sounding the "Four present and accounted for" to Jensen who would turn and report an "All present and accounted for" to Thorpe. "Recruit West, for example, will look down her row and make sure that all four members are in position. After third squad reports, she will form a salute to Recruit Jensen and report 'All present and accounted for,'" Drill Sergeant Thorpe acted out the event.

The cadre insisted that the accounting had to be accurate as if it were a life or death situation. No one could fib, which led to the lecture about knowing the location of the battle buddies at all times. The squad would eat together, study together, work together, and could only part to sleep in the separate barracks. Even bathroom breaks required direct permission by the squad leader, so the socially challenged needed to check their need for isolation at the door.

The drill sergeant elaborated on the concept, explaining that this particular arrangement would integrate them into the practice of submission. They would be forced to become a better follower, knowing that within a week's time, they would be at the helm of the squad, hoping for reciprocal cooperation. The consistency of the platoon leader would test their submission over an extended period while still allowing for the ever-present authoritative role of the drill sergeants who knew the in's and out's of the end game. To Hoyt's logical mind, the synopsis made perfect sense, in theory; however, the methodical thinker wished that the strategic tactics involved more impersonal components like chess pieces.

"Left face! Forward march! Mark time, march! Platoon halt!

The Recruits

About face! About face! Right face!" Jensen enjoyed his leadership position.

The platoon rehearsed their drill techniques along the pathways to the dining hall for breakfast where they scurried through the serving line, sat at their assigned table, and gobbled their food in silence within the twenty minutes allotted. Because Hoyt did not have to wait for an invitation to the popular table, he galloped to his seat and peeked with pride at the squad mates on his left and right. Being a part of that team, even if by default, meant more to him than whether the slop looked like it came out of a bucket, smelled like it came out of a can, or if he had enough time to taste before swallowing.

However, before the feeding frenzy began, the entire dining hall bowed their heads as Drill Sergeant Akpore gave thanks for their bounty, triggering the twenty-minute stopwatch upon the amen. As the hungry recruits shoveled in the mystery meat doused in gravy and ladled over toast, forced down by some mildly warm dark substance they were passing off as coffee, Akpore reiterated that at some point each soldier would take a turn praying for his own table. For now, the trainees could glean from the examples of the instructors.

With no time to ponder his fear of public speaking, Hoyt shoved the grub into his mouth and rushed to follow the others to the pass-thru window to turn in their trays. Garbage cans were not necessary because scraps were not an option.

Just as the company had filed into the building, the recruits hustled through the exit and back into their exact places in their platoon formations. Once again, they fumbled through the new marching maneuvers to a nearby building marked in plain black lettering, "Classroom." Their practice of study would commence there.

Encounter

"How could this happen again?" Mr. West yelled from the other end of the phone.

"I don't know, Bill!" Tina fought back. "You know she has a mind of her own!"

"We cannot endure another scandal! This is a small town! We won't survive it!" the father insisted.

"Oh, well, heaven forbid that you and your precious wife endure another scandal!" Tina chided.

"Are you even sure about this?" the outraged one probed over speaker phone.

"Yes. I took her to the doctor. It was positive!" the mother replied with a condescending edge.

"Was there one or two?" he inquired.

"Just the one," Tina answered, unsure as to why that was significant.

"Well, since there is just the one, we have to do something about it. If there were two, we would possibly consider other options, but if you are sure there is just one, there is no other way. This is ludicrous!"

"Well, I don't have the money for it. Are you going to foot the bill?" she enticed.

"Ugghhh, I guess I'll have to. You get the details, get it arranged, and I will give you a check. I want a receipt though!" he demanded.

The young seventeen-year-old felt like she had no other choice. The two people that claimed to care about her the most in this world had set the tone.

"Well, you heard him," Tina explained. "He is only paying for one thing in this, and you know that I can't afford to support a baby. We barely make due as it is."

"What about Alan and Shannon? Maybe they want another one, a sibling?" the young girl proposed.

"Oh, honey, do you really want to go through all of that again?" the mother suggested. "Walking down those hallways with a big belly? The talk? The looks? We all have to still live here, you know."

"Well, maybe I could go to their house or something in the meantime?" Darby tossed another line.

"Well, you obviously do what you want anyway, young lady," Tina turned angry. "But I'm telling you now that I want no part of this. If you go that route, you are on your own, and you know your father won't approve!"

On her own? She was a teenager, saving as much as she could to help pay for the basics. Did she have the courage to sever the only family ties that she had, albeit weak ones at that?

"Uh, yes. I would like to make an appointment," the adolescent quivered over the phone, trying to sound official. "Yes, I'm sure. Maybe a month or two. Yes, next week will be fine. Oh, could you tell me how much that would be?"

Just a pick from the phone book, and it was as easy as that. It felt as if she were just making an appointment for a dental cleaning. The scheduler asked for no other information, never questioned the decision of the youthful voice, not even concerned about the patient's mental health, maintaining the steady pitch the entire time.

Tina took off from work that day to drive her to the clinic, and as they pulled into the facility just past the picketers on the curb, Darby slid down into her seat mortified. The five people determined to weather the cold to promote their agenda flaunted their "Abomination" signs towards their vehicle, but even that did not break the solemn silence inside. She and her mother had managed to keep eyes forward and mouths shut with a determined intent to make this all go away with as little emotion as possible.

Thankfully, the entrance door was around the building in the back. The strategic business created as much privacy for their clients as possible. The solid plain orange door was unadorned, conveying the serious nature and permanency of the services provided on the other side.

As Tina took a seat amongst the few others in the waiting room, Darby paced up to the receptionist to check in.

"Okay, Darby," the middle-aged woman replied with the same robotic tone that the young girl had heard over the phone. "We will call you back in a few minutes."

As the teenager turned to take her own seat, she was surprised to find several men present as well as women. The older man appeared close to her own dad's age, and the distant daughter thought that odd and contemplated what brought him to this place. The young black couple kept their heads down as they fidgeted with their hands. The girl looked about the same age as Darby, but the boy looked just a couple of years older. The other single guy looked early twenties, and the white couple looked just a bit older. No one spoke. No one made eye contact. No one even made unnecessary movement.

After calling her name, the nurse led the child back to the sonogram room to once again confirm the pregnancy.

"Yes, there is a heartbeat, and it looks like you are probably about nine weeks along," the monotone approach continued.

From there, the girl was guided into the billing office where the clerk presented her with a formal list of all fees. After a cursory glance of the ultrasound fee, the physician fee, the office fee, the gas fee, the home medication fee, and the procedure fee, Darby lowered her head in shame and handed over the seven-hundred-dollar check that Mr. West had provided.

"I need a receipt," she whispered.

The same nurse then escorted her to another private waiting room, and young West glanced through the pamphlets on abortion and such. It struck her quite peculiar that no brochures on adoption were offered, and even yet, that no staff ever asked her if she was even certain about her decision. Obviously, they had reasoned that the less talk the better.

After the well-rehearsed nurse returned and guided her into the clinic room, the young patient downed a Valium and changed into her gown behind the curtain. Once she was situated on the table and the Darth Vader-like mask put over her nose and mouth, her mind fogged and faded off into oblivion. When she roused in her recliner with a tray of juice and crackers at her side, the teen was alarmed to find four other women recovering in their own stationed recliner. It was just a large, hollow, silent room full of high-end, leather chairs to start the gals off in comfort in their new reality.

That was it. West fought nausea on the drive home and had to pull over at least once to relieve her gut, but all of them did their utmost to put the ordeal behind them, never speaking of it again. Even Darby did her best to block the memories, telling herself over and over that it was just like when she had her wisdom teeth removed, only on a rare occasion allowing her heart to confess.

"I could have loved you!"

"Before I formed you in the womb I knew you." (Jeremiah 1:5, NIV)

CHAPTER 21

West

The classroom looked as ordinary as the sign suggested with three columns of eight-foot, brown tables arranged four deep, four metal folding chairs positioned on just one side, and all facing towards a three-sectioned white board that ran the length of the front of the room. A single wooden podium stood at the far left, cocked at an angle to allow the instructor to address the class while still being able to view the board. On guard at the entrance sat a large cardboard box sitting atop a gray stool.

Because they were considered first platoon, Drill Sergeant Thorpe gave her four squads the lead instructions on how to assemble into their study digs. "You will file in one at a time, first squad, second squad, and so on just as you did into the mess hall. Recruit Jensen will go first because right inside that door is a box of textbooks. He will hand one book to each of you as you secure the first column of tables. First squad will occupy the first table, second squad the table behind them, and so on. You will place your book on the table in front of your chair and wait behind your chair at at ease. Do you understand, recruits?" She never sounded like she expected any replies.

"Yes, drill sergeant," they all answered with enthusiasm, representing the esprit d'corps that was expected.

"Move!" Drill Sergeant Thorpe commanded.

Growing more accustomed to the maneuverings of this place, the unit complied. Almost gloating over the coveted lead role, Jensen played his part and handed each soldier a book as they crossed over the threshold.

After first platoon took their positions, second platoon rolled in with third platoon right behind. Silence and obedience fell across the room as a gaunt blond-haired man halted at the door. His pale skin and flushed cheeks appeared like the permanent variety, and he wore dark green dress pants with a black stripe down each side, a lighter green short-sleeved dress shirt, and black patent leather shoes. His long, thin, black tie remained in place with a pin, and the emblems above his left breast pocket looked impressive. As he remained at the door, waiting for the initiation of the protocol required for his high-ranking position, he rolled his eyes and released his gasp to reduce the rising redness in his face.

"Class, attention!" Drill Sergeant Akpore bellowed with his strong, deep voice and African accent.

The room shot into the stiff stance as the instructor avoided eye contact and marched to the podium. "Take seats." His soft voice lacked the commanding tone of the drill sergeants.

West relaxed her shoulders at the gentle nature of his order, but the entire room still adhered all the same as they removed their web belts with single empty cargo pouch on the front left and canteen full of water on the back right hip and slung them over the backs of their chairs. With no idle chatter, they took their seats, keeping their backs straight and taut to signal their readiness for the next directive.

Like the rest of the class West glanced down at the textbook entitled *The Bible* with *Student Version* as the subtitle. *How ironic*, she thought, expecting something more tactical or strategic. Having never cracked open the two Bibles that had been gifted to her, the recruit failed to comprehend the value in an ancient text full of unpronounceable words and extinct cultural references. Although she had not read it before, she had tried a time or two as a kid, but its copious lists of old names and confusing sentence structures baffled her mind. Figuring that God would not require His people to be literary scholars to understand Him, she never pursued it further.

With her messy life choices igniting an inquisitive fire on occasion, reason always won the final straw and quenched any lingering intrigue. Because the town folks and her own thoughts imposed enough guilt, the blemished one resented some old book making her feel worse. The touted message seemed so out of touch with reality, or at least her reality.

As she thought back on that day in the café, West remembered her knees shaking as she approached the sergeant. Her ploy involved bussing tables near his booth during the break in the rush. "Hey, there, sergeant. Are you done with your cup?" the unassuming employee attempted to sound diligent in her efforts.

"Thank ya kindly, West, that would be mighty nice of ya."

"Sergeant, I told you time and again that you can call me by my first name, Darby." The young adult never understood why he insisted on that formal practice in the civilian world.

"No can do, West. Told ya that I'm used to callin' soldiers by their last names. It's a hard habit to break," the sergeant grinned at her puzzled look.

"No soldiers around here, sergeant. Just town folks drinking coffee." West rather enjoyed this tit-for-tat that the two of them shared. "I know. I know, it is all in the eye of the beholder."

The apathetic woman never comprehended his quips, but she also never wanted to spend too much time with him to find out what they meant. Her personal boundaries maintained the required distance to keep her guilt on lockdown. "Say, sergeant, I could not help but see that Mr. Bradford left a bit shaken up. Everything okay? I mean, I couldn't tell if those were happy tears or sad ones," West was trying to be careful to lead the conversation without getting too nosey.

"A bit of both, West. A bit of both. Food for the soul," the sergeant always elongated his vowel sounds, making everything sound so smooth and inviting.

Normally West would have been satisfied with that level of response, wiped the table, and wished him good day, but something urged her on this time. "Food for the soul?" she asked with hesitation.

"Yes, West, when the Son sets you free, you will be free indeed," the sergeant looked deep into her eyes as if he were searching her very soul.

Part of her wanted to run, fearing he could see her internal dungeon, yet another part of her wanted that—to be free. She did not know what *sun* he referred to unless he meant perhaps that the sun needed to shine in that darkness deep within her. Perhaps somehow he had not been privy to the stories that circulated about her in this small town.

It had been six years since her major debut to the rumor mill, yet she still felt its sting every time someone came into the shop, recognized her as that young pregnant girl from the high school that gave her baby up for adoption, acted all polite and thankful for their drink, and then strode off to their table in hushed whispers. Telling herself over and over again that she did not care, West calloused her heart and perfected the art of acting. Some customers confessed with an angelic face and sad pucker that they thought her brave, giving her baby a chance at a better life. Although West knew the intentions were meant for good, aimed to help her feel better about her decision, it always hurt far worse than if they had just ignored her altogether.

"Some people just don't deserve freedom, sergeant. Some people deserve their sentence on death row, never again seeing the light of day," the server blurted, shocked at the verbal fight she rallied.

"Even murder can be forgiven, West. Isn't that what you really want?" the sergeant kept his calm, cool, and collected posture even at her slight attack.

Murder? Her heart ached and stretched as he pried at that dungeon door. *No, no, this can't be happening,* West thought to herself. *This is impossible. I never told a soul. Retreat, retreat. I'm not ready for this!*

Tears welled and her body quivered as all of those locked emotions crept out of the dark hole where she had buried them. The female target remained at an absolute loss for words, not knowing how in the world to respond to him, and the strong, independent woman never saw this coming. When he rose, the silent tension broke as he embraced her like a loving father and consoled her as the hurt won out and found its release.

"I've never told anyone. I have kept that to myself for so long," the recruit found such relief to even admit it.

"I know. I know," his words were comforting and kind.

"I just could not do it again. I could not be that pregnant girl again," she confessed. "I'm so sorry! I am just so sorry!"

"I know, West. You are forgiven. You have to believe that. He sent me to tell you that," the sergeant continued in his gracious response.

"He did?" Although West was not sure who he was referring to, she longed to be forgiven, never realizing how much until now.

"Yes, West. Jesus has always known, and He still loves you." The rugged sergeant seemed too manly for such affectionate talk.

"Jesus? Really? But how can He? I am not worth it," the defeated girl let out between sobs.

"No one is worth it by our own actions, West. That is both the mystery and the beauty of it all," the sergeant spoke truth back into that gaping hole. "*The Bible* is chock-full of undeserving witnesses throughout the ages, but He paid their ransom with His life once and for all. It is real, West. I can testify with my own life that it is real. You have to believe me, trust Him, and surrender your own understanding."

As Recruit West looked down at her study table, here it was, *The Bible*. Her lifeline lay cradled in her very hands. Although she still doubted her ability to understand its contents, she chose to believe the promise that the sergeant gave her about its transformational power. It was the handbook of all basic soldiering skills needed for life.

CHAPTER

Hoyt

Hoyt's confidence soared during PT that morning when his group conquered the cadence challenge, able to focus more on staying together and in step and less about their own aches, pains, or stomach growls. As the gaggle graduated to the next level of following cadences to their memory verse assignments like the second group, the drudgery they had endured seemed worth it. Even he had grown weary of the repetitive "left, right" that they were stuck with, but now that they could run as a unit, the gradual training had realized its full potential. The non-athletic trainee would never forget that first memory verse this morning.

"Not by might and not by power," Drill Sergeant Burroughs belted out.

"Not by might and not by power," Hoyt's group echoed back with beaming pride.

"But by my Spirit says the Lord."

"But by my Spirit says the Lord," the chants continued.

"Zechariah, Zechariah."

"Zechariah, Zechariah," the ranks sang as they held their heads high and even looked about.

"Zechariah 4:6." Drill Sergeant Burroughs always over-emphasized the numbers.

Hoyt reminded himself that it was four six and not six four. Six four rhymed with Lord, so he wanted to say that, but then he would rearrange the algebraic sequence in his mind. *I want to say six four, but I know it is the reciprocal of what I would normally think, so it is four six*, the devoted student rationalized.

The studious recruit loved all that they were learning in class with Captain Peters too. Methodical in his delivery, their study instructor resembled some of the better professors he had experienced at school. While the class first searched through the Gospels, looking for evidences of Jesus preaching, teaching, or practicing the various disciplines, the practical application involved role-playing exercises with peers.

Although the former Sunday school student recalled the location of the Gospels of Matthew, Mark, Luke, and John, he had considered them more as fabled stories of Jesus visiting people, performing miracles, or the miraculous birth story. The uninterested youth thought those lessons redundant and did not understand the real value of having all three of the Synoptics. As the enlightened adult learned more in this present setting, his softening heart confessed his ignorance beyond the colorful stories of vacation Bible school.

Beyond the obligatory attendance required of every child of an active member of the local congregation, Hoyt never read *The Bible* for himself, and he most certainly never studied it. The novice soldier did not even know how to study it or even realize that there were so many different ways to approach it. A lifetime of learning could be spent on this divine masterpiece, and Hoyt was thrilled to still have the chance.

The ministry of Jesus came to life for the young recruit as he searched for ways that Jesus worshipped or pursued solitude. Through these exercises Hoyt began to see how he could emulate Jesus and practice the disciplines as He did, growing ever mindful of his desire for less of himself and more of Jesus ruling and reigning in his life. Feeling a sense of real purpose for the first time, a new identity burrowed in fertile soil began to sprout.

The Recruits

A laid back type of guy, Hoyt never overreacted, but he figured his sisters expressed enough emotion for the whole family. Insignificant by comparison, his preferences seemed irrelevant, yet he still lacked overt concern. In so many ways, he followed along under the radar for the sheer pleasure of the ride, but with that, the young man stifled wonderful feelings like passion, drive, exhilaration.

According to his mother's assessment, the young Hoyt possessed the endearing gift of compassion and service. She often affirmed his willingness to help her with small tasks like carrying in the groceries or helping the girls bring in loads of laundry and bags from school. Although a picky eater from infancy, the tot downed a few token bites every meal to please his mother and respect his father. In an attempt to be gentle yet honest, the thoughtful boy never told his mom that he disliked her cooking unless she outright asked. Hoyt mowed the lawn, raked leaves, and emptied the garbage without constant provocation and kept his room tidy. To ease his mother's burdens, he even laundered his own clothes since the age of eleven.

"Brian, you're a good kid. Just a downright good guy," his father would tell him time and again.

"Thanks, Dad," he always responded.

Not much else needed to be said between the two of them. The patriarch was his best friend, and in many respects, his only true friend. When others teased that the boy used to proclaim that he came out of his dad's back instead of his mom's stomach, he believed the embarrassing tale although he did not remember it himself. Hoping his mother's feelings were not hurt with the constant reference to the legend, he redirected the meaning and insisted that his youthful comments stemmed from a reluctance to replicate the girls.

Every evening at six o'clock, nearly on the dot, Mr. Hoyt's red-and-white-striped Chevy Citation turned the corner. Waiting for the sighting on the front porch or in the sunroom, the anxious son wiggled and squirmed until he spotted the car, dashed to the edge of the drive, and hopped up and down as his dad eased out of the car with briefcase in hand. Full of zeal, the young Hoyt darted to his side, grabbed his free hand, and begged to carry the overstuffed luggage as he recited all that he had learned in school that day. Knowing that his father had a steel trap of a mind, Hoyt blurted out the details, excited to hear his dad relate to the topic with tidbits of stored information like a personal computer prototype. The effortless interaction flowed with relevant meaning and majestic quality.

A huge jazz fan, his father listened to his music on old-fashioned reel-to-reel tapes with enormous gray headphones covering his ears like an airplane pilot. Although the young boy never could relate to the enticement of the upbeat tempos, blaring horns, and scat runs, he envied his dad's passion and longed to be passionate about something himself one day. Although the youngster tried his hand at the art of collecting in the form of rare stamps, shiny marbles, or even eight-sided dice, nothing ever stuck.

An avid reader, Mr. Hoyt shared fantastical stories of faraway lands with the children each night before bed and offered an open invitation to accompany him during one of his frequent trips to the libraries in the area. "I am heading to the public library. Anyone want to come?" Mr. Hoyt called up or down the stairs, depending on where the kids were playing. With only his boy ever taking him up on the offer, the head of the household aimed to make interesting conversation and appeared enthusiastic about any topic his son was willing to share. The eternal optimist saw the glass half full, so their adventures on the pages or along the sidewalks conveyed his light-hearted view of fun.

During that first time at the public library, Mr. Hoyt migrated to the records section and let his boy hang behind in the kids' section. Beaming with the confidence imparted to him, the youngster squelched his fear of strangers lurking behind the deep and dusty cases and stayed in the well-lit confines of the comic book section.

On their walk home, his father offered a stop at Laesch's Dairy Barn for a cone. A rare treat for his frugal family to purchase anything outside of the grocery store, the plain vanilla cone solidified their bond, a sign of true affection.

"Now, no need to brag to your sisters about this ice cream cone," Mr. Hoyt was not one to cause a fuss. "If they choose to come sometime, they will get one too."

With the joy of the undivided attention filling his emotional tank, little Hoyt nodded in agreement, accepting the notion that more ice cream in the future would be icing on the proverbial cake.

Sometimes their travels took them to the university library across the parking lot from their house. Due to the short walk to that facility, the girls tagged along on occasion because they all played hide-and-seek in the multi-floored building. Calling the elevator off limits, the siblings traipsed up and down the dark and scary back staircase where every single noise echoed off the dull cement steps. When hiding, Hoyt slithered around on the first floor to avoid the creepy sensation that loomed around the steps, but whenever he had to seek, it never failed that the girls scaled the haunted path to alternate levels as a means of further torturing their timid brother.

Knowing his best friend would be fascinated by the history as well as the theology taught at Fort Gideon, Recruit Hoyt wished he could talk to his dad about everything that he was learning at basic. Without a doubt, Mr. Hoyt would be proud to know that his son finally found that passion. *Oh, Lord, I pray that my dad truly knew You as Lord and Savior*, Hoyt often thought throughout this experience. *I loved him dearly, and I now know that You must have loved him even more.*

BASIC TRAINING

Phase II: Qualification

Marching with the Master Minutes

September 2005

Cadre: Akpore, Thorpe, Burroughs, Peters

Recruiters: Riley

The group opened with prayer for each recruit in 1st Platoon, 4th Squad.

1. Bradford was selected as Squad Leader for the Confidence and Leadership Reaction Courses. Sergeant Riley felt he had the best leadership style to utilize the strengths of his other team members at this juncture. His past experience with similar physical challenges will also serve to give them a foundational game plan to be successful.

2. Hoyt will serve as Squad Leader for the range week. His lack of leadership will be bolstered during these tasks because these events are largely individual. His team will follow him to the zeroing range, the M-16 range, and the rappelling towers, but then the challenges are individual from there. His success here will prepare him for a more confident voice. His logical instincts to follow direction could prove to be the key to his personal success in this phase of training.

3. Sergeant Riley has selected Salinas to lead the Squad during the Land Navigation training. Again, other than movements to and from range sites, these activities are largely individual. Salinas has a lot of terrain experience in his past and should feel confident this week. His calmness will set the tone for the rest of the Squad. It will be interesting to see how the dynamics have evolved with any adversity in this phase.

> Bradford may struggle the most here, so we will see how his teammates respond to assist him. We will join them back together for the night portion since it will be their first time functioning in that type of limited visibility. We will be able to gauge how well they are prepared to respond without imploding.

4. West should perform well in each event, but she may struggle on the team portions. She is still learning how to trust men and to follow them. She is learning how the Holy Spirit moves and works in all different kinds of people, but her tendency to resort to her own personal experiences could be a road block for her and thus for the team as a whole.

The group closed in silent prayer as we listened for any further promptings of the Holy Spirit.

Godspeed,

Akpore

CHAPTER 23

Bradford

Bradford relished the hands-on training that they were learning outside of the classroom. Although he had experienced similar activities in his preparation with the Department of Corrections, he found new purpose in these exercises. As he related these types of challenges to those he conquered during his athletic prime, the oldest trainee thought it fitting that he would be in line for squad leader during their week at the Obstacle and Leadership Reaction courses.

The training began at the Obstacle course that boasted a wide array of monstrous contraptions erected from enormous logs. To orient the platoon to the course, Drill Sergeant Thorpe escorted the trainees along the path and explained each station while Recruit Jensen demonstrated the maneuvers with that same smirk on his face, appearing as if he was just being diligent while hints of righteous indignation oozed out of his pores. Bradford wished he could take him on, one on one, but Drill Sergeant Thorpe shared that this course was going to be a platoon versus platoon competition.

Over the last few weeks, the entire unit had come to know that Jensen was a PK, Preacher's Kid, a title spouted by Jensen himself, of course. The tall and lanky child-man assumed that he was chosen as their fearless leader because of the familial holiness that radiated from his high moral character.

Bradford could not stand guys like that because they competed for the limelight. The former football star's claim to fame would always win over the masses, but those judgmental overtones coming from the whippersnapper made him want to squeeze the victory right of his opponent rather than rely on his rehearsed smiles and clever jokes.

The experienced correctional officer knew that if he could just have five minutes with Jensen, he could force him into submission, but the gentle ways of Recruit Hoyt always knew how to calm him down. "We are supposed to be practicing our submission to others, Bradford, not demanding others submit to us." The hopeful Hoyt calmed the raging beast. "Drill Sergeant Thorpe subtly warned us at the beginning that we would have to exercise submission over time with Jensen."

"What about his need to learn submission?" Bradford almost demanded an answer. "Putting him in charge just feeds into his ego that he was somehow born better than us. That guy truly believes he never did any wrong."

"We have to remember to trust and obey just like that one cadence says," that naïve little Hoyt always resorted to that analogy, but it worked every time thus far.

"You're right. You're right. I am frustrated with him, but you're right," Bradford resigned his on-edge posture and recited the rehearsed expectations. "I know the drill sergeants have a plan for every part of this training, and I have to surrender to it, no matter how difficult it may be at times."

As per protocol, first platoon led the way, and the instructions directed each individual squad to tackle the entire course, ensuring that each member transitioned through each obstacle. Although the guidelines allowed for some autonomy in strategy and tactics, the team of four was required to start and finish as a unified squad, abiding by the boundaries of the contraption and following the premise of the challenge itself. Upon completion the times of all four squads would be averaged together for an overall platoon rating. The objective of the training prompted the individual groups to work together as a small team while encouraging the success of the other squads in their platoon as well. The challenge exercised their submission and service to each other while practicing encouragement and communication.

Practicing seemed to be the common thread of all of this training, and Captain Peters taught it best during his vices and virtues segment. "Virtues are a culmination of all of the aspects of God: love, kindness, mercy, compassion, and so on. Vices are the sinful aspects of our carnal nature that oppose those virtues. Some of the virtues come easier to some of us than others, but you cannot rest on those laurels. You cannot claim your strengths and ignore your weaknesses. You have to allow the Holy Spirit to transform those weaknesses as well, making them stronger and stronger," the blond-haired, blue-eyed teacher lectured from the heart. "The most common question, 'How do I become more virtuous?'"

Bradford replayed that series in his mind, opting to absorb its truths. If he wanted to love Jensen, he would have to be intentional and practice being more loving. The theory sounded so simple, yet the application proved to be very difficult. By nature the middle-aged bachelor lacked the skills to show more mercy, or more forgiveness, or more love, but Captain Peters highlighted some practical examples to, again, practice on each other. This obstacle course was going to be one of their first real field exercises.

At the call to ready themselves, fourth squad shuffled towards their position on the starting line where they could just make out the first two rungs of the obstacle before the surrounding woods hid them from view. With the advantage of seeing the first three squads take off down the dirt trail that led to the first contraption, a set of six horizontal hitching posts, standing about five feet off of the ground separated by about three feet of space, Bradford formulated his plan of attack. "Listen, you guys," the assigned leader rallied his team one last time. "From what I could see, each squad took off like they were racing against time more than anything else. I could see some of them leaving the slower ones behind, stuck on that first log, so I can only assume that they are going to try and meet up somewhere at the end to cross the finish line together."

"I noticed that too," West added. "If you are worried about me, I know I can handle it. You won't have to be waiting on me."

"No, that's not the point, West," Bradford explained. "I think we will do better to make sure that we work together through these obstacles. We need to start and finish each one as a team. I just know it will give us a faster time in the end."

"I don't know, Bradford," West struggled stifling her own two cents. "We don't know that the strategy of those other squads didn't work. If we all go our fastest, then it can encourage the slow ones to go faster."

"Why are you looking at me?" Hoyt surprised even himself that he spoke up. "Okay, okay, it probably will be me, but I will give it my all."

"That's okay, Hoyt. You guys are going to have to trust me on this one. I got a strong feeling this is the way we should attack this," Bradford asserted himself.

"Now, I know you have the gift of discernment and all," West tried not to sound rude, "but doesn't that work more with people, not situations?"

"This has nothing to do with my discernment, West," Bradford also practiced speaking with respect, making every attempt to mask his irritation with West's insistence on not being led. "I have just had to learn the hard way that a team is really more powerful than any individual. Believe me, I wish I had understood that when I was an athlete like I do now. Shoot, I wish even more that I had learned that in my marriages."

"I'm with you, Bradford," Hoyt cast his lot.

"I typically prefer to go it alone myself," Salinas broke his silence, giving West the nod, "but I also know that on my own, I am far weaker than I realized. I'm game."

"Well, I'm not going to be the one to hold us back," West recognized defeat. "I hope you're right, Bradford."

"At the ready," Drill Sergeant Thorpe's command broke into the planning. "Go!"

In a cluster, they sprinted to that first obstacle. Reaching the challenge first, Salinas and West bridged their hands together, giving Bradford an easy step up and over the first log. By that time, Hoyt arrived and stepped in stride up and over. Salinas then knelt down on one leg and braced himself as West sprung on top of his leveled thigh and right over the log.

As soon as she landed, she leaned forward and stepped right onto the platform that Bradford and Hoyt formed with their entwined hands. By that time, Salinas used his upper body strength to heave himself over the first rung and then used the man-made boost to get over the second. They continued through each horizontal log in this manner, ensuring that either Bradford or Salinas used their brute strength to tackle the single components. As their weekly leader suspected, they negotiated that obstacle with astounding efficiency and darted towards the next in no time. Bradford's chest swelled with true thankfulness as his team gleamed with pride at their strategic success while their newfound camaraderie quickened their steps.

The next obstacle demanded the recruits low crawl under some concertina wire. Maintaining their working pairs, West and Salinas dove for the entrenched path on the right while Hoyt and Bradford took the one on the left. On his belly Hoyt stretched and tugged at the packed sand above his head, peeking forward enough to see his next reach. He struggled and leaned towards his left side, scared of the jagged edges hovering just above his back and used his right leg to dig for footing as Bradford sacrificed his head against Hoyt's left foot to bulldoze him forward. Once West and Salinas scurried through their lane, they each knelt and grasped for Hoyt's hand to pull him through the rest of the wired tunnel. As they tossed him aside, they turned back to ease Bradford's burden as well and slid him through. The team moved like clockwork one obstacle at a time without any hesitation.

The third obstacle challenged their balance, hand grip strength, and arm endurance with a six-post stepping course at varied heights that ended at a set of rotating monkey bars. Without hesitation, Salinas negotiated the posts, displaying his soft footedness and low center of gravity. As he sat atop the metal ladder at the end of the first section, the gentle voice guided his teammates across the safest, most effective route.

"Hoyt, you come!" the Latino suggested. "I will help you cross this next part."

Placing his willful trust in his committed supporters, Hoyt stepped and turned as ordered. The youngest member wanted to contemplate the angles and the pain that might result after a fall, but his cheering section kept him focused, and his rather long stride proved advantageous. First one step, then two, and the momentum grew with each success until at the fifth post the gravitational pull kept him moving right off the course and into the pit.

"You're fine, buddy," the leader calmed the fallen one. "Just get back over here and start again."

Hoyt took a deep breath and set off on the narrow stumps again, feeling his accomplishment urge him farther. One step, then two, a third to the right, a fourth towards the left, the fifth, and then... back down into the dirt, his knees smarting something awful from the brief skid.

"Hoyt, you gotta slow down on that one!" West yelled from back at the starting line. "Are you okay?"

The athletically-challenged squad member knelt on the ground, rocking back and forth, wincing in pain.

"Hoyt, are you going to be all right, buddy? Can you make it back over here to the start to try again?" Bradford set the tone.

"Just give me a sec," Hoyt answered as he stood, raised his

pant legs to assess the damage, and reported, "No blood. I think I can make it, but it sure does sting. I think there may even be some pebbles wedged in there."

"You got this, buddy!" Bradford hollered.

"Hoyt, go slower, and before you get to that post, I want you to stop and look at me," Salinas encouraged with his cool tone.

Hoyt's nerves shook as he wobbled and tottered on every single post while West began to panic, growing leery of the squad's ability to conquer this obstacle. Her mind raced to formulate another plan of attack. "Maybe one of us should help him across these things too."

"No need," Salinas interjected. "He's got this."

"Uh, are you sure?" she offered, startled by the uncharacteristic response.

"You know I can hear you, right?" Hoyt added.

"You have this, buddy!" Bradford took over. "Just one at a time and then make connection with Salinas just like he told you."

"That's it!" Salinas guided. "Now, look at me. You need to step with your left foot over to that post, then throw your body towards me, towards this last one right here."

As he teetered and tottered on that fifth post, Hoyt thrust his movement forward and to the right winning over his lack of balance by a hair. Before the trainee hit the ground yet again, Salinas grabbed his shirt sleeve and yanked him across the ladder.

"Fantastico!" the Spanish one encouraged. "Now, put your right foot on that bottom bar before you fall off of this thing."

"Great job, Hoyt!" Bradford and West bolstered from behind.

"You two have to go ahead and cross those monkey bars because there is not going to be enough room for all of us to stop there," the leader shouted.

"Sí, I will help him!" Salinas called back. "Hoyt, listen. Some of these bars move, remember? But it is pretty wide, so I will go first. If I come to a bar that moves, I will hang there and wait for you. I am sure that I can hold it in place."

"Okay," Hoyt's hesitation showed.

"It will work!"

"What if there are two in a row that move?" the mathematical mind aimed to consider all possible outcomes.

"For those, we will move together," Salinas answered with boldness.

As the pair began their methodical dance across the monkey bars, Bradford rehearsed his strategy with West. "Do you think we should try that?"

"No!" she blurted. "I can cross them myself, even if they do move. I'm a lot more capable than you think!"

"Okay, okay," Bradford backed off. "After you!"

They learned a lot about each other during that course. No, first platoon did not win the competition, but Bradford's squad turned in the fastest leg. With the sweet relief of victory, he thought he would want to gloat to Jensen, pointing out that first squad had the slowest lap, causing the biggest drop in their average, but that desire had long diminished. The staunch competitor shocked even himself that he was far more concerned about their efforts than the win.

He also focused more of his energy on thoughts of leading his squad through the Leadership Reaction Course coming up the following day. They had started to build something solid during that challenge, and he knew he wanted to nourish that. He did not know when his care and concern for his teammates deepened, and maybe his age caused him to be so protective of them, but he wanted each of them to realize their worth to the overall success of the squad.

CHAPTER 24

West

Even West enjoyed the emotional high from the teamwork that her squad experienced the day before. Although she maintained reservations about these guys, she ignored her deep-rooted issues with trusting people in general, but men most certainly, for the sake of the mission. Prior to the field training, the rebel female envisioned she would be able to avoid submitting to their leadership. She figured she would either be able to convince them to follow her suggestions, or she would appear agreeable only to do her own thing and force them to see the error of their ways.

Raised by her mother with little to no relationship with her father, West mastered the art of manipulation to escape the pains of her home life. Her parents divorced when she was too young to even remember that they were ever together, and the two of them concocted the grand idea of splitting her and her brother apart, avoiding the need for the exchange of child support and thus communication altogether. Her brother lived with her father as it was proper for a man to raise a man, and her mother assumed responsibility of her, reciprocating the concept. While the divided couple avoided arguing over money or co-parenting, they managed to isolate the kids from one of their parents as well as a sibling. By some standards the unprecedented arrangement proved to be the perfect solution, yet it left West bitter and confused.

The devoted daughter loved her mother, sympathetic to the parent's failed attempts to secure the stability that she relegated to find in one man after the other. Sometimes they lived with a boyfriend that had a beautiful home on the ritzier side of town, and other times they shacked up with a guy that lived in a dump but drove an impressive Harley. In either case the common story involved her mother meeting some stranger at a bar that shared a mutual passion for wallowing in sorrows over joints or drinks. The setup lasted for a few years at a time until some explosive combination of the guy's aggressive nature and her mom's apparent inability to manage even the smallest amount of money blew up, sending the gals packing once again. Her mother at least retained the foresight to have another invitation waiting in the wings as the cycle reset.

West swore that she would break the patterns of her mother, so she always tried to have a job and worked hard to pay for the things that she needed. Sometimes she caved to her mother's pleas to help pay for a bill here or there. "Darby, sweetie, don't you love this house?" Her mom hinted that a move was imminent if she did not help hide her inability to keep up her side of the housing agreement.

"Of course, Mom. It's great. How much are you short?" West gave up reasoning with her mother about the path that led to this repetitive scene each time. The capable daughter just contributed her finances as best she could and began her savings all over again.

The scorned young woman also relinquished her unrealistic fantasies about what life would have been like with her dad. When West was still young, her dad remarried, and the blissful couple made no effort to maintain a relationship with the girl. Since a toddler, the striking beauty received praise about how much she resembled her mother, so she was not sure if the mere presence of her company caused more issue with her dad or his wife. All she knew was that he must have been weak and worthless to have agreed to the custody arrangement.

And so her struggle with a warped impression of men and their inability to love and serve for a lifetime took root. Even when the endearing sergeant shared with her that men too could live a life surrendered to Jesus, the target ignored the fantastical claim. Because West had never witnessed such a transformation, she resigned that belief stemmed from experience. Her survival depended on keeping the opposite sex at arm's length and relying on her own strengths.

At Ford Gideon during the previous day's obstacle course, the triumph seemed insignificant on the grand scale of life because in many ways, after all, the challenge was just a game, but the obligation to follow Bradford's lead loosened the chains of bondage within her. Convinced that she would find some way to take over along the path, West held her tongue, but after that first station, the new believer functioned in unison with her partners. As the persistent woman refocused on their collective strengths, the abiding camaraderie kept her glued to Salinas's coattails. When her squad crossed that finish line, she distinguished a cultivating conversion rattling within that answered the call to the mission and her new friends.

With her hands clenched at her knees, propping up her body while she caught her breath, her heart pounded as Bradford patted her left shoulder with his right hand and Salinas's shoulder with his left hand. "We did it, you guys. We did it," Bradford congratulated them as if they just survived a fierce battle.

Hoyt slid his arm off of Salinas's shoulders which had helped to support him across the line. "I can't thank you guys enough," Hoyt's words forced out between deep breaths. "I would have never been able to do that without you all."

"We all did it together," Bradford offered encouragement to Hoyt and then grasped West's shoulder, insisting that she look at him. "Thanks for trusting me, West. You were incredible out there."

With a simple nod back at him, she hoped that he thought her just too exhausted to form a verbal response. She trusted him. To her surprise, she trusted all of them. Their common goal had somehow managed to erase a life's worth of baggage if only for a moment, and the recruit felt peace. She admired each one of those men for their unique gifts to calm, motivate, encourage, and guide—an impossible emotion, she thought. West clung to the renewed hope, not wanting to reason it away, but instead bottled it for a rainy day that she assumed would come soon enough.

Perhaps this Leadership Reaction Course would put things back into proper perspective. The Obstacle Course could have been a fluke, and Bradford's true colors could permeate this new challenge.

As the squad bobbed to and fro on the cattle truck, Bradford laid out his strategy. "This course is going to be different than yesterday's," Bradford opened. "Drill Sergeant Thorpe is not going to give us a preview of the stations. We are going to have to tackle them on our own. All we know for certain is that they are more like puzzles than the obstacles were."

"Do you have any idea what we might be up against?" Hoyt sounded concerned.

"I have no clue," Bradford confessed. "But I am counting on your logical mind, Hoyt, to figure it out."

"Me? Oh, I don't know about that. I'm sure they're not going to be like any puzzles I deal with," Hoyt tried in desperation to diminish any expectations.

To her surprise, West felt protective of Hoyt. Different than most guys that she knew, he seemed so sweet and innocent, almost as if the world had not had its chance to corrupt him yet. She also saw that as a weakness, not certain that she wanted to rely on Hoyt's cerebral abilities either. "I'm sure we can figure it out," she attempted to relieve him of the uncomfortable spotlight while hinting that she was more than capable of taking on any challenge.

Bradford did not pick up on the subtleties. "Right, West. Just like yesterday, we are going to have to conquer them one at a time as a team."

With the path winding away into obscurity, fourth squad lost their advantage point as they shuffled up to the starting line. The thirty minutes of separation between each leg proved to be an added hindrance, giving each of the members more time to settle back into their individual identities.

The familiar voice of Drill Sergeant Thorpe shouted the command, "Fourth squad, at the ready…go!"

Off they went, the beaten path making its way through the thick of the woods. Their plan of attack required Salinas to hustle to the station, find their instruction bag, and lay out any tools provided. When Hoyt trickled in and caught his breath, West read the challenge instructions aloud to the entire group. From there, all options were presented for discussion.

"Okay, according to the rules of this one," West summarized what she read, "we have to get everyone over that twelve-foot wall using only that twelve-foot-high bar and this rope, but we can't touch the water."

At first, they tried to loop the rope around the bar to make a swing, but it was too short. Finally, Hoyt regained his ability to speak and chimed in. "We got to get someone on that high bar to tie the rope to it. Then we can make a swing over to the wall," he spoke with confidence.

"Okay, okay," Bradford appeared more than willing to give it a go. "But, how are we going to scale that wall? It's flat."

"I can do it." The quiet Salinas knew when to interject. "You guys boost me to that high bar so that I can get my hands on it, and I know I can get myself up. I will tie the rope, get to the wall, and then I can help you all up and over."

West wanted to offer some advice, influence the situation somehow, but she had nothing. Hoyt sounded so certain, and she could not argue with his logic, and Salinas presented his part as if he had done it a million times before. She had no choice but to go with it.

"Let's do it!" Bradford gave the green light.

West and Hoyt helped Salinas up and onto Bradford's shoulders, and then he jumped to the high bar and kept his momentum. As the agile recruit contorted his body, he forced a couple of giant swings until he heaved his core right onto that bar like a seasoned gymnast. The mighty Latino managed to straddle the rail, anchoring himself with his feet around one of the vertical side posts and then secured a sturdy knot. West thought he was going to use the rope somehow to get himself over to the wall, but he caught them all by surprise when he steadied himself atop the bar and then dove for the wall. The rest of them gasped when Salinas made the leap, catching the top of the wall with his hands and hoisting himself on top.

"Wow, dude, that was amazing!" Hoyt shouted, blown away at Salinas's ingenuity and strength.

"Well, okay then," Bradford echoed.

"West," Salinas ordered as he swung the rope back toward his comrades. "You first."

The determined trainee grabbed the rope at its peak and leapt without hesitation. The smack against the wall stung, but she shook it off, and Salinas reacted to take hold of the rope above her. He strained and pulled until he reached her hand, and then they worked together to get her over. To her relief, the other side of the wall had several wooden rungs which allowed West to secure herself a spot.

"Now you, Hoyt," Salinas showed such confidence in their present task.

Bradford held the very bottom of the rope so that Hoyt could get a higher grip. The kid swung and smacked, but this time both Salinas and West pulled to get him up. With just Bradford left, the last effort took all three of them to pull the sturdy giant, but his long wingspan helped.

"Okay, here I come," Bradford warned.

West wanted to laugh at the heavy grunt Bradford let out when he hit the wall, but she stifled her criticism and played her part in getting him up. They heaved twice until Hoyt locked arms with him, and then Bradford climbed the thin trainee like a rope to scale the rest of the way.

As they eased their way down the other side, even West wanted to bask in the glory of what they had just accomplished, but Salinas kept the steady clip and raced towards the next station.

CHAPTER 25

Hoyt

Hoyt felt alive. Although the physical demands of the camp produced innovative challenges unlike he had ever experienced before, he belonged. As his new friends helped him negotiate the obstacles, they sought him out for logistical advice. They valued his contributions and minimized his shortcomings, and he felt full in the face of adversity.

By the time the trailer reached the final obstacle, bending at the gut to concentrate on his huffing and puffing, Salinas had already aligned the three wooden planks side-by-side with the barrel rolled upright. Without having to hear the instructions, Hoyt hurried his belabored breathing to spout the plan of attack. "I know what to do."

"Don't you want me to read the task first?" West sounded, concerned that they may miss a detail.

"I'm sure we have to use these planks to get us and this barrel over to the other side," Hoyt continued. "Just read through it yourself, West, to make sure I am not missing anything. I will get started."

The notorious problem-solver forged through the tightness of his lungs, grabbed the longest board, and timbered it across the expanse of the shallow ditch. Directing Bradford to position the short plank perpendicular across the base of the first board and then stand on it with Salinas, Hoyt trusted his anchors and walked the plank, tucking the third board under his arm. Like a sloth, he sat on the end of the bouncy piece of pine, pushing the recent memories of falling out of his mind. Using every ounce of arm and back strength he could muster, the recruit grimaced and grunted as he guided one end of the third slat to the opposite side of the ditch, resting the closest end atop the board in between his legs. With the pieces in place, the loner glanced back at his team like a newborn foal, knowing standing up would require the utmost control of his balance.

"You got this, buddy," Bradford detected his need for support.

"We got you," Salinas added.

Hoyt nodded back like a malfunctioning bobblehead as if any unnecessary noise on his part might jeopardize the mission, pulled his feet into a tuck, rolled like an overgrown walrus onto his belly, and then teetered and tottered his way into an upright position. Although the animated maneuver succeeded in getting him up, he found himself facing his teammates instead of the landing zone. As the soldier breathed deep and exhaled his concerns, he executed the perfect about-face and lunged for the other side in fleeting vigor.

"Yes, you did it!" Bradford cheered.

"Now look who is amazing," Salinas reciprocated Hoyt's earlier praise.

Even West applauded her uncoordinated buddy. "Wow, Hoyt. You got it. Instructions all look good."

"Okay, guys," Hoyt curbed the adoration to direct his team across the muddy divide. "Now, West, you roll that barrel in front of you as you make your way across here."

West obliged as she pushed the barrel inch by inch, steadying herself with each step until Hoyt assumed the control on dry ground and moved it from her path. After West pranced her way to safe pasture, Bradford steadied the anchor, so that the nimble

Salinas could skirt across the wobbly bridge, straddle the hanging intersection, and reverse the supported position.

With Hoyt and West utilizing the weight of the barrel to help secure a perpendicular lock on the third board, the skillful immigrant relied on the weight and strength of the course leader to keep him out of the muck and endured an imposing bounce as he scraped the ends of the boards apart and back together again. Upon the successful transition with the first pine now resting atop the third, Salinas continued heel to toe the rest of the way. As directed, Bradford then picked up the short board and staggered with it across the overpass, his three teammates bearing the brunt of his steps with the help of the barrel.

To achieve the required goal, however, Salinas tiptoed his way back to the suspending link, took a seat, and slid that first plank across his head with the added support of his soft curls until his squad could offer relief. Once the agile recruit jumped onto the embankment, Bradford swiveled that last board to safety, and they all raced across the finish line.

With Hoyt as their mastermind, the motley unit conquered that course and radiated with plenty of high fives and you are the mans. The praise and adoration reminded the loner of that day at the recruiting office with the sergeant. "You are wonderfully made, and God wants to use everything about you for His divine purpose," the recruiter spoke life into the weary soul that day.

As belief began to take root, Hoyt considered the innate purpose of his intellect, his abilities, his experiences, waging their significance as much more than a means to secure a good job that paid well. The camaraderie in which his present circumstances bolstered him defied his imagination, his cornerstone of reason. *Oh, use me, Lord,* the tender heart prayed on the jolting ride back to the barracks. *Continue to use me, please.*

CHAPTER 26

Salinas

After an exceptional physical training session that morning, Salinas basked in the rejuvenation of their silent run amidst the beautiful creation of their surroundings. At first he thought the efforts of the demand futile because he had grown accustomed to keeping a watchful eye on the calculated movements in the background or deciphering the triggers of unwelcome signs and sounds. In Mexico he had trained as a lookout in the petty crime circles like pick-pocketing, shoplifting, and chicken snatching, and then graduated to the more intricate crime circuits later. In the US the illegal immigrant scanned the leering eyes of social circles, detecting the judgmental expressions of class discrimination or moral indignation.

Without provocation, though, he began to feel God's presence during those early morning runs, and as his paranoia eased, the trainee began to witness the majesty and splendor in all of creation. He marveled at the intricacies of trees, birds, and even the morning dew and the humility of his God-given authority.

After the first week when they muddled along out of an act of obedience, Drill Sergeant Thorpe challenged her ability group to consider the Bible verses that they were memorizing or some of the other aspects of the Word that they were learning. With the helpful hints to aid the mundane attributes of the quiet, sometimes Salinas thought about the covenants and how God structured relationships this way throughout history. Sometimes he used his imagination to replay the Gospel of Mark in his head as if he were Peter. Would he have thought or acted differently than the brash disciple? Sometimes he meditated on the beatitudes and rehearsed in his mind how he might act with love towards those he encountered. As the steady pace mellowed the movements of the pack, Salinas lowered his guard and started to treasure the solitude. Like a daily fill of joy, peace, and righteous fortitude, the dedicated act to meditate on the way of the Lord burrowed deeper and deeper.

Drill Sergeant Thorpe's subsequent change of direction elevated the intentional progression. "This morning, I want to move you all from meditation to prayer. Now most people assume prayer is a laundry list of needs or wants, but prayer is first listening."

The concept sounded foreign to the ritualistic ears because even his abuela and mama lit candles to this saint or that saint under the premise of a request. What would the convert be listening for?

Drill Sergeant Thorpe continued her morning lesson, "Prayer is communication with Jesus. It is having relationship with him. If you never listen to Him, well, now, that's just not much of a relationship, now is it?"

Their exercise leader had a point there. Although Anna accused him of not being a good communicator, the well-rehearsed performer sat in abiding silence, rarely adding to her lecture, because most times the sly one knew that if he said too much, he would trip over some of his lies. As an effort of concealment, he learned to just tell the wife what she wanted to hear and go about his merry way. Most times the elusive technique bought him at least a month of solace before the couple recycled back to the same old discussions about her unproven insecurities.

His communication with Jesus, however, had to be different. The novice soldier wanted it to be different. Desperate to shelve his clever cover ups and manipulative tactics to skirt the issues, the committed Christ-follower developed an unquenchable thirst for the never-ending supply of forgiveness and soul cleansing that accompanied the redeeming relationship of the Savior. No longer able to employ the decoys of a potential language barrier, the sinner embraced the pains of spiritual confrontation for the gentle comfort of conversing with the Lord of Lords and King of Kings, knowing that the new man germinated in the process of maturation.

Drill Sergeant Thorpe spoke again, "When you surrendered your life to Jesus, you heard His voice, so you know what it sounds like."

Salinas had heard Him that day at the restaurant with the sergeant. The inaudible voice of Jesus beckoned the runaway from within, and the new disciple found the experience difficult to explain to unbelieving ears. How could the indescribable be described? However, the gentle call fell silent as the trainee busied himself with preparations for camp, conversations with his wife and family, and the pursuit of study for the sake of righteous knowledge. Although his efforts of obedience and active participation in joining God's army answered his divine calling, the soldier had not heard Him often. Would the redeemed one still recognize His voice? With the demanding requirements of the camp stirring his emotions, how could he be certain it was Jesus anyway and not his own thoughts or even the enemy masking as an angel of light?

"Remember, if you hear something contrary to the Word, then you know it is not Him. Jesus is the Word, and that is exactly why you gotta know it, study it, hide it in your heart," Drill Sergeant Thorpe finished her instructions and continued the run in typical silence.

As Salinas weighed her comments against his own experience, he re-focused his attention on listening. At first the methodic footsteps of his unit and the patterned breathing of the soldiers to his right and left distracted his cerebral search for the voice of Jesus. In desperation for Him, the runner scanned the woodlands and begged his thoughts to unite with his eyes in meditation as a means of pleading for His presence. As he battled for control, the paranoia of the past reared its ugly head, the fading remnants of the old man wondering what others might be thinking.

"Dirty Mexican."

"Illegal. Go back to your own country."

"You are a liar and a cheat, and you will always be a liar and a cheat."

"You don't deserve to be here. You aren't good enough."

In defeat, Salinas stared down at his feet and bellowed from his heart, *Oh, Lord, help me. Help me.*

"I am here, Artemio. I am here, and I love you."

Jesus, is that you? Salinas was startled at the calm yet powerful presence that eased its way into his thoughts.

"Yes, Artemio. I love you."

That was it. Nothing else was said to him that day. Salinas did recognize His voice just as Drill Sergeant Thorpe said he would. Jesus did not preach him a sermon, condemn him for his lack of faith, or even usher him into some apocalyptic revelation. The Lord's words were short, simple, and powerful, and the recruit realized how much he needed to hear the affirmation. As he stayed the pooling of his emotional tears, the committed trainee raised his head and responded, *Thank you, Lord. Thank you.*

Encounter

Always tight on money, the Hoyt family participated in free activities like playing hot box at the park, sitting on the roof of the front porch to watch fireworks, or hiking along the trails around the lake just north of town. However, one day in late October when the youngest was in second grade, Mr. Hoyt announced that the whole troop was going to the haunted house on the south end. The kids piled into the car, radiating with pride, excitement, and anticipation as if the impromptu excursion elevated their social standing.

After waiting in the long line, Dad paid for the tickets, and the six of them squeezed into an elevator with two other families to begin the ascent to the great scare. When a grinding thump of the winch set the metal room to teeter and rock and the lights hissed and flickered, the ensuing darkness initiated a curdling scream from the entire group. The three sisters huddled together as if they loved each other so dearly, their feuds about clothes buried deep in the past, while Mom looped her arm through Dad's and leaned on his shoulder. Little Hoyt curled himself around his father's leg and gaped at the shadows of the other families, making similar embraces to protect their own. With a continuous rumble reverberating through the floor, the electricity sizzled and zinged as the lights sparked, battling their way back to their task to illuminate, when, out of nowhere, surfaced... Dracula.

The horrendous vampire roared at his captive audience with his hands grasping the edges of his cape while his arms rose into the air as if taking off in flight. Just enough red fluorescent light peered from beneath his chin to reveal his long sharp fangs, and the entire elevator shrieked with shrills of horror and alarming fright that dwindled into sighs of relief and approving giggles. Hoyt's lone, angelic voice continued to scream from the bellows of his gut as he turned his head to the ceiling, moving from side to side to rid his mind of the terror. With his eyes glued shut to eliminate any trace of the dreadful vision, he clenched his arms and legs around his dad like a frightened koala.

The bemused child was brought to by the return of the lights and his dad's stern yet reassuring voice that all was okay as he pried his son's pudgy fingers from their death grip. As the patriarch advised his mom to take the snickering girls on ahead, Dracula knelt down and confessed that he was just a college student doing this stint as a part-time gig, but the young Hoyt could not be convinced. Nothing was going to deter him from getting out of there, so he and his dad sauntered hand-in-hand against the grain of the line back to the car to wait for the rest of the family.

"Fear of man will prove to be a snare, but whoever trusts in the Lord is kept safe." (Proverbs 29:25, NIV)

CHAPTER 27

Hoyt

Although he had been apprehensive about the moment, Hoyt's turn as weekly squad leader had arrived. When his friends held the position, the timid soldier took mental notes of their strategies to encourage teamwork, emphasize strengths, and forgive weaknesses, but the practical application of his findings begged for more time for careful analysis.

With the firing range and the rappelling towers looming over his reign, the video-gamer hoped that the mechanics of the two challenges replicated that of the mock versions that he experienced. The only time that Hoyt even cradled a weapon in his frail hands involved a birthday and an adventurous game of paintball.

As a way to allow for a mixing of the genders while limiting opportunity for any hanky-panky, his folks scheduled the event for one of his sister's first guy-girl parties. The first round of competition pitted the males against the females, but the dopey brother got stuck with the girls to balance out the numbers. As the token tagalong, he envisioned serving his time at the video games in the lounge area, but when the gals ended up one person shy, his fate was sealed.

"Bri..." the sister closest to him always used that pet name when she wanted something, "please?"

"Please?" her girlfriends chimed in.

"Oh, okay," the pushover caved.

The crux of the rivalry mimicked capture the flag. Hoyt and the ladies started on one end of the tree line and the guys started at the other with the order to maneuver through the woods, capture the other team's flag, and then bask in the victory. The unassuming fill-in never knew what hit him.

To play it safe, the reluctant guardian hid behind a tree near the flag while the girls set out to annihilate the boys. While resting against the prickly bark of an oak, imagining the safety of a good game of Ms. Pac-Man, the rattle of incoming fire whizzed past his right and left flanks. Pulling his legs in tight to avoid the onslaught, the bouncing balls of paint ricocheted in rapid succession against the hard ground just inches from his feet and pummeled his shins. Although the force of the repeated blasts inflicted its pain, the plastic spheres never even broke. Convinced that the opposing force found greater pleasure in bombarding the keeper than capturing the flag that lay defenseless behind the next tree, the blow of the referee's whistle and the distant cheers of the girls ended the relentless barrage.

Oh sure, the appreciative gals doted on their brave and clever deterrent, thanking him for his sacrifice, when in all honesty, he was just downright stuck. With the welts on his pasty-white legs pulsating and growing by the minute, the stifled Hoyt bit his lip and hobbled all of the way back to the lodge until he secured himself within a bathroom stall. Once perched in seclusion upon the toilet, his battered legs out of view, the broken spirit just huddled there and cried, trying to make as little noise as possible.

With no concept of Fort Gideon's weapons qualification phase, the token leader squelched his fears and listened with forced optimism.

"You will keep your weapons directed down range at all times!" Drill Sergeant Akpore bellowed down the line "You will face your body in whatever direction you are moving, but your weapon will remain pointing down range at all times. Am I clear, recruits?"

"Yes, drill sergeant!" they all replied with fervent enthusiasm.

Finding their voice in this simple act of responding had become second nature to them now. Some recruits had no problem sounding off, but for others, like Hoyt who preferred to be seen and not heard, it was an uphill battle. Growing in confidence over the duration of the progressive schedule, he attempted to roar with the best of them.

The concept of this particular exercise involved an act of discernment, recognizing friend versus foe, and the M-16 served as a training tool. After a short stint at the zeroing range where the soldiers practiced the breathing, relaxing, aiming, and squeezing technique of firing and adjusted their sights based on the calculations of their hits, they graduated to the live rounds. With his nerves floundering like a fish out of water, Hoyt adhered to the drill sergeant's explicit instructions. Although the squeeze step proved bothersome because he kept jerking the trigger, the trainee managed three rounds in the target's perimeter and joined his patient squad mates at the next range.

As the man in charge, Hoyt led them, single file, onto the shooting ground as they marched in unison forward and to the left, keeping their weapons to the right in stoic compliance. Assigned a concrete foxhole, each soldier placed his M-16 next to the sandbags stacked two high in front of the rim of the chasm. Moving only when instructed, he eased into the hole and readied his position for the first shot.

Hoyt adjusted his sandbags to bear the weight of his barrel while still giving him enough maneuverability to pivot his sights to the right or to the left. Orienting himself to his lane, the shooter perused the well-manicured fairway that had been carved out of the tall, dark forest. Even in the daylight, the surrounding woods appeared hushed and eerie. Although the plush green center highlighted the smooth rolls in the terrain, the shadows of the looming trees cast an unnerving pattern near the back and the sides.

As Hoyt settled into his supported prone position, every breath rattled his ears as if it were on speaker for surround sound. His heavy Kevlar helmet forced the center of his glasses onto the bridge of his nose, and the dirt and dust stuck in his throat while the jagged edges of the loose rock poked into his elbows. As he tried to steady his hold, his eyelids blinked without ceasing, begging his ducts to maintain their moisture, and the rim of his glasses cropped the periphery.

With the first magazine clip of five bullets locked and loaded for the practice round, the dark silhouettes of enemy targets flipped up in random order across his lane. As the alarming blast of his weapon echoed in his ears with each conscientious squeeze of the trigger, the sporadic pops of the other rifles along the line clattered with surprising innocence, almost like firecrackers. The pounding of his chest urged him to keep his focus on the forward terrain. *"This is a dangerous exercise, recruits,"* Drill Sergeant Akpore's warnings replayed in Hoyt's mind. *"Look alive out there. Stay focused and stick to your training."*

The metallic rattles of the line switching magazine clips quieted as the alarm signaled that the qualifying round had begun and now friendly targets would appear interspersed amongst the foe. Hoyt pushed up his helmet one last time, ensuring his view was not further hindered by his equipment. The nervous Nellie breathed deep into his gut and controlled his exhale, scanning the lane from left to right without moving his head. He had to focus and not just react because, like spoken words, once that round left the chamber, there was no getting it back.

After qualifying with their weapons, fourth squad utilized their ride to the rappelling towers in the back of an old wobbly Deuce and Half to summarize the previous training event.

"I'm impressed, Hoyt," Bradford broke the silence. "I've had plenty of shooting experience in the DOC, so I was a bit cocky going onto the range. I'm more than satisfied with qualifying sharpshooter, but I will have to admit that I was pleasantly surprised to hear that you qualified expert."

"You and me both," Hoyt resounded.

"Yeah, good job, buddy," West offered her genuine support.

"I am impressed too," Salinas remarked as he patted Hoyt on the back. "Better than I could do."

"Thanks, you guys." Hoyt was so humbled by the adoration. "I really can't take credit. I was so scared, but I just kept remembering what Drill Sergeant Akpore taught us. I just did what he said."

"That is the real key, isn't it?" Salinas added, "It is putting what we have learned into action."

"Good point, Salinas," said Hoyt. "I mean, I don't have the gift of discernment or anything, but I did rely a lot on remembering just a couple different aspects of the enemy targets during that practice round. When the target would pop up, I just quickly went through that list in my mind and shot at any target that matched."

Bradford spoke up, "That is a perfect point, Hoyt. It is kind of like how we have to hold onto truths from the Bible and be able to recognize when stuff people say doesn't match."

"You're right," West said, intrigued by the conversation. "When they talked about discernment as part of the training objective, I assumed it had to do with the gift of discernment, like what you have, Bradford. I thought I was kind of being set up for failure since that gift didn't come up on my assessment."

"Right, right," Bradford understood. "I hear ya. It was about a different kind of discernment, wasn't it?"

"Sì, yes," Salinas provided his calm assurance. "This type of discernment is available to all of us. We all have to be able to sink our teeth into the Word and not be easily fooled."

"What do you think they really want us to learn about this place?" Hoyt nodded out the window as the cattle truck came to a slow stop at the base of the rappelling tours.

"I'm pretty confident that this one is as it seems," Salinas replied. "This one is about faith and trust."

Drill Sergeant Burroughs hollered for the squad to hightail it out of the parked truck, grab a rope, and form a semicircle in front of him for careful instructions on weaving a Swiss seat. "This lifeless piece of thick string might look like a scrap to most of you, but it will be your lifeline for this challenge," the trainer relished the dramatic significance that he described for his novice mountaineers. "Pay close attention and do just as I do!"

With the message received, the four teammates kept quiet as they mimicked their instructor's every twist and turn in knotting their rappelling harnesses. With a loop at the midpoint of the rope, each trainee started at the hip of his weak arm, around his waist, two crosses in the front, through the legs for a very awkward and uncomfortable crotch hold, back to the hips for a half-hitch, and a final return to the weak side for a square knot tied off with two final half-hitches.

"Looks good!" Drill Sergeant Burroughs praised. "Now, unwind it and do it again!"

Three more times the recruits created the single-strand harnesses until the complex contraption became almost second nature. With a careful final inspection, the instructor awarded each crew member with a carabineer, a word of wisdom, and a firm tug for good measure. "Screw down, so that you don't screw up!"

This basic training program was chock full of little quips to help a soldier remember a simple yet important aspect of safety. Hoyt was not clear why the closing of the D-ring needed to be rotated closed from the top down, but he had learned not to argue against the gems of wisdom shared by the veterans.

After some final directions on getting connected to the rappelling ropes atop the tower and the belaying components on ground level, the four-man squad climbed the forty-seven-foot ascent. Recruit Hoyt in particular found comfort that Captain Peters, a fellow scholar, conducted the sky-high operations. Perhaps their collective love for the discipline of study yielded a common reservation for the possible painful challenges of the more physical ones.

The cool breeze that rustled through the red, orange, and yellow leaves that prepared for their own fall from on high caused concern for the leader of the week. He was not scared of heights per se, but it was an affinity for avoiding injury that stifled his fluid movement about the wooden-railed platform.

"As you walk over towards me, raise both hands up and behind your head, so that I can hook you in without hindrance," Captain Peters ordered with the same serious tone that he utilized in the classroom. "You will sound off as you glance back over your shoulder to signal to Drill Sergeant Burroughs to reply with his belay status."

The process sounded simple enough, yet the whispers in the wind and the chants from the birds perched so near seemed to warn the frightful young man that danger lay just beyond the edge. Why was this training necessary anyway? Was he going to be required to scale tall buildings or be dropped into combat by helicopter to spread the Good News of Jesus? Faith? Trust? Couldn't those virtues be practiced easier with that one game where one person stands open armed behind another person and the other person closes his eyes, crosses his arms against his chest, and falls back? Wouldn't that practical application be just a bit safer?

"So, who's going first?" Captain Peters ushered an invitation.

"Me!" West replied with over-joyous enthusiasm. As she took a determined step towards their classroom instructor, Bradford raised his arm to block her path and halt her progress.

"Hoyt is our squad leader this week," the older one remarked. "He should lead the way here."

"Oh, I don't mind," the chosen one replied, hoping to mask his inner terror. "I can wait."

"No, it has got to be you. Set the example," Salinas chimed in certain of Bradford's intent.

"Really guys," Hoyt pleaded. "We are all going to end up down there in a few minutes anyway. It is not a big deal about who goes first."

"No, they're right, Hoyt," West conceded, realizing the need to support their friend. "We are here to follow you."

"Let's do this!" Captain Peters bellowed. "It is getting windier up here by the minute."

Knowing that he had no real escape route, the conscientious objector approached with his surrendered hands shaking behind his head and the click of his carabineer marking his doom.

"Now your left hand on top of the rope in front and your right hand tucked tightly behind, keep scooting back," Captain Peters directed. "That's good. Now sound off!"

"Hoyt on rappel," the high-pitched voice squeaked, exposing his disguise.

"Burroughs on belay!" the deep bellowing reply came from somewhere down in the bottomless abyss of pain.

"Now, just start leaning back! Keep those legs nice and straight until you form an L," the topside guide encouraged.

Hoyt took one final look at his three new best friends, certain their concerned faces just might be the last things he ever had the joy of seeing. West looked almost sad. Bradford projected that glad-to-know-you expression, and Salinas managed a wink and a thumbs-up.

"Get ready to start walking down!" Peters instructed.

The overwhelming angst of it all must have clogged the young recruit's ears because he just continued to lean and lean, certain a death-inducing fall was soon to ensue, until the breath-taking pinch around his sides and the blood rushing to his head broke his silence. "Owwww!"

"You got yourself hung upside down, recruit!" Burroughs chided. "Now, get your wits about you and get those feet against that tower and start moving!"

"But my ribs are going to break!"

"I will loosen my hold once you get moving!" the safety brake hollered up to his target.

Hoyt felt like an awkward tap dancer as he shimmied his boots against the slick wooden surface and managed to start getting his head back in the upright position. In his animated efforts, the awkward one rotated just a little too far as the full force of his face planted against the sanded planks. In a gut-wrenching attempt to ignore the bruising sting and without further provocation, the fancy dance began again, the embarrassed anger rising from within, and Hoyt wrestled back into his stiff L-shaped position.

When he glanced to the top to discern his progress down the enormous tower thus far, the challenged competitor rolled his eyes at his measly six-foot descent. With the helpful cadence calls of lefts and rights from his physical training instructor manning the bottom of the ropes, the timid rappeler made contact with the ground, scooted backwards off the main line, only tripping over himself once, and then voiced his final report. "Hoyt off rappel!"

"Burroughs off belay!"

CHAPTER 28

Salinas

"Recruit Salinas, this is you!" the stocky black bus driver peered back at him through the rearview mirror and smiled.

Salinas rubbed his eyes, fastened his web gear, slid out of his seat at the back, and headed down the black rubber aisle. Just before turning towards the exit, he grabbed the set of instructions from the driver's extended hand and stuffed them into his right cargo pocket. As the trainee reached that last step on his ride to the middle of nowhere, the friendly bus driver gave him one more send-off. "Godspeed, Salinas. Godspeed."

The recruit nodded his head in acceptance of the call and stepped onto the next playing field. When the keen observer scanned to his right and then back to his left with nothing else in view but rows of shriveling corn for as long as the eye could see, the bus door folded shut behind him, the air brakes released, and the tires rotated down the gravel dirt road toward the next recruit's drop station. As the lone navigator watched his ride disappear across the horizon, the sun making its final descent behind him, the astute listener never heard the bus halt again and reasoned that the next stop lay farther than the travel of sound. Wishing he had warded off the trance-like rhythms of the droning motor and paid closer attention to the recruits that had been dropped off before him, the soldier knelt down in the cracked dirt at the edge of the field to plot his points.

Over the last week the trainees learned how to read a topographical map, plot points, use a compass, and shoot an azimuth. They narrowed down their pace count, numbering only every left step, and even practiced their new skills on a few smaller land navigation courses around the playground equipment near the mess hall.

The experienced traveler negotiated the beginner modules with ease. In a flat piece of terrain closest to the ball diamonds, a hodgepodge of wooden stakes with round, white numbered disks created a non-sequential puzzle. One platoon at a time, the recruits crisscrossed paths as the directions led them to the points in varying order, challenging the soldiers to maintain an account of distance and direction while avoiding the potential collisions of organized chaos. The humorous scene of a gaggle of adults scurrying about from task to task resembled the arduous workings of ants running along the crack in the cement on a hot summer day.

The second practice course proved a bit more challenging as the participants hiked up and over a few hills and through some sparse woods set just behind the picnic area. Although the points hid from view, the trainees still ran across each other, stopping near bushes, stumbling upon numbers, and then setting off on another hunt.

Having loads of experience with the outdoors both back at home in Mexico and traveling about the States to get to his final destination, Salinas's confidence strengthened until he reached his present trial. The success seeker conquered the city, the mountains, the hills, and even some desert, but he possessed no familiarity with corn. "Well, I did not see this coming," he spoke out loud to himself. "Stick to the training, Salinas. Stick to the training."

As per the instructions, the soldier oriented himself to the map, plotted his points, determined his distance and direction, and shot an azimuth. Expected to meet his other squad mates at a rally point at an unknown intersection along their individual courses, the team would resupply with a rucksack full of Meals Ready to Eat (MREs), a five-gallon can of water to refill their canteens, and one set of night-vision goggles to aid them in completing the rest of the course. Although the orienteers started their journey alone in the daylight, they would finish as a unified squad in the dark. Their only safeguard if lost: travel due north to the blacktop road and wait for the straggler truck.

Salinas wanted nothing to do with that Deuce and Half truck because it would mean an automatic fail for his entire squad. Although he stifled some concerns with Bradford's weak sense of direction, the competitor wished he had the local celebrity's insight into corn mazes.

Even though the rigid rows blocked a clear path in the calculated direction from his starting stake, the recruit dove into the starchy sea of stalks headed due south, determined to compensate for the twists and turns as he went. Although the sprawling plains portrayed the sweet nostalgia of the historical spread of the American pioneers in paintings and photographs, the confines of the giant plants forging together to weed out infiltrators with the jagged edges of their defensive leaves that clawed at the eyes and arms like miniature swords contested the soldier to battle his way through their territory.

With as little as five minutes into the course, Salinas struggled to see patches of the darkening sky through the looming tassels while the drying foliage gated his movement forward. Grateful that the drill sergeants insisted the trainees wear their uniform top, sleeves down, the fighter guarded his face with his forearms and surged through the attacks of the razor-like antagonists to complete his mission.

Breathing deep and slow to counter the onset of claustrophobia and the nagging of defeat, the exhausted traveler penetrated the course for miles before he heard a scuffle up ahead. Through the thinning bases of the stalks, he spied combat boots dashing across his path into an airy green opening. In haste, the hopeful soul broke through the boundary of his enemy into a gap in the rows and sucked in the fresh air before noticing the fellow combatant kneeling down in front of a numbered stake, plotting another point on the map.

"Oh, Salinas, hey, it's you," the man spouted as he raised his head and glanced back at his visitor.

"Oh, hey, Jensen!" Salinas replied, surprised that he encountered someone from first squad. "I wasn't expecting to see you here."

"No kidding." Jensen turned back to finish his topographical work.

"Were we supposed to run into other squads on this thing?" Salinas asked, hoping Jensen had some kind of inside scoop as their token platoon leader.

"Uh, yeah, I think so," Jensen answered with a lack of conviction, too busy figuring out his own route to worry about what Salinas had to say.

"I mean, I know we are supposed to meet up with our own squad eventually, but I don't remember them saying that we would run into anyone else along the way." Salinas grew a bit annoyed that Jensen was blowing him off.

"Uh, yeah, uh, don't know, man," Jensen acknowledged. "I'm kind of busy here."

"Oh, yeah, sorry." Salinas, convicted at his irritation with Jensen, "Need any help with that?"

The proud platoon leader halted his calculations and eyed Salinas with a confused look on his face. "I don't need help from you." Then the cocky combatant gathered his belongings and headed off into the abyss of fading green, selecting one of the exit openings off to the southwest.

"Now I'm sorry that I was sorry," Salinas confessed under his breath.

The meticulous order-taker jotted down the number on the stake and shot his next azimuth as he had already plotted all of his points from the very beginning. Again, none of the exit options veered in a direct path for him, and he grew weary of trying to compensate for his corrections across waterways or other lanes. Although he felt some comfort in running into Jensen, the soldier hoped that his own squad roamed nearby.

As the navigator powered his way through the roughage, he located two other numbered stakes but never ran into another recruit or even heard one, for that matter. Heading due south, the night closed in while the doubtful orienteer fumbled along in desperate need of supplies. With his canteen near empty and his stomach growling, the famished trainee wished he had been clever enough to stash a couple of granola bars in his ammo pouch because a little pick-me-up would go a long way to boost his morale.

After an eternity of left foot counts, keeping track of veers to the right or to the left, Salinas paused in the middle of nowhere, engulfed by leaves and shadows of more leaves. The moon dimmed as the cool night air brought relief to the stifling fall heat that had insulated the field during the daylight. The isolated pathfinder could see just two steps in front now, and he knew he must have been long overdue for that rallying point. Soon the trainee would not be able to see his hand in front of his face, those night-vision goggles a welcome help at this point.

Drudging along in the dark, the soloist tried not to dwell too much on how hungry and weak he felt. After a quick calculation on how long it would take him to travel due north at this juncture and get to that straggler truck, the disoriented soldier was too far for that option.

As one who had survived far more grave situations, the recruit gathered himself, tried to quiet his breathing, and listened for any hint of other people. As he gasped and held his breath to eliminate any unnecessary noise, the ever-increasing pounding of the heart marched closer and closer to the ears. The accomplished meditator squeezed his eyes tight and tried to focus his mind on just listening, but he heard nothing. In defeat he released his air through his nose.

With the dull echoes of the turn of an engine breaking the

silence, the hopeful one jerked his head back to the south and started an all-out sprint for reinforcements. As the attacking stalks eased their slaps near the edge of the field, the recruit caught glimpses of a building with a dimmed light post illuminating a pair of lopsided wooden doors. When he had broken free of his confinement, resting his hands on his knees for a breather, the immigrant imagined his other squad members at the rally point, bargaining away the best bits of the MREs and relaxing next to their rucks, waiting for his arrival. The forceful slide of the shotgun bolt demanded his undivided attention as the illegal raised both of his hands in familiar surrender.

"Who's there?" the aged voice shouted out into the darkness.

Salinas dreaded having to respond, knowing his accent still lingered and doubtful that this farmer man was going to give him the time to explain himself.

"Answer, or I'll shoot!"

"Please, don't shoot!" the frightened trainee begged in his very best English. "I'm lost!"

"Who is that? Who are you? What are you doing around here?"

"Please, sir, I would love to explain, if you will just put down your rifle," Salinas begged.

"No can do, foreigner! You just hold yourself steady there while I call the police!"

The illegal immigrant contemplated the options: the weapon or the law. Would the cadre speak on his behalf? What would the other recruits think of him getting arrested during a Bible training camp, of all things? Should he take his chances and dart back into the covering of that blasted corn? *Oh, Lord, help me here!* the new disciple prayed to himself. *I don't know what I should do here.*

Although the attuned listener had heard the voice of Jesus, this time he heard nothing but felt a powerful urging from within to just be calm, direct, and honest with his confronter. "Sir, if you would just allow me to explain!"

"There is no explanation for you being here on my property,

and what in the world are you wearing?" the southern drawl of the captor sounding similar to that of Sergeant Riley's.

"Sir, it is a uniform. I am a trainee at Fort Gideon. Have you heard of it? It can't be far from here." The captive took his chance as he paced forward one step at a time, exposing himself in bits to the glow of the overhead light.

"I told you not to move!"

"Okay, okay," the intruder stopped dead in his tracks. "I'm not moving. I'm staying put, but please, sir. You must know of this camp that I speak of. Drill Sergeant Akpore? Captain Peters?"

"I don't know of any camp in these parts," the farmer scolded. "And you don't look like a camper to me."

"No, no, it is not camping," Salinas tried to explain further. "It is a basic training program for soldiers for Christ. I am a new Christian, and I am just trying to be obedient and learn more about how best I may serve Him in my life."

"A Christian? What does that have to do with dressing like that and trespassing where you are not wanted?" the old man gave audience.

"I made a mistake, sir. I got lost somewhere out there. I was on a land navigation course in the corn, and I made a wrong move somewhere. I mean no harm, sir, truly," the muscles in his arms began to quiver in tired agony. "I have a map and a set of instructions that I can show you if you just let me."

"Keep those arms up! I'm warning you! I have rights to defend what is mine!"

"Yes, sir, but in my right cargo pocket I have the map and the instructions. Please, allow me to show you," Salinas continued to beg.

"Well, no funny business or I'm shooting, and that will be that! No rightful lawman is going to fault me for that!"

"No, sir! No funny business!" the captive promised.

With absolute relief, Salinas reached down and into his right cargo pocket to retrieve his folded documents and kept his head lowered in submission as he held them out as a token of peace, easing his way up to the weapon. The skeptical farmhand grabbed the papers and moved back closer to the light. With one swift flick, he popped the instructions open, confirming the name and address printed in the top middle of the page. With the same skill, he cracked just the edge of the other document to concede that it was indeed a map. Finally, the barrel of the weapon lowered and the detainee leaned his hands against his knees in exhausting victory over a dangerous scenario.

"Well, what you gonna do now that you got yourself so cattywampus?" the armed man probed.

"Quite honestly, sir, I'm not sure what to do at this point."

"Well, it's too dark out here to get you redirected. Let's head into the house and see if we can't figure somethin' out," the old man reasoned as he led the way to the side door of the white farmhouse.

Salinas considered refusing his offer, but that nudging from somewhere deep within kept him moving towards engagement with this gentleman. As soon as the pair passed across the threshold, the trainee smelled the dampness rising up from the old cellar, felt the overwhelming sense of sadness in the barren kitchen, and saw the ragged, sullen exterior of the homeowner. Away from the cool breeze of the great outdoors, even the frail-looking fellow exuded a mild stench that conveyed that he had no one tending to him.

"I'll put on the kettle," the now-willing host proclaimed.

"Thank you, sir," the waiter accepted, removing his hat and taking a seat in the dingy yellow chair next to the speckled gray kitchen table.

After pulling out a box of Lipton tea bags, the aged man opened the narrow cupboard next to the stove to retrieve a mug and then grabbed another resting in the dish drainer. Salinas observed the surroundings, noticing the old and sparse but tidy accommodations. One plate, one small copper-bottomed pot, and one soup spoon still air dried next to the sink.

As the water began to rattle against the base of the blue speckled kettle and the lid started hissing its inviting whistle, the gentleman set down a crocheted pot holder in the middle of the table and handed his guest a cup. The obliging immigrant accepted the token of goodwill and plopped the bag into its place in preparation for the hot water.

"I'll let you pour your own," the farmer offered, taking his seat across from the night's intruder. "So, Christian you say?"

"Yes, sir," the disciple confessed, being careful not to spill.

"I used to be a churchgoer with my Geraldine, but since her passin', it don't seem fittin' to worship a God that would allow such heartache, such agonizin' pain," the host confessed.

"Um," Salinas paused, unsure how in the world he was supposed to respond to such rawness and vulnerability with a man he encountered by accident. "Was Geraldine your wife?"

"She was the love of my life!" the man corrected. "She was the most gracious, selfless, and God-fearing woman I've ever known. It just ain't right! If she had to go, she certainly deserved to die in her sleep or somethin' peaceful like that."

Oh, Lord, Jesus, the disciple pled, *help me! Help me!*

"May I ask how she died?"

"A head-on collision, of all things! She had headed up north for one of her brother-in-law's funerals. I knew I should have gone with her that day, but it was cold, windy, and I didn't rightly care for that fella anyway. She didn't harp on me about staying home, though. That's just how she was, but if I would have escorted my precious Geraldine like a good husband should have, maybe she'd still be with me, or better yet, maybe we'd both be gone together," the farmer picked at the gaping wound.

The lonely old fellow continued the adoring praise of his beloved wife buried out at the back hill next to their two baby boys that failed to survive childbirth. The pain in the storyteller's eyes was real and palatable, and it made Salinas regret his callous, self-serving attitude that he had practiced most of his life. The new faithful follower wanted to offer some comfort to the hopeless widower, but the desperate soldier was a brand-spanking-new believer himself. He did not know enough about the Bible or the workings of the Trinity to formulate some intelligent, moving response. *Why am I even here, oh, Lord?* his mind ushered up in boldness.

"Nope, I don't want nothin' to do with church goin' anymore!" the farmer resigned.

With no words coming to mind, yet his emotions welling up within to some form of attention, the soldier reached over and grabbed the man's hand. The affection caught the recipient by surprise, but then the weary soul lowered his head in submission as the two just sat there in silence for a few moments. The thankful old man finally wiped a fallen tear from his right eye and perked up to suggest that his guest pull out that map again so that they could get him back on the right path.

Salinas accepted the disguised transition from the more vulnerable encounter, released the hand, and dug for his map. In excited anticipation for the challenge, the old farmer cleared the kettle and used the two cups to hold down the curled edges. "Ah, I see right where you veered off too far," the gentleman advised, straightening his glasses to be certain. "Got a pencil?"

The friendly farmer identified the location of his homestead just off the brink of the course, outlined a quick and easy path back on track, and even escorted the lost trainee back out to the field right at the perfect entry point. The odd pair shook hands, thankful for their unlikely encounter, and before Salinas could escape into the darkness of the terrain, he turned back once more to his gracious host. "What's your name, mister?"

"Stevens, Chuck Stevens," the gentleman replied. "And what is yours, fella?"

"My friends call me Art!"

CHAPTER 29

West

"Well," Bradford advised, "we either got to keep waiting here in hopes that Salinas finds us sooner or later, or we got to take matters into our own hands."

"I had enough trouble getting here," Hoyt replied. "I am not so sure we can find him out there."

"Don't be so defeated, Hoyt," West corrected as she dug into the rucksack. "We have food, and we have these." She tossed her squad mates an MRE and held up the pair of night-vision goggles like a well-earned trophy. "Let's just down the crackers in those MREs, fill up our canteens, and get going," West laid out the necessities. "He has got to be around here somewhere."

"But I can't see well at night," Hoyt pleaded, "and, those night-vision goggles are horrible. They smoosh my glasses, and they have absolutely no depth perception to them."

"I will wear the goggles," West resolved. "Hoyt, you just got to plot the points and shoot the azimuths. You are the best at that map reading stuff."

"What should I do, then?" Bradford felt left out.

"Well, I don't know." West picked up on his sensitivity. "We could use someone to carry this rucksack and maybe even the water can so that we can bring the supplies to Salinas."

Hoyt interjected, "Are we allowed to do that?"

"Do what?" West tried not to show her annoyance with Hoyt's no-can-do attitude.

"Take the supplies. The instructions never specifically said that we could take them with us," Hoyt recalled.

"Well, they didn't say we couldn't," West retorted.

"She does have a point," Bradford added.

"Thanks, Bradford." West appreciated his efforts to get over his load-bearing role. "May I also point out that we are losing precious time debating this?"

In surrender, Bradford grabbed the water container and offered to fill the canteens while Hoyt searched for his red-lensed flashlight and analyzed the map. West opened up three of the MREs, retrieved the crackers, and inventoried the spreadable accompaniment: two tubes of peanut butter and one tube of cheese spread.

They huddled in a semicircle and listened to Hoyt's briefing. "Okay, we each came at this point from varying angles. West, you came in at about a hundred-and-thirty-five degrees. I entered at about two-hundred-twenty-five degrees, and Bradford, my guess is that you were supposed to have come in at about forty-five degrees," Hoyt pointed to the map as he spoke.

Offended again, Bradford interrupted, "How do you know that I wasn't supposed to enter where I did?"

His teammates eyed him in disbelief. "I'm pretty sure the purpose of this exercise was not to walk for fifteen minutes down the waterway in hopes that you would run into us," West attempted to square Bradford away.

"Hey, you guys," the logical one tried to re-focus the group. "Bradford, even you admitted that you did not stick to the points exactly, and you started at forty-five degrees, right?"

"Well, yes," Bradford admitted.

"Okay, then," Hoyt redirected them. "The pattern is that we all entered this rallying point at the same degree that we started the course, so I assume the intention was to have you enter at about here."

"Great job, Hoyt," West excited at the analysis.

"So, applying that same strategy to Salinas, he should have entered about here, at three-hundred-fifteen degrees." Hoyt marked an X on the spot.

They all looked up and over at the northwest corner. "Hoyt, I'm serious, you rock!" West patted him on the back.

"Well, I don't know exactly where he is since he apparently got off course, but I think that would be the place to start," the studious skeptic resigned to their new mission.

"Let's move out!" West ordered as she stuffed her cracker and peanut butter packages into her ammo pouch, took one last swig of her canteen, and headed that way with the night-vision goggles resting on her forehead.

Right before the trio stepped back into the shadows of the clattering stalks, the slight breeze brushing the drying tassels together, the self-designated leader gave the final thumbs up, turned toward the opening, and lowered her goggles. Confirming Hoyt's assessment that the newfangled contraption lacked the clarity of depth, she planted one foot near a stalk to her left, then stretched to plant her right foot at the edge of the row to her right, proceeding down the seeded path like an ice skater performing her initial stride around the rink while her ears concentrated on the kid's directions. "Hoyt, I love you bro, but you got to put those crackers away," West halted the movement.

"But I'm hungry, and I used all of my chow time coming up with our game plan," Hoyt whined.

"Here." She reached into her left pants pocket, pulled out a tube of cheese, and passed it over her shoulder while maintaining her forward focus. "Suck on this. It is quieter and we need to listen for Salinas."

"But that stuff is nasty!" Hoyt continued. "That's why I gave it back to you to begin with."

"Beggars can't be choosers, Hoyt!" West ordered. "We have to stay focused here, so you are going to have to either down something less noisy or deal with it for now."

"Okay, okay," Hoyt conceded, "but do either of you have any peanut butter left?"

"Really?" West replied.

"Here." Bradford reached over Hoyt's shoulder to offer a half a tube. "Have the rest of mine."

"But you ate off of it already," the youngster answered.

"Hoyt!" West growled, her lips puckered against the edge of the clunky contraption.

"Fine, I'll just wait."

"Suit yourself," Bradford tucked the peanut butter back in his right shirt pocket.

With the issue stymied for the moment, West continued her elongated gait along the route for another fifteen minutes and then halted the train of three. "I can see an opening up ahead," she whispered as if the enemy lurked in preparation for an ambush.

"Why are we whispering?" Hoyt mimicked.

"Because," West spoke between her teeth, jaw clenched, "we need to be alert, and we need to be listening."

"Okay, but wouldn't it be easier to shout his name?"

"Hoyt," Bradford finally stepped into the conversation, "we don't know what is out there. I feel something eerie."

"Really? Uh, I mean, thanks, Bradford," West appreciated the support but grew concerned with the commentary. "Now, let's move, but quietly."

"Okay," Hoyt whined.

The commanding front woman signaled for them to follow her lead as they crept out into the vulnerable expanse of the waterway. Unlike previous breaks in the course, this particular lane laid bare with no markings or signs of foot traffic. When she raised her fist to signal the halt and then lowered her opened hand, the team knelt down on one knee as she scoped out the surroundings. Unable to identify any dark patches that would indicate an established entry point, West slid her goggles back atop her head and turned to her teammates. "This one is different," the goggle operator reported.

"There are no entrances or exits, no stakes, and no sign of anyone having been here."

"Interesting," Bradford added. "When I came upon my big waterway, I could see points to my right, so I just started walking towards them. I even ran into second squad's rallying point, so I knew I would eventually hit ours."

Hoyt turned on his red light again to review the map. "I don't even see this one on here."

"Well, Salinas must have mistaken this thing as a regular lane, so he must have gotten off track because of this somehow," West insisted on whispering. "The question is, which way do we go from here?"

"I'm not sure," Hoyt whispered back.

"I say we go that way," Bradford pointed to the right.

"Is that some mystical notion?" West required clarification of which power Bradford relied upon.

He got the hint and instead suggested that they pray. West led them as they knelt together, held hands, and bowed their heads. They longed to hear from Jesus and set out on a path to find their dear friend.

Sensing the strengthening bonds of a kindred spirit, West relished this new form of brotherhood, regretting her tendency to belittle the men's suggestions and point out their shortcomings. The conviction of her words and her tone cut at her soul while the warmth of the presence of the Holy Spirit blanketed them. "I'm sorry, Hoyt, and I'm sorry, Bradford," followed the amen. "Bradford, you are right. I think we should go that way."

The team walked side by side along the open green, the moon lighting their way until an inviting sound waving across the coolness of the night air stopped them in their tracks. "Holy, holy, holy," the sweet chorus lofted above the tassels, "is the Lord, God, Almighty, who was and is and is to come."

The glistening blue of the night beamed across their faces as they looked at each other with complete adulation. Without any words, they knew they recognized that song, that voice, that accent. Their brother once lost was now found.

BASIC TRAINING

Phase III: Maneuvers

Marching with the Master Minutes

October 2005

Cadre: Akpore, Thorpe, Burroughs, Peters

Recruiters: Riley

The group opened with prayer for each recruit in 1st Platoon, 4th Squad.

1. Captain Peters will have two days to wrap up the classroom training. All recruits are responding well to the discipline of Study. It will be a bit of an adjustment for them to be focused on these finals, but they need to learn to continue to seek out the Word even in the midst of business. He will re-emphasize the three types of people groups found behind enemy lines as these Field Training Exercises (FTX) will put the soldiers' head knowledge to the test. The groups are: Enemy, Collateral Damage, and POW.

2. Burroughs will lead a one-day lanes training exercise as a practice run for the final FTX. We have selected a RECON mission and a movement to contact for this phase. It will give the entire platoon a chance to operate as a larger unit without making them react in enemy territory. Recruit Jensen will take the helm as the Platoon Leader for the Recon, so Sergeant Riley has selected Hoyt as the Squad Leader. It will be the easiest leadership position for Hoyt in the field, and Bradford is struggling with Jensen, so we want to keep them at bay for a bit. Although challenges make us grow, Bradford might need a bit more time of transformation as far as Jensen is concerned. Salinas has been selected to act as Platoon Leader for the movement-to-contact mission which will showcase

the collateral damage group. Essentially, in the enemy camp will be people that have accepted Jesus as their Savior, and the contact will move them from that camp to 1st Platoon who will secure them and simulate discipleship. With the long-term plans that the Lord has for Salinas, he needs to build a bit of confidence with larger-scaled operations, and he needs a chance to redeem himself with land navigation. First Platoon will run the lane first thing in the morning, then Second Platoon right before lunch, and Third Platoon right after lunch. When not running the lane, Squads should continue to prepare for the final FTX and get recuperated.

3. Thorpe will be spearheading the final FTX which will be an entire company- sized movement. The entire company will road march to the bivouac site, assume the defensive perimeter, and await taskings of squad-sized elements. Sergeant Riley has selected West as Squad Leader for this final mission. He wants them to get a POW mission because the Lord has called West to this type of service. Because POWs can be the most difficult to discern in the real Spiritual battle of life, this assignment is going to have to be subtle yet solvable.

The group closed in silent prayer as we listened for any further promptings of the Holy Spirit.

Godspeed,

Akpore

CHAPTER 30

West

After the thrill of the field training, West grew weary of the classroom environment again. The qualification phase got them out in the great outdoors, putting their knowledge into action. Although the female disciple developed an unquenchable thirst for the Word at the camp, the girl considered herself a doer. Once she knew better, she wanted to get out there and do better, and the transforming trainee resigned her previous tactics to make it up as she went along.

Throughout her childhood, West ran the show. From as far back as she could remember, Darby dressed herself, fed herself, and kept an eye on the clock before walking to school alone with the red yarn lanyard knotted around her belt loop and the house key tucked into her front pocket. Even as a tiny first grader, the young girl traipsed in solitude back and forth, taking her time to admire the landscaped homes all decorated for the appropriate season and wonder what life might have been like in each of them. The dreamer imagined big family dinners, friendly games of catch in the backyard, and gooey s'mores over a roaring bonfire. Although the lonely walker seldom crossed paths with others along her trek across pretend land, when the opportunity presented itself, West took a gamble, desperate to make a friend.

"Mary Beth," the mother on the other side of the street scolded her daughter for dilly-dallying. "Come on, now. We are going to be late."

"Oh, hi, Mary Beth," young West yelled.

"Mary Beth, do you know that girl?" the mother asked, pulling her daughter closer.

"See you at school!" Darby shouted back and then raced off before the little girl had a chance to respond.

The adrenaline rush caused by her boldness enabled her to keep her hurried pace until Mary Beth and her mom fell out of sight. Only then would young West reduce her gait to a fast walk as she finished the rest of the way to school with her head held high and face beaming with pride. In her mind, she had done it. She had made a friend. The marginalized grade-schooler knew that little girl's name even if that girl had no idea who the perpetrator was.

As per protocol, at recess West opted out of her usual game of tag with the boys to look for Mary Beth and solidify their bond. Finding the confused friend on the slide, West struck up a conversation as if they were long lost buds. "Oh, hey, I finally found you," she began with her hand against her chest as a sign of her contained concern. "How about you invite me over to your house for a play date? Can you ask your mom tonight?" Sometimes the brash tactic worked, giving her at least a school friend for a few months, and sometimes it fell flat on its face.

Her mild successes at some level of notoriety in first grade only spurred her on further in the second grade under the domineering eye of Mrs. Weede. When the class discussed the basics of city government like the police department, the fire department, city hall, and the mayor, West initiated another risky move and volunteered to get the mayor to visit the classroom.

"Yes, Darby?" Mrs. Weede pointed to the frantic girl raising her hand in the air from her desk in the back row as if it might separate from her armpit if ignored.

"I just wanted you to know that the mayor is my neighbor, so

I can get him to come visit our class if you want," West claimed with confident resolve.

"Really?" Mrs. Weede, skeptical of the young girl's antics, responded.

"Really!" West replied in earnest. "I just trick or treated at his house last month."

"Well," Mrs. Weede was unsure how to respond as the kids roared in delight, "maybe I can arrange something with your mom."

"Oh, sure. No problem," Darby smiled and rested in her victory while her mind calculated the moves. First, the latch-key kid had to circumvent communication attempts to her mother, and second, in order to save face in that class, she had to deliver the goods.

Wasting no precious time, the determined little lady skipped home, pulled out a spiral notebook and her stubby pencil with remnants of a useable eraser, and planned out her mission. After she stuffed her mouth full of popcorn, her dinner for the night, and downed a can of diet soda, Darby slid on her jacket, locked the door behind her, and journeyed into uncharted waters with the details still fresh in her mind. She remembered the street, and she was certain she knew which house too.

With hands tucked in her front pockets, West strolled down one block, up two, over three, and then up that driveway like she owned the place. "Ding-dong," the bell chimed.

"I'll get it," came a high-pitched, muffled voice from within. "Well, hello there. May I help you?"

Darby tried to use her grown-up voice. "Is Richard home?"

"Richard?" the woman looked amused.

"Yeah, you know, Richard, the mayor," the impatient eight-year-old added.

"Oh," the lady tried to hold in the laughter. "You mean Mayor Richard Godfrey?"

"Yeah," West puzzled at this gal's confusion. "This is his house, right?"

"Yes, dear," the conversation appeared to make this woman's

day as she held back a chuckle and smiled from ear to ear. "Let me get him for you. Would you like to step in?"

"No thanks," the rehearsed caller intended to stick to her script. "I'll just wait here."

The mayor approached the door with that same amused look on his face, but the serious grade-schooler struggled to comprehend the joke. Proceeding with her typical social call demeanor, Darby explained her promise to Mrs. Weede and her entire second-grade class. "I just live over there," the young girl pointed. "So, we are like neighbors. You may remember giving me candy at Halloween? I was a pink Power Ranger...anyway, Mrs. Weede said you had to give speeches and be friendly and stuff to be mayor, so I thought being a friendly neighbor would really help you out."

With no concept of the magnitude of her efforts, Darby leaned her head on her folded arms atop her desk as Mayor Godfrey greeted the kids the following week. As far as she was concerned, Richard came to her class, she accomplished her goal, and she secured herself a place in elementary history for the rest of the year.

"Huh, um," Captain Peters cleared his throat. "Hello? Recruit West?"

"Oh, yes," West lifted her head off of her arms and straightened up in her chair. "Sorry, sir. What was that again?"

Captain Peters rephrased his question to her about the three categories of people groups found behind enemy lines. "Yes, right," the recruit cleared her throat in preparation of her recitation. "The first people group behind enemy lines is the enemy. The enemy is the spiritual world against the Kingdom of God as the Apostle Paul outlined in Ephesians 6:12 when he said we do not fight against flesh and blood but against spiritual darkness. The second people group is collateral damage. They are those people that think they are neutral, not involved in the battle. And the third group is prisoners of war. A prisoner of war is 'a person who has been captured and imprisoned by the enemy in war.'"

CHAPTER 31

Bradford

Ready to migrate out of the combat service support phase involving intercessory prayer, stewardship of finances, and logistical support and into the nitty-gritty of the combat service role, Bradford imagined getting dirty in the trenches, maybe even trying his hand as a sniper.

Drill Sergeant Burroughs served as the primary field exercise instructor for this phase, the last before the final combat simulation and then commencement. As the idea of graduation became a reality, Bradford rallied for the last surge like the first round of playoffs.

Allowed to carry weapons on these maneuvers, the trainees were issued heavy laser equipment and fashioned them to their rifles with additional components for the web gear and helmets. Per the training, when the soldiers fired a blank round from their magazine clip, a red light at the end of the barrel would pierce through the atmosphere, follow the designated aim, and trigger the alarm of one of the target's receiving elements. A piercing squeal would ensue, and the hit combatant would have to halt and play dead until a cadre member with a key reset their power source.

Feeling like a modern-day Rambo, the burly athlete volunteered for the M-60, sacrificing his brawn for the good of the platoon.

Jensen maintained his position as the platoon leader, although Bradford questioned the squeaky-clean kid's ability to function out in the real world. First, Jensen had been homeschooled until he went off to some tiny Christian college. Second, he was raised in a commune of sorts out in the sticks of northern Minnesota. Third, he was artsy-fartsy, determined to be a worship leader of some sort. Finally, he worked in a posh environment, loaded with Christians, sitting behind a desk, helping people over the phone with some sort of medical insurance stuff.

"It's not insurance!" Jensen corrected. "It's like insurance, but it is not. It is medical sharing. It is a ministry."

The redeemed correctional officer bit his tongue and held his desired response inside, fearful of what might come out. First, his job existed smack dab in the middle of the worst of the worst, and he had been trying to surrender his potty mouth to the purification of the Lord. Second, he had grown up like most normal people, through the school of hard knocks in public education. Third, the cleanest and best he could come up with without blowing Jensen's mind was the gentle, "Could you be more sheltered?"

While this lanes training would be the first time they operated as a platoon-sized unit apart from their movements in garrison, Bradford preferred the autonomy of the squad. However, Drill Sergeant Burroughs insisted that the soldiers needed practice with larger forces. "Recruit Jensen," Drill Sergeant Burroughs ordered, "follow me for your briefing. You will then have ten minutes to prepare your operations order. After that, you will brief your platoon and make your final preparations for the assigned mission."

"Yes, drill sergeant!" Jensen answered loud enough to be heard but quiet enough to maintain the silence required for the training.

"Bradford," Jensen whispered to his gunner.

The frustrated soldier kept his prone position and peered back over his right shoulder.

"You stay focused with that thing," Jensen ordered.

The aggravated trainee just turned back around and continued to scan his field of vision. *Give me patience, oh Lord*, he prayed to himself.

After fifteen minutes, the scuffled scurries of long striding tiptoes approached the M-60 position. "Bradford," Jensen whispered his command again.

Appeasing him yet again, the obliging participant turned over his right shoulder and raised his eyebrows.

"Follow me to the middle of the AO for the briefing," Jensen continued.

The older member tried to sound respectful in his reply, "But I'm not the squad leader. Hoyt is."

"Hold questions to the end, Bradford," Jensen scolded.

"That is for the briefing, Jensen. Not now," the assigned follower could not help but try and correct Jensen's miscue of that command.

"Hold your questions to the end then too," Jensen ordered and then scampered off to gather a few others.

Oh, Lord, Bradford prayed again, *please, help me. This guy is killing me.*

The begrudged machine gunner had to obey his platoon leader's order, so he tossed a pebble at Salinas and motioned him over. Bradford explained his task as they exchanged weapons, and then the role player high-crawled his way over to Hoyt to let him know he had been beckoned to the middle. "I'm not sure what is going on here, Hoyt," Bradford tried to support his friend, "but I will let you know what I find out."

"Sure thing, Bradford. Sure thing," Hoyt's passive posture went with the flow.

"I exchanged weapons with Salinas, and now he is manning the M-60 position," Bradford explained.

"Oh, good thinking," Hoyt appreciated his friend's thoroughness.

"Yes, well, you will have to fill in at his spot until I get back so we don't have a break in our defense," Bradford offered.

"Oh, yeah, sure thing," Hoyt replied and moved to the gap.

Ah, Hoyt, the protective comrade thought to himself as he paced towards the center of their three-hundred-sixty-degree defensive position, *got to love that guy.*

Puzzled at his abundance of patience for Hoyt yet his shallow reserve for Jensen, Bradford considered the contrasting personalities. Hoyt presented himself as humble and caring while Jensen projected this arrogance as if his righteousness stemmed from his own ethical choices. Sure, Jensen had remained pure until marriage. He had grown up poor, his family only as well off as the gifts of the parishioners. He had lived a life surrounded by Christian people. He was responsible and innocent by most standards. So, why was it that he was at basic training now? Why had he not participated in this sort of training years ago? Why was he leading them when he could not seem to relate to them?

"Oh, good, Bradford," Jensen paused as the bemused gunner entered the inner circle. "I was just about to start." Jensen proceeded to brief their recon mission and left his five-point contingency plan with the acting platoon sergeant. All five of them would have just a few minutes to make their way back to their squad's section, convey the plan, and gather some supplies before rallying at the nine-o'clock position to head out into the unknown.

After leaving the security of the guarded exit point, the group followed Jensen's lead, skirting along the path, eyes peeled to the sides with an occasional glance at the front. The zealous platoon leader abused his controlling hand signals, commanding them to stop and take cover for no apparent reason only to order them to rise and continue forward once again. The excursion looked and felt like a woodland PT session with all of the ups and downs he made them endure.

Bradford debated over and over again in his head if he should do something stupid just to blow Jensen's operation. As the sixty gunner, he was supposed to remain with the primary defense because a leader's recon should have called upon Hoyt, so the instigator within wanted to make the annoying kid pay for his misstep. What could the sly operator do that would not be so obvious? Should he fake a coughing attack, alerting whoever they were spying on that they were near? Should he fake an injury, blaming all of the unnecessary stops and starts? Should he just play dumb to Jensen's overdone, animated hand signals? *I'm serious, Lord,* Bradford prayed within again, *I desperately need you! I desperately need more of you and less of me because I am getting vengeful here!*

"Brock," he heard a voice answer him, "*you know this is just petty foolishness. What is the point of all these shenanigans?*"

Sweat beaded up on his brow as he lay in cover next to some ferns that had sprouted up at the foot of a tree. Feeling uneasy about the eerie and condescending tone of the response, Bradford searched for the source and noticed the bluish-green aura that misted up near the lead position. *No, no, no!* the soldier battled in his mind. *I rebuke you, whatever you are, in the name of Jesus Christ.*

"*Come on, now Brock,*" it retaliated. "*You don't really believe that little phrase is more powerful than me?*"

Bradford felt fear trickle deep because the inexperienced disciple questioned his belief in the power of the rebuke, and this thing seemed to know it. He wanted to believe. He wanted to see the power of the Holy Spirit working in him like he had seen the power of darkness work. He longed to believe what Captain Peters had taught them. "You simply have to command evil to stand behind you in the name of Jesus."

Bradford recalled the counsel of Captain Peters as if it was just as black and white as that, conveying that the school instructor lacked a personal encounter with the evil side of the spiritual realm. Captain Peters talked as if it were something superficial like warding off temptation; however, the grandson of the Great Greta knew firsthand that it was much darker than that. This dabbling surpassed the disgust of lying or even sleeping around. Those sins Bradford chalked up to bad choices, but he knew pure evil.

When Hoyt retold some story about his earliest encounter with darkness, Bradford nearly cried from laughing. Shoot, he had worked the haunted houses as a college student because Halloween was his all-time favorite holiday. Like his father's side of the family, Bradford continued the tradition of decorating the house from head to toe for the annual event. Out of every nook and cranny poked a skeleton, a few bats here or there, or the token black cauldron, and the guests at the rambunctious parties loved dressing up in scary, political, or thought-provoking costumes. Before the adult entertainment kicked off, the gracious host handed out full-sized candy bars to the kids, his personal version of community service. "The kids love it," the condescending son attempted to explain to his righteous mother every year. "They expect it. We are not messing with tarot cards or conjuring up spirits, mom. Don't worry. It is just good fun. Besides, skeletons and stuff are supposed to be warding off the evil spirits. I'm actually doing a good thing."

Grimacing at the thought of his callous attitude, Bradford lay still in the thick of the woods surrounding Fort Gideon, nearing the end of his basic training in God's army, and wondered why this recent visit from the dark side reared its ugly head. He had not called upon it, and he had been ignoring his ability to decipher auras and such. *Lord,* the warrior pled as he burrowed his head in between his weapon and the ground, *I want to believe. I want to believe You are more powerful. Help my unbelief.* His heart jolted as he felt a tug at his left foot.

"Bradford, let's move," Jensen ordered with that condescending tone. "Did you fall asleep over here?"

Encounter

The first Latina chauffeur appeared pleasant and professional and insisted that Salinas speak English for the duration of their leg of the voyage to the north. After exchanging the basic pleasantries, she selected a pop station for some more practice with the culturally-relevant tunes of the land.

Given the extravagant network of committed employees that manned the key components and the considerate comfort of his travel, Salinas concluded that the outrageous fees associated with this tour to freedom were reasonable after all.

After fidgeting with the electric window opener and the automatic seat adjuster of the silver minivan at a scheduled stop, the passenger opted to recline his chair to allow for a much-needed nap until the screeching scrape of the sliding door slammed the handle into his headrest. "Move your seat up!" a hardened fellow dressed in a dark suit scowled.

"Lo siento!" the escapee begged his pardon and hurried to find the lever.

"Tirza, where is the car seat?" the brute demanded.

"It's in the trunk!" the driver touted back, eyes forward.

"Get it and get it in here!" he ordered. "Now! And get a movie going on that thing!"

After a sigh of displeasure, the chauffeur obeyed, pulling down a small TV from the ceiling just behind the center console and shuffled around the back to retrieve a booster. She climbed in the sliding door behind Salinas and finagled with the child-sized contraption until it was anchored in the middle space.

As the Latina strolled back around the front of the car and into the driver's seat, the well-dressed thug returned with three, scrawny, frightened little chicas with their hair combed and slicked back into ponytails wearing frilly, cream dresses and black shiny leather shoes. Each of the obedient young girls carried a small stuffed animal and climbed onto the bench seat at the stern request of their escort. "Get them buckled in, Tirza! They are precious cargo and need to get where they are going!"

"Fine!" she bellowed back as the man in charge took his leave. "Girls, everything is going to be just fine. I got a cute movie about dogs playing for you, and my husband is a kind man."

As Salinas caught onto the reference of his theatrical position, the decoy stared back at the deadened blank looks from the violated dark eyes of the three new passengers. His stomach turned and rolled as he contemplated the reality that likely brought these three little ones into his caravan. As a former carrier of the chemical sort of cargo, he had heard of the other avenues of money making involved with the influx of refugees desperate to cross the border, but the optimist chose not to dwell on the details.

Should he do something? Should he try and take over the vehicle and drive these girls to safety? Would the network be able to track him? Maybe he was being paranoid. Maybe there was a perfectly good explanation why that rough handler had a seven-, eight-, and nine-year-old in his care, passing them off to be driven to a destination accompanied by another escapee and a woman posing to be his wife and their mother. The desperate American wanna-be refocused his attention to the road and kept his mouth shut.

> "*Blessed be the name of God forever and ever*
> *To whom belong wisdom and might*
> *He changes times and seasons*
> *He removes kings and sets up kings*
> *He gives wisdom to the wise*
> *And knowledge to those who have understanding*
> *He reveals deep and hidden things*
> *He knows what is in the darkness*
> *And the light dwells with him*
> *To you oh God of my fathers*
> *I give thanks and praise*
> *For you have given me wisdom and might*
> *And have now made known to me what we asked of you*
> *For you have made known to us the King's matter.*" (Daniel 2:20–23, ESV)

CHAPTER 32

Salinas

"Good after-action review (AAR), Jensen," Drill Sergeant Burroughs commended the recruit on the successful leader's recon mission. "You got the necessary intel for the next lane. Let's see... Salinas!"

"Yes, drill sergeant!" Salinas sounded.

"You will be spearheading the next mission, so stay behind with me for your briefing," Drill Sergeant Burroughs directed. "The rest of you go back to your defensive positions and await further instructions."

As Salinas sat biting the inside of his lower lip, Drill Sergeant Burroughs set the scene. "Now that we have some intelligence about the enemy, Salinas, we need to get in there and take care of some collateral damage."

"Collateral damage?" the anxious recruit asked.

"Always remember your training, Salinas," the drill sergeant advised. "Some of the folks milling about the enemy AO are not purposefully fighting for the other side. They just got swallowed up in the mix when the Opposition Forces (OPFOR) moved in."

"Oh, yes, yes, one of the groups behind enemy lines," Salinas recalled the classroom lectures.

"Roger that," the drill sergeant confirmed. "They have no real concept of who is for them and who is against them. They are just existing."

"Right, right," the nervous trainee appreciated the reminder. "Now how am I supposed to recognize them?"

"Well, for the purpose of this exercise, we have placed a secret agent in the fray over there." Drill Sergeant Burroughs relished his role as facilitator of the lanes. "You will maneuver the platoon along the route cleared by the recon and establish a new AO at position Bravo."

"Okay," Salinas said with hesitation after getting lost during their last land navigation course. Questioning his ability to guide the entire platoon, he resisted the temptation to shake his head and hand in his resignation.

"You will make contact with the agent and finalize plans for smuggling some of those folks out of there," the drill sergeant continued his directions, giving Salinas authentication codes and code names.

The trainee shorthanded the key points and prepared his own operations order. Although the unit movement to position Bravo seemed a straightforward route as long as the cadre did not throw any surprises at them, the leader remained confused about how Agent Gideon was supposed to help him smuggle converts out of the enemy camp without detection. The immigrant would have to rely on his ability to adapt and overcome—a familiar experience.

* * *

Growing up in the lower foothills of Matehuala proved challenging for many in his small village. As poor, simple folk, they herded the animals of the larger ranch owners, worked construction jobs, or sold small handmade trinkets to put food on the table and clothes on their backs. As a young boy, Artemio's first job involved corralling the pigs and fastening the stringed collars with triangular wooden protrusions around their necks. Although the clever device kept the free-roaming animals out of the house, the stubborn pigs never seemed to learn their place. While the slew of chickens and stray dogs knew better somehow, the swine pushed the boundaries and insisted on cohabitating, and when one broke past the threshold, the beast wreaked havoc.

As he got older, Salinas followed in his brothers' footsteps and became a stable boy for a nearby rancher. The difficult but steady work strengthened his resolve and fostered his desire for more while bearing his father's financial burdens and bolstering his mother's pride. Although the long and dirty days strained his growing muscles and robbed him of more time for relaxation, Salinas did not mind his meager service to the family. His mother had taught him best.

Every morning after the men downed their coffee and set out to work, Mama fashioned the human yoke about her shoulders and meandered to the water hole. Although the main town had procured a truck to deliver fresh drinking water to the small cistern at the back of each little adobe house once a week and the blue plastic water box atop the roof caught any rain water, the tireless lady of the house kept her routine of retrieving water for the animals and to flush the toilet out back.

After setting the meat to roast in the clay stove outside the back door, Fortuna ground the corn for tortillas and concocted a delicious accompaniment with cactus leaves and any other vegetable she could gather. With diligent hands, the housekeeper swept their dirt floor and patched the clothes, working day and night to take care of her family, and Salinas adored her.

As the middle child, often lost in the mix, Mama stole moments to make him feel special by pulling him aside, squeezing his cheeks, gazing deep into his eyes, and offering him a heart-felt blessing. "Dios te bendiga, mi chu-cha," she recited and then pled for this saint or that saint to guide and protect him to the greatness that she knew was in store for him.

"Gracias, Mama. Gracias," the favored son managed, although

he hated that nickname. The term of endearment given to him by his father because he had a small face stuck, but he only tolerated it from her.

Although Salinas never wanted to disappoint his dear mother, he had another role to play along with the other men in the family. He recalled how his father called him out one day to help him and his uncle, visiting from El Norte. They hopped into his uncle's fancy truck, a huge treat since the villagers still walked or rode horses on lend from the ranch, and sped off down the rock-laden road towards town.

As they negotiated the ruts past women struggling to carry their heavy loads or young men waiting at the lone bus stop on the edge of town, he hoped that some chica would spot him in this expensive rig barreling down the incline and out into an exciting adventure.

Artemio kept overhearing Papi and Tio talking about some coyote. The quiet listener wondered if they were setting out on a hunting expedition, but they hauled no shotguns, and they were headed out towards the barren lands. When the vehicle stopped in the middle of nowhere and his dad rushed out of the truck and started clinking around under the bed, the curious teenager filed out of the cab behind him, jumping to miss the scores of rifles sliding out across the ground. The roaring sound of approaching vehicles echoed across the plains, but the two older men did not appear alarmed.

On that day with his first rendezvous with Coyote, Salinas understood that the title did not describe an animal, per se, but a position. As a smuggler, people paid him hard-earned money to get them safely to El Norte. Although the young man did not understand the full dynamics of the operation at the time or his family's involvement, he suspected Fortuna would not have approved.

★ ★ ★

Back at Fort Gideon, the chosen leader for this particular mission wondered if Drill Sergeant Burroughs had access to that mysterious manila folder that the sergeant had referenced back when he was first recruited. The file seemed to hold bits and pieces of his life that had far greater relevance than he ever had imagined, and the perceptive soldier no longer believed in coincidence.

As the platoon scaled the obscure woods in a staggered formation and reestablished their new base at point Bravo free of any unexpected encounters with corn, Salinas waited for Agent Gideon to make contact. Hoyt looked ridiculous as he tried to hunch and run at the same time to deliver information to Salinas from fourth squad's segment. As per usual, the kid's Kevlar fell cocked to the side and wobbled with each step while the brass clasp of his web gear clinked against the weapon slung around his head like a heavy weight. With both feet forward, Hoyt skidded into the dirt next to Salinas like a jet plane having trouble with the landing, pushed his glasses back at the bridge, and gasped for breath. "West spotted some movement."

"Is it Agent Gideon?" Salinas grasped Hoyt's arm to try and calm him.

"She thinks so. She gave the authentication challenge and he responded correctly," Hoyt tried to steady his nerves. "She has them halted just outside the perimeter."

"Them?" Salinas inquired.

"Yeah, them," Hoyt explained. "She said he confirmed three people to cross."

"Okay," Salinas understood. "Let them in and bring them here."

"WILCO," Hoyt uttered his new vocabulary.

Salinas tried not to laugh. Hoyt just never sounded convincing with this kind of encrypted talk, but he was zealous in his efforts. "Oh, Hoyt," Salinas called out in hushed tones, "make sure they are guarded all of the way."

"Oh, yeah, right. Good thinking," Hoyt confirmed with a thumbs-up.

Time seemed to stand still as Salinas waited for Hoyt's reappearance with the contact team, certain that the pounding of his heart echoed loud enough to expose their positions. "Drill Sergeant Akpore?" Salinas surprised to see one of his instructors approach with two others following.

"You mean, Special Agent Gideon," the drill sergeant played his part.

CHAPTER 33

West

With Rest and Relaxation (R and R) over, the recruits prepared for their final examination, a three-day continuous field training exercise (FTX). This last simulation would encompass all that they had learned both in the classroom as well as in the field, and the excursion would test their spiritual disciplines, their gifts, and their camaraderie. The final outing represented the culmination of their basic training and the conclusion of their stay at Fort Gideon.

For West, the time flew by, and she appreciated the break from reality. The trainee could not wait to begin her fresh start out there amidst the regular folks because the redeemed woman flourished in her new identity with a new and meaningful purpose. She wished she could have a genuine do-over for a lot of her sins, but those aspects secured a permanent spot as part of her testimony. They existed. They were real, and they were painful, but the hope she found in Jesus had triumphed, and the warrior felt victorious.

Because the entire cycle taught her so much about putting things into perspective, and because she understood how much the Lord had lifted her out of the mire, the gifted leader approached this last stage without apprehension or trepidation. The redeemed sinner would never forget her life before Christ. She could not forget that. It was a part of her as surely as she lived and breathed.

Back at the helm for this training, Drill Sergeant Thorpe gathered the platoon together outside the female barracks to brief them on their final mission of basic training. "For this final FTX, the entire company will road march to our bivouac site. Our platoon will man the twelve o'clock to three o'clock positions. From there, we will task squad-sized elements for various missions," Drill Sergeant Thorpe sounded serious yet encouraging. "All of the drill sergeants will be manning the Command Center. You will respond to tasks as well as do your part in maintaining the safety and integrity of the entire Company AO."

The even-keeled instructor did not further explain the details of the types of missions that would funnel down the chain of command, but she elaborated on the additional duties that would accompany this size of operation, like KP duty, CQ duty, and digging latrines. "Get some good shut eye tonight," Drill Sergeant Thorpe concluded. "We march at 0500 hours."

West tossed and turned in her bunk all night long. During those moments that she was awake, she tried to envision what this last challenge looked like. Would they get ambushed? Would they have movement to contact for an all-out battle? The imaginative soldier tried to play it out in her mind as she dozed in and out of consciousness. Every time she faded off, the battle came to life.

"What's that?" West, startled by some faint rustling, waking her from her slumber.

She held her breath and tried to listen. There it was again. Someone or something pried at the garage service door, so the awakened soldier eased out from underneath her covers onto the floor and slipped on her BDU pants. As she crept down the hallway and up the staircase, the intruder continued to pick away at the lock. In quiet haste, the young mother edged open her daughter's door and tiptoed to the side of her bed. "Lana," West whispered. "Lana, wake up."

"Mommy?" Lana turned and rubbed her eyes, unsure if she was dreaming.

"Yes, honey," West hugged the sleepy toddler to comfort her and spoke into her ear. "You have to listen to Mommy and do just as I tell you."

"What is it, Mommy?" Lana clutched her sheets and quivered her lip at her mother's serious tone

"Ssshhhh," West warned with her index finger over her lips. "Everything is fine, Lana. You must be quiet and do just as I tell you."

Innocent little Lana nodded and followed her mother's silent commands to grab her teddy bear and follow her out the bedroom door. The young girl clad in her soft, pink-footed jammies moved with soft steps but finally whispered again, "Mommy, I'm scared."

West paused, turned, and knelt down in front of her daughter. "Please, Lana," she begged. "You have to just trust Mommy on this one. Just do what I tell you."

The girl nodded in compliance again as the two tiptoed their way back out onto the landing to the peak of the staircase where a small window about six feet off of the ground shed some light from the street lamp into the lofted level.

"Lana, I'm going to lift you up and through that window," West directed in a whisper. "You will be on the roof, and you just sit there and wait for me. I will climb out after you, and then we will go from there. Understand?"

Lana nodded, tears forming in her pouty little eyes. "What about brother?" she whimpered.

"Brother?" West answered, confused, certain that she and Lana were the only ones in the house.

Precious Lana tilted her head to the right past her mom's shoulder, pointed her chubby little finger at the other bedroom door pulled closed behind them. "Yes, brother. Don't leave him here, Mommy," Lana urged and then turned with arms raised to be lifted up to the window sill.

Perplexed at her daughter's comments, West unlatched the

window and cranked the handle. She unhooked both sides of the rectangular screen and placed it on the floor next to her Marauder combat boots, although the soldier did not recall lacing those up.

"I love you, Mommy," Lana proclaimed with her lip still quivering as she clung to her teddy.

"I love you too, Lana," West whispered in her daughter's ear as she hoisted her up and out. "Mommy will keep you safe."

Once Lana crawled atop the roof and out of sight, West turned to face the last bedroom door with no idea as to what brother Lana referred. As she heard the intruder jimmy the door below, the escapee debated if she should save herself or take the risk of seeing what was in that room.

"Rise and shine!" Drill Sergeant Thorpe bellowed through the bay as she switched on all of the lights.

Recruit West opened her eyes and threw back the wool blanket that had covered half of her face; however, she laid there in exhausted relief for just a few minutes. She had been dreaming, but it felt so real. Her muscles ached from the tension and her thoughts still swirled in an attempt to understand the fictitious scenario.

In it the soldier wore her uniform and maneuvered around that house like an obstacle course. The stealthy combatant moved and spoke in hushed tones so as not to give away her position or her purpose, and she spoke truth to the little girl as if time was of the essence. West knew that little girl. In real life, Lana was not placed out on the roof but into the loving arms of Alan and Shannon from Arizona. West had saved her, but who was this brother, and better yet, how did Lana know about him?

"Move it, move it, move it!" Drill Sergeant Thorpe broke through the fog again. "Ten minutes and counting 'til our departure."

CHAPTER 34

Hoyt

Hoyt rehearsed the left, rights in his head as a meager attempt to distract his tired mind from the heavy load and chilly dampness that surrounded the morning. Every third step, the rail-thin recruit forced his dragging neck up high enough for his dry eyes to catch a quick glimpse of the distant horizon between the brim of his slipping glasses and heavy helmet. With no ready sign of the rising sun offering its warmth as well as its light, the defeated fighter drooped back into his drudgery.

In desperation the imaginative one lost himself in visions of family hikes and more pleasant trails. The young boy was never forced to lug the heavy load back then, and more often than not, Mr. Hoyt carried his son on his back or shoulders. An inexpensive and bonding trip for the family, they galloped and skipped along the wood-chipped pathways, playing games of I Spy or tag. For some of the steeper climbs, Dad hunted for the perfect fallen branch to fashion a makeshift walking stick for each of them.

The children pretended to be the Crusoes, nomads, or exploring pioneers, but the girls always ruined it for their little brother. Sometimes they poked him with their sticks, or worse yet, they made a game out of stepping on the back of his shoes, a coveted prize for whoever could get it to come off.

"Dad!" the wounded one would yell, hobbling on one foot as the conquering snickers rushed ahead. "Wait! Wait for me, you guys!"

Impaired by the darkness of the morning, Hoyt strained to see Salinas in front of him while Bradford urged him on from behind. Although he sensed the frustration in his elder's voice, the lack of sleep, lack of food, and ample supply of cold took their toll.

Oh how the weary one welcomed the thought of a cattle car ride about now, even with all of its bumps and throws. At least he could get a bit more shut eye and would not be expending so much energy. Why did the unit have to road march to their bivouac site anyway? The troops did not even march with cadence calls which helped to keep their attention away from their aches and pains, and the only thing drawing his attention right now was the nagging heat grating on his right pinky toe. He feared a blister was already forming.

"Hoyt!" Bradford called. "I'm trying not to step on you, bud, but you aren't making it easy."

In obliging response, Hoyt propped back his bulky Kevlar helmet, adjusted his glasses still wet from the morning mist, and secured his weapon with both hands to keep it from tossing him to and fro as he jogged a couple of steps to create some separation. From the front, Salinas slowed just a bit and came alongside. "Give me your ruck," Salinas prompted.

"What?" Hoyt replied, unsure of the meaning of that proposition.

"Give me your rucksack!" Salinas offered again. "I will carry it for awhile until you get your legs."

"Oh, no, thanks, Salinas," Hoyt appreciated his thoughtfulness. "I got it. I'm good."

"You sure?" Salinas presented it one last time.

"Yes, I got it," Hoyt answered as he rolled back his shoulders and quickened his pace.

"Okay, then," Salinas affirmed and hustled back to his place in the line.

"Hey, Salinas," Hoyt called up to him.

"Yeah, bro," Salinas looked back, keeping the pace with ease.

"Thanks. I needed that," Hoyt confessed.

"I got your back, Hoyt," Salinas acknowledged. "We're a team."

The youngster smiled back at his thoughtful friend, so thankful for that reassurance, and recognized that he had caved into his old habits of feeling weak, incapable, and alone. The fourth target retained some sort of misconception that when the sergeant promised him that he would be a new creation that all of those flaws would just disappear. While the practice of the disciplines helped him to focus on others, especially during those times that he wanted to think of himself, they were not quite the magic spell that he hoped they would be at first.

Transformation had progressed at a more gradual pace in more subtle ways, exemplifying the ever-present need of relationships to bolster the growth. That spirit of thankfulness perked his step as well as his demeanor as the line of trainees turned up the dirt path and into their bivouac site in no time. Platoon Leader Jensen directed each squad toward their appropriate sectors, and the trained recruits set out to improve their assigned positions.

Hoyt sighed in relief at the sight of the pre-dug foxholes, knowing that the soldiers only needed to add some camouflage and adjust their sight openings. He and Bradford manned the M-60 position together right at the three o'clock. Although Hoyt fired expert on the M-16 range, he knew that he could better serve as Bradford's assistant on this one, resupplying and feeding the ammo.

Immediately the duo located full branches for top cover and pushed handfuls of leaves around the sides of their hideout. Pine needles for some natural disguise and fresh scent, broken twigs for boundary stakes, and some sandbags from the supply tent helped to make their lair the envy of most.

On constant alert, the tired team of two sat in that hole for hours, unsure of what all the rest of the unit was doing. They heard tinkering back towards the main clearing and surmised that the GP Mediums were being erected for the command post and makeshift mess hall. Although the combatants had been issued enough MREs for each meal, Drill Sergeant Thorpe explained that they would be provided at least a hot breakfast every morning. Hoyt's mouth watered as wafts of bacon passed his nostrils.

CHAPTER 35

West

With confidence West marched over to the M-60 position while Salinas followed close behind. "Hoyt, Bradford," she ordered. "We have been tasked for a mission."

"But I just got done eating," Hoyt whined. "Can't they at least let our food settle a little?"

"Hoyt, be thankful that you got a hot meal," West added. "We need to take advantage of this daylight. Second squad will be over in a minute to man your position. When they get here, grab your gear and meet me at the Command Center."

West felt exhilarated as she took the lead for this last mission. Their task: navigate to a secure supply point behind enemy lines and rescue a Prisoner of War (POW). This was it. This was the final challenge for fourth squad, and the competitive crew could nearly taste the sweet relief of victory.

After their final preparations at the GP Medium tent that served as their company headquarters, fourth squad set out on their search-and-rescue mission. West took the point, Hoyt followed in the second position, Salinas the third, and Bradford the rear. With the utmost stealth, they all traveled together without incident through the wooded terrain and paused atop a small cliff. The scouts could see the enemy's position from there, armed uniformed soldiers pacing behind some concertina wire, and regularly dressed extras going about their business close behind. On the other side of this narrow valley, they spotted one lone tent with a five-ton truck parked at its rear. "That has to be the supply point," Salinas informed.

"I agree," West confirmed. "We have to carefully maneuver around their perimeter and get to that tent without being detected."

"How do you propose we do that?" Hoyt sounded concerned.

"Well, I definitely think our best bet is to do it from up here," Bradford advised. "I think it is too risky to try and go down there and then up the other side."

"I agree," West affirmed again. "I know down there would be shorter, but we just can't take the risk. Hoyt, take a look at that map and find the best route around."

After two soldiers popped up, rushed forward, dropped down, and rolled, then the other two followed in suit until fourth squad flanked the enemy's perimeter along the left upper crest and halted at a position just past the rear of the truck. Salinas zigzagged like a pouncing tiger towards the entrance of the tent, taking cover wherever he could find it while the rest of the support laid at the ready in the camouflage of the nearby tree line. The watchful squad held their breath as Salinas slid into the tent opening and out of view.

When Salinas reappeared with Drill Sergeant Burroughs and motioned for his teammates to move in, the trio rose from their hidden positions and hustled into the tent. "Welcome, my friends," Drill Sergeant Burroughs spoke with a horrible fake accent, trying to play his part. "May I offer you food and drink?"

As the leader, West responded, "Thank you, uh, Darius?"

"Yes, I am Darius," Drill Sergeant Burroughs confirmed.

"You are a supplier for the enemy?" West again verified her intelligence.

"Well, I do supply them with some needed items, but I also supply Gideon with needed items as well," Burroughs offered.

"Right, right," West understood. "You help Agent Gideon as well."

"Yes, I want to do my part in furthering the Kingdom," Burroughs added.

The startled visitors jumped and pointed their weapons at the opening as someone else entered, hunched just enough to clear the top. "Relax, dear friends," Burroughs calmed them. "Relax. This is my helper, Simon. He delivers the goods for me."

In utter relief, the group lowered their rifles and took a seat on the oversized red cushions. This Simon character did not appear friendly which left the squad a bit confused because he said nothing to them, simply entered the tent, grabbed a case of bottled water, and left as if nothing was amiss. "What's his deal?" Bradford asked.

"Oh, no need to worry about him," Burroughs replied. "He's harmless. He is not a convert, but I'm working on him. For now, the money he gets for working for me is enough to keep him quiet." The satisfied squad nodded, uncertain of how all of this information was applicable, but they had to carry on with their mission. "It is growing dark," Burroughs chimed in again, stumbling over his lines. "You will have to stay the night here. It will be safe. You may all sleep here in my supply tent tonight. Simon will keep guard and sleep in the truck."

West wanted more of an explanation. "Well, where are you going to be?"

The cheery contact answered, "Me, well, I will be sleeping in my house in the valley. I have some more business to do down there. Money does not grow on trees, you know. If I am going to help Agent Gideon at all, I have to do a lot of my own bidding down there."

Again, that explanation seemed reasonable to the visitors, so they bid him farewell and tried to make themselves comfortable in the tent. "What are we supposed to do now?" Bradford grew concerned.

"I'm not sure," West responded. "Per Drill Sergeant Thorpe's directions, we were to move to this point, identify a POW, rescue him, and bring him back to camp."

"Well, who is the POW we are supposed to be rescuing?" Hoyt pleaded.

"That's just it," West continued. "I'm not sure. They did not say."

"We probably have to use what we have learned to try and figure it out," Salinas offered.

"Well, how are we going to do that?" Hoyt whined, his voice cracking. "We have only met two guys so far. Burroughs is clearly our contact, and he said Simon was not a believer, so it can't be him. A prisoner of war is supposed to be one of us, remember?"

"I know," West affirmed. "Maybe we will run into someone tomorrow."

"Let's hope so," Bradford added. "We have to find him, somehow rescue him, and still get back to our base. We tear down that bivouac and road march back to garrison the day after tomorrow."

"I know, I know," West understood the logistical dilemma. "Should we run some night ops?"

"I don't think so," Bradford replied. "We have no idea what we would even be looking for, and we could see most of the enemy camp from the other side. Let's just get some good rest and get at it first thing in the morning."

They all felt comfortable with that suggestion and settled in for the night. Burroughs had stated that they would be guarded by Simon, so they felt secure in not setting up their own night watch.

Bright and early the next morning, Burroughs pushed through the tent entrance and welcomed his crew with some scrambled eggs, bacon, and fresh coffee. Hoyt was thrilled to have not missed his hot breakfast even though they were far from their own AO.

"Did you all sleep well?" Burroughs still butchered the accent.

"Yes, thank you," Salinas replied.

"Drill Sergeant Burroughs, I mean, Darius," West corrected herself, "we have to be heading out today, so… is there anyone else you might want to introduce us to?"

"Oh, you are heading out so soon," Burroughs played along. "I will be sorry to see you go. It is so nice to have some company. Anyone else? Well, let's see now. No, I don't think there is anyone else for you to meet. Simon and I run this operation. I don't know how many others there are that I can trust, you know."

"Okay," West was confused at this tit-for-tat.

"In fact, I will need to leave you all yet again. Simon and I have to use our truck to take a general down the road for some... 'special delivery'." He used hand quotes.

"What kind of delivery?" Bradford concerned that the information may be pertinent to their mission.

"Oh, nothing you need to concern yourselves with," Burroughs tried to calm him. "What I do with them down there is separate from what I do for Agent Gideon."

"Wait a sec," Hoyt stopped gnawing on his bacon. "I thought you said last night that you used those guys to fund your work with Agent Gideon?"

"Well, yes, of course," Burroughs entertained Hoyt's inquisition. "There is that, but I keep the two missions separate otherwise. Now, I must get to it. You all stay as long as you like." Burroughs bowed his head at them, turned back to the entrance, and left.

"I do not know what in the world is going on," Bradford grew even more concerned about their ability to complete this last mission.

"You and me both," West added. "Can't you use your discernment or something here?"

"West," Bradford barked, "they are role playing. This is all a big game of pretend. I can't pretend to discern."

"Well," West sounded desperate, "I'm trying to think how we can use what is at our disposal."

"How about we do some small recons?" Salinas suggested. "See if we can find someone else that is approachable."

"I don't think we have any other choice," West concluded.

"Salinas, why don't you go first? We will take turns if we need to, and then we will gather the intel and make our plan from there."

Throughout the entire day, the squad took turns setting out from their cover within the supply tent and scouted the terrain. Each time they returned with similar findings: guards stationed behind concertina wire and others just fixing their tent pegs, or eating, or playing dice on the ground. They saw no other leads, never encountered any other people, and had pretty much come full circle around the place. Panic began to set in as the sun made its final descent. "Well, West," Bradford frustrated at their useless efforts, "what do you propose we do now? We are running out of daylight."

"I know, Bradford," the assigned leader irritated as well. "I am fully aware."

"If we don't get this POW, we fail," Hoyt sounded defeated.

"We got to be missing something," Salinas tried to calm the rising tensions. "We got to talk this through. What have we learned about prisoners of war?"

Hoyt recited the lesson, "Well, we know that they are believers trapped behind enemy lines."

"Right!" Salinas affirmed. "But I think we all assumed that there would be some tent down there that was guarded, a makeshift prison like we are used to seeing in the movies. We would devise a plan to get that guy out of there and get him back to safety."

"Well, of course," Bradford confused at where Salinas was going with all of this.

"What if they don't need to be guarded like that?" Salinas suggested. "Remember, a prisoner of war is 'a person who has been captured and imprisoned.' They are at the mercy of the enemy. They are doing his bidding. Have you ever watched one of those movies when people remain in captivity too long and then sometimes they end up looking like one of them? It is not as if they say, 'Oh, hey, I've been brainwashed.' They sometimes just choose the path of least resistance. Remember when Daniel got carried off to Babylon? They offered him and his friends food from the King's table and trained them in their ways for three years. Yet we read that Daniel clung to God but others caved. Sometimes they think they are just going to get along until they have been freed, and sometimes they have forgotten the captivity in which they live. We have to remember the spiritual side of our opposition as well."

"Salinas, you're brilliant," West lit up at the insightfulness. "We got to act fast if we are going to get back in time."

West communicated her thorough plan of attack to the other members. Everyone understood their role to complete this mission as time was of the essence and improvisation was its partner. Just as the five-ton truck rolled back onto the scene, the group sprang into action. Bradford used his skills from corrections to strong-arm the POW into the back of the vehicle as Salinas dodged into the driver's seat. Hoyt took the passenger's side as the navigator, and West joined the keeper on guard in the cargo bed. They wasted no time, opting to drive that vehicle back to the AO instead of hoofing it back through the woods. The pumped-up group risked the unsecured road system to get back before their company moved out.

As the truck jerked with each shift of the gear, Hoyt wished they had a pair of night-vision goggles. "Are you sure you can see?" Hoyt asked Salinas while fighting to control his jitters.

"I'm fine, Hoyt," Salinas responded. "I have eyes like an owl."

"We getting close?" West yelled from the back.

"Almost there," Hoyt screamed back over the roar of the engine.

Salinas slammed on the brakes and threw that vehicle into park as the entire squad scurried in unison, POW in hand. The cohesive team jogged up the path, authenticated their way through the main gate, and clambered into the Command Post. The entire tent froze at the ruckus as Drill Sergeant Thorpe turned from the sand table positioned in the middle of the room. "Well, fourth squad," she congratulated, "about time you showed up. You got the POW?" Salinas stepped aside as West dragged their guest into view, front and center. Drill Sergeant Thorpe smiled her approval. "Darius, welcome back."

COMMENCEMENT

CHAPTER 36

Salinas

During this final ceremony, Salinas stood with shoulders back and chest out in the position as leader of the fourth squad first platoon. The entire company practiced their marching drills for the parade all morning long, and now the time had come for the live event. As usual, Drill Sergeant Thorpe's platoon took the unit's lead as they entered on the south side of the parade field, just behind the colors.

"Present arms," Jensen ordered as he and each squad leader turned and saluted the post commander as the entire unit stepped to the beat of the drum. "Order arms," Jensen bellowed again to signal the lowering of the salute.

The formation of trained soldiers marched in unison, passed the bleachers full of guests, across the yard at the post commander's house situated at the north side of the parade field, and then around into their final position facing the podium. Salinas peeked over the shoulder of the third squad leader without being too obvious, hoping that Anna and the kids would be seated in the crowd somewhere. He had written to her before their final week of maneuvers in hopes that she would come and watch his graduation. Although the unfaithful one did not deserve her attention, the new man wanted for her to see that he had begun to change. He wanted her to know that his conversion was real, and the graduate hoped that she could see in his efforts at this camp that he understood the seriousness. *Oh, Lord,* he prayed to himself, *please let her be here. Let her not have grown weary. I want to keep my family together.*

His toes cramped and lost their hold as the officiating post commander introduced their speaker for the day. "And without further ado," Drill Sergeant Akpore remarked, "I give you Sergeant First Class Hamilton Riley."

The polite guests clapped as the humble speaker ambled to his position at the podium. Fourth squad stood stoic with wide eyes and strained grins as the dedicated recruits peered out of the farthest corners of their eyes to catch a glimpse of their beloved recruiter. It was him, the sergeant.

Over the course of the camp as each shared their story, the undeniable connection rested in the comfort that he had been their collective, diehard beacon of truth, and together they grew to love, admire, respect, and even miss him.

As their very own recruiter addressed the entire company, their journey coming full circle, righteous pride welled up from deep within, and the squad of four hoped that they had made him as proud. As privileged representatives of a man who showed patient endurance during his pursuit of them, gratefulness overflowed. Sergeant Riley sought out each one of them in the miry muck of their self-driven lives as he followed the leading of the Holy Spirit to guide his targets to a place of confession, repentance, and then restoration back into rightful relationship with God. They did not deserve it, but they hoped that they could one day go and do likewise.

"At ease," the sergeant commanded the troops to change from their position of attention for the duration of his speech.

Keeping to the character that they had come to know and love, the sergeant's words generated power with precision, his southern twang ever-present. It sounded like sweet music to their ears, calling one home to rest. For the betterment of the guests as well as the troops, he shared bits and pieces of what this training entailed, explaining how the recruits experienced the very extremes of the spiritual disciplines while at Fort Gideon, not so that they might adhere to them out in the real world like some legalistic rulebook, but so that they could practice them without the interruptions that accompany life in a less controlled environment. The professional soldier offered brief examples of one training phase after another, comparing how the recruits' participation in the intense discipleship program at this specialty camp might be exercised in their day-to-day lives out there. It served as a summary of the purpose of sorts, a bridged scenario for their next steps. "Always remember, recruits," the sergeant pointed up as he summarized, "it is not by might, nor by power, but by His Spirit." The audience clapped again as the sergeant returned to his seat as guest of honor.

The post commander walked back to the podium to finalize the ceremony with the presenting of the camp awards. The medals went to the recruits that had the highest cumulative scores on all of the qualifying stages as well as reports from the cadre on aspects like following orders, leading as well as following, and success during maneuvers. Some soldier from Drill Sergeant Akpore's platoon was named for the third-place position. Next, the commander called, "For the Sojourners Award, the second highest score goes to...Recruit Salinas, first platoon."

With only three different awards, Salinas figured the cadre would give one to each platoon, so the illegal immigrant straightened up in shock when he heard his name called. He had no idea that he had done so well because he did not bother keeping track of how he was comparing to everyone else in that regard. The committed soldier just tried to do as he was told, learning as much as he could during the experience.

Salinas rose to attention, stepped back behind the squad, pivoted to his right, and then marched up to receive his medal. The changed man halted in front of the post commander, turned a right face, saluted, and then moved to parade rest. After lowering his head to ease Drill Sergeant Akpore's efforts in placing the award around his neck, Salinas stood to attention, returned the salute, and then marched back to his place in the unit.

Just as the surprised candidate settled back in position, he made one final effort to peek over the shoulder of the third squad leader. There she was. The rookie scout strained to identify her, but he knew it was her. Anna sat perched in the top left of the bleachers under the awning and appeared to be wiping tears from her eyes, concerned about smearing her makeup. That was her all right. The grateful spouse did not see the kids with her, but he did not care. The disciple needed her to hold on; the kids would follow their lead.

CHAPTER 37

Bradford

Bradford eased his way over to the bunks of Salinas and Hoyt, patting each of them on the back as the graduates packed their items back into their duffel bags. "Congratulations, boys," Bradford expressed with such genuine appreciation. "We made it, and it has been an honor and a privilege to serve with you."

"Thanks, Bradford," Hoyt paused to soak in the praise. "That means a lot."

"Likewise," Salinas smiled back as if viewing a prized treasure.

"I am happy to call you my friends," Bradford added.

Drill Sergeant Akpore cut into the moment as he ordered fourth squad to Drill Sergeant Thorpe's office for their active duty assignments.

"Well, this is what we have been waiting for." Bradford placed both arms around his comrades as they made their way down the bay of the barracks.

"Enter," Drill Sergeant Thorpe ordered from within the office.

Bradford, Salinas, Hoyt, and West filed into the room. "At ease," Drill Sergeant Thorpe commanded, signaling to her fourth squad that they could relax. "You are the last ones from my platoon to get their marching orders. I am so proud of the team you all became during this training. You have been inspirational."

The crew broke their stance and smiled at each other, so thankful for the esprit d'corps they managed to form, one that they would all cherish and hold dear to their hearts. "I have the orders right here for each of you, but as you now know, we have a very special guest here today that wanted to give them to you personally." Drill Sergeant Thorpe smirked as she waved the manila folders in her hands. "So, as we wait for him, I would like to give you a very special congratulations for that outstanding outcome on your final assignment."

"Why, thank you," West responded since she was the squad leader of that mission.

"I was beginning to have my doubts when you all were taking so long to get back to the AO," Drill Sergeant Thorpe confessed. "But I knew you would not give up."

"That was definitely a tricky one," West added. "I really have to give props to Salinas for breaking the code on that one."

"Ah, Salinas," Drill Sergeant Thorpe directed her praise at him. "How wise of you to figure out that sometimes prisoners of war are not bound by the chains that our eyes may expect to see."

"Yes, drill sergeant," Salinas agreed.

"How did you arrive at your conclusion?" the drill sergeant inquired.

"Well, I knew it could not be Simon because he was not a believer. He was more like collateral damage," Salinas explained.

"Very good," the drill sergeant confirmed. "Go on."

"Well, the only other person we met was Darius," Salinas continued. "At first, we assumed we needed to find someone else because Darius said a lot of the right things, like he was one of us. We felt pretty safe in his care, but the more I thought about a lot of his comments, I realized that he was a believer that got off track."

"How do you mean?" the instructor encouraged his thought process.

"Well, I don't know where he went wrong exactly," Salinas

added, "but somewhere he compromised himself, justifying his dealings with the enemy as for the good of the cause in the beginning, I guess. But the ends don't always justify the means."

"Well done, Salinas," Drill Sergeant Thorpe applauded. "I knew I was right in picking this squad for that challenge. You worked together, relied on one another, never gave up, and held to truth. Far easier said than done, I might add."

No one was surprised when someone knocked on the door behind them.

"Enter," Drill Sergeant Thorpe answered, certain of their next guest.

The door creaked open just as Captain Peters peered his head around the door just far enough to gaze into the room. "Oh, sorry," he apologized. "I did not mean to interrupt."

"Oh, that's okay, hun," Drill Sergeant Thorpe replied. "What do you need?"

"If you still need to finish up," Captain Peters looked right through them to Thorpe, "I can just meet you at home."

"That will be fine," Drill Sergeant Thorpe concluded. "I'll see you there."

With that, Captain Peters eased the door back closed and took his leave. "As I was saying..." drill sergeant continued her address to her squad.

"With all due respect," West interrupted, "are you involved with Captain Peters?" They all wanted to know, but only West had the guts to ask. It must have been a woman thing.

"I would not call it involved," Drill Sergeant Thorpe appeased her. "He is my husband."

The graduates all looked at each other in total disbelief. They had no clue. "Married?" West bewildered at the comment. "You never let on."

"We try to keep the PDA at a minimum during training," Drill Sergeant Thorpe explained. The interruption of another knock at the door came all too soon for the awkwardness in the room.

"Enter," Drill Sergeant Thorpe bellowed. "Thankfully, Sergeant Riley, you made it."

"Sorry about that," the sergeant apologized. "I needed to speak to a few guests before I could graciously cut out."

"Understood," Thorpe affirmed. "With that, I will leave you all to it." She gathered her keys from the desk and left the room.

The team fought back the urge to surrender their stance and form a big group hug with their recruiter. The sergeant also adhered to protocol and took his place behind the desk. "I hope y'all don't mind the delay," the sergeant began. "I just figured since I was the one that started ya'll on this leg of the race, and since I was gonna be here for the graduation address, that it would just be fittin' that I get you started on your next leg."

"Of course," Bradford enthused as he spoke on the entire squad's behalf. "It is our pleasure, sergeant."

"Now, I'm gonna hand each of you your folder, but I don't want you to open it in here," the sergeant explained. "I want you to take them out there, find some place comfortable under a tree or something, think about your experience here at Fort Gideon, and then open them up. The assignment will be on the top page." The squad nodded their heads in compliance. "I just don't have time to visit with each of you as I would like," the sergeant explained further. "My ride is waiting, and I was pushin' it to manage this much. I hope that we can cross paths again someday. We'll have to do our sharin' then."

The squad accepted his request, appreciating the time they had with him, although it was not enough for any of them. West was called first as she took her folder, thanked the sergeant, and held back her tears as she left the room. Hoyt was next, holding his shoulders back, standing tall, conveying to the sergeant that he was not wrong in recruiting him. Salinas approached the desk in his gentle, humble way, thanking the sergeant with such gratitude in his tone. Then Bradford, the last one in the room, moved forward, took his folder, thanked the sergeant, and turned to leave the room.

Just as the oldest recruit reached for the door, he paused and turned back with hesitation. "Sergeant?" Bradford asked. "I know you are in a hurry and all, and I know this may seem petty to take what little time that you have here to ask this, but I just don't know when I will get the chance again."

"Shoot, Bradford, what's on your mind?" the sly sergeant permitted.

"I feel horrible even asking this, but," Bradford hesitated, "what is the deal with Jensen? I mean, first place in the entire company?"

The sergeant chuckled at Bradford's confession. "I'm surprised you lasted this long with those questions, Bradford. I figured you would have caved about him a long time ago." The graduate was taken aback by the sergeant's apparent expectation of his inquiry. "You see, Bradford," the sergeant explained, "Jensen wasn't my recruit, as you have figured out. He fell into more of Sergeant Thorpe's expertise."

"He's Thorpe's recruit?" Bradford sounded more confused.

"No, but he was recruited by a dear friend of hers," the sergeant explained. "Ya see, like this friend, he joined as a mere child. He did not have to walk through the same kind of muck that you and I did."

"Yeah, well, no kidding," Bradford added. "That's obvious. He has been isolated his whole life."

"Not isolated, Bradford," the sergeant corrected, "insulated. Ya see, it is not about his upbringing. It's about his calling."

"Calling, what do you mean?" Bradford questioned.

"He was called so young, and he was given the gift of faith," the sergeant expounded. "He believed so easily and obeyed so readily."

"I know," Bradford commented. "It seems like he did everything right."

"Oh, Bradford," the sergeant scolded, "don't be so naïve. Jensen has his own challenges, his own flaws, his own sins. He is a man, after all. He is not perfect. He has the gift of faith but a terrible struggle understanding why others don't."

"Well, that part is obvious," Bradford grunted. "He is too good for his own good. He was our leader but could hardly relate to any of us."

"Bradford," the sergeant got serious, "to other believers in his walk of life, Jensen not only has the gift of faith, but also the gift of encouragement."

"Encouragement?" Bradford bewildered at the notion. "I can't imagine that."

"Believe it, 'cause it's true," the sergeant affirmed. "And here, at Fort Gideon, shoot, Jensen was being prepared for his toughest challenge yet. Jensen has one of the greatest and most difficult assignments out there."

"Really?" Bradford would not have believed it if it were not coming straight from the source. "What's that?"

"Well, I'm not supposed to be the one to share other's assignments, but Jensen has the job of raising his children in The Way," the sergeant offered. "As a child convert himself, he knows the benefit of that all too well. That is perhaps one of the most amazing testimonies to the world and an encouragement to all."

"How's that?" Bradford wanted to understand.

"Ya see, Bradford," the sergeant concluded, "there are plenty of folks like you and me out there that had to learn what life is all about the hard way. Shoot, we've got the scars to prove it. But guys like Jensen, they give hope to fathers and mothers alike. If they can truly train a child up in the way he should go, they just might save a child from having to take that same path. Wouldn't you want your son to be insulated if possible?"

CHAPTER 38

Hoyt

Hoyt looked up from his spot underneath the oak tree next to the dining hall and watched Bradford leave the office. The older, stronger graduate looked like he was in deep contemplation with his serious grimace and forceful steps as he trod across the cement slab and rested against the outside of the male barracks. The sergeant followed, secured the office door behind him, and hesitated as he reached for the passenger door of the waiting HUMVV. As he turned to gaze back at his squad of soldiers, the proud recruiter grinned and nodded.

Hoyt thought for sure that he saw the sergeant's eyes well up, almost as if his departure was final, a last good-bye. Joy and pride exuded from the faint curl of his lip and the sparkle in those mesmerizing blues as their recruiter turned back to his ride, mounted the vehicle, and sped off and out of sight. The young soldier reasoned that he would walk back down to that obscure little office on Broadway when he got home and catch up with the fatherly figure, but the pit that had formed in his stomach aimed to convince him that his plan would not be quite so easy. Hopefully the sergeant and he could sit down and chat more about his journey at Fort Gideon. Perhaps the veteran would even have some tips for his fourth target's active duty assignment.

Surprised by the fluttering of his nerves as he slid his finger along the frayed edge, Hoyt read the top page of ordinary copy paper with words written in the center as if a title page in a book, "Jarahueca". *Jarahueca?* Hoyt's eyebrows narrowed to a point. *I'm not even sure what language that is.* He flipped the page over, hoping for some further explanation, but the blank backside sent the curious one rifling through the rest of the folder's contents: marksmanship score sheet, land navigation results, his assessment, even that page that the sergeant must have read from when they first met, but nothing else about this next assignment.

As he glanced up at Bradford, still in quiet meditation, the graduate looked around and saw both Salinas and West rummaging through their folders with that same bewildered look on their faces. As the two moved in his direction, the compliant teammate rose and met them at Bradford's position. "Bradford!" West barked. "Did you look at your assignment yet?"

"I was just about to," Bradford replied, encouraging calm patience to his friends.

The trio hovered over their senior comrade as he took his time to open his folder, read his title page assignment, and then thumbed through his folder in much the same manner.

"Just as I thought!" West added. "You don't have any other info either."

"Let's not lose our heads," Salinas offered his best American dialect. "We are going to have to be patient and wait for further instructions, just like the sergeant said."

"Well, can I at least ask what you guys got?" West resigned. "I will tell you that I got Koscierzyna."

"Wow, cool!" Hoyt responded. "Sounds like Europe for sure."

"I got Reynosa," Salinas recited. "I know that is from my homeland in Mexico."

"Really?" Hoyt chimed in. "That is going to be interesting... I got Jarahueca. I'm not even sure how to pronounce that. Sounds African or something though."

"What?" Bradford questioned in frustration. "And I got Pontiac?"

United still, fourth squad broke out in laughter. Here it looked like three of them would be traipsing around the world somehow, and the correctional officer was going to be stuck in his own backyard. "Oh, the Lord really does have a sense of humor, now doesn't he?" Hoyt touted as the group came together arm in arm for one last team huddle.

The prayers and blessings of these cherished friends were the perfect send off. As recruits, they each answered the call, and now as soldiers, they would don the armor.

EPILOGUE

Sowing Seeds

Oh, Lord, how will I know who they are?

I will send you to them.

What will I say to them? How will I get them to listen?

I will give them ears to hear. You must just go and tell.

But I am so unworthy.

I want them to see Me, not you. Sow the seed.

But what if I miss it? What if I fail?

Based on *Mark 4:1-20* —

Sometimes as you spread the Good News, it will be snatched away before it is ever given consideration. The Word will be rejected. Sometimes people will respond eagerly, for the goodness seems desirable, but the gift never penetrates. There is no root. Others may hold to the idea of truth in their mind, but they never surrender their grip to controlling their own life. They cling to the world. But some seeds will sink deep within the soul. A marvelous transformation will take place as that dead seed yields to the power around it, the power to nourish it, water it, control its path. Some plants take a long time to grow into the mighty tree that can withstand the storms. Some of them sprout at once and even their roots bring nourishment as they replenish over and over. All have their purpose as you have yours. Sow! As you cast the Word, you do not know which one will sink deep. He brings the wind and the rain and the light. You just sow!

Thank you, Lord, for reminding me.

"Take heart. I am with you. I have overcome the world." (John 16:33, ESV)

ABOUT THE AUTHOR

J.M. Cranford is a Veteran logistical officer in the U.S. Army and served stateside in both active and reserve capacities during the First Gulf War, the Somalia Conflict, and the draw down in Bosnia. She holds a Master's degree in Bible and Theology and has served as Treasurer of a non-profit mission organization as well as a team member of a local church's mission board for many years. She and her husband have five adult children, many grandchildren, and live in Pontiac, Illinois.

CPSIA information can be obtained
at www.ICGtesting.com
Printed in the USA
BVOW03s1834100717
488994BV00001B/31/P